## About the Author

Joe Bagnall studied Ancient History and Archaeology at the University
of Wales Trinity Saint David. He now lives and works in the Lake
District with his fiancée, Deb, and their cat, Ned.

# The Last Son of Rome

**Joe Bagnall**

# The Last Son of Rome

Olympia Publishers
*London*

**www.olympiapublishers.com**
OLYMPIA PAPERBACK EDITION

A CIP catalogue record for this title is
available from the British Library.

ISBN: 978-1-80074-172-0

First Published in 2022

Olympia Publishers
Tallis House
2 Tallis Street
London
EC4Y 0AB

Printed in Great Britain

# Dedication

In loving memory of Ann Fox and Alan Bagnall, I hope you would have enjoyed the story.

# Acknowledgements

This novel started off as little more than a persistent thought in my head; the only way to shift it seemed to be to write it down. It likely would have dwindled after the first few pages if it had not been for the continuing support of my fiancée, Deb. Her encouragement and reassurance have seen this book through to fruition. Her perseverance and willingness to visit endless Roman sites and museums is worthy of a medal and she will now no doubt be glad to talk about something other than the Romans. I am immensely grateful to my mum, Katy, and sister, Ellys, for being the first to read through the completed manuscript and for their patience in editing my bad grammar. Thanks also to my dad, Tony, for producing the first hard copy of this novel and for his continued support. That you sat down and read through the first chapters gave me more encouragement than you could know. Thanks also to the team at Olympia Publishers for making this all possible and helping me share this persistent thought with the wider world.

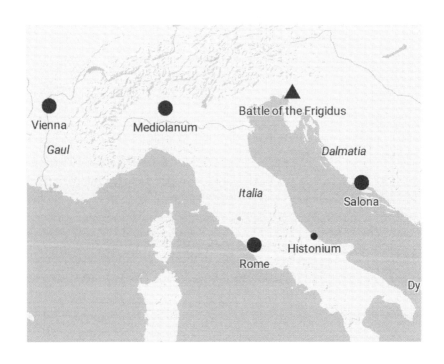

**The Western Roman Empire**

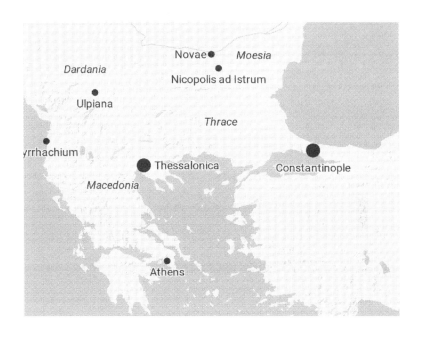

**The Eastern Roman Empire**

*392 A.D. The Western Roman Emperor, Valentinian II is dead. His successor is the puppet Emperor, Eugenius, installed by the Frankish general Arbogast, magister militum of the Western Empire.*

# I

The Emperor was dead.

The news hit Rome like a great wave, sweeping along all those that it encountered, flooding through the old city, filling lowly wine sinks and patrician mansions alike.

Though it had been some months since the first whispers arrived from the palace at Vienna, and the swift official confirmation that followed from the Imperial court at Mediolanum, the ancient city streets still had not quietened.

People spoke in hurried whispers in the streets, careful to avoid the newly arrived soldiers who patrolled the city; vicious looking men who spoke Latin with heavy Germanic accents.

The whispers carried tales that the young Emperor had not committed suicide as proclaimed but had instead died at the order of his protector, the Frankish general, Arbogast.

It was well known that it was the Frank, not the late Emperor, who truly ruled the Western Empire and now many said that he had grown tired of Valentinian, who had begun to challenge his power as he came into manhood.

Even the Roman Senate, once the seat of great men who had turned a small city state into a power that controlled most of the known world, was not immune to the rumour and intrigue surrounding the death of Valentinian. The appointment of the scholar and teacher, Eugenius, to the Imperial purple was a shrewd move on Arbogast's part. Though the power of the Senate was a faint shadow of what it once had been, they would not have accepted a Frank as Emperor without a struggle. Eugenius being Roman born was more politically acceptable, yet his obvious position as puppet ruler did not sit well with many in the Senate. Still, most knew to keep their mouths shut in fear of the new Emperor and the general who controlled him.

Upon his accession, Eugenius had installed his own men in positions of power and, despite his own faith, had taken measures to suppress to growing power of the Christian faith in the Western Empire, in favour of the old ways, to gather favour with the traditionally-minded Senators and citizens. The men who had served Valentinian had either retired to their homes in the country, or taken appointments in far off provinces; some had openly fled to the East whilst others had disappeared totally along with their immediate family.

A rift opened in the Senate house. Supporters of Eugenius and Arbogast formed around the newly appointed Prefect of Italy, Virius Nicomachus Flavianus and his son Nicomachus Flavianus the Younger, recently appointed Prefect of Rome.

Those who had been supporters of Valentinian and despised the new puppet Emperor and his barbarian master, gravitated towards Senator Publius Aelius Cotta, a descendant of one of the last true Roman noble houses, renowned for his unerring belief in the power of the Senate.

On an unusually cool, late August night, a small group of senators gathered in the house of Senator Cotta.

The Senators made their way into the tablinum where Cotta stood before his writing desk. The short-cropped curls upon his head were steel grey in the flickering light of the lamps; his clean-shaven face was creased in a smile as he welcomed his guests.

One by one, they settled themselves into the couches that had been arranged for them and accepted wine from the slaves that moved silently across the tiled floor.

Once all were seated and equipped with a cup, Cotta dismissed the slaves with a flick of his hand.

"It's good to see you, my friend., I feared when we left the capital we might never find ourselves in each other's company again," he said warmly.

"You left at a good time, Cotta," replied Senator Seutonius, an overweight man in his late fifties with a large purple birthmark on his left temple. "We followed shortly after you, but already Arbogast's brutes had begun going house to house, imprisoning any too slow or too foolish to leave."

"The dog shows its true colours once free from its master's leash," commented the aged Senator Gallinus in his steady, level tones, drawing murmurs of ascent from the gathered men.

"The dog has his own hounds now," growled Senator Ruga above the noise. "He's sending them to Rome, which means our time here must be short."

"Flavianus?" asked Cotta.

Ruga nodded, his bald head gleaming in the lamplight. "The new prefect has been appointed consul and means to address the Senate. No doubt his son has already informed him of our presence within the city."

The news clearly troubled Cotta. He began to pace before the seated men.

"Friends, surely you fret too much. Rome is not Mediolanum; we are not in the imperial court."

Ruga turned to the man who had spoken. "No, Varro, Rome is not the imperial court. But you would be a fool to think yourself safe here!" he barked angrily.

Varro opened his mouth to retort but Cotta interjected.

"Friends! We are not here to argue." He shot glances at both men and they fell silent.

"Then tell us why we are here," said Seutonius. He looked across at Ruga on the next couch. "I can't condone his tone but Senator Ruga here is right. Flavianus will not ride alone," he looked at Varro, "and things are no longer as they were when the emperor was alive."

All of the seated men looked up at Cotta, who had ceased pacing.

"I asked you all here because we have a decision to make. A plan was set in motion in Mediolanum but now the situation demands that we choose whether to commit or not." He took a deep breath. "What I am about to say is treasonous and I give you all this opportunity to leave now."

No one moved.

Cotta nodded. "Valentinian was murdered by Arbogast, on this I'm sure we all agree. There were too many amongst the emperor's household who said as much before disappearing for the truth to be anything else. Arbogast and Eugenius are usurpers; they have bitten the hand that raised them and soon there will be conflict."

"You believe Theodosius will make war?" asked Gallinus.

"I believe he will. He appointed Arbogast as Magister Militum and bade him be the protector of Valentinian. Now the boy is dead and the Frank is a rival emperor in all but title."

"The Empire is weak, why would Theodosius risk conflict within when there are so many threats along his borders?" Ruga asked.

"Because, my friend, he risks a greater threat emerging at his back. Theodosius had eyes and ears within the court; we all know this. He will know, as I know, that under Arbogast's governance there has been a steady trickle of Franks and other Germans from beyond the Rhine into Gaul, settling and taking up positions in Roman towns and cities. No doubt that trickle will be become a torrent now and a new Frankish kingdom will emerge. These people have no desire to be Roman! They eschew our traditions and laws and would see the Empire fall. That is why Theodosius will not make peace with Eugenius and that is why we have to choose a side."

"The choice is clear," stated Varro after a moment's silence, "Flavianus and Eugenius would see us dead, therefore we are with Theodosius."

Seutonius shook his head slowly. "I would not be so quick to proclaim our allegiance. Theodosius has proved a capable Emperor, a hard man, but he is a Christian! It's said he grows more hostile to our ways each passing day."

Cotta raised his hands to placate the Senator. "On this I am with you, Seutonius. However, I fear that is a battle for another day. Our duty is to Rome and the people; I believe that there will be no Rome under Arbogast's rule."

"Cotta speaks true," said Gallinus calmly, "I, too, see the Empire's demise at the hands of the usurper. Theodosius is the only man capable of uniting the two Empires under one rule, of making us strong once more."

Cotta looked to Seutonius and Ruga. He knew he could not proceed without their support, even if he wanted to. He alone did not have the power to sway the whole Senate; only united would their voices be heard.

Ruga was quiet for a moment before nodding his consent. Seutonius took longer. Cotta could almost see the arguments raging inside his head; the birthmark seemed to grow more vivid in the lamplight as he struggled towards a decision. Eventually, he seemed to reach a conclusion and raised his eyes to Cotta.

"Very well. Theodosius it is."

Cotta strode forward and raised an alarmed-looking Seutonius from his couch before embracing him. The gesture was so out of character and the look on Seutonius's face such a picture, that the other men could not help but chuckle at the sight. Their laughter somewhat eased the tension in the room, though it quickly subsided as Cotta released the embarrassed Senator and allowed him to return to his seat.

"What now, then," asked Ruga, "now we have agreed to our treason?"

Cotta held up three fingers. "First, we send word to Theodosius. Tell him of our fears and our support for him and call for his aid." He lowered one finger. "Second, the Senate. We have limited time; Flavianus's arrival will weaken us so we must move quickly to convince the rest of the Senate to support us in our decision. Our power is a mere shade of what it once was but if the people see us united on our course they will follow, and whoever controls the people controls the Empire." He lowered his second finger. "Third, Rome. We must hold Rome."

"Hold Rome?" Ruga scoffed.

"What do you mean, Cotta?" Gallinus asked quizzically.

"Like the Senate, Rome is not what she was," explained Cotta. "However, Rome is a symbol that men have fought and died for, for over a thousand years. If Theodosius has the Senate and Rome, then he has an advantage over Arbogast."

"You mean to employ the legion at Albanum?" said Varro.

Cotta nodded in surprise "How did you guess, old friend?"

Varro smiled, "I presumed you did not intend us to man the walls and they are the only troops near enough to reach the city before Arbogast's would."

"They would not be enough to defeat Arbogast's force," warned Gallinus.

"They would not need to," replied Cotta, "only to hold the city long enough for Theodosius's army to reach us."

Seutonius paused whilst refilling his cup. "This plan seems to hinge a lot on Theodosius sending help very quickly. I am no military man, but neither are any of you. How long do you think we could hold the city for, even if we do somehow manage to convince a legion of soldiers to fight for us?"

Cotta lowered his third finger and closed his hand into a fist by his side. Seutonius made excellent arguments. No Senator had held a military office in almost two centuries, a result of decrees issued by past Emperors whose rule had been threatened by opposition of the Senate. Cotta had expected such a response, as was his way, and responded calmly.

"This plan has stages, Seutonius. I intend to enact stage one immediately; I would send messengers at first light. In the event of this decision being reached, I prepared this dispatch today." He moved behind his desk and, from a shelf built underneath it, withdrew a rolled scroll. "This outlines what we have spoken of and asks that a positive response be accompanied by a man more qualified in the art of war than any of us to organise the defence of the city. The time between responses will allow us to enact stage two. With luck, if we can secure enough support, it will offer us enough protection from Flavianus."

Seutonius inclined his head. "You seem well prepared, Senator Cotta, I'll give you that. Which one of us will carry the message?"

Cotta shook his head. "We are all needed here, Seutonius, I had hoped Varro might be able to help us with our couriers. I know your nephews are back in the city."

"They are," Varro nodded. "They are experienced riders and loyal men; they will carry the message if I ask."

"Thank you, my friend. I have a favour to ask of you."

Varro furrowed his brows. "Anything!" he exclaimed. "What would you ask of me?"

Cotta was quiet for a moment; he looked down at the scroll and turned it between his hands. "I ask that your nephews take my son with them. To Constantinople. I will arrange for him to be tutored there whilst events unfold as they will here."

Varro stood and clapped his friend on the shoulder. "The boy will be welcome; they will see him there safely. He is not so much younger than you or I when we were sent away from home."

Cotta bowed his head in gratitude. Raising it once again he said, "I advise you send your son with them. Celer and he get on well and it is easier to travel with a companion you know when going far from home."

Varro frowned again. "I see the wisdom in your words; the boy would be safer away from Rome. However, I fear he is not as robust as your Celer. I do not think he is ready for such a journey."

Turning to the others Cotta said, "You would all do well to make arrangements for your loved ones. I cannot guarantee our safety, let alone theirs."

"Agreed," said Ruga, rising from his couch. "We had best make our leave and set about them."

Seutonius and Gallinus rose as well.

As they prepared to leave, Cotta issued his last instructions. "Speak nothing of this night to anyone. I will contact you within two days to enact the second part of our plan. Use that time wisely to prepare. May Fortuna favour us."

"May Fortuna favour us!" they echoed. They clasped one another's arms before making their way out into the atrium.

Before Varro left, Cotta beckoned him to the desk. He placed the scroll in a leather tube and placed a cap on the end.

"For you nephews to read. I would not have any man carry this unwitting of what was written within."

Varro nodded and took the tube from him. "Will you tell Celer?"

"No." Cotta shook his head, suddenly tired and drained from the night's events. "Celer is not to know of this. I trust him to secrecy but worry that knowledge may place him more at risk on the journey."

"Very well, at dawn then."

"At dawn, he will be ready," said Cotta.

Varro clapped him on the shoulder once more, then turned and headed for the door.

*** 

With the household quietened for the night, Cotta called his son into the tablinum.

Marcus Aelius Celer had just turned sixteen that winter. He was almost of a height with his father, though it was too soon to tell if he would develop Cotta's broad frame. He shared his father's curly hair, a dark brown in place of the grey, but had not inherited the proud nose of his father's family.

"Sit." Cotta waved a hand towards one of the empty couches.

Celer sat as his father dismissed the slaves and poured them both a cup of wine.

"I'm sending you to study in Constantinople," said Cotta as he handed one of the cups over.

"Constantinople?" Celer said surprised.

Cotta detected the nervousness in his son's voice. He nodded. "You're of an age where you need to experience more of the world than Rome or Mediolanum. Some of the finest tutors in the Empire, West or East, are in Constantinople."

"When do we leave?" asked Celer, more firmly, and Cotta was secretly pleased that the boy controlled his emotions so well. He shook his head with a sad smile.

"Like I said, you're of an age. Your mother and I will remain in Rome."

"Oh." At once, a look of worry flashed across Celer's face and Cotta remembered his own fears the first time he had faced leaving home without the guiding hand of his father.

"Do not be afraid, my son. An exciting chapter in your life is about to begin. I have friends amongst the Senate in Constantinople. You shall be well hosted, and introduced to all their daughters, no doubt," he teased and was gladdened to see the boy blush and smile in embarrassment.

"You shall have fine tutors and one day soon shall no doubt attend the court of the Emperor himself."

"Will I travel alone?"

"No, good Varro has informed me this very night that his nephews travel to Constantinople on business tomorrow and has graciously offered that you accompany them."

"And Young Varro," said Celer, eyes bright at the mention of his friend's family. "Shall he also accompany us?"

"His father has decided now is not yet the right time for him," said Cotta gently. Discomforted by his son's crestfallen face, he hastily added, "But I have no doubt he intends to send him soon. You shall have time to get to know the city so that you may show him its wonders when he arrives." The thought seemed to comfort Celer and he nodded with a small smile.

They sat in silence for a moment with nothing but the slow crackle of the fire and the night noises of the city drifting in from the terrace.

Cotta thought hard about the commitment he had made that night; it would affect all his family, his son maybe most of all.

"Tell me, son. What do you know of the Republic?"

"Father?" Celer looked up at Cotta; there was an unusual tenseness in his father's posture, almost hidden behind his usual noble rigidity but there plain enough for those few who knew him best to see. Celer wondered if it had something to do with the Senators' visit earlier that night. Whilst it was not unusual for his father to host members of the Senate it was unusual in that only a small number had come and without the usual retinue of sons, wives and other followers.

For a moment, Cotta thought about telling him. A part of his soul yearned to share its deepest secret with his only son but a colder, more rational part of him said no. Not yet; the boy was too young to bear such a burden. It weighed heavily on a man, as Cotta knew only too well.

He blinked once and his expression lightened, his body relaxed marginally. "Forgive me Celer, the eccentricities of old age." He tapped a finger to his greying hair.

"Now, the hour is late," said Cotta, glad to see his son smile. "You should get some sleep; you leave at first light."

He laughed as Celer pulled a face at the thought of rising so early and left his chair to stand in front of his son.

"Do not make such faces! You may have to arise before your usual time but I have the task of consoling your mother as her only son leaves home!"

They both grinned as they faced one another. Cotta laid both his hands on his son's shoulders.

"Before you make for your bed, I would say one last thing. Something that my father said to me before I left home for the first time. A man's duty is to his family and to Rome. Our forefathers have served Rome since before the days of Augustus and you are the next in that long line. Let your actions be worthy of their memory and bring honour to your family and to Rome herself."

Celer looked at him solemnly. "I will, Father, I swear."

"I know you will, Celer" he said, embracing his son.

"Now, to bed with you," he said, releasing him. "You have a long journey ahead of you and you will need your strength."

After his son had disappeared to bed; Cotta sat alone in the tablinum.

Though the empty wine cups of the senators had been taken away, the couches remained in a rough semi-circle facing his desk and the single brazier that kept the chill of the night air at bay.

Cotta sat hunched over the desk, his left hand wrapped around a cup of wine, whilst the fingers of his right drummed lightly on the polished surface of the desk. The weak flickering light of the brazier caused the colour of the wine to deepen, so that to Cotta's eyes it looked like blood and he pushed it away.

He worried for the safety of his family; the course that he and the other Senators had set upon was treasonous, of this there was no doubt. Failure would result in all their deaths and even if they emerged victorious, would the cost to the survivors be worth it?

He knew that sending Celer to Constantinople was dangerous. If his plan succeeded, he knew full well that Theodosius would not hesitate to use the boy as leverage against him, yet he could no quell the fear that if his plan did not succeed then Rome itself may not be safe enough.

No, Celer was safer in the East, he decided, determined to be resolute from now on.

The message to the court of Theodosius would soon be on its way, carrying a hope of a new age.

Dawn's first light would guide Varro's nephews and his son away from Rome but it would still take weeks to reach the court in Constantinople. Cotta drained the last of his wine and nodded slowly to himself before rising slowly and padding quietly towards his bed. He eased himself between the blankets next to Marcella, his wife, careful to not disturb her. His last thoughts before sleep took him were that there was still time to make preparations for the trials to come and to ensure the safety of his family. There was still time.

# II

A deafening crash woke Celer from his dreams, making him sit bolt upright, rubbing the sleep from his eyes.

At the second loud crash, followed by a splintering noise, he threw himself out of bed, grabbing his tunic from where he had flung it over a chair before sleep and quickly pulling it over his head.

He made it to his door, which opened out onto the atrium, in time to hear a terrific blow that resonated through the house, making dust fall from the ceiling and objects rattle on the wall shelves.

An axe head smashed through the heavy timbers of the door, only to become caught on one of the iron strips that strengthened it.

A second object hammered into the door, but did not break through as the head of the axe was untangled for another strike. His father was striding across the atrium, a long robe flowing about him as he bellowed at two bewildered slaves to drag one of the stout wooden benches in front of the door. His mother appeared at the doorway to his parents' room, hair wild from sleep. The slaves had barely grasped the thick wooden arms before the door gave in.

A mighty blow from a heavy stone cutter's hammer slammed into the wooden boards, cracking those where it struck, but the iron strips did their job, and the door remained intact. The force, however, was too much for the socket cut into the door frame that the iron locking bolt slotted into. A spray of masonry flew into the room, showering Cotta and the two slaves, and huge dark shapes rushed in.

They got to the slaves first.

One went down screaming, trying to cover his head with his arms as blows from axes and swords rained down upon him.

The other slave, Zardan, a tall man with skin the colour of teak tried to fight back, whipping a large painted jug off a side table into the face of one of the attackers, staggering him.

"Quick, boy! Out the back," his father roared at him, as he grabbed his hysterical wife and dragged her through the curtains that separated the atrium from the tablinum. Celer darted after them as Zardan was run through with a sword; another jug raised above his head tumbled from his hands as his life slipped away.

Cotta was pushing his wife across the mosaic floor of the tablinum and out into the garden at the rear of the house. He grabbed Celer by the shoulder and pushed him after her before grabbing the bronze stand of the brazier, spilling the still hot coals out onto the floor.

Marcella had fallen on the tiled floor of the garden, just in front of the small pool that collected water when it rained. Celer was trying to lift her, but she was a dead weight. Her eyes were wide and she gasped for breath as if the air was suddenly too thin for her. Cotta pushed his son further into the garden and, with desperate strength, hauled his wife to her feet and half carried her after their boy.

Screams chased them across the tiles towards the back wall, as the rest of the house slaves were dragged from the corners where they had tried to hide. The coals from the brazier had caught on the curtains surrounding the tablinum, and now the flames silhouetted the frames of the armed men that pursued them. The wall at the end of the garden rose to the height of a man, and half as much again. Cotta carefully lowered his wife to the ground and shot a glance at the approaching men. "Quick, over the wall," he commanded Celer.

"No father I wo..."

Cotta slammed him against the wall before the words could fully form. "You will do as I say!" he shouted, staring madly into Celer's frightened eyes. "Now go!" He turned away, back toward their pursuers, the brazier stand in his hands. Celer turned to the wall looming above him; it was too high for him to jump and reach the top. He took a few quick steps back then ran at the wall, planted a foot on it as he jumped; fear gave strength to his legs and he managed to grab the top of the wall.

There was a clash of metal on metal as he struggled up to straddle the wall; he looked down to see his father fending off four men, swinging the bronze stand wildly. The men spread out slowly, all with drawn swords held low and menacing. In the flames from the burning curtains Celer could see the long hair, thick moustaches and heavy builds of the Frankish soldiers that were becoming more and more common throughout the Empire following Arbogast's rise to power. Celer had seen their like many times in the streets and court at Treverorum. They had scared him then but now took on a more terrifying aspect, illuminated by the flames.

"Mother, quick, reach up to me!" Celer called down to her. His mother lay slumped at the foot of the wall and, in horror, Celer realised that she had fainted from the shock.

One of the Franks pointed up at Celer on the wall and Cotta risked a quick glance back. For a brief moment, their eyes met in the flickering light; the frightened wide eyes of the boy met the steady, senatorial gaze of the father.

"Run."

It was said in a level tone, as if Cotta was speaking to him across his writing desk, yet for a moment there was silence amongst the chaos and it was all that Celer heard.

A Frank in a mail shirt took advantage of the glance to dart forward. Cotta heard the man's footsteps and the eye contact was broken as he wheeled and swung the stand wildly at his foe. The Frank stepped in close, his armoured forearm soaking up the blow, as he slammed the hilt of his sword hilt into Cotta's face.

Celer cried out as he saw his father crumple, but then the Franks were coming for him.

He swung over the wall and dropped down the other side. His bare feet made little sound as he landed awkwardly in the dark of the alley. Light flared from the windows all around him as the noise and flames from his home roused the neighbouring households.

Celer darted off along the alley and heard a shout in a language he didn't know, then a thump as something heavy slammed into the alley behind him, followed by more of the strange language in a more strained voice.

He didn't look back, just sped down another alley and kept going, twisting and turning though the dark streets, leaping over or swerving around anything that loomed out of the darkness. He ran for what seemed like hours until his senses came back. All at once he was aware of his laboured breathing and the cold dawn air on his sweat-soaked skin. He stopped and leaned heavily on a wall, panting as his eyes darted about but he could see no one, nor hear the sound of anyone chasing him.

He was near the Forum. Dawn's light was creeping over the rooftops of Rome and as he watched he saw a few people begin to gather to set up stalls.

As his breath returned, so did the feeling to the rest of his body. He shook uncontrollably, a mixture of shock from the night's terrors and the unfamiliar strain upon his body. His feet were filthy and felt tender, but mercifully had not been cut on his wild flight through the dark city streets. His body was cooling quickly in the chill morning air, his unbelted tunic swinging loosely on his thin frame.

Celer suddenly felt very vulnerable in the ever-growing light. Would the Franks be looking for him still? He did not understand what had happened to make his family a target for such a brutal raid, but he thought it may have had something to do with the senators his father had hosted during the night.

Celer shook his head and gathered himself before moving slowly down the street away from the Forum, hugging the shelter of the wall. What reason the Frankish soldiers had for hunting him he did not know for certain. What was certain was his fate, if the soldiers, or any of the emperor's men for that matter, were to find him. The histories that had gripped his mind as a child left no delusions about the brutality of Roman politics.

The dangers the city now held for him were great, but it was also his only hope for help, and so he found himself moving cautiously towards the house of Varro.

The sun had risen above the city walls, and the morning rays shone through the spaces between the buildings by the time he was a few streets away. A space across the street had been cleared for the building of one of the tenement blocks that crept ever closer to the areas once occupied only by the elites of Rome.

The work gang had not yet arrived, so Celer hurried over to the mound of rubble and tiles that was all that remained of the previous building. He was hoping for something he could use as a weapon, but the work gang obviously took their tools with them at the end of their day. He began picking through the spars of wood, trying to find one short enough for him to use, when his foot scraped against something sharp in the rubble pile. Celer dug around quickly and retrieved an iron nail about half as long as his forearm, with crudely squared edges from the blacksmith's hammer. He cast about and found some tattered scraps of cloth, grey with age and the dust from the demolition. He bound the nail near its head to protect his hand and used a second strip to belt his loosely hanging tunic around his waist. The rubble was biting cruelly into his sore feet, so he wrapped them in more rags. There had been no time to grab his sandals from his room; the attack had happened so fast.

Gripping his makeshift weapon, he hurried out onto the street. His worries about his appearance drawing attention were soon dispersed. The streets of Rome now hummed with the sounds of humanity; a multitude of languages swarmed his ears and the people swirled past him in a sea of colour. No one paid a second glance to the dust covered youth, the expensive cut of his tunic disguised by the grime and stains from his sweat, as he forced his way through the press toward the house of his friend.

He knew something was wrong as soon as he saw the roof of the house of Varro above the heads of the people packing the street. Even though he was now in a wealthier district, the crowd in the street had deepened and people were no longer pushing their way along the street, but instead craned their necks to try and catch a glimpse of Varro's front door. As he tunnelled his way forward, the nail grasped tightly in his hand and laid flat against his forearm, the cold hands of fear gripped him tighter and tighter.

Frankish soldiers.

Six of them stood facing the crowd. At the sight of them, Celer froze. Someone shoved him from behind and he stumbled forward. Fortunately, luck was on his side and his face, disguised by a mask of dust, was just one among many in a crowd that surged and retreated from the raised shields of the Franks, as those at the back pushed forward to gain a look, whilst the front row strained to distance themselves from the shield wall and menacing sword points behind it.

The front door had been broken and through the gaps in the shields, shadowy shapes could be seen moving in the house. Suddenly, an armoured man, blood spattered across his mail armour, backed out of the house dragging something behind him. He threw a body on the ground and stood over it as another soldier followed, dragging a smaller body.

Young Varro! His friend was bloody and blackened by soot, and lay limply on the ground. The first man who had been dragged out tried to crawl to him but the Frankish warrior kicked him hard in the ribs so that he flipped over onto his back. Celer vaguely recognised him as one of Young Varro's older cousins.

Two more soldiers came out, carrying Varro the Elder between them. Celer barely recognised the face of his father's closest friend. He was so badly beaten that his face was swollen and purple. His jaw hung open loosely, and long tendrils of blood and spittle stretched almost to his chest.

A final Frank herded two women out with the point of his spear; he forced them to their knees where they cried and wailed, Young Varro's mother, Fausta, clutching his twin sister, Varrina, to her. Both were sobbing in terror.

Celer was suddenly aware of the thunder of heavy boots on the paved streets, and the crowd forced themselves apart as Virius Nicomachus Flavianus the Elder, Prefect of Italy, marched through in full military attire, surrounded by about fifty elite Auxilia soldiers.

Celer shrank back further into the crowd. His father and Flavianus despised one another, and Celer's face was well known to the Prefect. Celer knew little of what had sparked the feud between the two men, for it had happened in their youth and Cotta had never spoken of it to him. Cotta had often remarked to his son that it was men of Flavianus's character that had been the main cause of the Senate's downfall, an unforgivable trait in his father's eyes.

Slightly behind the Prefect marched his son. Flavianus the Younger had been made Prefect of Rome by the new Emperor, and was resplendent in gleaming, ornate armour.

The young Prefect scanned the crowd with an arrogant gaze and Celer felt the usual wash of hatred as his gaze passed over him.

Whilst their father's enmity was shrouded in mystery, Celer had good cause to hate the son of the Prefect of Italy. Flavianus was older than him, and was handsome and charming to his social superiors, but to all others he was a fiend who delighted in cruelty to those beneath him. Celer had suffered, along with the other young children of Rome's aristocracy, at Flavianus's hand over the years. There had been evil rumours of incidents with slave girls and daughters of lesser houses that were spoken of in hushed tones, though never when his father was near, and nothing ever seemed to stick to the young nobleman.

Flavianus the Elder drew up in front of Varro, and Celer thought he heard him chuckle. Flavianus said something quietly that Celer couldn't make out, even though the crowd had hushed to a low murmur. Flavianus turned and spread his arms wide. "Citizens!" he cried, and the crowd hushed.

"The man that kneels before you is a Senator of Rome, sworn to serve you, the Roman people. Yet he has betrayed his sacred purpose, and betrayed you, by plotting treason against his Excellency, Emperor Eugenius." He paused, expecting a response from the crowd, but apart from a dull murmur, the crowd gazed silently back with wary eyes.

"This family of vipers," Flavianus continued unperturbed, "and others of their ilk, plot to invite the Christian, Theodosius, to bring his armies to our lands, and wreak death and destruction upon you!"

This time the crowd broiled with angry shouts and several spat past the Auxilia who screened Varro and his family from them, riled by their loyalty to the old faiths.

Flavianus smiled at the emotions he had stirred, before half turning back towards Varro.

"And yet!" he raised his arm for quiet and the crowd obeyed at once.

Celer was both horrified and in awe of the power he seemed to wield over them. "And yet, our good Emperor is merciful!" He turned to look down on Varro. "If you will name all of your fellow conspirators, then you and your family shall be exiled, stripped of your wealth and title, but free to leave and go where you will."

As he finished, Varro's nephew pulled himself up onto his knees, and spat a large globule of blood onto Flavianus's boot.

Without turning, Flavianus raised a finger in his direction, and the Frankish soldier behind Varro's nephew grabbed him by his hair in one hand and hauled him into a kneeling position. The soldier then rammed a dagger into his neck.

As the crowd exploded with cheers of "Kill the traitors!" Celer watched in horror as the body jerked on the floor, blood pumping out onto the paving stones.

Varro the Elder was staring up at Flavianus with hate-filled eyes.

The Prefect met his gaze and said with a voice full of malice. "Do not test the emperor's mercy again; name your pathetic band of traitors, and the rest of your miserable family may yet live."

Varro, his breath rasping through broken teeth, looked down at the limp form of his son, and his crying wife and daughter. He was about to meet Flavianus's gaze, his mouth opening as if to speak, when he suddenly stopped. His eyes seemed to look straight at Celer, his gaze locked with such intensity that the Prefect began to turn.

Varro lashed out like a viper, and struck Flavianus a terrific blow to the groin with his fist.

As the Prefect crumpled, Varro was pierced by swords and spears from the Franks and Auxilia. His wife screamed hysterically at the sight, gripping her daughter's head even tighter to her chest.

The Frank with the spear took careful aim, before ramming his point through Varro's wife's back. He then leant all his weight onto the spear haft and pushed it through into her daughter's body, pinning the two together in an eternal embrace.

Young Varro's guard stooped to lift the unconscious boy to his knees, his sword raised in his other arm. At the site of his friend's peril, Celer took a step forward, uncaring of the armed spearmen blocking his path. He had barely taken another step, when a vice-like arm folded round his neck, and hauled him backwards into the tumultuous crowd.

He tried to struggle free as his captor forced his way through the crowd, but the arm only tightened, and his vision began to darken. He tried to raise the nail to stab at the arm but it snagged on a passing cloak and was ripped from his grasp. Stars exploded before his eyes and darkness gathered at the edges of his vision.

The last thing he saw was Flavianus the Younger, laughing as he scanned the crowd. Then the darkness filled his eyes and he saw no more.

# III

He was only unconscious for a few seconds.

His legs had begun to fold under him as the blackness momentarily enveloped him, but the arm around his neck was removed and a strong hand clamped the back of his tunic, keeping him on his feet.

To Celer, it seemed like he had blinked and jumped twenty feet down the street; his throat felt bruised, and bright stars filled his vision.

The hand gripping the back of his tunic pushed him roughly through the crowd, not minding whether he knocked people out of the way, and a chorus of angry shouts followed them down the cobbled street. Being pushed along was forcing him to bend slightly, so he had to look up and to his left to take a look at the cloaked and hooded figure who had grabbed him. He thought the man – for it was a man; he could see a thick beard in the shadow of the hooded face – stood a similar height to him, around six feet.

"Who ..." he managed to croak.

The man's left hand shot out and clamped over his mouth.

"Not here." The hooded face didn't turn in his direction but the pace quickened as the crowd thinned.

They pushed on in silence as the sun continued to rise above the rooftops and the citizens of Rome began another day, ignorant of the terrors of the night. Perhaps they wouldn't care anyway, Celer thought to himself, as he was forced along, even if they knew what had happened to his family and friends - for all he knew, the families of every man at the meeting last night. Celer was not ignorant of the marriage of grudging respect and general loathing the general populace felt for those of Senatorial rank. It was much the same across the Empire; in all the towns and cities he had visited he had picked up the same impression from the citizens he had encountered.

Generations of his forefathers had led armies, built great public works and held games for the people, his father had told him. But they had also made power plays and taken sides in the struggles for power that had led to civil wars. They had held feasts and flaunted their wealth, whilst others starved and sold themselves and their children into slavery to pay debts, and that was what the people remembered in what his father called their "civil memory".

The sight of the city's New Wall, raised almost a century before, snapped him back into the present. He recognised where he was and began to struggle.

"No!" He tried to rip free. "No, I can't leave. My parents, I can't leave my parents!"

The man just shoved him on faster, as they neared the Appian Gate, his left hand gripping something hidden in the depths of his cloak.

Then he stopped.

The abrupt halt jerked Celer upright from the near horizontal position he had been forced along in, and he saw what had made the man draw up. The gateway through the high walls swarmed with men. The city guard who manned the gate were there in larger numbers than usual. They went about their usual routine of checking all people and goods coming into the city, or stood about with their spears leaning against their shoulders. But their large numbers weren't the reason that Celer's captor had stopped dead.

As well as the larger body of guards, there were perhaps twenty Frankish soldiers. Whilst the guards checked all coming in, the Franks were checking everyone and everything going out. Celer saw a wine merchant pulled roughly off his cart as heavily armoured Franks, with long braided moustaches, climbed up with drawn swords and began searching amongst the amphorae.

Celer shot a glance at the hooded man and saw that something between rage and fear burning in the darkened pools of his eyes, and Celer instantly knew who he was, despite the hood.

The man dragged him off the main street, which was thankfully crowded due to the slow progress through the gate; their sudden halt and rapid move to the side was missed in the turbulent mass.

The back of his tunic was finally released, and Celer sat down heavily on a low wall, rubbing his sore throat, whilst the man leant against the building and peered around the corner at the armed men that had spoiled his escape plan.

"You're Varro's cousin, Attianus," Celer stated rather than asked.

Attianus turned towards him and pulled off his hood, revealing raven black hair that hung in curls almost to his shoulders. Combined with the thick beard, his entire face was framed in black curls. Bloodshot brown eyes stared at him from amongst a face darkened by the sun. Celer had met him and his brother often enough in passing to know them by name, but they had always been too old to join in his and Varro's boyish games.

"Cousin of the Younger and nephew of the Elder." He nodded.

"Then that man was..."

"My brother Atta, yes," Attianus interrupted brusquely.

"I'm sorry." The words sounded empty to Celer, remembering the brutal manner of this man's brother's death, but he said them anyway.

Attianus didn't respond, he merely continued watching the gate.

"We can't leave!" Celer blurted out.

"No," Attianus replied, with a tone of grim humour. "No, we can't."

"My father and mother might still be alive; I have to help them!" Celer cried, trying to get up.

At this, Attianus turned back to him and forced him back down, his mouth a grim line amongst the beard.

"Did your father give you instruction before you left?" he asked.

Celer shook his head, remembering the noise and confusion of the night.

"No, there was no time. We had no warning, he just told me to run, so I did." At these last few words Celer hung his head.

Attianus made as if to place a comforting hand upon him, but stopped himself; the boy would have to make do without comfort now. Instead he nodded and spoke slowly. "He told you to run, so that's what we're going to do. We still have a job to do; you were supposed to accompany my brother and I to Constantinople with a message for Theodosius." He reached into a leather bag that hung from his shoulder under his cloak, and pulled out a leather tube with a wax seal at either end. "I still have the message," he said, holding it forward so Celer could see it clearly enough to see a mark had been pressed into the wax end, presumably the mark of Varro.

"What does it say?"

Attianus looked at him worriedly. "Your father told you nothing of this?"

Celer shook his head. "I was to go to Constantinople to continue my studies, that's what he told me last night. He said you and your brother travelled there on business."

Attianus swore and looked away, considering. "Senator Cotta will have had his reasons for not telling you. However, those reasons may no longer be valid; much has changed and I need you to understand our situation," he said, turning back to the frightened boy before him.

"Your father and my uncle, along with several other Senators, were planning to convince the Senate to oppose Eugenius with an army. They needed an alliance with Theodosius to fight alongside them," said Attianus, grimly turning back to watch the gate again.

"That doesn't make any sense," urged Celer, shaking his head. "My father is a loyal Roman."

Rage flared across the older man's face. "They were all loyal Romans, boy! Their loyalty was to Rome and her people, not to a puppet dancing on the strings of a Frankish warlord," he hissed vehemently.

"Your father wanted the Senate's powers restored. He and my uncle believed the Senate could give the Empire the stability it needs to regain its strength."

Celer was speechless; he could not imagine his stoic father orchestrating such a grand scheme.

"Your father never mentioned such things to you?" Attianus asked, looking at him dubiously for a moment, as if he questioned who Celer was.

Celer struggled to respond; his mind seemed to be racing, and yet fixated on the memory of his friend's dead body all at once.

"We need to leave the city," Attianus said, not waiting for a reply, "and make for Constantinople. We'll be safe there, and we can gather support to seek vengeance for our losses at the hands of Eugenius and Arbogast." He spat the two names.

Celer was shaking his head.

"I can't leave without knowing that my parents are still alive."

At this, Attianus thumped a palm against the crumbling plaster of the wall he had been leaning on, knocking chunks to the floor of the alley.

He seemed to gather his thoughts for a moment before speaking, and Celer was momentarily aware that whilst Attianus was grieving for his own family, he was now tasked with taking care of him and felt, in that moment, a brief flash of shame.

When Attianus spoke, he did so slowly and softly, as if it might lessen the blow of his words.

"If your family were taken by the Emperor's men, then they will have either been killed in the street, as my family were, or they will have been taken for questioning. If they survive that, they will most likely be executed, for neither the Emperor nor Arbogast would risk leaving your father alive."

He gripped Celer's shoulder; not to offer comfort, but as if by doing so he could impart some strength into the boy.

"I am sorry about your parents. Truly, I am. But to stay in the city is to invite capture and your own torture and death. We need to leave, to gather the support of Theodosius as we were instructed. With luck, some of your father's allies in the Senate will have survived the night and will continue their work. Once our task is done we shall return and wreak retribution on those who have broken our families."

Attianus's words leant full weight to Celer's grief, and it now struck him with such force that it robbed him of his breath. His eyes shone with tears but by sheer force of will, he restrained from crying. He would not cry in front of Attianus, nor in front of any other from that day forth, he vowed to himself.

This struggle of will and emotion played out on Celer's face and Attianus nodded approval as he saw will win out.

"We look to our own safety now," Attianus said, looking around. "Let's get out of the open, give me time to think." He shot another glance towards the gate in time to see the back of the wine merchant's cart disappear into the waiting crowd beyond the city.

The Franks were slowly working their way through a mass of foot traffic that had built up behind the merchant's cart. Attianus made sure they were busy before looking around the buildings that crowded the edges of the main street.

Immediately next to the gate the cobbled street widened, its edges dominated on one side by a stables with a blacksmith's attached and on the other by a three-storey inn. The owners ran a wagon repair business between the inn and the city wall; Attianus could see several in varying states of repair under a large awning and watched as a boy rolled a newly crafted wheel across the street, nimbly dodging the crowd, and into the blacksmith's. He supposed that both businesses were owned by one wealthy citizen, or family, who would catch all the passing trade entering the city via the gate. The inn looked comfortable, but was too close to the guards and Franks for them to get in without risking being spotted. The rest of the buildings lining the main street were a mixture of wine shops, brothels, inns and small food vendors; everything a traveller or trader needed before heading to the larger markets deeper in the city, near the forums and Emporium.

Attianus spied a wine shop on their side of the street, heading away from the gate. He grabbed Celer by the arm and hauled him from his seat, pushing him into the street, falling in behind him so that his cloak masked them both from any Franks who might happen to look up the street.

He pushed Celer ahead of him into the wine shop, and paused a moment to allow his eyes to adjust to the gloom.

It was a low-ceilinged room, long and narrow, with benches and tables lining either wall. It was almost deserted apart from a few of the previous night's clientele, who were slumped over the tables, snoring amongst wine stains and vomit splatters. Celer stumbled past the tables. Even in his dazed state, the rancid tang of wine and other nameless things that hung heavy in the air made him want to gag. There was a counter at the far end with a door behind it, from which the smell of baking bread wafted through. A staircase rose above the counter, leading to the upper floors. Attianus slipped past Celer, and led him down the narrow isle to a table near the counter, sliding in so that his back was against the wall. Rather than sit opposite and not be able to see the entrance, Celer slid in next to him.

A dark-haired girl, close to Celer's age, stepped through the open doorway. Her passage wafted the smell of the fresh bread towards them and they both turned from watching the entrance for a moment.

She looked up and examined them before turning back through the doorway, calling out so softly that Celer couldn't make out what she said.

A man appeared in the open doorway. Like the girl, his arrival carried the smell of fresh bread and, like her, his hair was also dark, albeit streaked through with grey. But the similarities ended there. He stooped and turned sideways to fit his massive frame through the doorway before straightening, laying hands like masonry blocks on the top of the stone counter.

Celer could see traces of the girl in the man's face and by the similarity of their hair colour he guessed the man was her father.

Attianus rose and went over to the counter and ordered food and watered wine.

The girl's father listened to his order impassively, his eyes quietly examining these unusual early customers. Attianus looked every inch a man preparing to leave the city; the wine shop owner had seen his kind countless times over the years. The boy, however, was an oddity. Clearly on the verge of manhood, he sat with a posture and stillness that the shop-owner associated with his few wealthier patrons and the military personnel that frequented his establishment. Yet the boy looked nothing like a soldier, could barely pass as one who served in the city guard let alone as someone from money judging by his dirty appearance and feet bound in rags.

Yet he had long ago given up trying to understand the flow of humanity that came through his front door. The coins that Attianus placed on the counter were enough for him, so he scooped them up with one large hand, turned, and shouted the order through to the kitchen before reaching down for the cups.

Attianus placed the cup of wine before Celer and sat down. The boy looked at it dumbly for a moment, before wrapping a hand around it and taking a sip that turned into a gulp; before Attianus had a chance to raise his own cup, Celer had drained his.

"Better?" asked the older man.

Celer made no reply but instead stared into the empty cup, his face blank. The boy looked tired, Attianus thought, as he drank his own wine; it would be some hours before either of them could rest. Despite both escaping the raids on their families' homes, they were by no means safe. The speed with which Arbogast's forces had moved frightened him tremendously. He knew that his uncle and the boy's father had taken all precautions to ensure the secrecy of the meeting's purpose the previous night. Even he and his brother had only been informed upon Varro's return. The meeting had not been kept a total secret but instead talked about openly as a social gathering of friends and political partners, a common occurrence amongst the political elite. He cast his mind over the Senators who his uncle had told him had attended and could think of none who would betray Varro, or Cotta, who was held in such high esteem by all. Yet one of them must have, he thought, staring into the dark liquid as if he would find the answer there.

The dark-haired girl reappeared after a short while, bearing a jug of well-watered wine to refill their cups in one hand and two platters of food skilfully balanced in the other.

Whilst she placed the food and drink on the table before them, Attianus found himself admiring her. She was a rare beauty, no doubt, a trait that could be both a blessing and a curse, he thought. She was closer to the boy in age than him, and he was briefly amused to see that she had captured Celer's attention, despite the ordeal he had suffered. The girl would have turned the head of even those pious Christian priests he had met who had sworn to a life of celibacy, Attianus thought to himself.

The girl, for her part, kept her head low as she placed the platters and jug down and refilled their cups. Her eyes briefly darted to meet Attianus' as she poured his drink, but when she met Celer's gaze, Attianus would have sworn her lips twitched into quick smile. The boy tried to return the smile but the grief and tiredness was too fresh upon him, and it spoilt his attempt. The girl hurried off.

Attianus pushed a platter in front of the boy, then began eating hungrily.

He eyed the door as he ate, conscious that they could not linger long, yet all the while his mind broiled with the terrors of the previous night.

He and Atta had woken at the first crash upon Varro's door, bunked together in the same room as they had since they were children. Attianus had been first to the bedroom door. Atta had grabbed him then; his brother had been carrying the bag that contained the letter for Theodosius, and he had thrust it into Attianus's free hand.

Varro's door had not held up long against the axes and hammers of the Franks; a vicious slaughter had erupted in the atrium. Attianus had thrown himself at the press of men surging through the door and managed to knock one of the Franks over with his shoulder. Atta quickly grabbed the axe from the man's hand and threw himself at the bodies forcing their way through the splintered door. His uncle was there, wielding an ancient-looking sword, an heirloom that the brothers had both coveted as children.

Seeing that Attianus carried the bag containing the letter, Varro shouted at him to make for the back gate. At first, he had ignored the words of his uncle and turned to help his brother, but Varro was not a man to be ignored. He had seized Attianus by the back of his tunic, dragged him backwards and thrust him towards the rear terrace.

There was a small gate that led out to the street behind the house; his aunt and cousins, along with most of the house slaves, were already heading to it as he stumbled out into the cool night air.

A slave girl went through first, and instantly screams rent the night air as she quickly ran back in, slamming the gate shut behind her. The gate shook as something heavy slammed into it, and several of the slaves threw themselves at the gate to stop it being forced open. He remembered the look on his aunt's face as she turned, grasping both her children tightly to her; a look of almost animal fear. When she saw him, she seemed to steady herself. She knew what was in the bag, and from the look on his cousins' faces he guessed that they knew also. She glanced quickly at the wall separating them from the terrace of the next town house along, and he caught the meaning in her gaze.

The food on Attianus's platter was bread and beef; the bread was fresh but the beef tough, probably from the previous night, but he didn't care. He relished its toughness as he chewed angrily in silence.

Why had he not given his cousin the bag instead, and forced the boy and his sister along with his aunt over the wall instead of him? He knew the answer, of course, they all did. Getting the scroll to Theodosius was more important than them, and neither his cousins nor his aunt had a better chance of reaching Constantinople than him.

So he had jammed his foot into a crack in the wall, boosting himself up onto the top.

As he hauled himself up, the terrace gate was forced and armoured men flooded in, hacking at the slaves. More soldiers arrived from the atrium, where they had subdued his brother and uncle. Attianus had reached down to his aunt, who pushed her daughter towards the wall, but one of the Franks hurled a throwing axe at him and he had to twist awkwardly to avoid it and toppled backwards off the wall. He never saw his family captured, only heard his aunt and cousin screaming, a crash, shouts, and the sound of heavy blows on soft flesh.

There was a sickening crunch, and the thump of a body collapsing. Hands grasped the top of the wall, so he had grabbed the bag, quickly checking the tube containing the letter was still in it, before fleeing over several more terrace walls and dropping into a side street, disappearing into the dark city. The bag had yet to be made ready for travel, containing only the cloak he now wore, a small coin purse, an empty canteen, and a dagger. He had slumped down in a dark alley that stank of shit and rotting vegetables, and waited for the dawn before heading back to see what had happened at his uncle's house.

He had spotted Celer instantly; the boy naively trusted the crowd to hide him and Attianus had had no problem moving quietly up behind him. His brother's death had almost paralysed him, but then his uncle's stare, for it had been aimed at him and not Celer, had steadied him, and allowed him to grab the boy in time.

The thought of his brother's jerking body and the blood pumping onto the street filled him with hate and rage, robbing him of the last of his appetite, and he pushed his unfinished food away from him with an angry grunt that made Celer jump and shoot him a questioning glance, but the boy said nothing.

In truth, Celer had been watching Attianus out of the corner of his eye the whole time they had been eating. He had noticed the thousand-yard stare, and the tight jaw muscles as the older man chewed the tough meat a little more forcefully than Celer thought necessary. He had not wanted to eat himself, but Attianus's example made him force down as much of the meat and bread as he could, although he went easier on his second cup of wine.

They sat in silence for what felt like an age. Celer stared at the door to the street, fully expecting a helmeted head to appear through the door and shout their discovery. Attianus merely stared at the table, rolling his empty cup between his palms. When Celer finally drained his second cup of wine and didn't reach for the jug to refill it; Attianus put a hand into the bag he still wore looped over one shoulder and pulled out the canteen. He poured the rest of the jug into the canteen and placed it back in the bag, then pulled out a scrap of linen and wrapped the rest of the meat and bread into a bundle, stowing it alongside the canteen.

"We can't stay here," said Attianus, rising to his feet.

"How are we going to get through the gate?" asked Celer, his voice low, as the owner had put his huge head through the kitchen doorway at the sound of the bench scraping.

Attianus raised a hand to him. "Our thanks to you, for the food and drink."

The owner dipped his head in reply and disappeared back into the kitchen.

"I don't know yet," Attianus replied, keeping his voice low as well, "but we had better get moving." They made their way back towards the door.

"I do not have enough coin to clothe you," said Attianus as he neared the door. "So..." He paused by the table closest the entrance and checked to see if the shop-keeper was watching.

He quietly reached over a drunk lying slumped over a table, and picked up a bundled up cloak. "We will have to find other ways to acquire such things." He handed the cloak to Celer and walked out onto the street.

The sun had risen high, and with it, the temperature; as they stepped out onto the street, Celer guessed it to be near midday.

The street heaved with people, largely due to the backlog of people trying to leave and those coming in, forcing their way through the crowd. The day was growing hot, the sun's rays quickly blasting away the coolness of the night. The bottleneck had attracted dozens of street peddlers, who either roamed through the crowds with anything from beaded necklaces to flavoured meats on wooden skewers, or spread their wares on gaudily covered rugs on the sides of the street.

As it was, Celer and Attianus emerged between two traders; a Jew who was selling trinkets and baubles, and a Syrian selling garlands of flowers, who hailed every woman and girl that passed. Celer quickly put the cloak on, despite the heat, and was pleasantly surprised to find it fit him well and that apart from a small tear and smelling strongly of wine, it didn't seem in bad condition.

Attianus forced his way into the flow of people, one hand clamped over the leather bag to deter any pickpockets in the throng, and Celer quickly followed. They headed back towards the city centre, but just as the crowd was beginning to thin and Celer was about to question his companion's choice of direction, they veered off to the left into a side street.

"Where are we going?" he asked.

"To find somewhere to hide until nightfall," Attianus replied.

"Is it not too dangerous to stay so long in the city?" asked Celer, hurrying to keep pace with him.

"It would be more dangerous to attempt to leave in broad daylight."

Attianus slowed his pace slightly to let him catch up, constantly checking behind them and any streets that joined the one they were on. "The gate is out of the question and will be for days; the others are likely also guarded. The only other way in and out, short of wings, is the river. Can you swim?" he asked.

"Yes, I can swim," Celer said, already dreading the idea of having to swim in the murky brown waters of the Tiber, a common dumping ground for the city's waste and other more sinister refuse.

They came to a wider street surrounded by tenement blocks. The area was quiet; the residents would be out in the city, scratching a living in whatever profession they had. Attianus picked one and led the way in, climbing up the staircases until they arrived at the top floor. The top floor was half the size of the one below, and Attianus climbed out through a window from the stairwell onto the roof. Celer followed, and was surprised to find a small jumble of broken amphorae filled with soil. Looking around, he saw the roofs of all the blocks had similar groupings of jars and wooden troughs, filled with soil, many showing the stalks and leaves of whatever plants the tenants were growing there to supplement their meagre incomes.

Attianus said nothing about the broken pots but merely led him around the corner of the roof to the side that was shaded by the wall. Here there were no pots and Celer guessed that they would be undisturbed.

Attianus squatted down with his back resting against the wall and wrapped his cloak about him and Celer did the same. "If you need to sleep, do it now," said Attianus, stifling a yawn himself. "I will wake you in a few hours, then you can go on watch until nightfall."

Celer said nothing. He lay down and drew his knees into his chest, wrapping the cloak about him tightly.

Though he would never have admitted it, he was bone tired, and his feet ached terribly from walking, even with his makeshift foot wrappings. The rooftop was uncomfortable and gritty, and he thought that sleep would elude him, so he was surprised when Attianus shook him awake a few hours later.

The older man stood and walked over to one of the planters, urinating amongst the leaves, before coming back and slumping down.

He passed the bag to Celer.

"The rest of the wine and food is yours, eat as much as you can," he advised before he rolled over and fell asleep.

Celer sat and drank the last of the wine, then worked his way through the food. The bread was already going hard, and the meat felt tougher than the bag that he held between his knees, yet he forced himself to eat it all.

Afterwards he, too, rose and went around the corner of the upper floor and pissed in one of the soil-filled amphorae.

For the rest of the afternoon and into the evening, he sat with his arms wrapped round his knees, his feet and legs tucked into the cloak to shield them from the sun.

Attianus rumbled quietly in his sleep. Once or twice, Celer thought he heard the tramp of boots that would signal the arrival of soldiers or guardsmen, but the sounds quickly disappeared amongst the other sounds of the city.

From the rooftop, he could see small portions of the city between the roofs of other tenement blocks, and small sections of the walls with occasional figures silhouetted on its ramparts.

Looking into the heart of the city, the view was dominated by the Baths of Caracalla, the city's second largest.

Beyond that he could make out the stands of the Circus Maximus. To the left of the Circus were the slopes of the Aventine Hill and beyond them was the Emporium, the river port of the city, and main entry point for the city's grain supply.

He guessed Attianus's plan was to head for the Emporium, and then, by some method, escape down-river towards Ostia.

He could not bring himself to look to the east towards the slopes of the Caelian Hill where his home was; he was terrified of what he might see. The memories of fire and smoke, and the terrible screams of his family and household were still loud in his ears.

The moon seemed to rise slowly that night. He watched it, brooding on the fate of his family. He felt a near overwhelming urge to head into the city to try and find them, though he knew it would likely be suicidal.

He hoped desperately for them to be alive somewhere, imprisoned maybe, but alive. Yet, if what Attianus said was true, and his father had dared to challenge the Emperor, he knew that his parents were likely dead.

The brutal executions of Varro's family haunted his mind as the darkness of night closed in, and in his mind's eye, their faces were replaced with his family.

Tears threatened him again, and he angrily dug his fingernails into his palms until his eyes were dry, and there was blood on his palms. He looked around at the gathering dark, and shook Attianus. The older man woke instantly without a noise, looked around, and rose stiffly, stretching.

They climbed back into the stairwell; any noise they made was drowned out by the noise from the tenement rooms. People shouted at one another from behind rough wooden doors, above the din of squalling babies and shrieking children.

Four women were cooking on the ground floor over a communal hearth, but none so much as glanced at them as they stepped out into the night.

The street was busy, but not enough to hamper their progress. As they neared the Baths, they saw a patrol of city guardsmen coming their way. Fortunately, a group of men partially blocked them from sight and they managed to slip down a side alley to avoid them.

They saw many more patrols as they skirted the slopes of the Aventine; once, Attianus forced Celer quickly down another street to avoid a large group of men sitting on the steps of a tenement block. When Celer asked why, Attianus told him in hushed tones that officials often paid local gangs to help them hunt down fugitives.

By the time they neared the Emporium, Celer's nerves had been strained by all the near misses and his heart was hammering in his chest.

Even at this late hour, the docks were busy with cargo coming up river from Ostia. They would only quieten for a few hours around midnight, before work began to open the Emporium for dawn.

Groups of guards patrolled the main wharfs, so Attianus stealthily led the way through maze of cargo and wagons. He had hoped to find a small boat tied up at the lesser wharfs, either side of the main docking area, but they too were patrolled by guards and customs officers, who supervised the loading and unloading of the big river barges. They headed downriver, through a large holding area, avoiding more patrols until that too petered out, and they were once again amongst a residential area close to the city walls.

The gap between the riverbank and buildings narrowed until they could only just walk side by side. Celer could see the squat towers of the city walls that loomed either side of the river. The walls looked thick with men, clearly lit in the darkness by torches and lamps that illuminated the river below. Wooden platforms projected out from the towers, and men with burning torches held high stood on them, closely scrutinising each barge as it quietly drifted in and out of the city.

Attianus gave a hard look at the towers and wooden platforms and cursed. He scanned the riverbank for anything that would float, cursed again, and slapped his thigh. They could hear the distant tramp of boots behind them that heralded a patrol coming their way; the dull melody was slowly getting louder.

"Take of your cloak and tunic," Attianus hissed at Celer.

"What?" Celer was hugging his cloak tight to him; the night air was cool after the heat of the day.

"Your cloak and your tunic," Attianus repeated, pulling off his own, "quickly!"

Celer did as commanded, and stood still as Attianus put both tunics and cloaks into the leather bag. Then, they both slithered naked down the riverbank, and crouched just above the waterline.

Celer tried his best to ignore the putrid stench of the river, and was glad of the darkness that hid the layer of scum and debris that he knew floated just inches below him.

Attianus let two barges drift past before he saw one that fit his purpose. A huge barge, long and wide, riding low in the water bearing bales of wool, probably from the dye tubs on the Aventine, drifted towards them. It was so heavily laden that some of the bales protruded over its sides, with scraps of twine that bound them trailing in the water.

He let the front of the barge pass before wading into the water. They had to be quick, so he kept one hand on the boy's shoulder, knowing he would hesitate. He was surprised when Celer swam strongly and quietly out to the barge.

Celer tried to climb onto the barge, but Attianus held him back, instead pushing the leather bag into a gap between two bales. Then, holding onto the barge with their right hands and holding onto the bales above their heads, they drifted slowly towards the towers.

The river was cold after the heat of the day and the still night air, and Celer had to clamp his jaw tight to stop his teeth chattering. He tried to focus instead on not breathing too deeply the noxious fumes that rose from the Tiber, and resisted the urge to pull himself out onto the barge.

As they crept closer to the towers, the urge grew stronger and stronger. Something brushed against Celer's foot beneath the water, and he felt a slimy tendril begin to wrap around his arm making him want to cry out, until he realised it was nothing more than a loose strand of twine from the bales.

Then they were under the towers, and the water shone black like oil in the flickering light of the torches and he pulled himself closer to the barge and the wool bale a little closer to his head.

He heard shouts between the boatmen and the guards on the wall, though for some reason the combination of the chill water and the stench of the river seemed to make the words unrecognisable; Celer sent a wordless prayer to Tiberinus, the god of Rome's river, asking that he would deliver them safely in the river's cold embrace, free of the city walls.

The shouting stopped, and the light began to dim until there were only small pools of light from the torches at the front and rear of the barge, and they were drifting into a dark landscape, the walls of Rome silhouetted behind them against the night sky.

Attianus reached for the bag. His fingers felt like stone and would barely grip it, so he clamped his chattering teeth into the leather.

He tapped Celer on the shoulder and felt the boy recoil from his touch in surprise; thankfully he did not cry out, and the pair of them pushed off silently from the barge and began to swim towards the bank.

The pole man at the back saw them and shouted something, but they trusted in the darkness to hide them as they hauled themselves up the slippery bank and onto the grass above it.

"Here, dry yourself," Attianus said, his voice shaking from the cold as he threw Celer his cloak.

Celer scrubbed vigorously at his body, feeling like the filth of the river had crept into every pore. He felt better once he pulled his tunic on, and swung his arms to force the blood to flow into his chilled hands.

His legs, Attianus said, would warm as they walked. They were on the east bank of the Tiber, with Rome to the north, and so they set off south, away from the river and the city.

# IV

A light wind rustled the grass at their feet as they made their way from the city. Crickets buzzed and chirped noisily all about them whilst the familiar noises of the city, oddly muffled by the walls, faded behind them.

They kept clear of any path they came across and gave wide berths to any pinpricks of light that suggested a farmhouse or villa; Attianus didn't want to risk encountering any guard dogs and alerting the countryside to their presence.

They reached a stand of trees just after the moon had passed its peak. They were several miles from the city and Attianus thought it safe to rest a while. They both shrank down and instantly fell asleep. They both slept fitfully, waking often, and at one point Celer cried out, waking them both, and Attianus had to stem an urge to tell him to be quiet.

The dawn found them both red-eyed and awake. They were about to leave the trees when Celer froze.

"What is it?" asked Attianus.

Celer had cocked his head, "I thought I heard..." he clamped his mouth shut as he heard it again and this time Attianus heard it also "... horses," the boy finished in a whisper.

They both dropped to the ground and began scanning the countryside.

Dawn's rays slowly illuminated the field systems around them.

A quarter of a mile away ran a main road and Celer realised that in the dark they had stumbled close to the Via Ardeatina which ran south to the town of Ardea.

Four horsemen had appeared on the road coming from Rome, all clad in steel with scale armour shirts and tall conical helmets. They carried shields and long spears, the points gleaming in the morning rays.

They trotted along the road in a line and Celer could see that they were searching the fields either side of them. A small farm lay close to the road and the horsemen turned down its dusty track and disappeared into the small courtyard formed by the house and barn. As soon as they were out of site Attianus rose up from the leaf litter.

"We have to move, now!"

They both set off at a run; Attianus led them towards the road, his eyes fixed on the farmhouse, only glancing at where he was going. Celer followed him gamely, bare feet making no noise in the dewy grass. They both leapt the side ditch of the road onto its paved surface.

Celer felt the cold, worn stones beneath his bare feet for a moment before leaping across the far ditch into the field on the other side.

They were now on the opposite side of the road to the farm and Attianus slowed to a crouched run, trying to keep low in the crop of wheat as their line of sight into the farm's courtyard grew with every step. When he saw the rump of a horse in the yard he dropped to his belly and began to wriggle, snakelike, through the wheat stalks, pushing the bag before him. Celer quickly followed his example, pressing himself into the stalks.

Crawling quickly exhausted them both, tired as they were from lack of sleep for two nights, yet when a woman's screams and men's shouting rang out from the farm, fear fed new energy into their muscles and they wriggled forward faster until they hit a drainage ditch. Attianus slithered down into its boggy bottom and Celer followed.

They crouched, panting, ears straining for any sound of man or horse but they heard none. Attianus motioned with a hand for Celer to stay put then slowly raised himself up until he could see through the wheat.

The horsemen had left the farm; two sat upon their horses on the road scanning the fields, the others had broken off and headed towards the stand of trees where he and Celer had hidden but moments before. He watched as one rider dismounted and stalked amongst the trunks whilst the other, still mounted, circled the stand. The two mounted men on the road had were not looking in his direction, so Attianus took a quick look around to make sure there were no more patrols before dropping down into the small safety of the ditch.

Celer tapped his arm and, mouthing, asked if the mounted men were Franks. Attianus shook his head grimly and mouthed "scholae", noting the colour drain from the boy's face as he turned and began crawling down the ditch away from the road.

Celer quickly followed him, making sure to keep low, ears straining for the sound of hooves in the field above. The scholae cavalry units were the elite bodyguard of the Emperor. Chosen from Germanic tribes for their superior horsemanship and physical prowess, the tall, blonde warriors were feared fighters who had replaced the Praetorian Guard of old. The city had filled him with fear at every corner yet now the thought of being hunted across the open countryside by those mounted warriors made him wish for the tangled labyrinth of Rome's streets.

He glanced back over his shoulder in the direction of the city. Rome was hidden from his view by the ditch but he could see the plumes of smoke rising from thousands of fires. Somewhere just outside the city gates his horse would be tethered in the stables outside one of the main gates, no doubt arranged by his father for his journey. How he wished to have his swift gelding beneath him; his horse was from fine stock and he thought he would have been able to outrun the armoured guardsmen.

Instead, all he could do was keep low and blindly follow Attianus, his hands and knees sinking into the mossy base of the ditch. He thought that they were heading east, away from the road and the scholae, yet their path would eventually lead them to the Via Appia; surely the road would be heavily patrolled?

If Attianus shared the same fears he made no sign. The older man moved with steady pace, trying hard not to make a noise, the leather bag clamped in his left hand and held clear of the water.

Attianus did share the same fears. The scholae truly terrified him; they were formidable fighters and even if there had just been one, he would not have dared alert them to his presence.

The involvement of the elite guard of the Emperor did not surprise him. By all accounts, Eugenius was not a stupid man; he had proved that by increasing his support amongst the Senate by declaring his support for the old Roman Pantheon of gods over the Christian God.

Were it not for the Frank, Arbogast, at the man's back, pulling the strings like a children's puppeteer, Attianus thought his uncle and the boy's father would potentially have supported Eugenius.

As it was, the message that they carried in the bag was treason against Eugenius's rule. No doubt the new Emperor wanted them caught as much as the Frank did. War between the East and West seemed inevitable in Attianus's mind. Two opposing ideologies would eventually clash no matter the cost. The letter that they carried, however, could mean the difference between Arbogast facing a war on one front or two. Eugenius and Arbogast stood to lose if the army of the Eastern Empire were to be aided by forces raised by the Senate at their backs. Without opposition to their rear the contest between the two Empires was more even.

As he crawled along in that ditch for what seemed like hours, Attianus hoped for war. He swore to himself that if he ever made it out of that ditch and lived to deliver the letter and boy to Constantinople as instructed, he would return with the army that Theodosius sent and he would face his pursuers across the battlefield. He would look for the face of Flavianus the Elder in particular and he would gut the spineless bastard who had murdered his family.

The thought of exacting his retribution brought a terrifying smile to his face as he crawled on.

They crawled all morning. The first ditch ran out, so, after looking about, they hauled themselves out and set out across the fields heading eastward. The fields were hot and thankfully quiet as the farm labourers waited for the harvest, yet they saw many patrols, so they stayed low and dropped to their stomachs when necessary and made good use of the field drains to cross the undulating plains.

By midday, they had come upon the Via Appia. It was busy with foot traffic but free, for the moment, of any patrols.

They dared not risk approaching the road from the fields for fear that someone would remember and report them, so they crept down to some farm buildings and made their way to the road from the farm track.

They risked travelling south for a short time then took the first path leading east from the road. The path skirted around the northern shore of Lake Albano and was pitted with ruts. That no one had bothered to fix them, Attianus pointed out, hopefully meant that the road was little used, which suited them fine as it took them away from the town of Albana.

By the time they reached the Alban Hills, night had fallen. They had not seen a patrol for hours and they were also both starving so Attianus took a risk and led them to a small farm holding nestled in a valley.

An elderly farmer answered the door and immediately tried to shut it, but Attianus begged him to let them enter, claiming to be lost travellers. The farmer relented upon seeing Celer. The boy swayed where he stood, almost too tired to keep his eyes open. The farmer was called Ennius; his wife, who presented them each with a bowl of thick stew and a hunk of bread, was called Albina, a common name in those hills, she told them.

As they wolfed the food down, Ennius explained that his two sons were in Rome on business but would return within a couple of days. Neither of his guests gave much by way of a response; they were both busy making sure they extracted every scrap of food from their bowls. When they were done, Ennius led them outside to the small barn attached to the house. He kicked a few pigs aside and threw some fresh straw down for them to sleep on.

Attianus began to thank him but Ennius raised his hands to stop him.

"No need for thanks, friend," he said. "If I ever saw a boy in need of a good night's rest it would be that boy of yours." He motioned to Celer who had already sunk onto the straw and pulled his cloak over his head.

Ennius chuckled quietly at the sight and turned back towards the house. "Stop by the house after dawn and there'll be food to see you on your way," he called over his shoulder. There was no reply; Attianus lay curled up asleep, wrapped in his own cloak.

In the end, they slept through the dawn and only woke when Albina brought two steaming bowls out to them. It was a simple porridge with a few chopped figs in it but to Celer it was the best food he had ever had. Albina placed a loaf of bread at their feet. "I'm sorry it isn't much," she began, but Attianus raised a hand to stop her.

"It is more than enough, good lady. Much gratitude."

"Good lady," Albina repeated with a wide smile, "well aren't you well spoken; could teach my two boys a thing or two, my husband also, for that matter!" she said with a laugh. "Well spoken you may be," she continued, "but well dressed you are not." She said this directly to Celer, eyeing his dirty bare feet.

He said nothing, instead concentrating on devouring his porridge.

"The boy's shoes wore out on the road," said Attianus to break the silence.

It was a lame excuse and Albina no doubt saw through the lie instantly but she did not push the subject. Instead, she produced a pair of worn and much repaired boots.

"They looked about your size and my youngest won't miss them. Still a bit of wear left," Albina said holding them out.

Celer took them and put them on and stood to test the fit.

"Much gratitude, Lady, for your kindness."

"No need for that, young master," she said with a smile. "They're only old boots after all."

"Lady," Attianus rose to his feet, "we cannot thank you and your husband enough."

"Some day, we shall find a way to repay you," added Celer.

Albina's tanned faced blushed with their words, making them all smile.

"There's no need to promise such things," she said. "I'll not ask where you go, for I think its best I don't know. But I wish you a safe journey; may Mercury guide and protect you in your travels."

They refilled the canteen they carried from a small stream by the farm then made their way out of the valley, heading south; Ennius and Albina watched them until they disappeared over the brow of the hill.

Their progress through the hills was slow, though they travelled lightly, and so it took them two days before they reached the southern foothills of the Alban Hills. In the distance, across a wide plain, they could see the Apennines range, peaks rearing dark against the evening sky.

Attianus lay awake that night, exhausted as he was, the worry gnawing at his mind making sleep impossible. They were travelling far too slowly; they had covered barely thirty miles in two days. He would not allow himself to blame the boy who lay curled in an exhausted ball next to him. Celer had never travelled in such conditions in his life and had yet to complain, yet Attianus could see that the boy lacked the stamina to maintain even their sluggish pace for long. He could only hope that Celer would gain some strength in his legs before they reached the Apennines. He cursed the thought of his horse sitting in a stable somewhere close to Rome; mounted, they could have been three times the distance from the city.

Their pursuers had no such worries, he knew. They could cover much more ground more quickly and the noose around them would be drawing shut quickly. They had to make it to the mountains and hope to lose themselves amongst the peaks where it would be all but impossible to track two men.

The thought gave him some comfort and he clung to it as he willed away the demons of his mind and willed his body to sleep.

They had spent the night hidden away in a small wooded valley; it was a pleasant enough evening but for Celer the night was torturous.

The constant drone of crickets as well as the shrieks and barks of much larger animals and the creaking of the canopy in the breeze kept him awake for hours, and when exhaustion finally did lull him to sleep his dreams were vivid recollections of the murder of Varro's family. He dreamt of being trapped in a dark alley whilst the tramp of armoured boots rose to a deafening thunder in his ears, gathering pace until they turned to the hammer of hoof beats which would rip him back to consciousness with a start.

Attianus, who had barely slept at all, woke at dawn to find Celer awake, huddled in his cloak. He said nothing to the boy but instead passed him the last of the bread given to them by Albina. Celer took it wordlessly and ate without emotion. He accepted the canteen in a similar fashion when it was offered and, when he was done, Attianus went down to the small stream that ran past where they had slept and refilled it.

When he returned, he drew the dagger he now wore on his belt and found a young ash tree. He hacked away for a while until the trunk was cut then he busied himself trimming the branches from it and broke off the thin upper end. He was left with staff roughly five feet long and sturdy enough that it did not bend unless he leant heavily on it.

Celer was watching him with a vacant look that Attianus did not care for. He was worried about the boy; their journey would be a hard one and they would both have to endure hardships they had never dreamed of before it was over. Unless Celer pulled himself together soon, he might not make it.

To break him out of his sombre mood, Attianus tossed the dagger so that it landed an arm's length from the boy.

"Cut yourself a staff," he said, breaking their morning silence. "You will need one when we get to the mountains." He pointed his own staff at the looming slopes that were still dark as the morning sun rose behind them.

For a moment, he thought the boy wouldn't get up, but then Celer reached for the knife and hauled himself to his feet. He wandered a little way down the slope until he found an ash similar in thickness to the one Attianus had cut and began to hack away half-heartedly. It was tough work as the dagger was small and light and Celer quickly discovered he had to swing every blow with all the force he could muster. The work warmed him quickly and seemed to ease the tenseness he felt in his body; all the fear and grief of the past few days leant his arm strength and soon he had hacked huge chunks out of the tree.

Attianus came down and pulled the tree towards him to stretch the fibres so that they might be severed easier and Celer hacked through the last bit of trunk with ease. He was breathing heavily as he began to trim the branches but by the time he had finished and turned to Attianus with his new creation, he was calm. His eyes still had bags under them but they were now focused and alert.

Attianus re-sheathed the dagger at his belt and they set off downhill, walking briskly to keep warm in the cool morning air. They soon emerged at the foot of the valley and the trees gave way to pasture land and they could see the whole plain before them.

Gently rolling hills were covered with small villages and outlying farms; they seemed to sit along a line running from north to south and Attianus guessed that they straddled a main road, possibly the Via Labicana.

As they set off across the fields, the dawn light revealed small herds of cattle and goats, each minded by a young boy, being driven towards the hills for the days grazing. Some simply stared in silence as they passed whilst others waved and called out greetings. The first farm they came too was a few miles from the road and looked so rustic that Attianus wondered if it had ever received visitors from outside the valley. They met the farmer in the well-beaten farmyard, milking a cow. After assessing their coin, he pointed them in the direction of the farmhouse where his wife gave them freshly baked loaves and strips of dried meat in return for some of their dwindling supply of coin.

Despite the hunger pangs gnawing at his belly, and the hungry stare of the boy, Attianus carefully wrapped the food into separate bundles and stowed it away in the bag. His hands momentarily closed on the sealed tube, as was becoming his habit to check it every couple of hours.

They followed the farm track out towards the main road. Both of them slowed as they drew close; their eyes scanned the distance looking for mounted men or the glistening spear points that would mark an armed patrol. They saw nothing.

The road was well maintained and already busy with traffic. Carts loaded with goods and animal fodder rumbled past and more than once they had to move over to allow herded animals, destined for the town markets or even the great markets of Rome itself, to pass.

Travelling on the busy road made Celer nervous; although few of their fellow travellers bade them a second glance, it felt horribly exposed. He could tell Attianus felt the same way by the way he protectively hugged the leather bag to his side. The one benefit that he could see was that their progress towards the foothills of the Apennines was greatly speeded by the road. For the moment it was taking them on a diagonal line across the basin between the Alban hills and the Apennines. Off to his right he could make out rooftops and see the curling smoke of a town or village and he guessed at some point the road would swing further south to meet it.

Shortly before noon, just as he was beginning to feel comfortable walking out in the open, Celer felt the unmistakeable drum of hooves through the thin soles of his new boots. Attianus heard it too and he threw a worried glance over his shoulder before grabbing Celer's arm and pulling him to the side of the road. They fell into step behind a slow-moving cart piled high with amphorae. Attianus released Celer's arm and placed his palm on the back of the cart as if he was helping it along. Celer quickly copied him.

The cart driver remained oblivious; he was whistling an off-key tune and didn't notice the two strangers suddenly assisting him, but Celer hoped that they appeared to be part of the small convoy.

He gripped his newly-made staff tightly as the hoof beats grew to a low thunder and briefly wondered what use it would be against an armoured cavalryman.

The horseman was right on top of them now and Celer dropped his head and tensed, ready to hear a triumphant cry and a blow to the back of his head, but to his great relief the horse thundered on by, its rider low over its neck.

Attianus had kept his head up and he got a good look at the rider as the horse flew past. From his attire Attianus pegged him for an imperial courier; a dispatch bag securely fastened to the back of the saddle confirmed this. As he took all this in, the rider turned and looked at him.

For a moment Attianus thought he saw the man's eyes widen, but the horse did not slow and in a few heartbeats it was already growing smaller as it tore along the road.

Celer gave an audible sigh of relief from his side but Attianus could not share the feeling. He had no reason to feel suspicious. There were thousands of riders in the courier service, many stationed in Italy, yet the man had looked back and he had looked right at him and Attianus had a grim idea about what might have been in that dispatch case. No doubt the bargemen that had seen them slip off towards the bank had reported back to Rome which would explain the scholae patrols outside the city. Following their failure to find the fugitives, the Emperor would have issued orders to all corners of Italy demanding their capture. By now, every town and, more worryingly, every port would have officials and patrols looking out for them.

He turned to the boy next to him. "We have to get off the road," he said quietly.

Celer nodded in agreement and pointed towards a small track that branched off the main road and headed straight for a small village about two miles from the road.

They hurried over to the track. Attianus tried to judge the distance to the town that sat on the main road, hoping to gauge how much time they had before the courier would reach it and round up some troops. He thought they would make it past the small village at the end of their track before any riders would make it back to where the courier had passed them. After that it would be a game of cat and mouse.

They kept up a fast pace along the track, neither of them keen to be out in the open.

"Who was that on the horse?" asked Celer.

"Imperial dispatch rider," Attianus huffed in reply.

"You don't think he was looking for us?" the boy sounded worried.

"I think there's a good chance he may be carrying orders for our arrest. I imagine there have been hundreds just like it sent out all over Italy. They're going to try and close any escape route we can think of."

Celer had no response to that, but he threw a fearful glance over his shoulder and hurried his pace to a trot so that they almost ran the last mile and a half to the small village.

The sun had just passed its zenith as they passed through the village and many of the villagers were stood about talking in between their daily chores. Many stopped their conversations as the two strangers, breathing hard, passed through the single street. Celer felt their inquisitive looks and tried to keep his head down as they hurried through.

Several tracks ran from the rear of the village; most were small and clearly led to farms that radiated out from the village like spokes on a wheel. Attianus chose a wider, more worn track that seemed to lead to woodland about a mile from the village. The track wove its way through open fields of wheat, dotted here and there along their borders with the mossed over stumps of trees and he guessed that in the past the woodland had reached much closer to the village before a farmer decided he needed the land for crops more.

By the time they reached the trees, they were both breathing heavily and Attianus could feel a stitch developing in his side. He cursed his lack of stamina, wishing again for his horse and looking darkly up at the hilltops that rose above the trees. They would both have to get fitter, he thought as he took two strips of dried meat from the bag and gave one to Celer who was leaning on a tree, red faced from running nearly three miles from the main road.

"I don't think we're being followed," panted Celer between bites of the meat.

"No, not yet," agreed Attianus, "but word will soon get around from the villagers that we came this way." He swallowed the last of his strip and took a swig from the canteen, then passed it to Celer. When the boy had drunk and passed it back, they set off again.

At first, they followed paths made by the villagers through coppiced stands of trees, but as the afternoon wore on the paths petered out and they had to push their way through denser undergrowth. By late afternoon, the ground had begun to rise noticeably.

"We're climbing," commented Celer.

"The foothills of the Apennines," Attianus explained breathlessly. "When we come down from these mountains we'll be on the Adriatic coast."

"Then once we cross the Adriatic, we'll be safe?" asked Celer.

"That's right. Once on the other side, we're beyond Eugenius and Arbogast's reach," said Attianus, hoping he sounded as confident out loud as he did in his head.

They struggled on until they cleared the tree line. They were close to the summit of the first hill and still within the farmland of the villages.

Attianus allowed them to stop for a moment to catch their breath when Celer suddenly straightened, staring back down the slope to the distant village.

"What is it?" Attianus panted.

"There are horsemen in the village," Celer replied, fear plain in his voice.

Attianus swore and strained his eyes towards the distant village. By all the gods, the boy must have the eyes of a hawk, he thought to himself.

"How many?"

Celer paused a moment, raising a hand to shield his eyes from the sun's glare.

"Maybe ten, it's hard to tell, there are villagers gathered around them."

Attianus cursed under his breath. "No doubt telling them that they saw two travellers pass through heading east," he said a bit louder.

"They're moving!" Celer cried, taking an involuntary step back. He looked across at Attianus with terror in his eyes. "They're coming this way!"

They forced their tired legs into a run towards the summit of the hill. Ahead, they could hear sheep bleating somewhere over the crest. Not wanting to give away their presence, they contoured around the side of the hill and entered a valley. By early evening they had followed the long ridge line to the head of the valley. The ground began to climb steeply, taking them up to the summit of a huge spine of mountains running north to south and they were both grateful for the extra purchase from their ash staffs. The air was cold at the summit, despite the late summer sun, and the wind blew up the valley in gusts, making them hug their cloaks to them tightly.

Celer led the way over the top, both of them glancing back in the failing light, but they could see no pursuers. They had walked up onto a long plateau and now had to make their way across, stumbling across its rock-strewn top.

When the ground finally began to fall into a valley on the far side, the sun was just a sliver on the far horizon and the slopes were cast into deep shadow. They carefully picked their way down, their aching limbs making it difficult, and at last reached the gentler slopes of the valley bottom. It was dark now and they could just make out a clump of bushes below them, illuminated in the moonlight.

The temperature was dropping at this altitude and Attianus was about to suggest they push on further to find better shelter when the long moaning howl of a wolf sounded somewhere above them. They both froze in the darkness. Attianus felt his balls draw up as a wave of primal fear washed over him; they stood and listened, ears straining to hear over the gusts of wind that rustled the grasses around their feet. The wolf remained quiet. Attianus felt about in the dark and found Celer's arm; he pulled the shivering boy close to him and whispered in his ear.

"Head for the bushes, quietly."

Celer tried to reply but fear and exhaustion had stolen his voice. His legs, however, obeyed the order and he crept towards the bushes, Attianus keeping one hand on his shoulder all the way.

The bushes, or stunted trees, Attianus couldn't tell in the darkness, had grown amongst a rocky outcrop, protected from the hungry mouths of sheep and goats that grazed this high up. There was a slot between three boulders that was big enough for both of them and as soon as they slipped in they were sheltered from the wind. Attianus didn't stop to enjoy the sensation; instead, he drew his dagger and felt about in the dark for the base of the prickly plants that grew amongst the boulders. He hacked and slashed away until he had cut all within reach of the slot and he used the thorny brash to barricade the entrance. One of the boulders leant over, leaving only a small gap above their heads, but Attianus took no chances and used the remainder of the brash to fill the space. Finally, with his hands bleeding from the thorns and spines of the plants, he slumped back into the space and hugged his cloak about him. They lay in silence for some time, straining to hear any movement from outside but the wind moaned around the rocks and drowned out any noises from beyond them.

"The thorns will keep anything out," Attianus said after a while. "Try and get some sleep."

"OK," came the hoarse whisper from his right. He doubted either of them would sleep much that night but he was exhausted and his body felt heavy and numb with tiredness and cold.

He lay there with his eyes closed and listened to the wind moan and whine above their heads, willing for sleep to come. Eventually he drifted off and all too soon a shaft of weak morning light filtered through the branches of their rough shelter. The light shone through his eyelids and woke him; he raised his head groggily and looked around.

Mercifully, the wind had dropped and when he raised a hand to the shaft of light he could feel the warmth of the morning sun on his skin.

Celer lay beside him still as a corpse and for a moment Attianus did not hear the boy breathe or see him move and was gripped with the irrational fear that the boy had somehow died in the night.

He was about to reach out and shake his companion when he saw his cloak stir slightly and a small murmur issued from his mouth. He contemplated waking the boy so they could set out but it was the first time Celer had slept for more than a few hours since they left the barn belonging to Ennius and Albina. His own body craved more rest and the sunlight, weak as it was, was creeping into their makeshift shelter, slowly warming the rocks about them. He lay his head back down and closed his eyes; he would rest a few moments longer then wake the boy.

When Celer woke the dawn had long since broken. He, too, considered sleeping more but them he saw how high the sun had risen and he forced his aching body to stir. He reached over and shook Attianus; the older man started and grabbed for the dagger at his belt. Celer drew back as Attianus looked around, eyes wide before he remembered where he was.

"Sorry," the older man mumbled slumping back.

"That's OK," said Celer. "We should get going; it must be nearly mid-morning."

Attianus nodded and rubbed his face with both hands. His beard that had been neat when they fled the city was now going wild with several days' growth.

Celer felt his own face and felt the soft hairs on his upper lip and along his jaw line; he had only begun shaving the year before and the hair still grew patchy and soft.

With the howl of the wolf still fresh in his ears, Celer removed the brash from above their heads and cautiously stood up. The outcrop sat on the head slope of a short, tight valley. Behind him he could make out the ridge line they had descended from in the dark; the landscape was bathed in sunlight, a far cry from the wolf-infested darkness they had stumbled along the night before.

He removed the crude barricade that separated them from the outside world and Attianus followed him out. The older man squatted down and examined the ground just beyond where the brash had been piled. Celer saw his brow crease into a frown and he too squatted to get a look at the ground. There, clear in the dirt, was a single wolf print.

Their eyes quickly scanned the slopes and the valley bottom but they could see nothing amongst the rocks or scattered trees. Gathering their staffs, they hungrily chewed at one of the loaves and some dried meat as they walked. The valley bottom was marshy and despite the late summer warmth their feet still sank, so they hugged the south side and soon neared the valley mouth. The valley ended abruptly in a steep drop, cut perpendicular by a larger river valley running north to south. Opposite them, the eastern valley slope rose to a sheer, rocky cliff face. Scaling it would be unquestionable but Celer could see that if they followed the river north a short distance there was a low pass to the east that led into what looked like a fertile plain nestled in a bowl rimmed by peaks.

The descent down to the river valley was treacherous. Thorny scrub tore at their skin and clothes as they scrambled down loose scree that gave beneath their feet at every step. They both fell repeatedly, only saving themselves from greater harm by jamming their staffs into the rocky ground.

About half way down they hit a broad shelf and they followed it north, relishing the respite from the steep hillside. They had not gone far when Celer spotted the hut. It was cunningly built up against a larger boulder and its stone walls blended into the scree slope behind it. However, as they neared, Attianus raised his hand to slow Celer and shifted the staff in his hands so that he held it like a club.

The body lay perhaps twenty feet from the hut's crude wood door. It was a man, perhaps in his twenties, wearing the rough spun clothes of a peasant and Celer guessed he was a shepherd that minded one of the many hill flocks that grazed in the mountains. Close by lay the mangled headless body of a dog.

Gingerly, Attianus rolled the body over with his boot; they saw the bite and claw marks and that the man's belly had been ripped open.

"Wolves," said Attianus grimly, covering his nose and mouth against the stench of the man's open stomach. Celer stumbled over to the hut and leant heavily on the wall, retching. When he had finished he came back to the body. Attianus had pulled the shepherd's cloak over the body, hiding the wounds.

"We should burn him," said Celer, his voice rough from the retching.

"We don't have enough wood for a pyre."

"Then we should bury him."

Attianus thought about it for a moment. The gods frowned upon those who did not treat the dead with due respect, his own father had once told him and his brother, many years before. They would be likely to curse any such trespasses with ill fortune and he and Celer could not afford more misfortune.

"The ground is hard and the wolves may return," he said.

"Still, we should."

In the end they raised a stone cairn over the body; Celer laid the decapitated dog next to its master. He also found the shepherd's staff lying where the man had dropped it as the wolves pulled him down. The crook was formed from a sheep's horn, cleverly fitted to the shaft; its point was bloody and matted with fur. Celer wiped it clean on the grass and placed it on the shepherd's chest and folded his hands over it, carefully keeping his own hands clear of the red ruin of the man's belly. Once this was done, he joined Attianus in carrying over chunks of rock until they had covered the body.

They searched the hut; the remnants of a fire smouldered in the hearth so Attianus added logs and breathed into the pile until flames reared up. Celer took a burning log and used it to light up the hut, for there were no windows and the walls were so thick the only light came from the open doorway.

They found another cloak and a crudely fashioned sheep fleece jerkin as well as a leather bag, similar to the one Attianus carried but of plainer craftsmanship, hanging from a jutting stone above the sleeping platform. They found a few hard loaves and a pot of olives in oil. Dried meat hung from the ceiling and there were small pots of dried plants and vegetables. Attianus found a battered cooking pot and filled it with water from a carved stone bowl. He threw in handfuls of whatever he could lay hands on and when Celer found a small amphorae of wine he splashed a quarter into the pot.

They feasted on the stew, meagre as it was, soaking the bread in the juices until it was soft enough to chew and packed the rest of the shepherd's stores into the bag Celer now carried. He also now wore a long knife at his makeshift belt and Attianus carried a worn hatchet he had found.

A rough track zigzagged down to the river and they crossed a rickety wooden bridge and found themselves on wide track. There was no one in sight as far as they could see so they followed it north and found that it split into two, one smaller track leading east up to the pass they had seen that morning.

The path zigzagged up to the pass and, although they were both bone tired, Attianus pushed them hard towards the top. He was worried about the pursuers from the village; there were many valleys and ridge lines that they would have to search but they would be moving a lot quicker than Celer and he could.

He was so lost in his worries that he failed to notice that they were being tracked. They had just rounded the last bend before the summit when they heard rattle of falling rocks in the scree above their heads.

Attianus was pulled from his thoughts by the noise and looked up just in time.

"Oh shit, Celer look out!"

Three wolves were tearing down the slope towards them, a cascade of small rock preceding them; more were coming from either side. A wailing howl went up from the wolves as if Attianus's shout was the signal they had been waiting for and they all raced forward to close the gap.

Attianus quickly guessed there were about eight in total. He swapped the staff to his left hand and ripped the shepherd's hatchet from his belt.

Celer stooped and picked up a fist-sized rock from the path and hurled it at the wolf leading the group. By the luck of the gods his throw was true and the leading wolf ran head-on into the rock and tumbled down the slope with a yelp before crashing into a large boulder.

The wounded cries of the downed wolf caused the other wolves to hold back for a moment. The two wolves coming down the slope checked their headlong rush; they came forward more slowly, lips drawn back to reveal long yellow fangs in wicked snarls. When no more rocks came their way, they hurled themselves forward at the two Romans in a grey blur of snapping jaws.

Celer recoiled from the attack, his insides turned to ice and his breath caught in his throat. He had been around hounds all his life, had played with the puppies of his father's hunting dogs as a child and followed the same dogs as they chased deer across their country estate for most of his teenage years. Never once had he been afraid of them but the wolves were different creatures. Huge and shaggy, with cruel, scarred muzzles above the rows of fangs.

His limbs were suddenly so weak he didn't know how he remained standing and the staff almost slipped from his numb fingers.

He turned to flee but more off the pack were closing in from behind them; long rangy strides carried them across the broken ground far faster than he would have believed possible.

One of the beasts darted in low and fast with jaws wide open. Celer's arms moved independent of his mind; he saw his numb hands rise up before him, swinging the staff at the wolf's head. It connected, but so weak was his swing that it did little more than turn the snarling jaws so that they missed him by a hand's width before the wolf's body crashed into him. Staggering from the impact, he was forced to the edge of the path as the wolf landed and turned with deadly grace and launched another attack at him.

Attianus had weathered the attack better, holding out his staff horizontally as the nearest wolf lunged at him and fending off the animal's attack. The large jaws had clamped on the wood, threatening to tear it from his grasp. The animal's strength terrified him and almost threw him to the ground as it shook its head from side to side but he managed to bring the hatchet down on its head with a wet crunch. He ripped the axe free but the wolf's jaws had a death grip on the staff and he had to release his hold on it and jump back as the rest of the pack arrived.

Celer knew he was going to die. The rest of the pack had arrived; all around him, the grey bodies bounded and skidded on the loose stones, snarling and yelping. The wolf that had leapt at him was coming back. Its head was low with ragged ears pressed flat against its head. Its jaws hung open and he could see its pink tongue stark against the yellow of its teeth.

Whether it was the knowledge that his death was imminent, or the reality that he couldn't outrun the pack, he didn't know, but his body suddenly came back to life. He felt every limb shaking as sensation returned, every fibre filled with a terrified, crackling energy. The ashen staff was rough in his hands, the snarls and cries of the pack filled his ears drowning the heavy pounding of blood in his ears.

The beast leapt again at him and again he swung. This time the fear leant him strength behind the blow and it caught the wolf in the jaw with a loud crack; the beast fell away with a dog-like yelp but he had no time to see where it went. More of the pack closed in, three darting jaws coming in fast from his right. The staff scythed across in a blur. He felt it connect and the wolves checked their advance; one turned and bounded away as he swung again at the remaining two.

"Stay with me, boy!" He heard Attianus's warning cry and risked a look over his shoulder. Two wolves were angling around him, aiming for the gap between them to get at their unprotected backs.

Celer and Attianus quickly backed up to one another whilst the five remaining wolves began to circle them. The death of the wolf on the track had made them cautious and they darted at the Romans individually, looking for a weakness.

Celer went to pick up another rock but the wolves nearest him surged forward the moment he began to bend down and he had to slash with his staff furiously to repel them.

He looked about desperately for a way to escape and saw a huge boulder near the summit of the pass. It was part of a large scatter from some ancient rock fall and Celer thought that if they could make it to that they might be able to climb out of reach of the snarling jaws of the wolves.

"Attianus, I think I see a way out!" he shouted over the din of snarling, snapping wolves.

"Where?"

"Up ahead, in the boulder field. I think if we can climb up onto that big one, they won't be able to get near us!"

Attianus slashed at a wolf, causing it to draw back, and risked a look up the slope.

"It can't be worse than staying here!" he shouted back, swinging at the next wolf that darted in.

He now wielded his dagger in his left hand and used it to stab the muzzle of a wolf that tried to lunge between him and Celer; the wolf yelped and retreated, a bloody gash running from its nose to below its eye.

They inched up the track towards the boulder field. Attianus kept his back tight to Celer's, his companion warning him about any obstacles that might trip him. They managed to wound three more wolves by the time they neared the boulders. Celer jabbed one on the muzzle as it lunged in to snap at his legs and Attianus managed to draw blood from two with his hatchet. The injured wolves backed off, licking their wounds; the rest of the pack eased off their attack and merely watched the Romans edge their way amongst the rocks.

As they entered the boulder field it became harder for the wolves to encircle them so that by the time they were thirty feet from the big boulder, the Romans stood side by side and felt their way backwards.

The wolves seemed to sense their prey would soon be out of reach; they nipped and yelped at one another, seeming to build their courage to launch one final attack. The boulders forced them to come in a single mass of fur and teeth. Celer stabbed forward and was rewarded with a gasping whine as he caught one in the throat, but he had exposed himself and another beast leapt at his open side.

Attianus saw the danger and rushed forward with a bellow. He rammed his dagger forward and the beast went down before it could reach Celer, taking his weapon with it. A dark grey wolf, larger than the rest, threw itself at Attianus's throat. The Roman swung his hatchet but missed and the animal's jaws closed around his shoulder.

Celer's fear of the wolves disappeared in an instant, replaced by the overwhelming fear of losing Attianus. He drew his own knife from his belt and stabbed the big wolf behind its skull as it dragged Attianus screaming to the ground.

Celer scythed his staff into the wolf pack, scattering them. Screaming at the top of his lungs, he drove them back as Attianus hacked at the dying wolf that was still trying to maul him. Two swings of the hatchet and the beast lay slumped atop him and he barely managed to heave it off one-handed. He struggled to his feet, his wounded arm unable to bear his weight, gripping the axe tightly but the pack had retreated.

Celer did not turn his back until the wolves were clear of the boulder field. When he turned, he saw how Attianus's left arm hung limply and he rushed to the older man's side.

"Can you climb?" he asked worriedly.

Attianus slipped the bloodied hatchet into his belt and hurried over to the boulder. He couldn't move his arm but Celer boosted him up so that he could get a hand hold on the top of the rock. He jammed a foot into a crack and hung on whilst Celer climbed up past him to haul him up.

They both lay panting on top of the boulder for a moment, finally safe.

Celer moved himself to a kneeling position and almost retched. His body was shaking uncontrollably and he felt utterly drained. He almost lay back down to let the feeling pass but then Attianus uttered a small gasp of pain and he instead reached for his companion's wounded shoulder.

Attianus flinched but then beckoned the boy to carry on. As Celer prised away the torn scraps of his cloak and tunic, he quickly checked the leather bag, making sure that it had not fallen foul of the wolves' snapping teeth. The bag was unmarked, their supplies and more importantly the scroll were safe.

After wiping the blood from the knife he had stabbed the big wolf with, Celer used it to cut open the remnants of Attianus's sleeve. The man's shoulder was slick with blood that pumped from multiple large puncture holes and a section of skin flapped loosely.

"How bad is it?" asked Attianus, wincing as the tunic was pulled away.

"Not that bad," answered Celer quickly, reaching into his own bag.

"You're a terrible liar, Celer," said Attianus. He groaned in pain as Celer doused his shoulder with wine from a skin he had carried from the shepherd's hut.

He clamped his teeth together as Celer poured more wine onto a strip he cut from the cloak they had found and bound it around his wound.

"Think we can make it to that village?" he asked as Celer finished the crude dressing.

Celer looked where he was pointing. The small cluster of dwellings lay at the foot of the pass and could barely be called a village, but it offered more shelter than their rock and there might be a healer down there.

He said as much to Attianus, who looked around to see what the wolves were doing. They were clustered just outside the boulder field; most were licking wounds but some snapped at one another and the two Romans watched as one was knocked over and fled, whining, from its attacker, head and tail low.

"They seem to have forgotten us," said Celer.

"That big bastard down there was probably the leader of the pack." Attianus spat in the wolf's direction. "They'll fight now for dominance until one emerges as the new leader; some might die, others will be driven off."

"They sound like Romans," said Celer grimly.

"That they do. Come, let's get off this mountain before they remember us."

They slipped off the rock and down into the boulder field. The path zigzagged as it had on the ascent but by unspoken agreement they took the direct line down the slope. Celer kept a wary eye on the slopes behind them, waiting to see grey flashes amongst the rocks. Attianus, for his part, concentrated on not stepping too hard; every jolt sent pain lancing through his shoulder. Drops of blood dripped from his fingertips, leaving a small red trail behind them.

It was late afternoon by the time they reached the cluster of dwellings. Shadows were gathering around the feet of the slopes as the sun fell below the heights above them.

Despite the cool evening air, Attianus was sweating. He was also getting dizzy. The bandage on his shoulder felt wet and sticky and the steady drip of blood continued from the fingertips of his wounded arm.

They saw a man outside the nearest building and Attianus was about to shout a greeting when the world span and he stumbled. Celer, who had been watching him begin to wobble, rushed forward and caught him before he hit the ground. Attianus heard him shouting for help as the world grew dark but the boy sounded far away. He was aware of other shapes joining Celer, who cradled his head as the darkness enveloped him and then he thought no more.

# V

When Celer woke, the house of Decimus was deathly quiet. He rose from the mat he had been shown to late in the night and padded barefoot into the kitchen area where Attianus lay upon the big table.

His upper half was naked under a blanket apart from his wounded shoulder, which was heavily bandaged.

A girl – Lucia, Celer remembered – sat on a bench next to the table, asleep. Her head and forearms rested on the table-top near Attianus's waist. The backs of her fingers were still crusted with blood from the night and Celer thought back on how she had worked hurriedly over Attianus's sweating body, snapping instructions at her father and sister as Celer stood helpless by the door.

When Attianus had collapsed, Celer had caught him and lowered him to the ground best as he could and called out to the man, Decimus, who was chopping firewood outside his home.

Together they carried him into the house where Lucia had been preparing the evening meal with her little sister. Seeing Attianus's bloody and limp form she had quickly cleared the table and told her sister to boil water then fetch some old linen. She had plunged a red-hot poker from the fire into a jug of wine, then poured the wine straight into the wounds. Attianus had screamed out and lashed his good arm at her and Decimus had to pin him to the table, whilst Lucia shouted to hold him still before he faded mercifully into unconsciousness once more.

Once she had sponged the wounds clean, Lucia had neatly sewn them closed. The linen strips which her sister had added to the boiling water were lain over the stitched wound and had shrunk as they dried, forming tightly to his shoulder.

Attianus had slipped in and out of consciousness for a time as she worked but he had ceased to struggle. When he was sure he would remain unconscious, Decimus had turned to Celer and questioned him about who they were and what had happened.

In his exhaustion, Celer had babbled something about being travellers and the wolves attacking them on the pass. He had slumped against the wall, staring at his hands, crusted in blood from the wolves and his companion. Lucia chastised her father and pushed him aside, insisting on cleaning the blood from him. Her sister prepared a simple meal of bread, cheese and olives and, once he had eaten, Celer was led to the sleeping area where the mat and some old blankets had been laid out. He had been asleep in moments and had not awoken when Decimus and his youngest presumably stepped over him to get to their beds.

Reassured that Attianus still lived, he backed quietly away from the table, dressed, and headed out the door.

He found the younger sister feeding some hens and pigs to the side of the house.

"Good morning."

The girl turned but said nothing, merely staring at him with big eyes.

"Where is your farther?" he asked.

Again, the girl did not reply. Instead, she pointed a grubby finger past the house at the pass they had come over. When Celer looked back to the girl, she had run off. He cast about, trying to see where she had gone, and noticed a woman standing in the doorway to another house watching him.

"Don't mind her," the woman said, "she's just shy with strangers."

"Her father has gone to the pass?"

She nodded. "Him, my husband and all the other men and boys. Gone to see if there are any more of you up there."

Celer shook his head. "It was just us."

"Won't be long till they come back then. Are you hungry or has my cousin fed you already?"

"Your cousin?" Celer asked confused.

"The little one's sister, Lucia," the woman said, pointing to Decimus's home. "Decimus is my mother's brother," she explained.

"She's still sleeping."

"Not surprised; sounded like your friend kept her busy for a while last night. How is he?"

"He lives," said Celer, though from the look of him it was not safe to say for how long, he thought.

"She has healing hands, that girl," said the woman proudly. "Got that from her mother."

She stepped back into the house. "Come in, there's still porridge left," she called over her shoulder.

The woman's name was Fontia, she explained whilst Celer ate. Her uncle Decimus was the headman of their small hamlet. They had heard reports of a wolf pack in the area from other farmers but this was the first instance near their farms.

The men and eldest boys, nine in total, had gone out at first light armed with bows and spears. A wolf pack in the area was bad enough; one with a proven taste for man flesh could not be allowed to live.

When he had finished eating, he listened to Fontia as she chattered away, bustling about her chores, but his mind kept drifting back to the prone figure of Attianus stretched out in the next house. When Fontia went out to feed the animals, Celer rose and followed her out. Dark clouds hid the mountain tops and the pass was obscured from view by the cloud that seemed to pour down the slopes like thick smoke. He remembered the smoke that had billowed through the curtains of his father's tablinum and shivered. He crossed the wide yard to Decimus's house and tentatively opened the door.

Lucia was awake and was checking Attianus's wounds. She looked up and gave him a tired smile as he drew near. The stitches held the wounds shut but blood and pus now seeped from them, accompanied by a foul smell that made him want to retch. Attianus's closed eyes shook and twitched and his face looked haggard and ashen. Sweat beaded on his brow.

Lucia changed the soiled dressing after wiping his wounds clean, then beckoned Celer to follow her and led him back outside.

The air felt wonderfully fresh and they both breathed deeply for a moment, clearing their lungs of the smell of blood and infection.

"My gratitude, lady. For all that you have done for Attianus," he said.

"My name is Lucia, not 'Lady'," the girl replied with another smile. "I only hope that it was enough and that the infection does not take further hold. His wounds are at the limit of my knowledge for healing."

"He stands a better chance than without you my la... Lucia."

She blushed slightly and Celer saw her pride at his praise.

"Does everyone from Rome speak so well as you?" she asked.

Celer was instantly on his guard. "I never said we were from Rome," he said carefully.

"Oh, are you not?" she missed the caution in his tone. "My father thought you sounded like you were from the great city. He has had some dealings with magistrates and tax collectors from there before."

Her explanation eased the fear in his gut somewhat and he felt guilty for being wary of the girl who had helped his companion.

"My apologies, your question surprised me. We are both from Rome, yes."

Lucia's face lit up.

"What is Rome like?" she asked excitedly. "Is it as grand as they say?"

"There are grand buildings," said Celer, nodding, happy to talk of his home rather than their present situation.

"Are the buildings really built of marble and the streets paved with gold and gems from across the Empire?"

He smiled at the notion, picturing the worn paved streets, the cracked and dirty facings of the buildings, weathered by centuries of exposure, people and bird droppings. "Some of the buildings are made from marble, as well as fountains and columns and numerous statues. All different colours; whites, reds, greens and yellows. Some are even purple, but no streets of gold, I'm afraid."

Lucia laughed with delight and clasped her hands together.

"Oh, what I would give to see it, to live in such a place!"

Celer thought of the putrid smell of the Tiber on a hot day, the beggars crowding the streets like flies and the grim tenement blocks that he and Attianus had hidden in as they fled the city. He wondered how many of the occupants had arrived at the ancient capital with dreams such as this girl's, only to be rudely shattered by the realities of Rome.

"You have a beautiful home here," he countered, looking out across the plain to the ring of mountains beyond it, wreathed in cloud.

Lucia shrugged. "It's home. We get plenty of trade along the road that brings news of other places and we are lucky to have good land but..." she trailed off.

"But?"

"There must be more to life than this?" Lucia swept an arm about the houses about the yard.

True, Celer thought. The hamlet lacked many of the comforts of his own homes in Rome or in the country and the people here would never enjoy the great spectacles of a city and all its delights. Yet, Lucia and her family would never be in a situation like the one he'd found himself in, far removed from the dangers of politics and high society. Nor could he see how they would be affected by the civil strife that plagued much of the Empire. Here, nestled in the mountains, they would be spared much that the people of Rome would have to endure.

"I think it would surprise you how many would be jealous of a life such as yours," he said sincerely.

Lucia looked at him strangely for a moment before something behind him caught her eye.

"My father returns!"

Decimus and the other men strode back towards their homes. As they neared, women and children emerged from the houses to great them. The men met their wives and children with smiles and kisses. Celer saw a young man about his own age duck out of his mother's embrace, awkward in a bid not to be embarrassed in front of the older men.

In the daylight, Celer got his first proper look at his host.

Decimus was of middling height, perhaps a few inches shorter than Celer but well built. A short-sleeved tunic bared tanned, brawny arms and large calloused hands that gripped a hunting bow and bundle of arrows. He had thinning grey hair, closely cropped above a lined face that had a noble bearing about it that reminded Celer of his father.

Lucia hugged her father and her little sister ran out from the house and threw herself at Decimus's legs. He laughed and kissed both quickly before turning to Celer.

"Good to see you looking rested. I would have words inside." He gestured towards his door. Celer nodded and followed the family in.

The noise of their entry caused Attianus to wake and he groaned and mumbled something incoherent. Lucia went his side and shushed him; she raised his head and tilted a cup of water to his lips. Most ran into his beard and his spluttered and choked but managed to drink some of the liquid.

Decimus hung his cloak and bow on a peg by the door and motioned Celer over to some stools by the fire. Lucia poured some wine from a flagon from a shelf and brought her father a cup before offering one to Celer.

"Thank you, daughter."

Decimus drank deeply then looked across at Celer.

"We found the wolves near to where you said you were attacked. They won't be harming anyone else."

Celer nodded, relieved.

"We found no other bodies?"

"It was just us."

Decimus nodded slowly and looked over at his daughter, tending Attianus on the table.

"You come from Rome?"

Celer nodded.

"That man on the table..."

"Attianus," Celer supplied.

"Attianus. From the cut of his clothes I would take him for a man of some wealth and rank. Are you his slave?"

Celer snorted at the absurdity of the comment but, noticing Decimus's frown, he looked down at his attire.

His once expensive tunic, worth more than half the animals in the yard outside, was stained and torn and flapped loosely. The rag he had employed as a belt was so frayed that it barely held together. The cloak held bundled in his hands still smelt of the drunk it had been stolen from mixed with his own sweat and was as equally torn and dirtied. The boots given to him by Albina still held but were clearly inexpensive.

Celer raised his eyes to meet the farmer's gaze.

"My name is Marcus Aelius Celer and I am no man's slave."

Decimus looked the boy over once more. The tone of his voice and the way he spoke did not fit his appearance and his body, though dirty, carried no sign of a slave's brand.

"Very well, then tell me, Celer. What brings two men from Rome into the mountains, on foot with no guides or guards?"

Celer had been dreading this question. He steeled himself before replying; the lie he was about to tell would be seen through in an instance if his tone was not believable.

"Attianus and I were dispatched from Rome some days ago on a diplomatic mission to Constantinople in the East."

If Decimus was taken aback by this response, he did not show it. Instead he asked, "Then why do you travel alone? Surely such important men as yourselves would not be without an escort?"

"The nature of our mission dictates that we travel unaccompanied," said Celer, inwardly seething at Decimus's inquisitiveness. "Our presence is not supposed to be missed in Rome and therefore we are not to attract attention to ourselves."

Pre-empting the farmer's next question, he said, "Our horses bolted two nights ago; the wolves followed us since then."

"They bolted?" Decimus did not sound convinced.

Celer hung his head. "It was my turn to hobble them that night. I must not have tied the knots correctly," he lied, trying to invoke some shame into his voice.

Decimus seemed about to pursue him further about their journey but then he relented and instead nodded acceptance of Celer's story.

"Then we are pleased to offer any help to servants of the Empire."

"My gratitude," said Celer with a strained smile. "Your assistance will not be forgotten."

Attianus chose that moment to moan loudly and tried to roll over. With a cry of alarm, Lucia grabbed him and hauled him onto his back once more.

"I think it is time we moved your friend somewhere more comfortable and with less risk of falling," said Decimus, rising from his stool.

With Celer's help they lifted Attianus from the table and carried him through to the sleeping quarters of the house.

"Place him on my bed," grunted Decimus as they carefully manoeuvred the sweating body.

Celer spent the rest of the day minding his companion.

He helped Lucia mop his brow and lift his head for water every couple of hours and had to roll him onto his back several times after he deliriously tried to roll over. He almost retched when Attianus loosed his bowels, late in the afternoon, but he could not show weakness in front of

Lucia and helped her clean up the foul smelling slick from the bedding.

That night Celer ate with the family at the freshly scrubbed table. He thought Lucia would ask him more about Rome but, when she went to speak, her father gave her a stern look and she dropped her attention back to her food. Decimus offered prayers to Ceres for the bounty on their table, glancing at Celer after he was finished. Celer was startled for a moment, wondering what more Decimus wanted him to add but then he realised the man was waiting to see if he offered prayers of his own and guessed his host was politely trying to divine whether he was a Christian or not.

In response, Celer offered a quick prayer to Empanada, the goddess of hospitality, thanking her for such gracious hosts.

Decimus met his eyes once he had finished and gave a small nod before turning to his food. Lucia gave Celer a dazzling smile for a moment before ducking her head once again before her father noticed.

After they had eaten, Celer went back to watching Attianus, but it was not long before his eyes began to grow heavy, weary as he was still from their trek from the Alban Hills.

The next two days passed in similar fashion. Celer slept fitfully at night, his dreams full of fire and smoke and his parents' cries. He relived the murders of Varro's family over and over, only now wolves stalked amongst the crowds outside Varro's house too. And when his friend was cut down, a laughing spectre of Flavianus the Younger raised a bloody sword in his direction and the wolves leapt from amongst the shadowy spectators, yellow fangs bright in the flickering light of the flames.

On the fourth morning since they arrived at Decimus's farmstead, Celer stumbled out of the house, finally unable to stand being in there. Attianus's fever had raged for days but now it seemed to be abating and he slept peacefully for the first time. Lucia thought that his wounds seeped less pus and were on their way to healing.

He found Decimus and several other men outside; they were splitting thick tree limbs and trunks into posts and rails to repair the stock pens surrounding the houses.

"Can I help?" he asked the men.

Decimus was about to find a way to politely refuse, explaining how inappropriate it would be to allow a diplomat from Rome to work on a farm when he saw he strained look in the boy's face and he relented. The other men looked to him and didn't object when he nodded and beckoned Celer closer.

The farmers showed him how to trim the tree trunks and limbs of any smaller branches then how to fashion wedges from small logs. Once the limbs were prepared, a heavy axe was driven into one end, causing the wood to split a little. The new wedges were then driven into the split with hammers and the back of axe heads. The deeper they hammered them the more the wood split. More wedges were hammered home until the timber lay in two halves. This was repeated until each limb or trunk had been quartered. The thickest of these were kept for posts whilst the others were split again to make rails. It started to rain as the men worked, so they retreated to a small barn behind Fontia's house where Celer was handed a chisel and wooden mallet and shown how to fashion the holes that the rail ends would slot into.

Once all the posts had been chiselled, Decimus led them out into the rain, which was now falling heavily, and they began the exhaustive task of replacing all the old fences.

For another two days, Celer toiled in the rain alongside the farmers, first digging up the old posts then replacing them with the new and packing the bases with stones from a nearby river so that they would not be knocked over by the cattle that watched the men sweat and curse, chewing grass with a dull indifference.

Celer's expensive tunic had already been ruined by the journey from Rome and was deemed beyond repair by Lucia. He continued to wear it during the day, no longer caring how dirty or torn it became. Each evening he would wash himself from a weathered stone trough and change into a much-patched tunic that had belonged to Decimus. The farmer tried to insist Celer took a newer, finer garment but he politely refused. The patched tunic was worn but comfortable and they found him an old belt to replace his rag. Decimus lent him a finely-honed knife to shave the patchy wisps from his cheeks. Not only was it good to feel clean again but he hoped the new clothes would help mask his identity should they encounter any soldiers on the road.

As the family went through their evening chores, Celer would sit by Attianus's side for a while, watching over his companion. Fever had raged within the older man for days and he had only taken in the smallest amounts of water and a dribble of honey between his lips for nourishment.

Late one night, when most of the family had retired to their temporary beds by the hearth, Celer was mopping Attianus's brow with a dampened cloth. Wearied by the labours of the day, he did not hear Lucia as she approached from behind him.

"How is he?" she asked.

"Much the same," replied Celer quietly.

Lucia reached out and gently removed the damp cloth. She laid her wrist against Attianus's forehead, his cheeks and throat.

"His fever does not burn as hot tonight," she said. Celer felt a warm glow of hope at her words.

The damp cloth had slicked Attianus's dark hair back so that it was near plastered to his scalp. With deft gentleness, Lucia teased the raven curls free so that they framed his face once again.

"He's quite handsome, your friend," she said softly, the back of her hand lingering on one cheek. "A little wild, perhaps," she added with a tired smile as her hand ran over the bushy tangle of Attianus's beard.

Celer did not know what to say to that. Fortunately, Lucia saved him from any awkward response. With another smile, she tiptoed over to her blankets by her father and sister.

Attianus seemed to be sleeping peacefully before him and his eyes were growing heavier with each passing moment. Wearily, Celer placed the cloth by the bedside and pulled a blanket up to cover his companion. He blew out the small lamp that illuminated the small sleeping area before gratefully sinking into the blankets that made his bed on the floor beside Attianus, surrendering himself to sleep.

The sixth day after they had arrived at the hamlet found Celer and Decimus lying flat on their stomachs packing the base of one of the last posts with river rocks. So intent on their work were they that they didn't hear the sound of the horse's hooves until the rider was in the yard. When the sound reached Celer's ears, his first instinct was to run into Decimus's house and grab Attianus. It took a moment before the rational part of his mind took over; it would only look suspicious, after all, and Attianus, though on the mend, was not yet back to his full strength.

Instead, Celer slowly rose to his feet and followed Decimus into the yard where the rest of the men had gathered before the rider. Celer's heart began to pound at the sight of the armoured rider who was dressed similarly to a city guardsman.

"I bring word from Appius Buteo, magistrate of Marruvium and all surrounding districts."

Decimus stepped forward. "I know who magistrate Buteo is," he said in a tone that suggested the rider was wasting his time. "What word does he send?"

"The magistrate has received a missive from Mediolanum," said the horseman grandly. When the gathered men looked back up at him with unimpressed gazes he swiftly continued.

"The magistrate and the citizens of Marruvium are to aid the Emperor in the capture of two fugitives."

Celer's heart froze and he felt some of the men shoot glances at him. Fortunately, the horseman had not noticed and continued.

"These men are considered enemies of the Emperor and the Roman people."

"And how are we to recognise these men should we see them?" asked Decimus.

The horseman grinned. "They should stand out well enough; these men are sons of Roman Senators."

There was a noticeable intake of breath from several men around Celer and there were mutters amongst the group. The horseman, happy that his words had drawn such a reaction looked about the men gathered before him. Celer felt his eyes upon him and forced himself not to drop his head and instead stared at the man's horse.

Decimus waited a few moments for the murmurs behind him to die down before he spoke again.

"I fear that magistrate Buteo would do better looking closer to home for two such men. No soft son of a Senator would last long out here." This drew chuckles from the men around him and the horseman frowned.

"I doubt the magistrate needs the advice of a common farmer in order to catch these fugitives," he sneered. "In any case, the Emperor's soldiers arrived in Marruvium yesterday and are already searching the town."

Celer's mind reeled at this news. Could these be the men from the village on the other side of the peaks? It had been over a week since they fled from the riders in the village and horsemen would have made much better time on surfaced roads than travelling cross country as he and Attianus had. He did not know if it was a blessing or spelled doom for them that their pursuers were now ahead of them rather than behind them.

Decimus smiled back at the rider. "Well if your master ever does need my advice, he knows where to find me. In the meantime, we have not seen the men you speak of, nor are we likely to; we are far from any main road."

The horseman shot a glance at the pass then looked back towards Decimus. "Very well, I shall report back to the magistrate."

When Decimus said nothing, the horseman took one last look about the yard before turning his horse and spurring it towards the road.

In the yard, the farmers turned to look at Celer and eyed him warily. Decimus pushed his way through them and stood before him with his hands on his hips.

"I can explain," said Celer.

"I think you had better." Decimus turned towards his house and led the way with Celer following.

Decimus bade them both sit in front of the hearth.

Celer sat on a stool in his dirty tunic, feeling self-conscious. Attianus, who looked pale and thin after days in bed with little food, held a cloak tightly about himself.

"Who are you, really?" asked the farmer.

When the two Romans looked at one another and said nothing, he snorted angrily.

"I have shared my house, my food, my daughters have seen to your wounds," he pointed at Attianus. "I deserve to know the truth."

"We did not mean to deceive," Attianus raised trembling hands to placate him, "we only wished to keep you from danger. We owe you that," he paused. "I owe you my life."

Decimus grunted and waved off the remark.

"What do you mean 'keep me from danger'? What danger?"

"We are hunted by the Emperor and his men."

Decimus twirled his hand impatiently. "I know that already, thanks to the disciple of Mercury out there. Why is the Emperor hunting you?"

"My father," Celer began, the words catching in his throat slightly, "and Attianus's uncle, along with several other Senators, objected to Eugenius's appointment as Emperor."

"Why, what do they have against the man?"

"Not him, as such," replied Attianus, "but the fact that his power is based on the whim of the Frankish general, Arbogast."

Decimus shrugged. "So what? Roman generals have long held power over the Emperors if they are not strong themselves, even I know that."

"Arbogast is no Roman," said Attianus bitterly. "A good general he may be, but his heart has remained that of a Frank. He uses his position to gain land and power for his people and them alone. Word comes from Gaul each week telling of growing numbers of Franks in the towns and cities. They keep their own language and customs and they have no care for Roman law. My uncle's associates say that the Franks intend to create their own kingdom within Rome's borders."

Decimus sat quietly for a moment, allowing Attianus's words to sink in. He cleared his throat and looked at Celer. "What did your father and these other Senators do?"

"They did nothing," said Celer angrily. "They had taken no action, they merely spoke of opposing his rule in favour of Emperor Theodosius."

"They are dead?" the farmer asked quietly. Both man and boy nodded.

"Easiest way to stop a fox getting at your lambs is to kill all the foxes first," mused Decimus. His eyes widened as he saw the angry scowls his words brought and quickly carried on.

"Your mission to the east, is that true?"

"Yes," said Attianus at once, keen to keep at least the scroll a secret. "Our mission was to go to the court of Theodosius and extend the good will of the Roman Senate to him."

Decimus sat back on his bench and leaned against the table with his arms folded and eyed them shrewdly. When a short time had passed with no words spoken, Celer ventured a question.

"What do you intend to do?"

Decimus seemed to debate his answer internally before replying with a grim smile. "Well, I'm not going to turn you in, if that's what you mean. There's little love for the Emperor or his tax collectors here, and it wouldn't do to treat guests in such a way, anyway."

Decimus's words relieved some of the anxiety that gripped Celer's body.

"You can't remain here any longer," Decimus continued, "Buteo is a fool but he will still send out more men soon and they will likely be carrying swords rather than messages."

Celer looked outside; the night was drawing in and the yard was filled with long shadows. Decimus caught his look. "Don't worry, you can stay one more night. That messenger will not reach Marruvium until late tonight. You can leave at first light; I will have Lucia make up some supplies. Your work the last few days has earned you that, at least."

They ate the evening meal in silence that night. Afterwards, Lucia presented Celer and Attianus with a bundle each that they stowed in their bags. Decimus led them out to the yard and took them to the barn where the wooden posts had been prepared days before. "You'll sleep here tonight." He passed them a blanket each. "Be ready at dawn."

That night Celer slept fitfully, his dreams full of wolves and armoured horsemen, all against a backdrop of smoke.

When they woke, he saw the mountains were pale and grey in the faint light of dawn.

By the time Decimus arrived at the barn door, they were ready to leave, cloaked in the cool morning air. He handed them a walking staff each and refused to accept the blankets back. Instead, he led them from the farm and onto the road heading east. As they walked, the sun slowly rose above the mountain tops but the land around them seemed to remain asleep; animals in the fields lay clustered in tight groups with lone herdsmen watching over them. When they came to a fork in the road, Decimus took the southern branch without hesitation. As the morning drew on, they began to see people in the small villages they passed through. Decimus would raise a hand or nod a greeting and the farmers would reply without sparing a glance at the man and boy who walked behind him.

When they reached the far side of a village much the same as the ones before, Decimus drew up at the side of the road. "I will go no further," he stated.

Attianus nodded and held out a thin hand which the farmer took after a moment's hesitation. "Our deepest gratitude, for all that you have done for us."

"Repay it by not mentioning my name or that of my family, should Buteo's men find you."

Attianus nodded his assent and then stood aside so that Celer could also clasp the farmer's calloused hand.

"The land from here on is owned by the wealthy in Marruvium. Their estates are run by stewards who work the slaves and are patrolled by their own guards. You should be fine on the road but take care at night; you will find few villages from now on and all will be suspicious of anyone who is not a trader or local."

He pointed a calloused finger north and Celer could see the wisps of smoke from many fires in the far distance.

"Marruvium lies that way. Stay well clear of it; the roads close to the city are likely to have many patrols."

They thanked him once more then watched as he turned and walked away.

"I hope we can trust him," said Celer quietly as Decimus disappeared back into the village.

"We trust no one," replied Attianus firmly. "For now, though, we take his advice and follow the road, try and keep our heads down and make it to the other side." He pointed south-east at the far-off peaks, the summits wreathed in cloud, and Celer shivered at the sight of them.

# VI

They heeded Decimus's advice and stuck to the road as they crossed the plain. By day the road was heavy with traffic and aside from the rumbling wagons there were plenty of travellers on foot, so Celer and Attianus managed to pass the regular patrols undetected. At first, Celer thought that Fortuna was surely watching over them as they merged into a large group of farm hands as a patrol rode past. He said as much to Attianus as they continued walking but the older man shook his head. "I don't deny we have been lucky so far," he conceded, "but those men are not real soldiers, more like enforcers for the local magistrate and his tax collectors. Had we been nearer to Rome or in one of the heavily garrisoned frontier provinces we would be forced to travel far from the roads and even then we would have had to watch our backs."

They walked for days through large agricultural estates, quiet in the late summer heat, and only occasionally did they see a slave gang at work.

From his short time with Decimus and the other farmers, Celer thought that the land occupied by the estates was far richer than the meagre holdings of the farmers who generally occupied the periphery of the plain surrounding Marruvium in the foothills of the mountains that ringed the plain.

The road took them through a low-lying pass and into a series of valleys. Stone mile markers, badly faded with age, indicated that the next major settlement was called Aufidena. Celer had never heard of it before. This was rural Italy, far from the intrigues and plots of Rome or Treverorum where life continued much as it had for several peaceful centuries.

The road was quieter now they had left the plain and the thinning cover provided by other travellers began to make Celer nervous. From the way Attianus kept checking behind them and carefully eyeing any groups in the distance, Celer could tell he felt the same.

On the third morning since they had parted with Decimus, they sighted a large cloud of smoke, fed from many smaller plumes that indicated a large settlement.

"Aufidena?" asked Celer.

"Must be," nodded Attianus wearily, still bundled in his cloak despite the growing morning heat. He was still pale and gaunt, the bones of his face showing more sharply than they had before. Lucia had taken a small pair of shears to his wild beard before they left, returning it to its neat lines that Celer had seen when they first met. Even with this, Attianus looked ten years older than when they had first escaped Rome.

They had spent the night alongside a lake that filled most of a small valley. A tiny village sat at the head of the lake but, to avoid encountering any locals or patrols that might spend the night there, they had camped in the dense woodland that hugged the hills on the south side of the lake. The long miles on foot and living rough had stripped any fat from their bodies. Attianus still suffered from the infection in his shoulder and now had a rasping cough that shook his thinning frame.

By midday they had left the valley after an exhausting climb over another pass. Weak as he was, Celer had taken Attianus's pack from him as the older man struggled up the slope, leaning heavily on his staff with every step. Celer stood at the top of the pass and looked towards Aufidena. The town was large and sprawling, with an industrial area just outside the city's low walls. He could see the road that they followed as it ran straight and true towards the west gate of the town where it met another major route that ran north to south.

A hacking cough made him turn back to Attianus. His companion was bent double with his hands on his knees. Celer patted him gently on the back and was alarmed to feel the man's ribs through the layers of wool. The food that Lucia had packed them was almost gone and, though they still had a few coins that Attianus had brought from Rome, it would not buy them enough food or a room to rest in.

At length, Attianus straightened and took several deep breaths. He drank deeply from a wineskin Celer offered then eyed the town before them.

"We stand little chance of gaining entry; if Marruvium had word to watch for us then so will they."

"What do we do then?" asked Celer glumly. "We're almost out of food."

"There will be inns outside the town, safer, though it will cost us all the coin we have."

"And then what, do we head north or south?" Celer gestured to the two roads that disappeared off into the distance.

"Neither, we keep heading east. There should be a road that follows a river valley out to the coast."

Celer raised his eyebrows. "Should be?"

Attianus nodded. "Should be. An old friend of mine is the magistrate of a port town called Histonium; I remember last time I visited him he showed me the road, said it ran to Aufidena."

The wind gusted about them and there was a distant rumble that threatened an autumnal storm, making both of them cringe and huddle tighter into their cloaks. They set off down the other side of the pass.

"Can we trust this friend of yours?" asked Celer whilst they walked.

Attianus nodded slowly. "He will hear me out, at least. We have known each other a long time."

"Very well," said Celer, "how far to Histonium from Aufidena?"

At this Attianus shook his head. "Two, maybe three days?"

Three days, thought Celer grimly. They would be lucky to last another night exposed with no fire and little food. Attianus walked stiffly beside him; by his small steps and the way he held his injured shoulder Celer could tell that his wounds still pained him and, in his weakened state, there was a risk that his infection would return.

A fine drizzle began to soak them, growing in strength as they trudged towards Aufidena. The roads gradually broadened and began to fill with traffic and they kept watchful eyes out for any patrols of soldiers.

Celer had never been so miserable in all his life. Everything they carried, bar the leather scroll tube, was wet. The tattered remnants of the cloak Attianus had stolen for him no longer protected him from the damp and he could feel the tunic from Decimus he wore beneath it grow heavy, as the rain soaked in.

They ate the last of Lucia's supplies beneath the sagging roof of a dilapidated barn barely a mile from the city. The bread was stale and would have been hard as iron were it not as sodden as he was.

Swallowing the last mushy mouthful, he found he had not the will nor the strength to stand back up. His companion lay huddled in his own ragged cloak; only the occasional shuddering cough indicated some form of life remained.

The misery and despair of their position became too much. He was too young for this. Too young to have his family destroyed. Too young to be forced to flee and hide like an animal, pursued by Germanic warriors that haunted his nightmares like the wolves that had tried to tear him apart.

It was hopeless! How could a boy barely into manhood and an injured man hope to escape the far reach of the Emperor?

Should they somehow manage to avoid their hunters, the lack of food and shelter would surely finish them off before they reached the coast.

A gust of wind blew droplets into his face as the rain began to fall harder and he tried to edge away but his body would not respond.

He would die in this barn. The thought forced its way to the fore of his mind and he wanted to scream. His mouth opened but no sound came out. His eyes grew hot with tears and with their heat he grew angry.

If he were to die then so be it, but he would not die like a snivelling child trying to hide from rain. With an immense force of will he cuffed his eyes. Had he not sworn to not shed another tear? His hands and arms were leaden with fatigue and his touch was numb from the rain that robbed heat from his body, so he rubbed his arms furiously to generate some warmth. He worked his arms until they ached and he began to regain feeling in them. It came painfully; blood seemed to fizz and boil in his veins like molten bronze and he gasped at the pain but kept his arms working. He rubbed his legs until the numbness left them then forced himself to his knees. Using his walking staff as a crutch, he found his feet and staggered to the barn door.

He was about to force it open when he heard voices amongst the hammer of rain drops.

He cautiously peered through a gap in the leaning door and saw two men leading horses thirty paces from him. He immediately drew his head back inside; the men wore woollen military cloaks and helmets and carried spears and small shields.

Celer hurried over to Attianus and shook him vigorously and at first the older man did not stir. Celer shook him again as the voices drew nearer and Attianus's eyes snapped open and he shot out a hand that gripped Celer's arm with surprising strength. He made to speak but Celer hurriedly shushed him with a finger to his lips and hauled him up. With his staff and both their bags in one hand and the other supporting Attianus, Celer crossed the barn to where a section of wall had fallen away. He pushed Attianus out into the rain and had just scrambled over the rubble when the door to the barn groaned as it was pulled open.

They lay panting in the rain as the two soldiers entered. Peering through a gap in the tumbled rocks, Celer could see that whilst they carried spears and shields, neither man wore armour or a helmet. Both were older than he and Attianus and he could see streaks of grey in the dark curls of both men.

"Don't you bring that fucking animal in here!" one of the men shouted above the sound of the rain. "It's bad enough that I have to be out in this looking for two patrician ponces without having to sit in here with those stinking animals."

"As you wish, Metellus." His companion sighed with the tone of the long-suffering member of the relationship and led his horse out of Celer's sight. The two men reappeared moments later and sat down heavily where Attianus had been slumped not moments before.

"Anyway, where was I?" asked Metellus.

"You were telling me how your son had knocked up the butcher's daughter," replied his companion in a bored voice as he leant his weapons against the barn wall and leaned back, his eyes half closed.

Metellus laughed. "That's right. Little shit, takes after his old man. Of course, similar thing happened to me with his mother. Now the little slut's father wants my boy to marry this girl, says he's disgraced her and her family."

Metellus spat. "If you ask me, I bet the bastard put her up to it in the first place. Got four other daughters, no doubt costing him a fortune, getting one in the oven is an easy way to get one out of his house and into mine."

Metellus continued to rant about his son's future in-laws with his companion merely nodding or grunting in response.

Celer slowly sank down until he couldn't see the soldiers. Attianus looked at him with questioning eyes. Rain poured off his face running in rivulets from his beard.

"Two men," Celer whispered, raising his fingers to reinforce his words over the downpour.

Attianus nodded. He wiped the rain from his face with a shaking hand then drew Celer close to him. "Horses?" he rasped in the boy's ear.

Celer nodded and gestured towards the end on the barn where the two men had entered.

Attianus retrieved his bag and made sure it was secured over his back, then he began to crawl over the rubble towards the door end of the barn. Celer gave him a moment before following, taking care not to slip on the wet stones. They cleared the rubble pile and, though the wall now stood between them and the soldiers, Attianus did not stand and Celer wondered if he could, weak as he was now.

The pair of them crawled and slithered through the mud as the rain beat down on their backs. So loud was the deluge that the horses did not notice them until Celer rose up, a horror of mud and rags. They shied away nervously as he approached with arms outstretched, but he whispered to them as loudly as he dared, the way he had been shown as a boy, and the horses quickly calmed and allowed him close enough to take their reigns. Celer turned to help Attianus up but the older man had found his feet unaided and leant heavily on the barn wall. He helped him across to one of the horses, a brown mare, boosting him up with trembling arms. From within the barn, he could hear Metellus's continued ranting and Celer hoped fervently that he would continue a while longer. The other horse, another mare, darker than Attianus's, was thankfully docile as he struggled up into the saddle, suppressing the excited thrill to be riding once again. They kicked their heels in and trotted the horses away from the barn towards the road. Celer rode at Attianus's side, fearful that the older man would fall in his weakened state.

The track to the road was a little more than a muddy stream now so they walked the horses, not wanting them to slip. Celer sat twisted in his saddle, eyes locked onto the door of the barn as it gradually faded into the sheets of rain.

They made the road without issue and, by unspoken command, they kicked the horses into a canter.

Aufidena slowly came into view through the grey, a dark mass looming before them. Attianus did not slow his horse but instead veered right onto the road south. The weather had driven all inside and as they rode past the inns that flanked the main approach to the city, Celer could see they were crammed with people. None looked out at the two filthy riders as they passed and he saw no one step out to follow them.

The rain did not lesson as they rode into the afternoon, turning their world into all that existed within thirty feet of their mounts. They almost missed the road that led towards Histonium. Attianus had kept his eye to the left of the main road as Celer kept watch for any pursuers. He suddenly reined in so hard hat he almost toppled from the saddle. Celer managed to catch him and steady him before turning to see what had caused him to halt. A milestone leant drunkenly by the side of the road. Despite the moss and lichens that clad it, Celer could just make out the letters H S VM and a rough arrow below. The track that the arrow indicated was so rutted and potholed that Celer wondered why anyone would use it at all.

They had begun to tire the horses by pushing them hard to get past Aufidena so they slowed to a trot and followed the track east in single file.

Celer quickly lost all concept of time or where they were. He guessed that they followed a series of valleys or perhaps one long one. Time was hard to determine, for the world was a sea of grey with no hint of the sun's passage in the sky. He sat limply upon his horse, mirroring the slumped form of Attianus ahead of him. When the day did eventually begin to grow perceivably darker, he thought the older man would call a halt, but they continued to plod on. The horses now walked with their own heads low. His body was numb with cold and his first attempt to dig his heels into the horse's flanks merely caused the animal to toss its head. Summoning his strength, he kicked again and this time his mount reluctantly increased the pace and drew alongside Attianus.

"We have to stop," croaked Celer.

Attianus's head lolled towards him. "Can't. Stop," came the laboured reply as the older man blinked away raindrops.

"It will be dark soon." Already it was becoming hard to make out the features of his companion's face. "We can't ride in the dark; the horses could fall."

Attianus just shook his head. "Can't stop," he said again. "Close now."

Celer thought about grabbing the reigns and forcing him to stop. Part of him longed to stop, to get off his horse and just curl up and sleep despite the cold and the wet. The rest of him knew, however, that if he dismounted he would likely never have the strength to get back on, let alone lift Attianus back into the saddle. There was a good chance that men would be on their trail soon if they already weren't. Better to risk a fall in the dark than give up precious miles to their pursuers.

Attianus's head had rolled back to its previous position, his chin hovering above his chest; there would be no further discussion. The track narrowed again. Branches reached out from the darkness, so he steered his mount in behind Attianus and followed him into the night.

# VII

The rain stopped during the night. Celer did not know at what point, as the moon remained hidden by thick cloud, but he was grateful nonetheless. As dawn broke, the cloud began to thin and a strong breeze swept in, carrying the smell of salt upon it. The track wound its way out of a small woodland and into pasture land; small huts dotted the hillsides around them, cooking fires already smoking as the farmers prepared for another day's work.

Celer was staring blankly at the dust kicked up by Attianus's mare with red eyes when a lance of sunlight broke through the cloud just above the horizon and drew his gaze eastward. The valley they were in widened out before him into a broad plain cut by a wide river channel. Beyond the plain, illuminated in the dawn sun, were the deep blue waters of the Adriatic.

Attianus rode ahead of him, slumped in the saddle. Celer tried to call to him but his throat was too dry, so he kicked his heels into his tired mount and urged it alongside the brown mare. He reached out and shook Attianus's shoulder as vigorously as he dared, not wanting to tip him from the saddle. Attianus raised his gaunt face and looked at him with weary eyes. Celer raised his staff and pointed it down the valley. Attianus followed the direction until his eyes fell upon the shimmering blue in the distance.

The sight of the coast renewed a little of their strength and they forced their tired mounts back into a trot. They crossed the river on an old stone bridge with an inn beside it and followed a wide road south along the coast.

The port town of Histonium soon came into sight and they rode through quiet orchards and vineyards as the sun broke up the clouds and revealed the clear blue waters lapping at the port.

Histonium was not a large settlement, the port seemed empty and Celer guessed that it housed mainly fishing boats rather than large mercantile vessels, though he knew little of boats. What drew more of his attention was an imposing customs building, squatting to one side of the harbour, with a small naval vessel docked beyond it. The town was quiet as they rode through, the fishermen were already out on their boats for the morning catch and the rest of the town was slowly waking. The streets were empty as they made their way towards the magistrate's residence in the town centre. The smell of baking bread made Celer feel faint as his stomach growled at the thought of a warm loaf.

The magistrate's house sat behind the town's small forum. They rode through a low archway into a spacious courtyard with stables on one side and several ovens on the other. A slave was tending one of the ovens when the sound of hooves on the cobbled floor of the yard made him turn. Years of habit made him step out to take the reins of Attianus's horse before he looked up at the two riders. When he caught site of their ragged appearance and the two pairs of wild red eyes staring at him, he suddenly changed direction and backed up towards the ovens.

"Solena!" he called out over his shoulder, not taking his eyes from the riders who had halted in the centre of the yard.

An old woman stepped into sight from a doorway that Celer guessed led to the house kitchens.

"What is it, Porcius? You better not have burnt them loaves again." She raised a threatening hand towards the slave.

Porcius, however, paid her threat no heed; instead he spoke quickly in a shrill voice.

"Never mind the bread! Go and get Nekar!"

Solena took a step out of the doorway, irritation giving way to confusion when she saw Celer and Attianus. Her hand shot to her mouth as if to try and catch the gasp she let out.

"Quickly!" hissed Porcius.

Solena disappeared without a word, leaving Porcius with the two bedraggled strangers.

Half hidden behind one of the columns holding up the covered walkways that surrounded the courtyard, Porcius nervously addressed them.

"Can I help you gentlemen? Perhaps you are lost?"

Attianus shook his head. "Water," he croaked.

Porcius seemed surprised by the request and seemed to think about it for a moment. Then a lifetime of servitude kicked in and he scurried round to the well, keeping the columns between himself and the riders.

Whilst the slave drew water to fill a pitcher resting on a table beside the well, Attianus began to dismount. Celer moved to help him but was too late as the older man's legs, weakened through weeks of rough living and sickness, buckled beneath him and he collapsed with a loud thud that made Porcius jump and drop the bucket back into the well. Celer had just managed to dismount onto his own unsteady legs and was helping Attianus to his feet when Solena returned with Nekar.

Nekar turned out to be a towering Numidian with a powerfully built chest and arms thicker than most men's legs. He held an ornately carved cudgel in one of his massive hands. Celer had seen such a man once before. A friend of his father had kept a similar man in his retinue after serving as Proconsul of Africa. Men like Nekar came from the militarised zone in the south of the province and were a popular choice as bodyguards.

Swaying on unstable legs, Attianus raised his hands to show he was unarmed as the Numidian approached. Nekar stopped several paces short of them and planted the heavy head of his cudgel between his feet and rested both hands upon its leather wrapped handle. "What do they want?" he asked Porcius in a deep booming voice of accented Latin.

Attianus tried to speak but his voice failed and he could only manage a hacking cough instead.

Nekar ignored him and waited for Porcius's answer.

"They never said what they wanted," said Porcius hurriedly, "only asked for some water."

Nekar looked at the ragged figures before him with a frown. "There's a fountain in the Forum if it's water you need," he said, pointing a finger toward the archway they had entered through. "Now be gone before you disturb my master."

Celer licked his dry lips and willed his voice not to crack. "We are here to see your master. My companion is an old friend of his."

Nekar snorted at his words and hefted his cudgel, taking a step towards them. "Ha, nice try, boy, but I have heard that one before. You two aren't going anywhere near the Magistrate."

Attianus raised his head and fixed the bodyguard with as firm a gaze as his sleep-deprived eyes could manage. "Go give word to your master, slave, tell him his friend Caius Maximus Attianus is here."

Nekar took another step towards them and for a moment Celer thought he might beat them to death there in the courtyard. But Attianus held steady and stared him down and Celer saw doubt creep into the big man's eyes.

Nekar spat to one side and motioned to Porcius. "Porcius, go and tell the master that he has visitors." He paused, eyeing Attianus up and down. "Tell him one of them claims to know him."

"Caius Maximus Attianus," Attianus repeated as Porcius carefully stepped around them and made for the main entrance.

Nekar took a step back, then planted his cudgel and stood watching them, solid as a mountain. Celer left Attianus leaning against his horse and went over to the well and carried over the pitcher Porcius had left. They both drank deeply, though both by unspoken consent made efforts not to appear too desperate in front of Nekar.

They did not have to wait long. The main doors to the house were hurriedly thrown open as a well-built man with dark hair already going grey strode out.

"What is going on here?" the man barked at Nekar. "Porcius told me an old friend was here. Who are these people?" He raised a finger at the two bedraggled forms leaning heavily upon their tired, mud spattered mounts.

Attianus pushed himself away from his horse and took a step towards the Governor on his unsteady legs.

"It has been too long, Helva..." he said, sweeping away the greasy locks that obscured his face with a shaking hand, "...if you do not to recognise your old friend."

Magistrate Helva stared at Attianus, appalled.

"Attianus?" he whispered, stepping closer warily.

"What's left of him," came the croaking reply as Attianus sank to his knees, tears beginning to flow freely from his eyes.

Helva immediately went to one knee beside him and cradled his old friend as a hacking cough shook Attianus's bony frame.

"Fetch the medicus!" Helva shouted over his shoulder to Solena who was stood in the doorway. "Nekar, help the boy inside. And you, Porcius!" he shouted at the slave who had tried to slink off after Solena, "make yourself useful and stable their horses."

As Porcius rushed to do his master's bidding, Helva gathered up Attianus and, with a grunt, rose to his feet. Nekar gripped Celer's upper arm in one of his powerful hands and supported the boy as they followed the magistrate up the stairs and into the house.

Attianus was carried off into a side room, Helva reappeared momentarily to tell Nekar to see that Celer was fed and washed and given something clean to wear.

The big Numidian bowed his head at his master's orders and led Celer in the opposite direction. He was pushed down onto a rough wooden bench in the kitchen and given a platter with a few flat loaves with oil to dip them in as well as a small piece of cold fish and some cheese. He ate quickly and the platter soon lay empty so the old Greek, who he guessed to be the governor's cook, pushed two more of the flat loaves across the table to him. Celer muttered a quick thanks before tearing into them.

When he was finally sated, Nekar took hold of his arm again and lifted him from the bench and guided him to the bath house at the rear of the building.

Two more slaves were waiting for them and they moved to begin stripping Celer's clothes from him. One of them made to take the battered leather bag that hung from his shoulder but Celer brushed his arm away and shook his head, he removed the bag and placed it to one side where it would remain in reach before allowing them to continue.

Nekar disappeared as the two slaves led him into the pool and began to wash the grime from his body. Celer was horrified to see how pronounced his ribs had become and was grateful to see when Nekar returned that the Numidian carried a clean tunic folded in his hand.

Once he was dressed Nekar led him back into the house to a room not far from the kitchens. It was a bare room with only a small cot against one wall beneath the single narrow window and Celer realised that this was where the slaves of visiting guests were likely allowed to sleep. For a moment the insult to his station stung but the cot looked inviting, despite its small size, and the bath and food had made him so tired he could barely keep his eyes open. He allowed himself to be guided to the bed, pausing only to lower his bag to the floor beside it, and was asleep before Nekar left the room.

It was dark when he woke. Someone had lit a small candle on the table beside his cot and its wavering light confused him for a moment before he remembered where he was. He lay still a moment, relishing the warmth of the bed despite its worn sheets and poor construction. When he swung his aching legs off the bed and rose into a sitting position, he saw that whoever had brought the candle had also brought him a belt and some light sandals which sat upon a folded blanket. He took the belt and sandals, pausing a moment to relish the warmth in the room. This far into the house, it would not be just from the strength of the sun, but most likely his room was close to where they fed the hypocaust system for the magistrate's rooms.

He quickly checked the bag to ensure the leather tube was still in there, then he stood up unsteadily. Despite the rest, his body was stiff and tired and he was hungry again. He opened the door and jumped back immediately as a large dark figure loomed in the doorway.

"My apologies, master," said Nekar in his deep voice, head bowed. "I did not mean to startle you. If you would follow me, please."

The Numidian did not wait for response but instead led the way through the house. Celer followed, noticing that the bodyguard no longer carried his ornate cudgel.

Nekar led him through to the triclinium where the governor and another man were already reclining on two of the three couches arranged around a low table laden with food.

At the sight of Celer, Magistrate Helva rose to his feet.

"Good evening, Celer, please come and join us." He indicated the third couch.

As Celer approached, Helva turned and gestured towards the man who had risen beside him. "Allow me to introduce another old friend of mine, Flavius Vegetius."

Vegetius, a tall, thin man with neat brown curls and inquisitive grey eyes, nodded politely to Celer as all three took their seats.

"How are you feeling?" asked Helva. "Hungry, I imagine?"

"Better, Sir," replied Celer, "and yes, very."

Helva smiled. "I never met a lad who wasn't. Please, help yourself, have as much as you like."

Celer needed no further instruction and worked his way through the contents of the table whilst the magistrate and Vegetius politely picked at their food in silence.

When he was done, he washed his hands in the bowl by his couch and wiped his lips on the linen napkin that a slave handed him. He was surprised to find that it all felt slightly unnatural, despite being brought up in a house similar to this and having eaten in such a way all his life. He suddenly ashamed at such luxury compared to the poor existence of people like Decimus and his family who had helped him and Attianus on their way from Rome.

The thought of Attianus suddenly made him feel guilty.

"How is Attianus? Can I see him?"

Helva's expression became sombre. "Attianus is being attended by my personal medicus and is resting for the moment, but you can see him in the morning."

Celer nodded his acceptance and gratefully took a cup of wine offered by a slave.

Helva continued. "I must also apologise for the way in which you were treated upon arriving in my house. A room befitting your station has been prepared and Nekar shall be punished for the insult to yourself."

Celer shot a glance at the Numidian who was standing still as a statue by the doorway looking rigidly ahead.

"You have no need to apologise, Magistrate. I am indebted to you for your hospitality."

Helva smiled, "You are too kind, Celer; your manners are a credit to your father."

At the mention of his father, Celer was instantly alert.

"You know my father?" he asked.

Helva shook his head. "I met Senator Cotta several times in passing but never had the pleasure of knowing him well."

Celer's head sank dejectedly. "I don't suppose you have heard any news of him?" he asked quietly. "Or my mother?"

With his head bowed, he missed the glance between Helva and Vegetius.

"Why don't you tell us of how you came to be in Histonium?" suggested Helva gently. "I have already heard some of it from Attianus, though much I find hard to believe. I would appreciate your version of events."

Celer sat silently, suddenly nervous of disclosing the nature of his and Attianus's mission.

Helva must have guessed his thoughts. "I already know of the message to Theodosius," he said in his gentle tone. "Let me assure you that you are amongst friends here and have nothing to fear from us."

"You are not the only ones who have reason to flee from our new Emperor," added Vegetius. "We only wish to help."

Celer looked at Vegetius questioningly, noting how the fingers on his right hand seemed to be stained black as if he had dipped them in ink, wondering what he could have done to be on the run from Eugenius as he and Attianus were. He looked back to Helva, who was now sitting upright and waiting patiently. He gathered his thought and began to recount the tale of how he came to Histonium.

He began with the night-raid on his family home, with how his father had to carry his mother away from the house as it began to burn and how he forced Celer over the wall to flee the swords of the Frankish soldiers. He spoke tonelessly, trying to keep the emotion from his voice lest it betray him and bring tears to his eyes. He told them what happened to Varro and his family, ignoring the muttered curses of both men as he told how Attianus's family were killed in the street and how Attianus had saved him and eventually led him out of the city in the turgid waters of the Tiber.

The journey from the countryside outside Rome was harder to tell; days seemed to blur into one and he struggled to make sense of the time it had taken them to cross first the Alban Hills and then the Apennines. He spoke little of the people that had helped them along the way and mentioned no names. Some small part of him was determined that if this was some clever trap by agents of Eugenius then those that had helped him would remain safe. He told them how Attianus came to be wounded as they fought for their lives on the pass above the plain of Marruvium and how they had managed to steal the horses from the soldiers in a barn outside Aufidena.

At this point in the tale, Helva held up a hand to pause him and beckoned Nekar over.

"Make sure that the horses are removed from Histonium before first light; there will be people looking for them. See to it." Nekar bowed and left the room.

Helva turned back to Celer. "My apologies, please continue."

There was little left to tell and Celer struggled to make sense of the blurred memories of the night ride from Aufidena and there was little to say about the ride into Histonium.

When he was finished, he sat quietly watching Helva. The Magistrate regarded him with sharp brown eyes for a moment before speaking.

"Thank you for telling us of your ordeal, I know it must be hard to go through it all again. You have given me a great deal to think on and the hour is late. I shall summon someone to take you to your new room."

"No need, Magistrate," interjected Vegetius. "The boy's room is next to mine and the hour is indeed late, I think I shall retire and can show young Celer here the way."

"Very well," Helva nodded, "I shall see you both in the morning."

He rose with them and remained standing until they were out of the room.

Vegetius led Celer up a flight of stone steps to the upper floor of the house and showed him to a room three times the size of the one he had slept in during the day.

Vegetius turned to him in the corridor. "I just wanted to say how sorry I am for what happened to you and your family and that of your friend. You have shown great resilience in getting here, Cele. I shall be keeping an eye on you. I believe you capable of great things."

He clapped Celer on the shoulder and crossed the corridor into the room opposite. Celer stood dazed in the corridor a moment, trying to think about what Vegetius had said. However, his tired body cried out for rest, so he closed his door and stumbled towards the large bed. His had had barely touched the pillow before sleep claimed him once more.

# VIII

Celer woke to the morning sun streaming through the open window and the sound of crying gulls outside. For the first time in weeks he felt rested although his body still ached. He dressed quickly and left the room hoping to find Attianus and check on him. He went downstairs to the room just off the entrance hall that Helva had entered when they arrived at the magistrate's house. Behind it there was a long corridor with a series of small rooms leading off it. He found Attianus in a large room at the end of the corridor. His companion was lying in a spacious bed swamped in blankets and sweating profusely. A slightly built Greek was bent over a table with his back to Celer as he entered.

"…upon first treating an open wound it should be treated with acid vinegar or strong wine; if this is not possible then the use of hot iron is acceptable.' I think we are well past that stage, my friend, don't you?" The question was directed over the Greek's shoulder at Attianus's swaddled form.

"In caring for wounds caused by arms or beasts, ensure that the wound is frequently cleaned and the dressings changed. Should decaying skin be sighted, the application of leeches to the affected area has been shown to be most efficient at remedying this."

The Greek began to rummage amongst the collection of glass vials and wooden boxes that covered his table and Celer could see the unrolled scroll he had been reading from. The Greek turned, muttering something about leeches, and saw Celer standing in the doorway.

"Ah, dear boy!" he cried out and clasped his hands together, smiling. "You must be this young fellow's companion that I have heard about?"

Celer nodded and stepped into the room. "I am. My name is Celer."

"A pleasure." the Greek bowed. "My name is Timaeus; I am Magistrate Helva's household physician."

"How is he?" asked Celer, taking a step towards Attianus's bed.

"He is very weak, half starved, which isn't helping his body to heal, but his wound was well treated initially. I have seen men recover from worse. Tell me..." Timaeus turned to Celer. "What was the name of the physician who first treated him? I would very much like to praise him on his excellent handiwork."

"He was treated by a farmer's daughter in their house at the foot of the pass where we were attacked."

"A farmer's daughter!" Timaeus exclaimed. "Well, wonders never cease. In that case, he is exceptionally lucky to be with us still."

Timaeus moved around the bed to where a small table stood beside it. He took a small piece of clean linen and wet it in a bowl of dark vinegar. The Greek folded down the layers of blankets covering Attianus's naked chest and peeled back the dressings covering his wounded shoulder. The shoulder and chest was a mass of purple bruising, with the puncture wounds and tears to the skin standing dark against it. Several of the holes made by the wolf's fangs were surrounded by rings of yellow and purple skin and some leaked dribbles of white fluid.

Timaeus carefully wiped all of the wounds clean, ignoring Attianus's groans as the vinegar stung the unhealed wounds.

"What was that you were reading?" asked Celer.

"A manual on wound treatment written by a Veturius Priscus of Aquileia. An old text, I'll grant you, but he was renowned for his work on gladiators in the Great Flavian Amphitheatre during the reign of Emperor Marcus Aurelius. Still one of the best of its kind in my most humble opinion."

Timaeus finished cleaning Attianus's wounds and placed fresh dressings on them before pulling the blankets back up under his chin.

"Now then, young master," he said, turning to Celer, "you must leave my patient to rest. Besides, you look like you're in need of a few more meals yourself. Come, I'll walk with you to the kitchens, see what that old cook Gemellus has got this morning."

Gemellus, it turned out, had prepared much the same fare as the day before, only this time there was dried fruit and a small clay pot of honey to accompany it.

Celer took his food through the house and out onto the small terrace at the back. The magistrate's house sat atop a small outcrop so he had a clear view over the Histonium all the way to the docks. There was smoke from maybe a hundred morning cooking fires and ovens and he could see the crowds in the forum as the first fishermen returned to sell their catch amongst the other stalls and traders. He could make out the helmeted forms of soldiers outside the customs building by the dock and the sight of them almost made him duck down behind the terrace wall before he chastised himself for being foolish. A single merchant vessel was now anchored in the water next to the squat building and Celer watched as a small boarding party of officials made their way aboard.

Celer was so engrossed watching the town that at first he didn't hear the footsteps behind him. He turned finally to see Vegetius walking towards him.

"Good morning."

"Good morning," Celer replied.

"It promises to be a fine day." Vegetius nodded out to sea where the sky was a clear blue. "How is your friend?"

"The medicus is looking after him; he seems hopeful."

"Good, that is good news." Vegetius came to stand beside him, looking out at the town.

They stood in silence for a while as the sounds of the seaside town drifted up to them over the rooftops.

"Why are you here, sir?" asked Celer. "If you don't mind me asking."

Vegetius smiled sadly. "There's no need for the 'sir' any more, Celer, Vegetius will do." He sighed before continuing. "I have spent the last two years in Mediolanum at the court of Valentinian working towards gaining an office as a Praesides." He chuckled dryly. "I was hoping for somewhere with a good climate, possibly southern Gaul or even Hispania."

Celer just nodded but was quietly impressed. A Praesides was high civil office, the first rung on the ladder for provincial governorship; Vegetius was clearly a man of ability.

"Obviously, just when the appointments were due to be made, the Emperor was killed and that put an end to that dream."

"Wait." Celer raised his palm, frowning. "The Emperor was killed? The Senate was told he committed suicide."

Vegetius snorted. "Unlikely. The Emperor was a young man, full of vigour and ambition, and that was his undoing. Arbogast had ruled for many years in his stead as the Emperor grew up, but Valentinian began to make his own decisions and the Frank saw his power begin to slip away."

Vegetius shook his head angrily. "Anyway, it matters not. The Emperor died and history will remember it as a suicide; there is no proof to lay the blame at Arbogast's feet and none would dare anyway."

"So why did you leave Mediolanum?" asked Celer.

"Arbogast raised Eugenius to the purple and he instantly installed his own lackeys to positions that other men had spent years working towards. Then there was the matter of returning to the old gods which presented a problem for many of us in the capital."

He eyed the confused look on Celer's face.

"I'm a Christian, you see."

Celer looked out over the town and shuffled his feet, instantly feeling awkward.

Vegetius nodded. "That's pretty much the response the Christians in the Imperial Court received from our peers. The response from Arbogast and his Frankish soldiers was worse; people were rounded up in the night and exiled or worse."

Celer, face flushing in shame at his reaction, turned back towards him.

"Vegetius, I apologise, I meant no offence."

"None taken," the older man responded. "I am quite used to it, especially amongst men from the Senatorial classes. I appreciate that you hold to your traditions stronger than most of us. And why not!" he exclaimed. "The Empire was built under the auspices of the old gods. Our troubled times do often call into question the righteousness of God the Almighty."

"How so?" Celer asked.

"For over a thousand years we Romans have conquered new territories and landed on new shores and in all that time we have accepted those we conquered, merged our beliefs with theirs and found peace in common understanding. Then a new sect comes along, following the teachings of a man who lived barely three hundred years ago, and they demand that their belief is the right one. That their god is the only god and all other are false idols - it's no wonder so many resent us."

"Yet you are a Christian yourself?" Celer said, intrigued by Vegetius's words.

"You believe what you believe, Celer, because it feels right, do you not?" He waited until Celer nodded his agreement. "I believe what I believe for the same reason; we should be left alone in these choices for they are our own. I dedicated a work to this topic back in Mediolanum."

"You write?" Celer asked, relieved to change the topic.

"A great deal, since I was about your age. Unfortunately, much of my work has been destroyed," he said sadly.

"Destroyed?"

"Yes, alongside my religious affiliations I had one more reason to flee the court of Eugenius and Arbogast. Whilst working towards becoming a Praesides I penned a work comparing Roman troops with those of foreign lands in which I concluded that foreign troops were inferior in that they lacked, amongst other things, proper devotion to Rome and instead were led by baser desires such as financial reward."

"And they burned your books because you wrote this?"

"Arbogast..." Vegetius looked suddenly uncomfortable at the memory. "Arbogast took personal offence when I mentioned his Frankish soldiers amongst the foreign forces."

Celer was saved having to reply by the arrival of Nekar. The Numidian bowed his head respectfully to the two Romans.

"My master bids you both join him. He has urgent matters he would discuss with you."

They met Helva in his tablinum. The room was so similar to that of Celer's father that it instantly made him homesick. He pushed the thought of his family from his mind and listened to the magistrate.

Helva held a wax dispatch tablet in his hand. "I have received an official command," he began. "'From Nicomachus Flavianus, Prefect of Italy, to lend all forces at my disposal towards the capture of two traitors of the Empire'." He glanced up at Celer. "'C. Maximus Attianus and M. Aelius Celer are considered enemies of the state and are wanted alive if possible'." He sighed and placed the tablet on the desk where they could see it.

"It arrived this morning?" asked Vegetius, bending forward to read it.

Helva nodded. "It states that the Prefect is on his way south and intends to establish a base of operations at Brundisium. No doubt someone reported the horses you stole and they guessed it was you."

"Wait," Vegetius was still reading the dispatch. "This says that you are being replaced as magistrate?"

Helva sat heavily in his chair and nodded. "It seems that the Emperor is not satisfied with purging Christians from just his court. I expect my replacement is travelling with Flavianus."

Celer felt the sense of safety he had begun to feel start to slip away. "We have to leave," he said to Helva.

The magistrate nodded. "I agree, the sooner the better."

"What about Attianus? He is still weak."

Vegetius pointed an ink-stained finger at the dispatch. "No one else has seen this yet?"

"No one," Helve replied, shaking his head.

"Then you still have authority over the patrol ship at the dock?"

Helva's eyes brightened "I do, yes."

Vegetius nodded and began heating the end of a bronze stylus over a candle on the desk. "Then we forge a new dispatch with orders to assist three dignitaries on their crossing to Dyrrhachium. One of whom has fallen ill and requires us to make all haste in the crossing,"

"Won't sailing to Dyrrhachium take us close to Brundisium?" Celer interjected.

"Very close," nodded Helva. "However, if we leave now, we should beat Flavianus's party by a day or two."

Vegetius finished writing the new orders on the wax tablet. Celer noticed he had been careful to leave the impression left by the seal of the Prefect in the top corner. Helva cast a careful eye over the document. "You have done this before," he said disapprovingly.

"Written orders, or forged Imperial documents?" asked Vegetius wryly. "I will go pack my things; we should leave at first opportunity."

Helva summoned Nekar from where he had been standing by the door.

"Instruct Timaeus that Attianus is to be prepared to be carried by stretcher to the docks." Nekar bowed his huge head and left the room.

"Before you leave, Celer, I'm afraid I have one unpleasant task left to perform." He reached into a draw in his desk and drew out a second dispatch tablet and handed it to Celer.

"It arrived several days before you."

Celer opened the tablet and read the dispatch. It was a generic document, no doubt sent to the magistrates of all the towns in Italy. It stated that several Senators in Rome had been found guilty of treasonous activities and so had been put to death along with all other conspirators. Beneath the brief passage stating this was a list of the Senators named. Second from the top his father's name was written. Resisting the urge to hurl the tablet across the room and smash it against the wall, he forced himself to adopt an expressionless mask and continue reading. Following from the list was a short section stating that all property and ranks or titles associated with each conspirator had been seized and now belonged to the Emperor. Stamped in the corner of the tablet was the seal of the Prefect of Italy.

"Celer, I am so sorry," began Helva.

"Can I keep this?" Celer interrupted, holding up the dispatch.

Surprised, Helva nodded.

"Thank you, I will go get my things."

He left the tablinum and made for the stairs. Several slaves he had not seen before smartly stepped out of his way. They noticed the cold expression on the young nobleman's face and quickly fixed their gazes upon the tiled floor.

Once in his room he roughly stuffed the tablet into the bag alongside the now battered tube that contained the scroll from his father. Celer stared at it angrily for a moment, thinking about all the people who had died because of what was written on that scroll and the implication behind it.

The clothes he had travelled in had been taken away so he had little to pack. Nekar had removed the hatchet and his staff from him when he arrived and he had not seen them since but his dagger had been returned to him. He held it by its rough handle and stared at the blade and imagined Flavianus the Elder kneeling before him at his mercy.

His rational mind told him it was fantasy. He did not know how to fight. Apart from a few scuffles as a boy and the mad scramble for survival with the wolves he had never had cause too. And the prefect was surrounded by hundreds of armed men; he would never get close by himself. Yet his irrational mind cried out for vengeance. Vengeance against Flavianus the Elder for killing his parents and Varro and his family and vengeance against Arbogast, for all the lives ruined by his lust for power.

When he heard movement from the corridor he put the knife in his belt and picked his bag up and left. Vegetius was following a slave wearing a bag similar to Celer's and carrying a chest to the stairs.

"Ready to go?" asked Vegetius nodding towards his bag.

"Ready." Celer nodded. "What's in the chest?" he asked, trying to distract himself from murderous thoughts about the Prefect of Italy.

"Just some things I have been working on during my time here," said Vegetius, waving a hand dismissively.

"Oh really," Celer eager for the distraction. "Like what?"

"Nothing that would interest a young man such as yourself," said Vegetius, as they descended the staircase. When he looked back and saw Celer waiting expectantly, however, he relented. "You must understand it is by no means complete, but upon arriving I met a man in the forum who piqued my interest in medicine for animals..."

Celer quickly discovered that Vegetius had been right and it wasn't a very interesting topic, but the writer talked with such enthusiasm that Celer did not stop him and instead listened with as much interest as he could muster as they walked out into the courtyard. Vegetius was still talking when Attianus was carried out on a stretcher, looking pale in the weak sunlight. Helva walked beside the stretcher.

"Let's not waste any time," said the magistrate as he led the way out of the courtyard without a backwards glance.

As they walked down the street towards the harbour, Celer walked alongside Vegetius behind the stretcher whilst Helva led the way in front. "Does the Magistrate not have a family to say goodbye to?" asked Celer quietly, realising he had seen no sign of a woman or children in the house.

Vegetius shook his head and replied in a similar tone. "The Magistrate lost his wife giving birth to their son. The boy lives with family elsewhere. I have never met him."

They said no more on the subject and walked in silence until they arrived at the customs building.

The soldiers on guard duty recognised the magistrate and snapped to attention, looking straight ahead as the procession passed between them through the arched gateway to the waterfront behind.

The merchant vessel Celer had seen from the terrace earlier that morning was being unloaded. The officer supervising it came hurrying over when he saw the magistrate. He snapped to attention as Helva turned to him with a smile.

"At ease, Optio."

"Thank you, sir," said the officer, relaxing a fraction. "Can I help you, sir?"

Helva shook his head. "Not today, Optio, I have business with the captain of our patrol ship." He waved the closed dispatch tablet.

The optio knew better than to ask what was in the orders and instead snapped another salute as Helva led his party towards the anchored liburnian.

The captain of the ship – officially known as a triearch, Vegetius later informed Celer – was an old man with a weather-blasted face. He and the optio in charge of the small contingent of marines briefly looked over the dispatch that Vegetius had written whilst Helva tapped his foot impatiently.

"And you want to leave now, sir?" the captain asked when he had read the dispatch.

"Is that a problem, Triearch?"

The captain looked out to sea and scanned the horizon with a professional eye whilst the magistrate waited impatiently behind him.

"No problem at all, sir," the man replied finally. "To Dyrrhachium?"

"To Dyrrhachium," confirmed Helva. "With all haste."

"You heard the magistrate, lads!" the triearch bawled out to his crew who scrambled into action.

As the sailors made ready, the marines helped load the baggage as well as get Attianus aboard upon his stretcher. They laid him out on the deck and erected an awning from an old sail cloth over him. It did not take long to load their small amount of belongings and the supplies the crew and passengers would need for the short trip. Once they were all aboard the marines lifted the boarding ramp and stowed it away. Helva had dismissed the slaves that had carried Attianus so now the four Romans were accompanied only by Nekar and Timaeus, who squatted beside his patient as the ship pulled away from the dock and headed out to sea.

"How long will it take to reach Dyrrhachium?" Celer asked Vegetius.

The older man only shrugged.

"Should be there sometime after noon tomorrow, if all goes well," said the triearch from behind them as he finished his inspection of the deck.

"I'll probably keep at the oars until the wind picks up a little, then we'll make good progress."

"How do you know the wind will pick up in the right direction?" queried Vegetius.

"I don't," conceded the triearch, "but we've had warm southerlies for the past few days. Now that they've died off the bora is sure to follow."

"What's the 'bora'?" Celer beat Vegetius to the question.

"Strong wind from the north-east," explained the triearch. "Blows all the way down the Adriatic from Noricum and Pannonia. I wouldn't normally sail when it starts but if we judge it right, we can ride the head wind before it picks up too much."

"How much can it pick up?" asked Vegetius nervously.

The triearch smiled back at him. "Let's hope we don't find out."

Sure enough, in the early morning the following day they felt a cold wind begin to pick up behind them. The triearch called out for the crew to ship oars and erect the liburnian's rectangular sail. Celer stood at the bow and watched the coast of southern Italy be bathed in the dawn light as the sun rose above the mountains of the Illyrian coast.

# IX

The triearch was proved right in his prediction. By mid-morning the winds began to build in strength until it was a roaring blast of cold that penetrated the cloaks of the men huddled aboard the ship.

The sea became choppy and the sail strained above their heads as the ropes of the liburnian sang with the strain and the timbers creaked and groaned as she picked up speed. At first Celer was terrified; the ship seemed unstable as she skipped across the wave crests, sometimes rolling forward as the gusts stalled for a moment before a fresh blast would catch the sail and send her hurtling forward. Yet there was no air of panic among the crew. The triearch bawled continuous orders, straining to be heard above the wind, and the marines under their optio staggered across the deck making sure all the loose equipment was tied down as the skilled sailors eased or tightened the sail lines and soon Celer began to enjoy the rush as the wind drove them south.

With the bora behind them they made good progress and sighted Dyrrhachium as the sun reached its peak the day after they left Histonium.

Nekar gazed longingly as the port crept closer. With a cry from the stern, the triearch ordered the sail taken down and the crew manned the oars.

The big Numidian, normally so silent and imposing, had become a different man as soon as the first breath of wind had caused the ship to surge forward. Celer had heard Helva shouting above the wind to Attianus that his bodyguard had but one weakness and that was a deep-seated fear of any water he could not stand up in. The sailors and marines who had given the Numidian a wide berth when he first came aboard had picked up on this quickly and now one of them happily told him they would be docking within an hour or so and slapped him heartily on the back as Nekar sat shaking by the mast, gripping his knees tightly to his chest

Despite the roughness of their voyage, sea air seemed to have had the opposite effect on Attianus. He alone had slept soundly through the night and was now awake and cohesive for the first time in days. Celer had been delighted to have him back in the world of the living and had happily watched as Attianus managed to eat some flat bread and wine.

Dyrrhachium was a thriving, bustling port town, a far cry from the sleepy Italian coast they had departed from. The triearch guided them past the commercial shipping and made for the military harbour on one side of the port. The wind was still building in strength and Celer eyed the waves crashing against the docks with apprehension.

The sailors rowed harder, each muscle and tendon standing out on their arms like ropes as they battled to slow the small ship's speed. Celer watched as a unit of soldiers on the dock ran forward dragging what looked like large nets filled with something unidentifiable. As the ship neared, the soldiers quickly dropped the nets off the side of the stone docks and held them at the water line on ropes. The liburnian thumped into the nets; all the crew and passengers had braced at the triearch's shouted warning but most were still thrown to their feet. The marines were quickly on their feet again, swarming forward with ropes to lash the ship to the iron cleats set into the stonework of the dock.

As they disembarked Celer saw that the nets were stuffed with fleeces and even with the powerful wind the scent of damp animals was strong.

A duty officer had followed the soldiers out with more men, these armed with swords and shields. He approached them and saluted the marine optio.

"Welcome to Dyrrhachium!" he shouted in the wind. "We were not expecting your ship?"

The marine optio snapped a salute in return. "My apologies, sir..."

"I'm afraid the fault is mine, Centurion," interrupted Vegetius as he climbed from the ship onto the jetty.

The centurion noted Vegetius's fine clothes and quickly threw another salute.

Vegetius acknowledged the salute with a tip of his head. "Yes, I must apologise," Vegetius continued, "my colleagues and I are on an urgent embassy to the court of your Emperor and, as such, there was no time to send word ahead of our arrival."

The centurion eyed them as they disembarked from the liburnian.

"Do you have any documents proving this, sir?" he asked stiffly.

Vegetius snapped his fingers at Celer and beckoned him over. They had discussed this scenario as the liburnian had crawled into port and Celer now reached into his bag for the wax tablet containing the forged orders. He handed them over to the centurion and stood there quiet and expressionless as the soldier read the tablet.

After what seemed like an age the centurion nodded and snapped the tablet shut and tucked it under his arm.

"Everything seems to be in order, gentlemen. If you would like to follow me I will have your baggage brought to the depot." He motioned to his men and half of them broke ranks and made their way to the boat as the marines handed up the travellers' few bags. The rest of the legionaries formed up as an escort behind Celer and the group as they followed the centurion to the customs depot that sat between the dock and the town.

The centurion led them through the depot to the colonnaded courtyard at its centre and bade them take a seat next to a burning brazier before disappearing into a busy clerk's office.

"What's happening?" Celer whispered to Attianus as he helped him ease down onto a wooden bench.

"They're making copies of the orders," Attianus whispered back as he leant back against the wall with a sigh. "The infamous bureaucracy of the Empire. You get used to it," he added with a dry chuckle that turned into a cough.

They were sipping from cups of the sour wine brought to them by a navy clerk and drying their cloaks as best they could by the brazier when the officer returned with one of the depot's clerks.

"Here you are, sir," he said as he returned the wax tablet to Vegetius. "If I could just get your mark here, sir, then you can be on your way."

Vegetius made a scratchy signature on the parchment that the clerk held out to him and took the wax tablet from the officer.

"Thank you, Centurion, for your haste."

The soldier stiffened into one final salute which Vegetius matched this time with a slight bow.

As they left the depot the marine optio was waiting for them.

"The triearch says the weather will not permit us leaving right away, Magistrate," he said to Helva.

"There's been a change of plan, Optio. I shall be returning at a later date; my business is not yet concluded here."

The optio's eyes brightened. "Shall I give the order for the lads to disembark, sir?" he said happily at the thought of shore leave in Dyrrhachium and its bars and brothels.

"You may, Optio." Helva suppressed a laugh at the obvious glee on the optio's face. "As a reward for your speedy deliverance of our envoys and myself, allow me to get the first drinks for you and your men." He tossed a small coin purse to the optio who caught it deftly with a grin.

"Yes, sir, thank you, Magistrate."

"Where to now?" asked Vegetius as they cleared the customs depot.

Celer looked about them. They were still in the harbour area. Sailors, marines, slaves and merchants swarmed around them, heads bowed against the blasts of wind and rain, and carts laden with goods rumbled past, bound for the ships riding at anchor or up the paved street towards the town's forum.

"Follow me," said Attianus and took an unsteady step into the throng. A passing sailor caught him with his elbow and nearly sent him sprawling. Celer and Helva each took an arm and supported him as Nekar cleared a path through the crowd for them.

The main street leading from the port was just as busy as the harbour area had been but eventually the crowds thinned and Nekar no longer had to use his great size to force a passage for them. Following Attianus's directions they headed to the east side of the town, stopping only to buy food from one of the vendors lining the street.

The courier station was on the edge of the town and Attianus was breathing heavily by the time they reached it. Typical of imperial buildings, it was solidly built and whitewashed in contrast to the poorly maintained shops and houses nearby. A large stable area lay beyond the station and Celer could see horses, mules and even two oxen as well as several carts and wagons.

Helva and Vegetius went into the station to procure some horses, going through the process of showing the forged documents and waiting whilst they were checked and duplicated by the clerks.

Eventually they were taken round to the stables where six horses were waiting for them, held by three young stable hands who gave them dirty looks at having been dragged out into the wind. Nekar had recovered from his ordeal at sea and was beaming when he was presented with his mount, clearly sharing in his people's notorious love of horses. Attianus had to be boosted into his saddle, but once there he sat well and Celer was struck by the difference in him; it had been less than two days since they had arrived at Helva's house, half-starved and weak from his infected wounds. Timaeus, whilst skilled at healing wounds, had never ridden a horse and had to be shown how to mount into the saddle and how to get the horse to obey his commands. When they had loaded their bags into the horse's panniers Attianus led the way out of the station's yard and onto the road heading east.

The turned onto the Via Egnatia, a wide, paved road that ran from Dyrrhachium all the way to Constantinople.

"You still have the scroll for Theodosius?" Attianus asked Celer, shouting to be heard above the wind that continued to increase in strength, as they rode side by side a little way behind the others.

"It's safe!" Celer patted the pannier behind him.

"It should take us three weeks to reach Constantinople as long as we don't get held up by early snows in any of the passes!" Attianus nodded in the direction of the distant mountains.

"If we can convince Theodosius, between us and the message from your father and my uncle, to declare war on Eugenius then we shall have our revenge on those who murdered our families!"

Celer thought of the dispatch in his saddle bag with his father's name and all the other names of the murdered Senators. He thought of his mother and desperately hoped that she hadn't suffered before she died. He felt the rage building inside of him and gripped the reigns tightly until it hurt. Looking out over the flat, wind battered fields dotted with farms and villas and the mountains beyond, he looked forward to the arduous journey that would make him feel something other than the hate that boiled inside of him.

"Let's pick up the pace!" He kicked his heels in and his mount sped up to a trot.

Attianus noted the grim mask on his young companion's face and nodded approvingly to himself. Ignoring the throbbing of his shoulder, he urged his own mount after him.

# X

A cold morning breeze tugged at Celer's cloak, carrying with it the salty tang of the sea. He pulled it tighter about him and yawned, already missing the spartan comforts of the courier station outside Perinthus where they had spent the night. Timaeus had shaken him awake before dawn in the cramped room they all shared. They had eaten a quick meal alongside the soldiers coming off the night watch at the communal hearth attached to the accommodation block, then saddled their horses and rode out into the approaching dawn.

Now they trotted along the Via Egnatia to warm the horses, the leather caps that protected the horses' hooves drummed upon the paved road, breaking the quiet stillness of the morning. As the sun steadily climbed above the horizon, Celer felt a thrill of anticipation. The journey from Dyrrhachium had been hard but nothing compared to his and Attianus's flight across Italy. Several of the passes had been almost impassable from the early winter snows but they had driven their horses on through biting winds and blizzards of sleet. None of them were used to such conditions, though Celer liked to think he had coped with the cold better than the others, now that he was properly clothed and fed. Timaeus and Nekar had always lived in warmer climates and suffered bitterly in the mountains. The little Greek medicus had the added hardship of having never travelled by horse before. Whilst the others dropped from their saddles at the end of each day, weary and aching, Timaeus had to be lifted down and had resorted to concocting draughts from his medicinal herbs to counter the pain. Relief had been clear on all their faces when they finally descended to the northern shore of the Aegean Sea. With the last of the mountains behind them, they had spent two days recovering at Thessalonica.

Celer had found Thessalonica strange. In many ways it had reminded him of Rome, a thriving metropolis with a large mix of peoples from across the Empire and busy marketplaces worthy of its position on several of the major trade routes. Yet beneath the vibrant atmosphere there was an undercurrent among the people that unsettled him. There was a strong military presence in the city; the streets were heavily patrolled. To Celer, the soldiers looked more serious than the city guardsmen he was used to.

One night, Celer mentioned this to the older men, curious at their exchanged glances.

"The people here have little cause to love Theodosius," Helva explained in a low voice. "Two years ago, there were great riots in the city. The magister militum, whose actions had caused them in the first place, was slain by the crowds along with several of his staff and much of the garrison." He paused to make sure no-one else at the inn they were staying at was listening. Confident the other patrons were involved in their own conversations, he continued. "Theodosius ordered an example be made by executions of the ring leaders, but the soldiers he sent took retribution for their murdered comrades. In the end they killed thousands."

"It was an unholy act, by a Christian Emperor," added Vegetius darkly. "One he was rightly punished for by the Bishop of Mediolanum."

'A man of God' Celer thought to himself as he watched the rising sun turn the sea from dark steel to a light blue. Soon he and Attianus would have to face Theodosius himself, armed only with the scroll he carried, to somehow convince this Christian Emperor to enter into a bloody civil war.

Troubled by his thoughts, he slowed his horse to a walk until Attianus drew alongside him. The journey had been hard on Attianus. Timaeus fed him a steady stream of concoctions whenever they stopped to ease the pain in his shoulder and the wheezing in his lungs.

"A fine morning," the older man commented as Celer brought his mount up to a trot alongside his.

Celer grunted in reply, trying to marshal his thoughts. Attianus had grown used to the way his young companion's mind worked and sat patiently, enjoying the warmth upon his face from the weak sunlight.

"How do we do it?" Celer asked eventually.

"Do what?"

"Persuade Theodosius to declare war on Eugenius and Arbogast."

Attianus thought a moment. "We have your father's letter."

"My father and Varro wrote that letter with the intention of being alive when it was received."

Attianus nodded and they rode in silence for a moment. Celer waited expectantly, noticing the way his face no longer looked sunken, though it was thinner than before and Celer was sure there were flecks of grey in his hair that had not been there when they first met in Rome.

"They could not have foreseen their fate; no doubt much of what they have written is no longer possible. Yet it does not diminish the truth of their words. Eugenius is still a puppet and Arbogast seeks power for himself and the other Franks, not the Roman people. Theodosius will see that."

"You seem confident that we shall succeed?"

Attianus looked him in the eye. "I am confident that if we do not then there shall be no vengeance for my family, or your own."

"Very well," said Celer meeting his eyes, "then we shall not fail."

Attianus reached out with his hand. "It has been a long road, Celer, but tonight we will sleep inside the walls of Constantinople."

Celer reached across his body and clasped the offered arm. "Finally, it will be good not to sit upon a horse all day."

"A good observation, Young Master!" called out Timaeus from behind them. "One I would heartily second."

Celer turned and saw the little Greek bouncing along behind them. Although greatly improved, the medicus's riding style left much to be desired and the sight of him caused a laugh to burst from Celer's lips. Timaeus adopted a mock expression of offence before readily joining in the laughter and soon they were all laughing. It felt good to laugh once more after weeks of hard travel and the strain of their mission, which had cast a shadow over the mood of their small band. Even Nekar, who rode with an enviable grace despite his size, was seen to crack a smile at the Greek's efforts.

As the sun climbed higher, the road grew busy, yet they managed to maintain a steady pace and wove their way past wagons and carts whilst anyone travelling on foot made room for the six travel-stained horses.

The mood between them was light and they chatted to one another as they rode. Celer felt as if a weight was being lifted from him with every step towards Constantinople. Between Rome and Histonium he had felt hunted, little more than an animal in the wilderness where everyone and anyone might be a threat. Crossing the Adriatic had felt like he put a barrier between himself and his pursuers. He knew Attianus had felt the same. With each mountain pass they crossed and every mile from Dyrrhachium, he felt freer. They both stopped checking over their shoulders on the road and Celer managed to sleep most nights without vivid nightmares filled with smoke and blood.

The road widened before them and there was a break in the traffic. With a hoarse shout and a slap to his mare's rump, Attianus upped the pace to a canter. The others followed suit and Celer found himself riding alongside Nekar. Not for the first time, Celer was impressed by Nekar's poise in the saddle; he rode like he was an extension of the horse beneath him.

Celer watched him a moment longer. He was envious of the Numidian, not for the big man's horsemanship but for his calm confidence and the feeling of security he inspired in those about him. It was more than just his size, thought Celer. There had been a few men amongst the soldiers garrisoning the courier stations that had the same air about them without the towering height of the bodyguard. Whatever the quality was that these men possessed, it was one he knew he lacked, and he was surprised to find that the knowledge made him feel jealous.

The horses had been pushed as hard as their riders since Dyrrhachium and after a short while at a canter they began to tire, so they slowed the pace to a walk, not wanting to exhaust them and have to stop. Though the cool morning breeze slowly died away the day did not grow hot and the horses soon recovered and they picked up the pace once more into the trot that the horses could hold for hours.

By late afternoon the roads had become busy with people and animals once more. As they drew ever closer to the city, they began to pass large flocks and herds of animals being driven to markets and slaughter houses in the Eastern capitol. They overtook several companies of soldiers tramping along the road that caused major disruption as the slow-moving wagons and animals ahead of them had to be moved off the road to allow the soldiers to pass. Vegetius mused aloud that they must be units from General Flavius Stilicho's victorious army, fresh from fighting the Gothic rebels in the northern provinces. Indeed, Celer could see that many of the men wore dirty bandages and several had strained faces as they coped with the pain of unhealed wounds. Their armour was thick with dust from the road and their shields were battered and he could see the vicious marks left on the painted surfaces where blows had rained down.

Though he knew little of military matters, Celer did know that a full-strength century should consist of eighty men, yet many of the units they passed had far less. One of the units had a bare eighteen men in a motley of mail and scale armour.

By nightfall they passed a mile marker that Celer's young eyes could just make out stated they were three miles from the city. In the distance they could see the sky glow orange as if the sun had decided to set in the east that night. Fortunately, the sky was clear and, although it quickly grew cold, there was enough light by the moon to guide their tired horses on. They passed several marching camps where the units from the road would be billeted outside the city. Despite their closeness to Constantinople Celer could make out the dark line of defensive embankments with the figures of sentries silhouetted by torch light upon them.

Like many major roads outside a Roman city, the Via Egnatia was lined with tombs as they reached the outskirts. Both Vegetius and Helva whispered prayers under their breath as the passed amongst the tombs and Nekar muttered under his breath in a strange language Celer guessed was his own.

For his part Celer, took one of the flat loaves he kept in his saddle bags and drew up at a neglected-looking road-side shrine. He quickly dismounted and placed the loaf in the depression carved into the top of the stone alter and, after a quickly muttered prayer to Pluto offering the bread in exchange for protection from any malevolent spirits of the dead, he remounted, conscious of the looks the Christians gave him. Attianus swiftly dismounted and gave similar offerings and, thus protected, they rode on towards the dark mass of the city walls.

"A word of warning," Helva addressed them both when they were back in the saddle, "you would do well to keep your faith to yourselves in Constantinople, especially in the Imperial court. You cannot give them cause to mistrust you."

"Wise counsel, my friend," agreed Attianus as they began passing through the residential area that had grown up outside the city walls. The air was thick with the smell of cooking fires and raw sewage; they could see people sat in doorways and around communal hearths eating and drinking.

An area roughly a hundred paces wide had been kept clear of buildings in front of the walls and as they approached the gates Celer shuddered suddenly, feeling exposed as he made out the helmets of the soldiers in the towers flanking the gate.

Celer saw to his dismay that the heavy wooden doors were barred shut and they reigned in a short distance from it.

"Who goes there!" came the challenge from above.

"We are envoys," responded Attianus, "bound for the court of Emperor Theodosius. We have come from Rome."

"Envoys from the Western court arrived three days ago by ship," shouted the officer of the watch. "We were not informed there would be a second party."

"Shit." Celer heard Vegetius curse quietly from behind him as his stomach churned. Somehow, Eugenius and Arbogast's agents had beaten them there. They would have already held an audience with Theodosius no doubt and may have reached an outcome agreeable for both sides already.

Attianus ignored his companion's curses from behind him and replied in a steady voice. "We do not represent Eugenius; we stand here on behalf of the Senate of Rome and her people."

The officer laughed harshly. "The Senate has no power any more; rumours are that their numbers have dwindled recently."

If Attianus shared the same flare of hatred that Celer felt at the officer's words he did well not to show it when he shouted back his reply.

"I represent men who name Eugenius a usurper and the General, Arbogast, a traitor! We carry with us the words of a great many men who believed him as such and died for that belief. The Senate is a symbol to the Roman people and would be a great ally for Emperor Theodosius. Now, I ask again, will you allow us to enter?"

There came no reply for a moment and the six horsemen stared at the battlements above them waiting for an answer that could doom their mission.

As it was, no answer was shouted from the walls. Instead, with a heavy groan, the great gates swung inward revealing a centurion in full armour with a half century arranged in double ranks either side of the gate.

Celer and the others followed Attianus's lead and dismounted and led their horses though the gate. Soldiers came forward to take the reins as they removed the saddle bags.

"Search them!" ordered the centurion.

"Centurion, I hardly think that's necessary," said Vegetius.

"I'll decide what is necessary, sir," said the centurion with the deadpan tone Celer had noticed soldiers used when dealing with civilians.

Vegetius looked as if he might respond but Attianus caught his eye and gave a minute shake of his head. The writer clamped his mouth shut and allowed the soldiers to search him whilst he fixed the centurion with an angry glare.

The officer ignored Vegetius and watched as the contents of the travellers' bags were emptied out before him. One of his men held a torch close as he examined their meagre possessions. He gave their knives a cursory glance but was far more interested in Nekar's cudgel, running an appreciative eye over the leather handle and ornate carvings that covered the weapon.

"Knives are permitted within the city but not within the palace, so we'll confiscate them now, and that," he pointed at the cudgel, that is not permitted within the city walls and shall be held alongside your blades. Optio!"

The centurion's second in command had been stood behind him with a small wax tablet which he now handed to the centurion. The officer quickly scanned it then made a few quick scratches with the stylus before handing it to Attianus.

"Your receipt for the weapons; show it at the gate when you come to leave the city and they shall be returned to you."

"If you would follow me, gentlemen, I shall escort you to the palace. Optio Pertax, you have the gate until I return; Aculeo and Vinicus, your

126

sections with me!"

The optio saluted as the centurion marched off into the city with the six travellers close behind, flanked by the two sections.

Constantinople seemed to be a very spacious city, Celer thought as they followed the centurion towards the Imperial palace. Compared with Rome or Thessalonica the streets were not crowded in by the buildings either side and here and there he could see open spaces amongst the buildings, something he had never seen in the cramped and often haphazard tangle of Rome. It made sense, he thought, as the city was still new, having undergone major rebuilding works in the reign of Constantine, for whom it was named. It was clear to see the influence of the first Christian Emperor of the Roman Empire in the busts and statues of various saints on every street corner in the place of the traditional gods and spirits. It was more comparable to Mediolanum, he thought, a modern imperial city but on a much grander scale.

The streets were deserted and Celer was reminded of the late hour and suddenly felt bone tired after their day-long ride. He was pleased when the towering complex of the Palace came into view and they could see the wall that separated it from the rest of the city.

A small unit of scholae guarded the palace gates and their commanding officer stepped forward to meet them, a towering German who rivalled Nekar in size, resplendent in bronze scale armour that had been heavily polished until it shone in the flickering light from the torches.

Celer felt a stab of fear at the sight of him, instantly transported back to the fields outside Rome where he had crawled through ditches to avoid these terrifying German warriors.

"Halt!" cried the scholae officer in accented Latin. "Identify yourself."

The centurion took two paces forward before slamming his heavy military boots down as he came to attention.

"Centurion Lucullus, duty officer for the Golden Gate. These men here claim to be envoys of the Senate in Rome and request an audience with the Emperor."

"Come forward," beckoned the guardsman.

The weary travellers stood before him as he stroked his blond beard in thought. He shouted something in a Germanic tongue over his shoulder and one of the guardsmen behind him placed his spear and shield carefully to one side then turned and disappeared into the Palace courtyard.

"We wait," said the scholae officer.

They stood in silence like two sides facing off before a confrontation. Celer listened to the sounds of the sleeping city behind hi; dogs barked and cats screeched and every so often the night was punctuated by echoing shouts. The scholae stood before him like gold and silver gods of war. The men behind the officer were dressed as he was, only their armour was polished steel instead of bronze. They wore conical helmets topped with a white horsehair plume and their faces were hidden by a sheet of mail that hung from the top of their cheek guards. They wore articulated arm guards that covered from above their elbows to the backs of their hands and their short-sleeved shirts of scale armour hung to their thighs. Silvered greaves protected their lower legs. Each of them carried a tall oval shield and a large spear with a gleaming leaf-shaped blade and they all wore long cavalry swords at their hips.

Thankfully, Celer heard the sound of hurried footsteps and tore his gaze away from the faceless guardsmen to see the soldier who had left returning with a man dressed in expensive robes.

The guards on the gate parted without a word in an impressive display of synchronism to allow the robed man through. He came and stood by the scholae officer's elbow and Celer could see from the tangled mess of his receding hair that he had been woken up.

"Who are you?" asked the robed man irritably.

Attianus stepped forward. "My name is Caius Maximus Attianus. My companions and I have travelled from Rome with a letter from the Senate to Emperor Theodosius regarding the ascension of Eugenius to the throne of the Western Empire."

The robed man regarded Attianus with a calculating eye.

"I had heard that you might show up in Constantinople, Attianus, and you, Celer." He fixed Celer with a piercing gaze.

"As you have probably heard by now, we have already received the envoys sent by the court of Eugenius."

Attianus shook his head. "With all due respect, we do not represent

Eugenius."

"No, you represent members of the Senate who are no longer of this world," said the robed man harshly. "Yet," he continued, "the Emperor has decided to afford you the audience you seek. You will appear before him tomorrow evening. Until that time you will remain confined to the guest quarters in the east wing of the Palace. If you are found beyond these quarters you will all be executed, is that clear?"

Celer, still unnerved at how the robed man had known his name, nodded along with the others.

"Very well. These men shall show you to your quarters." With that the robed man turned on his heel and disappeared through the gate. The scholae officer barked an order in his harsh German tongue and two guardsmen stepped forward.

"Follow," said the golden warrior, raising an armoured arm towards them.

As they followed the guardsmen through the gate, Celer heard Centurion Lucullus ordering his men to fall in behind him but the tramp of their boots was cut off as the palace gates boomed shut behind them.

# XI

The quarters they were shown to were lavish even by the standards that Celer had been used to in his father's house. The east wing of the palace was massive, and they were taken to its very edge. Their rooms were arranged on three sides of an internal garden with a sculpted fountain at its centre; the fourth side of the garden became a tiled terrace which looked out over the city, the great Church of Constantine dominating much of the view. All this Celer barely acknowledged as their guards escorted them to their rooms. He was so tired that he murmured a brief goodnight to Attianus and Vegetius who had the rooms either side of him and sank onto his spacious bed. Within moments the gentle sound of running water and the comfort of the bed had robbed the last of his willpower and he fell into a deep sleep.

Given the weeks of exhausting travel, Celer should have slept the rest of the night and most of the next day. However, the weeks of pursuit through Italy and nights sleeping in rough way-stations throughout northern Greece had instilled an alertness that he had not possessed before. As it was, his unconscious mind picked up the light pad of feet and noticed the brief break in noise from the fountain as something entered his room through the doorway from the inner garden. His eyes snapped open; fear honed his senses in the darkness. His senses at once attuned to every noise and smell and his body tensed, ready to react.

He was lying face-down across the bed where he had dropped just hours earlier. His head was closest to the garden but his view was obscured by the silk drapes that hung at the head of the bed. Slowly, so as to not make any noise, he lifted his head and looked to his left, past the drapes, trusting that the movement would be hidden by the darkness of the room. Fortunately, the room was large and the doorway to the garden was at least ten paces from the edge of the bed, for he saw the shadowy figure of the intruder at once. The shadows meant he could not see if they were armed or not.

Ever so slowly, Celer tensed his arms and waited to move, the figure padding closer faster now, not caring about the noise.

He watched as the figure's right arm rose up and he saw the slim shape of a dagger briefly profiled against the moonlight from the open doorway. Celer thrust down with his arms and threw himself backwards off the bed and onto his feet. The intruder was momentarily startled to see him rise up so suddenly, giving Celer time to seize a glass vase from the bedside table and hurl it towards the shadow. His aim was off and the vase missed and shattered against the marble floor; the sound was explosive in the still night but it broke through the intruder's stunned surprise and the figure rushed at him. The light from the doorway was blotted out as the intruder leapt onto the bed to get to him and Celer quickly grabbed the silk drapes and snatched them across his side of the bed, the brass rings shrieking as they slid along the rail. There was a loud tearing noise as the attacker hurtled into the drapes and crashed to the hard floor. Celer staggered back from the flailing figure on the floor and leapt across the room to grab the chair from the writing desk. He whirled about in time to see the intruder had rid themselves of the silk and come rushing after him. Celer swung the chair with all his strength and it connected solidly with a large crash and his attacker stumbled heavily with a cry. Celer pressed his attack, raining blows upon the intruder until the chair splintered into pieces. He brought the solid seat of the chair crashing down on the man and heard a large crack as he connected with the attacker's head.

The crumpled shape at his feet was still and he could smell the coppery tang of blood. He dropped the remnants of the chair and scrabbled around on the floor until his hands found the dagger. He snatched it up, the handle sticky from the spreading pool of blood, and backed away, panting.

Where were the guards? he thought frantically. They must have heard the crashing coming from his room. Only then was he aware of shouting coming from the courtyard garden. Gripping the dagger tightly, he rushed over to the doorway and carefully peered out. The courtyard was lit by several braziers; one of these had been knocked over and the hot coals lay smouldering in the flower bed. For a moment, Celer was back at his family's house and he saw his father silhouetted against the flames. He shook himself and darted out. The sounds of shouting and crashing furniture were louder now and came from Helva's room. Celer almost hurried straight past Vegetius's room but as he passed he heard a strangled cry. With a glance towards Helva's room, Celer ducked through the doorway, keeping low so that he would be harder to see in the moonlight and weak flames from the remaining braziers. His eyes were well adjusted to the gloom and he instantly saw a writhing mass upon the bed and he could see one of the drapes had been torn down in the struggle.

Vegetius was locked in a vicious struggle for his assailant's knife which was hovering just above his breast.

With a wordless cry, Celer rushed forward.

The assassin turned at the shout and Vegetius managed to force the dagger to the side where it sank harmlessly into the mattress. Celer slashed at the attacker, laying open their arm whilst Vegetius pummelled them with his fists from below. Attacked from two sides, the assassin fell back, clutching their wounded arm to their chest. Vegetius ripped the dagger from the mattress and together he and Celer moved towards the assassin. The intruder backed away, their features lost in shadow, then feinted towards Vegetius before making a break for the door.

"Stop him!" cried Vegetius, lunging after them.

Celer threw himself at the escaping assassin and they both went down in a tangle of limbs. The dagger flew from his hands and went spinning across the marbled floor.

The assassin recovered first and struck Celer across the face with his elbow as he struggled to find his feet. Despite the dark, stars exploded across Celer's vision and he hurriedly raised an arm to protect his face as the assassin struck again and again. Suddenly there was a gasp from above him and the intruder struck him again but without any force this time. Celer fought through the grogginess and lashed out and to his surprise his blow knocked the assassin to the floor. Only then did his see the dark hilt of the dagger projecting from the assassin's back.

"Thank you!" Celer gasped.

Vegetius only panted in reply, his hands on his knees, then he retched and turned away to vomit as Celer slowly rose to a kneeling position, one hand braced against the bed post for support as his head swam.

After a few seconds Vegetius spat and straightened up. He crossed over and helped Celer to his feet before bending to pick up the dagger Celer had dropped. He paused over the body as if deciding to whether to pull out the weapon buried in the assassin's back but couldn't seem to bring himself to do so.

They both started for the doorway when the moonlight was blotted out by a huge shadow filling the doorway. Vegetius threw andarm across Celer's chest and they backed away as he raised the dagger in his other had.

"Master Vegetius?" came the deep rumble.

Vegetius breathed a sigh of relief and lowered the dagger. "Nekar, you had me worried there a moment!" he admonished.

"Sorry, Master," the big Numidian stepped aside and Helva entered the room. Celer could see the small figure of Timaeus behind them.

"Are you all right, my friend?" asked Helva. "Is that Celer?"

"It is and we are," said Vegetius. "You were attacked also?"

Helva nodded, then, realising that they couldn't see the gesture in the dark, he said, "Yes, Nekar dealt with them."

"Where is Attianus?" asked Celer, brushing past them into the courtyard.

He hurried back past his room with the others close behind. The door to the palace boomed open and he could hear the metallic sound of the guards' armour as the rushed into the courtyard. Celer was the first to the doorway as the air was filled with the shouts of the guardsmen. He was about to rush inside when he caught a sign of movement in the dark and hurled himself to one side as a figure hurtled out of the dark, a dull dagger blade held low.

The assassin lunged at Celer but his quick reaction saved him and the blade sliced open his tunic rather than his flesh. Nekar had been close behind Celer and the Numidian caught the assassin with a colossal blow that drove them to the floor. The assassin recovered and, quick as a cat, rolled clear of Nekar's follow-up kick. With a parting look at Celer, the assassin turned and ran for the terrace. They had almost made it to the low wall when a spear whistled through the air and sank into their back, just between the shoulder blades. The blow knocked the assassin over and they slid across the tiled floor, coming to a rest against the wall, leaving a smear of blood across the tiles.

Celer's tunic was wet with blood where the blade had cut through it and he cautiously peeled back the flap to see how bad it was, but his shin was unmarked.

Realisation struck and he realised that the blood was not his.

"Attianus!" Scrambling to his feet, he rushed into the room. A guardsman arrived with a torch and by its flickering light Celer could see that the bed was empty. Slowly, he circled around until he saw his companion.

Attianus lay naked in a tangle of bed sheets. The wounds he had suffered from the wolf attack had healed under Timaeus's care and now the puckered scar tissue stood out against his pale skin. Below his bitten shoulder, his chest was awash with blood; there was a ragged hole that looked black in the badly-lit room.

"Timaeus!" Celer heard his own shout, as if from far away. The medicus was already in the room and quickly sank down beside Attianus. He pressed the already soaked bedclothes to the wound to stem the bleeding and laid two fingers against Attianus's neck. Helva knelt by his friend, cradling his head as the Greek tried for a pulse again but to no avail. Eventually, Timaeus straightened and eased the pressure off the wound; Celer could see that blood no longer pumped out of it.

The guards gathered them all into Nekar's room. The Numidian had chosen to sleep outside his master's room and so his room, along with Timaeus's, were the only ones absent of bodies. Timaeus had been answering a call of nature in the bushes of the garden when the assassins had climbed over the terrace wall and they had missed him in the dark. Likewise, the assassin aiming for Helva's room had stolen right past Nekar; the Numidian's dark skin had rendered him almost invisible on the low couch he had dragged to the door.

Celer smashing the vase had woken everyone. Nekar had awoken as the assassin aiming for Helva had just stalked past him and had risen, a demon in the dark, and swiftly dispatched him. Timaeus had rushed over to wake the bodyguard when he heard sounds of fighting and that was when the three of them were cornered by the two assassins who had gone into the medicus's and bodyguard's rooms.

By the time Nekar had dealt with the two assailants, suffering a wound to his side in the process, Celer was in Vegetius's room and the three of them had rushed over to help.

"The vase must have woken Attianus also," said Helva quietly, holding his head in his hands.

"For the assassin to be leaving as we arrived, he must have struggled," suggested Vegetius, "much like I did, only Celer came to my rescue." The writer placed a hand upon Celer"s shoulder. "Had you not come no doubt I would lie dead, also; I owe you my life."

Celer did not know what to say he was so numb. How could they have survived so much for Attianus to die in bed in the heart of the Imperial Palace?

They could guess at least who the assailants were. Celer had gone back into his room, much to the protest of the guard officer, not willing to leave the scroll unattended. Vegetius and Helva had briefly looked at the body on his floor. The face had been smashed beyond recognition by the seat of the chair and the pulped remains made Vegetius turn away, retching. Helva was made of sterner stuff and had searched the body, finding little, but had exposed tattoos on the would-be assassin's arms that Nekar recognised as military tattoos.

"If they were soldiers sent as part of the envoy from Arbogast, we will soon find out," muttered Helva darkly. "The guards will know how many were in the party when it arrived; any absentees will be noticed quickly."

Vegetius slapped his thighs in frustration and stood up. "How did they know?" he exclaimed, starting to pace up and down. "We arrived in the dead of night; they could not have known how far along the road we were even if they knew we were coming towards Constantinople."

"I agree," said Helva. "They must have spies in the palace to have known where we were staying."

Vegetius stopped pacing suddenly. "Unless they were under orders from someone in the palace."

"No," said Celer quietly from the couch by the door.

"How do you know?" asked Helva.

"They came in the night, same as when they took my parents. Same as when they killed Attianus's brother, his uncle's family; it was Arbogast's doing."

"Very well," the writer slowly sank back down onto the bed. "We'll find out soon enough."

Morning broke on the grim scene. A steward and a train of slaves arrived to clean the blood from them as the guards dragged the bodies from the rooms. Slaves immediately began mopping the blood from the marble floors as weak dawn light illuminated the horrors of the night.

Celer allowed the blood to be scrubbed from his limbs and accepted a new tunic with a patterned hem but he refused the breeches they presented him. Whilst most of the Empire had adopted this barbaric fashion, it had never caught on in Rome and Celer saw no need to start now.

The slaves never once spoke, nor did he even look at them, instead keeping his eye on the bag and the scroll it contained. When he was clean and dressed the steward appeared at the door to his room.

"His Excellency requests your presence in the audience chamber," said the steward with a deep bow.

"Just me?" asked Celer warily.

"Yes, Master," said the steward. "His Excellency desires to speak with you in private."

He said it with a tone implying that the Emperor had bestowed a great honour upon him and Celer supposed that a private audience with the ruler of the Eastern Empire was an honour few ever received.

"Very well." Celer took the leather scroll tube from his bag and followed the steward out into the garden courtyard. As they headed for the door leading into the palace, Helva stepped out from his room. He saw the steward leading Celer towards the door and took a step forward, the frown that creased his brow deepening. Celer gave a slight shake of his head and Helva stopped but he watched as Celer stepped through the double doors after the steward and flanked by two guardsmen, with an expression of concern.

Unlike when they had arrived, the palace now swarmed with activity. Not only Theodosius's residence but also the administrative hub for the Eastern Empire, the palace was a bustling hive filled with slaves, clerks and courtiers. Tales of the Emperor's devotion to his faith seemed true, for they passed many groups of priests and monks in the marble halls, almost more in number than the scholae guardsmen who patrolled with their faces hidden behind sheets of mail or gilded face masks.

The audience chamber where Theodosius held court was a vast room. Towering marble columns ran either the length of the chamber, holding up the vaulted roof, and Celer's footsteps echoed on the pink marble floor.

The area behind the columns, normally occupied by the members of Theodosius's court, was ominously empty. No preening nobles in all their finery or stern-faced, battle-scarred officers in gleaming armour along with the usual abundance of priests, clerks, slaves and freedmen that made up the courts of Emperors; all were missing.

Emperor Theodosius sat in a low backed chair upon a dais looking out over the empty chamber. He was not an overly big man but he radiated power. His dark olive colouring, a reminder of his family's origins in northern Hispania, stood out in stark contrast to the white marble of the wall behind him. Celer had seen him once before, several years ago, as he celebrated a triumph through Rome with his youngest son at his side and he saw that Theodosius still wore the same stern expression on his face. The face bore a few more lines now but there was no grey in his hair and he looked fit and strong. Sitting beside him on a plainer chair was a boy of around a similar age to Celer. Celer surmised that this would be Arcadius, eldest son of the Emperor and his co-ruler of the Eastern Empire. Arcadius shared his father's colouring but possessed none of his aura of authority. His face was fleshy and round with a petulant look fixed upon it that Celer instantly recognised from the spoilt children of several of his father's friends. Such children were often petty and given to cruelty towards others but Celer knew from experience that more often their cruelty was matched by a cowardly nature.

Theodosius sat still as a rock as they walked towards the dais. Arcadius fidgeted in his chair, eyes darting between Celer and his father.

The steward halted twenty paces from the dais.

"Bow!" the steward hissed, he himself bending deeply at the waist, so that his torso was almost horizontal. Celer gave a dignified bow as he had been taught to as a child.

Theodosius leant back in his throne and studied him closely between steepled fingers, Celer stood with his feet slightly apart and hands clasped behind his back, respectfully waiting to be addressed.

After an age the Emperor spoke, his powerful voice echoing slightly off the vast marble walls.

"My condolences for your friend." He looked directly at Celer. "For such an atrocity to occur to guests under my protection is a grave insult and those responsible will soon face justice, you have my word."

Celer bowed his head. "Thank you, Excellency."

"I am told you have brought me a message from Rome, from your father."

Celer took a step forward and raised the leather tube. Instantly the two scholae guardsmen at the foot of the dais, who until that point could have been mistaken for statues, so still were they, drew their swords and advanced a pace towards him.

Theodosius frowned and raised a hand. "Enough! Let him through; enough blood has been shed this day."

The guardsmen, expressionless as ever behind the mail that covered their faces, stepped back and sheathed their swords but Celer saw their eyes follow him as he slowly approached the steps leading to the throne.

Theodosius leant forward and took the tube from him himself then held out a hand to a steward who hurried across from the shadows of the dais with a small knife. Celer watched as the Emperor deftly cut away the wax seal at the end of the tube and tipped the scroll out.

No one ordered him to move so Celer stood and waited two steps away from the most powerful man in the world whilst he read the scroll, feeling vulnerable and exposed.

It did not take long for Theodosius to read the scroll.

"Do you know what is written here?" he asked Celer, tapping the vellum page with a blunt finger.

"I have not read it myself, Excellency," conceded Celer.

"But you have a notion of its contents?"

"Yes, your Excellency."

"And your companions, do they also have a notion?"

Celer suddenly felt that he had walked into a trap, yet the piercing hazel eyes of the Emperor were now locked onto his own and he knew that any lie would be seen through in a heartbeat.

"Some, your Excellency."

Theodosius gave another of his slight nods and the hazel eyes fell back to the parchment on his lap.

"Allow me to enlighten you fully. On the face of it, this scroll condemns the claim of the usurper, Flavius Eugenius, to the title of Emperor of the Western Roman Empire.

"The Senate of Rome claim that he is merely a pawn of the general Arbogast, Magister Militum of the Western military forces, who seeks to better the cause of his own people over that of the Roman Empire. The Senate of Rome therefore asks that I, Theodosius, now the sole legal Augustus of the Roman Empire, march west with my armies and liberate them from the unlawful rule of Eugenius and Arbogast. This effort on my part will be matched by the Senate, who request military advisors from my court aid them in forming a military force of their own in order to seize the city of Rome and hold it in my name."

Theodosius raised his gaze from the scroll and fixed Celer with his fierce gaze once more.

"It then goes on to suggest a series of candidates from their own ranks who they consider suitable to fill the position of Augustus of the Western Empire and act as co-Emperor alongside me; your father is named as one of the candidates." He took a moment to scrutinise the shock on Celer's face before continuing.

"Furthermore, they suggest a repeal of the reforms enacted by the Emperor Diocletian prohibiting their involvement in new legislation and the appointment of new officials and magistracies."

Celer stood rooted in shock; his father had never mentioned the slightest hint of such ambition. A cold hand gripped his chest as he also realised the danger of his position now. The second half of the scroll was a barely veiled attempt by the Senate to restore its lost powers. Attianus had said as much the day he saved him from capture outside the house of Varro, but he had barely acknowledged his words at the time, so desperate with grief and fear as he had been. Now the cold reality hit him in this vast chamber. Its marble walls suddenly felt so close that it might as well have been a tomb.

The Emperor's eyes had never left his face all the while.

"Perhaps it is best your father lies dead already, boy," growled the Emperor. "Such Republican ambitions have existed since the days of

Caesar and will undoubtedly remain long after we are gone from this world, yet such ambition threatens the stability that I have struggled to maintain over this Empire for the good of all Romans!" His voice had gathered in volume as he spoke so that he roared the last word in Celer's face who did his best not to flinch.

Theodosius was not done. "I will not tolerate such attempts, especially from men with ancient names and dreams of day's long past and sufficient wealth to act upon them."

He paused and seemed to compose himself, for when he spoke again it was in the steadier tone he had begun with.

"By rights, I should have you all executed for playing your parts in this. There are those amongst my court that strongly advise me in this." Hazel eyes roamed over Celer, watching him wince at his words. "Yet I think you are little more than a messenger in this, not a player in a greater scheme, am I correct?"

He watched as Celer responded with a nod, not trusting himself to speak.

"Very well," he folded his hands over his lap, covering the parchment scroll. "I try to follow in the teachings of Christ as best I can, and He teaches us the value of mercy. Therefore, I will spare your life and those of your companions."

Celer felt the knot in his bowels loosen slightly.

"However, I am not done with you yet."

Celer felt his legs begin to tremble slightly as adrenaline coursed through his veins and he willed them to be still. Arcadius was watching him with a cruel smirk upon his face and Celer took strength from the sudden flush of anger he felt. Though there was likely less than a year between him and Arcadius, he felt in that moment very much older. He remembered his father's words that night before he fled Rome and resolved to face the Emperor's judgement like a man, without showing fear and shaming the memory of his forefathers. Forcing his legs to cease their trembling, he focused his gaze at the spot between Theodosius's feet.

Theodosius lowered his fierce eyes to the scroll in his hands and spoke slowly.

"Despite the blatant plots behind this," he shook the scroll, "I think

140

it may still serve a purpose. Arbogast's treason shall not go unpunished." He said the last words quietly, almost to himself as if he sat alone in the vast marble chamber. Arcadius obviously thought his father's mutterings strange, for the mocking gaze was replaced with one of confusion as he looked to Theodosius.

The Emperor, feeling his son's questioning eyes upon him, snapped his attention back up to Celer.

"You will remain here in the palace until I decide what to do with you. You shall all have the freedom of the palace but you will not be permitted to leave; any attempt to do so shall be considered an act of treason and you will be caught and executed." He looked Celer up and down once more and Celer felt as he had when he had been surrounded by wolves as he felt the weight of those hazel eyes.

"Bury your friend. My stewards shall see to the arrangements and give him the full Christian burial a man of his birth deserves."

Celer stiffened at this, remembering Helva's warning on the road outside Constantinople. He did not dare to correct Theodosius about Attianus''s continuing faith in the Roman gods. Instead he swiftly ducked his head and gave a slight bow.

"My gratitude, your Excellency."

In a fluid movement, Theodosius rose. Arcadius was caught off guard by the sudden change and stood with much less grace. The audience was at an end. Celer and the stewards bowed quickly as the Emperor and his son strode from the dais through a highly decorated door to the side.

Celer felt a tug at his elbow. He turned to see the steward stood a step below him.

"Does the young master require guiding back to his room or would he like to be taken elsewhere in the palace?"

"No." He felt dazed by all that had just happened. "No, I can find my own way back."

"As you wish." The steward bowed another of his deep bows and turned and left him alone in the chamber.

The grand walls and columns surrounding him suddenly felt stark and cold and he felt a sudden need for daylight and fresh air. Remembering a portico they had walked past on the way to the chamber,

Celer hurried out into the palace. Back-tracing his steps, he soon found the covered terrace that looked out over the city and part of the circus. Already some of the seats below were full as the crowds eagerly anticipated the races of the day and far below him the streets seethed with a great crush of people.

A pair of priests were talking in hushed tones, pausing only to stare at him as he sank onto a stone bench, but the terrace was otherwise deserted. He tipped his head back against the smooth stone of the column behind him and stared in the cloudless sky.

It was Vegetius that found him, hours later, still staring into the endless blue.

"They've prepared Attianus for burial," said the writer quietly.

Celer slowly lowered his head; his neck gave an audible crack that made Vegetius wince.

"He's dead because of my father." Celer's voice was cold and bitter.

Vegetius lowered himself onto the bench beside him. "What do you mean?"

"They were traitors, taking an opportunity to claw back their lost power." He shook his head and rubbed his eyes with both hands.

"Those are the Emperor's words, not your own," said Vegetius gently.

"And he's right!" Celer said angrily. "They committed treason and now they're all dead. Attianus, Varro, the god's know how many others. My father, my mother. They killed my mother!" He almost shouted the last words and Vegetius felt his heart wrench at the sorrow in his voice and the agony plain upon the boy's face.

Thankfully, Celer turned his grief-stricken face to the cityscape before them, sparing Vegetius his terrible expression.

"I had the pleasure of meeting your father once, and Senator Varro," said Vegetius quietly. "They were good men, with good reputations. A rare thing amongst the Senate these days, I am afraid to say. They struck me as men of a different age, who still believed in honour and duty. I would not be so quick to believe what Theodosius says. You know your father better than any of us, Celer; make your own judgement on who is to blame for all the loss that has been suffered."

Celer continued to look out over the city. From down below there came a roar from the circus as a race began. After a moment, he looked at Vegetius. The writer saw that his face was now calm and, though his eyes were red, he had shed no tears. "Thank you," Celer said quietly.

Vegetius clapped a comforting hand upon his shoulder. "Come," he said, standing. "The others will be waiting."

They buried him outside the city walls.

Under a heavily armed escort of scholae, they marched out of the palace. Attianus lay in a simple wooden coffin, carried by unarmed soldiers from the city guard. The procession was led by several Christian priests; Helva whispered that one more lavishly dressed than the others was the Bishop of Constantinople. He and Vegetius both obviously considered the Bishop's presence a great honour so Celer kept silent as they followed the coffin through the streets. As well as the scholae, a century of the city guard had turned out to clear the street ahead. The populace's disgruntlement at being forced to the sides of the street turned to curiosity and then awe at the strange procession. Celer saw many making a strange gesture, sketching a cross in the air before them and calling out the Bishop's name as he passed.

They walked a short distance from the city gate, past rows of tombs that lined the road of wealthy and important citizens of the past.

No grand tomb for Attianus, Celer thought sadly, for the Christians favoured simple burials. There was a small temple; Vegetius called it a chapel, upon a rise not far from the road. Behind it was a graveyard surrounded by a low stone wall. The Christian priests who resided there had already dug a grave and were stood waiting with their hands clasped together and their heads bowed.

Attianus's coffin was placed upon a table that stood by the grave and the Bishop stood at his head and offered prayers to his God, whilst the priests that had walked in the procession chanted in the background, swinging thuribles from which plumes of incense smoke rose.

Celer half listened to the Bishop, all the while looking down on the face of his companion. They had survived so much. He had survived largely due to Attianus and he knew full well that he would never have made it out of Rome alive without him.

The Bishop had finished his prayers. Accepting a silver chalice from one of the attending priests, he poured a libation of blood-red wine into the grave. With the offerings done, the Bishop said one final prayer and sketched the sign of the cross in the air above Attianus. He stepped back and beckoned the gravediggers forward to seal the coffin.

"Wait!" Celer stepped in front of a priest who carried the coffin lid. Carefully, conscious of the gaze of the Bishop, Celer stepped up to the coffin and reached in. One of the priests moved forward to stop him but Nekar stepped in front of him and the priest yielded to the big Numidian. Celer reached in and prized Attianus's jaw open as he had watched his father do at his grandfather's burial. It was hard work; Attianus''s jaw was seized like iron and Celer had to use two hands to prize his cold lips apart. Holding his chin with one hand, he reached into the pouch at his belt and took a silver siliqua out. He placed the coin in Attianus's mouth to pay his fare to Charon, the ferryman who ferried his passengers from the world of the living to that of the dead.

He struggled a moment more to force Attianus's mouth shut over the coin before he stepped back. With a quick gesture, the Bishop signalled to the gravediggers to close the coffin and lower it into the ground. As the coffin was lowered with cloth straps, dyed red and white for such a purpose, Helva took a pace forward and delivered Attianus's eulogy. He began with his immediate forefathers and their exploits and positions in life before listing Attianus's own accomplishments and positions he had held. The gravediggers had almost refilled the grave by the time Helva finished. As was the custom, he listed the names of the living who would miss Attianus but remember him in their prayers. Helva named himself, Vegetius, Celer and Timaeus. Nekar as a slave wasn't named, so as to not shame the spirits of Attianus's ancestors. Celer was startled when Helva also mentioned a woman's name, Festia. He wondered who she was as the gravediggers tamped down the loose mound with their shovels. Listening to Helva's eulogy had made him realise how little he knew of his late companion's life.

As they were escorted back to the city, he asked Helva who Festia was.

"They knew each other from childhood," Helva explained. "Her father was an equestrian, high ranking, a count of the second order I think."

"What happened to her? Is she his wife?"

Helva smiled sadly. "No, they didn't marry. Though nothing would have made either of them happier."

"Then why didn't they?" Celer asked.

"They were forbidden, in the end."

"Attianus's father?"

Helva shook his head. "No, he was dead by then. It was Festia's father who forbade it; he claimed Attianus was an unworthy match."

He eyed Celer's look of astonishment.

"It's more common thank you think," explained Vegetius. "Once upon a time an equestrian would have jumped at the chance for his daughter to marry up the social hierarchy to a Senatorial family. These days, those distinctions matter little; the true power in the Empire's lie with the equestrians now and they know it. Few patricians are granted the position of count and all are forbidden to serve in the armies, as you already know."

Celer was frowning. "But Attianus was from a well-respected family; their name has been known for centuries."

"Maybe amongst patricians, yes," said Helva gently. "Such things matter little outside of your class and Attianus's family had little else otherwise. They were not poor, but nor did they possess the wealth of many others, Festia's father included, and that is why her father forbade their marriage."

"So what happened to her? Where is she now?"

Helva shrugged. "I don't know. I heard she married but Attianus never spoke of her and I did not like to ask. I do know that he loved no other woman in the same way since."

The sombre procession trudged back to the city; once more the crowds parted before the armed escort but this time Celer payed no attention to their inquisitive looks.

When Celer got back to his room he found that it had been searched whilst they were outside the city. All the drawers had been pulled out and the bedding torn apart. His few possessions lay in a heap by the battered leather bag. The searchers had found what they wanted though; the dispatch Helva had given him, declaring his family traitors to the Empire, was gone.

Nine days after they had buried Attianus they held the funeral feast.

Their request to visit the grave had been denied so Helva poured the libation of wine off the edge of the terrace instead. Whilst they had not been allowed to visit the grave, the palace had put on a great deal of food and wine, so they feasted long into the night. Celer woke late the next morning with a thick head and thicker tongue. As soon as he sat upright he felt overwhelmingly sick and only just made the quick dash out of his room to throw up in one of the flowerbeds of the courtyard. He knelt there a long time until his stomach heaved its last and he felt safe enough to straighten. He stumbled on shaky legs to the fountain at the centre of the garden and washed his sweating face in it.

Nekar, who hadn't touched the wine the night before, brought him a cup of water that Celer gratefully accepted, sipping from it tentatively. Timaeus was also awake early. Annoyingly, the Greek seemed unaffected by the night's drinking, though Celer had a hazy recollection of the little medicus going cup for cup with Helva and Vegetius.

"Come here and try some of this, young Master," he beckoned to Celer.

He was heating an iron poker in the coals of a brazier still hot from the night before. When the tip glowed cherry-red he plunged it into bronze jug he held in the other hand. He poured a cup of the dark steaming liquid and handed it to Celer with a hunk of bread leftover from their feast.

"An old family remedy for the one cup too many," the medicus winked at him.

Celer sniffed at the vapours rising from the cup warily.

"It smells like wine," he said wrinkling his nose.

Timaeus laughed. "Because it is wine, young master, well-watered, amongst other things. Trust me, I'm a medicus!"

Celer mistrustfully took a sip. He could barely taste the wine beneath whatever combination of herbs Timaeus had mixed in and he burnt his tongue on the hot liquid, but to his surprise his churning stomach quietened almost instantly.

"Better?" Timaeus looked at him expectantly.

"It's good," Celer said, blowing on the drink before taking another sip.

The three of them turned at the sound of retching coming from

Helva's room. Nekar hurried off at once. Timaeus followed with a cheerful grin. "Sounds like my next patient is awake!"

Celer grinned despite himself at the Greek's infectious good humour and went over to the terrace. He leant on the stone wall, feeling the cold beneath his hands and feet sober him up. The morning sun was hidden behind cloud and the whole city was dark and quiet in the cold morning air. When he began to shiver he drained the last of his lukewarm remedy and returned to his room. Taking up a razor and copper bowl of water, he stood in front of a burnished silver mirror and shaved off the wispy mourning beard he had attempted to grow.

He then dressed, putting on two tunics against the cold of the day but he still shunned the trousers he had been given. His battered boots that had borne him so many miles had been taken and presumably burnt so he laced up the light sandals he had been given and walked back out into the courtyard.

Vegetius and Helve were both seated at the feasting table. The writer smiled and pushed a plate of food across to him whilst Helva sat huddled in a cloak gripping a steaming mug of Timaeus's remedy between his hands.

"Good morning," Celer greeted them both. "I was going to walk the palace, clear my head a little."

"An excellent idea; I find a walk always does wonders after a night of drinking," said Vegetius. "Mind if I join you?"

Celer shook his head and Vegetius rose to his feet, using the table to stop himself swaying.

"Care to join us, Helva?" asked the writer.

Histonium's ex-magistrate's face looked pale, with an unhealthy waxy appearance in the weak morning light. He shook his head, then seemed to regret even that slight movement, for he reached hurriedly for a bowl that he promptly threw up into.

Vegetius made a face at Celer and jerked his head towards the door to the palace.

They strolled slowly through the maze of the palace complex, pausing occasionally to admire the breath-taking views of the city from its terraces, or the statues that adorned every courtyard and alcove.

As they passed the grand doorway to the imperial library, Vegetius slowed.

"I fear I must abandon you at this point, Celer, unless I can entice you inside?" he asked.

Celer shook his head. "Thank you for the offer, but I would like to walk a little more. Maybe later?"

Vegetius dipped his head graciously. "No rush, I shall likely be here most of the day. Do you know that they have the entire collection of Julius Frontius? I have found his work on military matters most interesting. Indeed, he refers several times to his campaigns in Britannia whilst governor there, most fascinating."

Celer shook his head as he watched Vegetius disappear muttering into the cavernous room, walls thick with scrolls.

The imperial library, alongside the records and treasury, was in the heart of the palace. Blindly, he picked one off the corridors that ran away from it like a spoke of a wheel. Here the palace was always busy. The needs of an empire required huge efforts at all hours of the day and night and he passed many clerks either arriving at or leaving their posts. Those leaving rubbed their sleep-deprived eyes in the daylight, a short respite from their candlelit world.

Curious, Celer followed a pair of clerks down the marble halls until they crossed a courtyard and disappeared into a large building fronted by outdoor bread ovens that he guessed were barracks of a kind. Gathering his bearings, he realised he must be near the gate that they had entered the palace by on their arrival.

Sure enough, he rounded the corner of the clerks' barrack and saw the gate guarded by the scholae. There were four stood in the gateway and another two on the walkway above, watching the crowd through the gap above their mail face masks.

In the space behind the wall more guardsmen were training. Some trained against thick wooden posts set in the dirt, delivering cuts and thrusts with their swords or heavy spears and stepping in close to punch their large oval shields forward. Others faced off in pairs; armed with wooden swords, they circled warily before launching a quick exchange of blows. If neither won the encounter, they broke off and resumed circling, looking for a weakness.

It was an impressive display and Celer watched with a mixture of fear and awe. Similar men to these had hunted him and he still saw them in his dreams. Giant warriors, armoured in gleaming scale, hounding him through the fields outside Rome.

In his dreams he always ran and whenever they finally caught him he would try to fight them off; always he failed.

Standing there watching the scholae train, he felt suddenly angry. All his life his father had bought him the best tutors so that he might learn the necessary skills of rhetoric, law and languages. He had sat at his knee as Cotta dealt with patron's' complaints and rectified disputes and sat bored as his father patiently explained the finances that were generated from their vast holdings and paid for their lifestyle. None of it had been of any use. Apart from the ability to ride a horse and to swim, nothing had prepared him for anything that happened the moment the soldiers broke down the door to his home. Sheer luck and a desperate will to survive had seen him through starvation, exposure, wolves and an assassination attempt but, watching the scholae train, he knew that no amount of luck or will would save him from those swords if they were turned upon him.

He knuckled his eyes until he saw stars, then turned away from the training ground. His dark thoughts did not help his hangover, so he forced them from his mind. Instead, he set himself the challenge of finding his way back to the library.

To his private delight, his sense of direction proved true and he took no wrong turns and when he rounded a corner to see the large doors of the palace library his mood improved considerably.

The library was a series of vaulted rooms, each one crammed with shelves of parchment and papyrus. The vast majority of people in the library seemed to be Christian priests and monks. Some were seated alone whilst others crowded around tables strewn with texts and argued loudly. From what he could make out, most of the conversations seemed to revolve around theological arguments, some quite heated, and he wondered how anyone could read in such a place. He was musing about how nice it would be if a library were a quiet place when he spotted Vegetius in a corner, seemingly as far from any noisy monks or priests as he could get.

Celer was surprised to see he had company in the form of a

powerfully built man. Their heads were bowed in deep conversation so Celer took a step back and made to leave. The man's head shot up and Celer saw a stern, unlined face with a neatly trimmed beard.

"No need to leave, boy, I don't bite," said the man. Celer saw that he wore a military tunic and belt; intrigued, he walked towards the desk they were sat behind.

"Ah, Celer!" cried Vegetius. "This is the young man I was telling you about, Stilicho."

Flavius Stilicho looked him up and down and Celer returned the scrutiny with equal curiosity. Somewhere in his early thirties, the general was a rising star in the Empire, spoken highly of in both the East and the West. Celer knew from listening to his father that Stilicho was the son-in-law to Theodosius, his wife being the adopted daughter of the Emperor. Despite his high status, Stilicho appeared at first glance very similar to many of the military men Celer had met on the journey from Dyrrhachium. The stern face was tanned, as were the hands that rested on the table. Celer noticed that the knuckles on his right hand were scarred. Stilicho wore a simple military tunic with long sleeves and, as he sat back in his chair, Celer saw that it hugged his chest and torso, indicating he was a man of some strength.

"No need to stand on ceremony for me, boy," growled the general. "Take a seat." He gestured towards an empty chair.

"Vegetius was telling me of your escape from Italy," said Stilicho when he was seated. "Wouldn't have made it far if you were running from me; seems Arbogast is losing his touch," he said with a dry chuckle.

Celer's fist's tightened at the mention of the Frank but he said nothing. Stilicho continued. "I don't suppose you know the number of troops stationed in Rome at the time of your escape? Their condition, how well armed they were?"

Celer was taken aback by the question. "No... no, sir," he managed to reply.

"I hardly think Celer's priorities at the time were to reconnoitre the forces pursuing him," said Vegetius smoothly.

Stilicho shrugged. "Worth asking. No matter, we believe Arbogast has had to dispatch troops to various towns and cities anyway to quell dissent within Christian populations unhappy with the new regime."

Celer snatched onto the thread of news. "There are many who are against Eugenius's rule?"

Stilicho laughed, a great booming laugh that even hushed a few of the groups of priests for a moment. "We both know that it's not Eugenius who rules, boy, so let's not pretend otherwise, eh? No, there are plenty unhappy with Arbogast. Mainly Bishops, who have incited their followers against him, but also a few of the Senators and their followers who survived the purge that got your father, as well as a few members of the old regime of Valentinian like Vegetius here, all quietly stirring up trouble, which suits us just fine."

Celer looked to Vegetius when Stilicho said nothing further.

"The Emperor has declared war upon Arbogast and Eugenius, Celer," said the writer quietly.

"Is preparing to declare war," corrected Stilicho. "He's called his council and is delivering the news to them right now. Nothing official, yet, not until we've strengthened our defences, but nothing stays secret here for long, anyway." He cast his stern gaze over the library and Celer thought the groups around them seemed to converse a little louder. Stilicho grunted at the pretence of innocence before continuing. "I've spent all morning sending dispatches to begin gathering and resupplying our forces. You still haven't given me an answer." This was directed at Vegetius.

"I accept, of course, general. I would be most honoured." Turning to Celer, he explained excitedly, "The general has asked if I would accompany him to his forward camp to help with the instruction of new recruits to the army, purely from an academic perspective of course. We often discussed the training methods of the ancients in the court at Mediolanum and both concur that our modern methods may be somewhat lacking in areas."

"Take me with you," Celer blurted out.

Stilicho boomed another laugh. Vegetius frowned. "But, my dear boy, you're safe in Constantinople, just as your father wanted. I tell you, when the fighting starts, I shall be as far away as possible. What could you possibly gain from accompanying an army?"

Celer shook his head angrily. "What my father wanted no longer matters. Attianus and I swore that we would avenge our families by

151

bringing the scroll to Theodosius and then we would watch as his armies destroy those who killed our families. Attianus may not have lived to see it but I accept his oath alongside my own and I would see them pay for what they did to us."

Stilicho heard the anger in his voice and now looked at him, no longer laughing.

"So, you wish to avenge your family? I can understand that, respect it even. But no-one marches in my army without serving a purpose, so tell me, how much military training have you had?"

"None," said Celer fuming.

"And your father, how much fighting did he see? What wisdom did he bestow on you regarding war?"

"None," said Celer again, beginning to feel foolish.

"You made it here from Rome, survived Arbogast's soldiers, the mountains and everything else, and I respect that; maybe there is more to you than meets the eye. But every man under my command is a soldier, born and bred. Their fathers and their grandfathers were soldiers too. It is all they know, and men like them will win this war and all those that follow. I have no need for boys who grew up in comfortable houses with expensive tutors. My advice, leave revenge to those who know how to wield a sword."

Stilicho regarded him a moment longer then stood up to leave.

A vision of Flavianus the Elder stood over Varro's lifeless body flashed through Celer's mind. He heard his mother's screams ringing in his ears and his father telling him to run.

"Then teach me!" he shouted after Stilicho. The general stopped and turned back towards the table.

"What did you say?" he asked, bemused.

"Teach me how to wield a sword, how to fight. Let me come with you.I will do anything you command, all I ask is that when the time comes I will be allowed to wreak vengeance upon those who butchered my parents and friends, who killed the man who saved my life!"

Vegetius leant across the table towards him. "Celer, please, this is preposterous! You have a chance at a peaceful life here. You can leave your past behind you and forge a new destiny for yourself."

"A peaceful life?" Celer responded angrily. "My home was attacked in the night, my parents taken from me and murdered. I watched my best friend bleed to death in the street alongside his family. They hunted me like an animal across Italy and when we finally made it to the one place we thought we would be safe, they sent assassins who killed Attianus and would have killed us all as well. You included!" He pointed a finger at Vegetius, chest heaving he went on. "How likely is it do you think that Eugenius or Arbogast will let me live?" He aimed this question at Stilicho, who stood, dumbfounded, unused to being spoken to in such a manner. "Would I be allowed to live and gain wealth and position, the surviving son of a man they declared a traitor and had executed? No, I think not! Sometime soon, more men will be sent to kill me and I will not likely survive again. This is why I beseech you, please, let me come with you!"

Stilicho had regained his stern composure. "You would do well to remember, boy, who you are speaking to," he growled menacingly, taking a step forward. Then he relented. "Even if I could, for I have no need for another junior officer, the Emperor would never permit you to serve on my staff or even as a minor officer. He does not know you and he does not trust you. There are many within the walls of this palace that whisper in the Emperor's ear that he would be better off executing you now, least you become a problem in the future. My answer is no."

Celer slumped back into his seat. I tried, father, he thought to himself despairingly, I tried.

"Who whispers in the Emperor's ear?" asked Vegetius, worry written across his face. "Celer has only been here a short time, who could he have earned the enmity of bar the agents of Arbogast?"

"Rufinus, for one," said Stilicho darkly. "Presumably the boy's presence threatens one of his little schemes somehow; the snake does not act unless it benefits somehow."

Vegetius began tapping his ink stained fingers against the table top, a sign Celer recognised after weeks of travelling with the writer as one that meant Vegetius was deeply concerned about something.

"Who is Rufinus?" asked Celer. The name seemed somewhat familiar but he could not remember why.

"The Emperor's Magister Officiorum," Vegetius supplied, looking about them nervously, "a powerful figure here in court."

"A bureaucrat," growled Stilicho loudly, causing Vegetius to wince. "Soon to be Prefect of the East if he has his way, which he usually does. Best step carefully, boy," he looked Celer in the eye, "Rufinus's hands may be soft and powdered but he has blood on them nonetheless. General Promotus could have told you that, were he not lying in a cold grave."

A silence fell upon their table. All about them priests babbled and scraped their wooden chairs on the polished tiled floors as they vigorously argued about their God.

Vegetius looked across at Celer. The worried look was gone, replaced by something that might be sorrow. "You need men," he said quietly.

"What was that?" Stilicho cocked an ear his direction.

"I said, you need men, General," replied Vegetius, louder this time. "Only moments ago, you were informing me that you were having to raise men from the city to bolster the number of recruits from the garrison towns."

"Your point, Vegetius?" asked Stilicho impatiently.

Vegetius paused a moment before replying. He suddenly seemed uncomfortable. "What if Celer was your first recruit?"

The general folded his arms and stared stone-faced at Vegetius for a long moment.

As the writer began to squirm beneath his iron gaze, he turned to look down at Celer through narrowed eyes.

"Now, there is a test for you. How desperate are you for a chance to carry the sword to Arbogast, Eugenius and all the rest responsible for your family's deaths?" he asked Celer.

The question reverberated around Celer's mind. How desperate was he? How far was he willing to go?

"I took an oath..." he started.

"This is no small decision, Celer," Vegetius interrupted. "Your wealth and birth would mean little; you would be subject to the same rules and discipline as the most base-born soldier. Your life would be at the disposal of the army." His eyes seemed to plead at Celer as if regretting his own idea.

"I think that the lad has less to lose than you think, Vegetius," Stilicho said, still watching Celer.

"What do you mean?" asked the writer.

"The envoys from Arbogast presented the Emperor with a document stating that the boy's family, along with all the others declared traitors and enemies of the state, had their property and wealth seized by Eugenius and all ranks and titles removed. No doubt Arbogast has used all that money and property to secure the loyalty of many to Eugenius as well as serving as a warning to everyone else."

All this Celer and Vegetius knew already. The document must have been stolen from his room by the envoys and given to Theodosius and he momentarily cursed himself for keeping it in the first place.

"Then I shall take back what is rightfully mine." He thumped a fist on the table.

Stilicho laughed. "Not likely." The general shook his head. "When we win this war, the Emperor will find better uses for your lands and property. They will be given to men who will be important in restoring peace and stability and to buy political favour from those who might oppose his actions. Short of an old family name, you have little to offer in such circumstances. An old family name," he continued, "that by law forbids you from serving in the military."

Celer clenched his fists at the bitter truth. Stilicho was right, gods curse him. He had little to offer the Emperor. Any support amongst the elite of Rome he might have been able to raise had likely died the same night as his parents. The seizure of his family's wealth also meant that if he stayed in Constantinople he would be destined to live the life of a beggar, living on the charity of distant acquaintances of his father until he was married to a lesser daughter of a family that valued his family name more than himself. The choice in his mind was clear.

Celer rose to his feet and stood before Stilicho.

"By law, no patrician may serve in the military," he said, "but you said it yourself. I have been stripped of my wealth and titles, which frees me from such restraints."

"Very well," the general raised a hand. "I must warn you, the army is not what you imagine nor what you read in the histories or what your tutors or father may have told you. Many men from military families find it hard, some too hard, let alone a Senator's son."

Celer looked him in the eye. "I understand."

"You have made your decision then?" the general asked.

"I have."

"Good, you can give you decision to the recruitment officer at the palace barracks tomorrow." Stilicho turned his head to look at Vegetius, who was still sat at the table, chewing his lip. "Vegetius, I will send you your orders this evening."

"Orders?" Vegetius seemed alarmed at the word.

Stilicho grinned at him. "Yes, orders, my friend. Academic or not, your contribution makes you a part of this army from now on, which means you will follow my orders. Don't worry, I'll make a soldier out of you yet."

As he finished speaking, he looked Celer in the eye and Celer wondered if the general was speaking solely to Vegetius.

They broke the news to Helva when they returned to their apartments and the ex-magistrate erupted with anger. "I have no doubt that you are the smartest man that I know," he growled at Vegetius, "which is why it staggers me that such a stupid idea could fall from your lips!"

"Helva please..." Vegetius raised his arms to try to placate his friend.

"And you!" Helva yelled, rounding on Celer. "I expected more sense from you. What would your father think? What would Attianus think? He would have wanted you to live, not march right back towards the men who wanted to kill you!"

The mention of Attianus only stiffened Celer's resolve at his decision. "It is because of Attianus and my father that I choose to do this!" he shouted back. "I swore retribution for their deaths; if this is what it takes then it is what I shall do." He took a breath, trying to calm himself. "Besides, I have nothing here for me apart from waiting for an assassin's blade whilst I sponge off the means of others. No assassin would hunt a common soldier; it's the last place they would look."

Helva glared at them both for a moment then stormed off. Moments later Celer heard a muffled string of curses from his room. Celer looked to Vegetius, unsure of what to do.

"Don't worry," the writer said, wearily shaking his head, "he'll come around." Vegetius excused himself and disappeared into his room. Timaeus stepped forward and clapped him on the arm.

"You are sure about this, young master?"

Celer looked down on the kindly face of the Greek medicus and nodded. "I am sure; I could not forgive myself if I did nothing whilst my parent's' killers still live."

Timaeus gave him a sad smile. "I understand. May the gods watch over you, young master, and help you find the peace you seek."

Nekar loomed behind the medicus. "Master, if I may?"

"Yes, Nekar?"

The bodyguard took a moment before speaking in his accented rumble. "You have courage, Master, and that is good, but remember to always fight with your head, not your heart. There will be great warriors amongst the soldiers. Find the best and learn from him; do as he does so that you might also become the best."

Timaeus chuckled. "Wonders never cease. I never dreamed of hearing such wisdom from you."

Nekar frowned and looked down at the Greek, unsure if his words were meant in mockery, but Celer stepped forward and surprised both of them by holding out his arm to the big Numidian. Startled by the gesture, Nekar reached out and grasped Celer's forearm, his huge hand almost encircling it.

"Thank you, for your wisdom," said Celer and the bodyguard bowed his head deeply in reply.

"And thank you for your prayers," he said, turning to Timaeus and taking hold of one of the medicus's bony shoulders. Timaeus grinned and shrugged off the hand and embraced him instead.

That night they dined together as they had every night. Helva had emerged from his room last and the others had quietened as he approached the table. He took a deep breath before speaking. "I wish to apologise for earlier." He held up a hand as Vegetius and Celer both tried to tell him not to. "No, I need to. My behaviour shames me. I am sorry for what I said." Turning to Celer, he said, "I understand your reasons for doing this and I respect them. I doubt I would have the courage to do so if I were in your place. I said what I said out of fear for your safety, but I see why you must do this. Please forgive me."

Celer stood up and walked over to him. "There is nothing to forgive, Helva," he said, gripping his forearm. Helva nodded and turned to Vegetius. "Will you forgive a fool, old friend? For words said in the heat

157

of the moment?"

Vegetius stood. "How could I not forgive the man who declares me the smartest man he knows!" They all laughed as the two men embraced. The mood lightened. They ate and talked late into the night until Helva chivvied Celer and Vegetius to their rooms, declaring loudly that the army waited for no man.

Though he was exhausted, Celer lay in bed staring at the dark ceiling. Suddenly he was gripped with fear of what he had chosen to do; he wrestled with the fear for a while before reasoning with himself that his fear was natural. He would not let it stop him, however, not now he had a purpose. Once more, he remembered that morning on the street outside Varro's house, saw the dagger plunge into Attianus's brother's neck and the swords that pierced Varro. He heard his mother's screams and his father's cry and his fists clenched beneath the blanket. Quietly, he mouthed a prayer to Mars Ultor, the Avenger, and promised he would make sacrifices if they helped him achieve his purpose.

Feeling calmed by his prayers, he quickly succumbed to sleep.

# XII

Celer woke shortly after dawn. He lay still in bed for a moment. By the end of the day he would be in the army, he thought to himself and a wave of nervousness washed over him.

Angry with himself, he threw back the blankets and swung his legs out.

Rain had fallen in the night and the flags beyond his room shone wetly in dawn light. He pulled on his two tunics and strapped on his sandals. A slave was waiting by the door to the palace and as soon as he saw Celer step from his room he opened the door and spoke quietly to someone on the other side before hurrying over to Celer with jug of watered wine.

The wine was heated to ward off the morning chill and Celer sipped gratefully at it, wondering if he would enjoy such luxuries as a soldier.

Vegetius arrived soon after, also dressed warmly. He accepted the hot wine with eager hands as he wrapped a cloak about himself. "My orders," he said to Celer over the steaming rim of his cup, tapping a hand on a wax tablet he had laid on the table before him. "It seems I am to be assisting the recruiting officer over the next few days. The General has concerns over the quality of men to be recruited from the city," he explained.

"Ah, I see," said Celer quietly, his eyes on his food.

Vegetius sensed his tone and placed his wine down. "You have nothing to worry about," he said gently. "By my estimations, you have all the makings of a good soldier." Celer said nothing in reply, but Vegetius's words had helped to quiet his nerves and so he focussed his attention on his food.

Vegetius left as soon as his wine was finished and Celer waited a short time before following. None of the others were awake yet but Vegetius had said that all the successful recruits would be told to reassemble at the palace barracks in three days' time so there was no need for goodbyes yet.

The palace seemed busier than usual as he headed for the barracks. Clerks and slaves hurried back and forth carrying stacks of wax tablets and rolls of paper.

The high numbers of priests seemed to have been replaced with greater numbers of men in military attire; some even wore armour as they marched down the corridors, metal hobnails creating a deafening racket in the enclosed space.

The recruiting officer was easy to find. A leather tent had been erected just inside the gate next to the barracks parade ground where he had watched the scholae train the day before.

The practice posts stood lonely vigils this morning as the heavily armoured guards manned the gate in greater numbers, searching any would-be recruit before they were permitted entrance to the palace.

A young man, only a few years older than Celer, had just finished talking with the recruiter as Celer approached. As he turned to leave, the new recruit caught Celer's eye and gave him a slight nod as they passed. Celer nodded back uncertainly; the familiarity with a commoner felt unusual. To his surprise, the recruit responded with a quick grin.

The recruiting officer was a squat Centurion with dark features that suggested his home lay in the Eastern provinces of the Empire, Syria perhaps, Celer thought to himself as he heard faint traces of an accent as the officer spoke. He was conversing with Vegetius who sat with him behind the campaign desk. Both men had several wax tablets before them and Celer watched the centurion spin the one open before him back to face him. He inspected what was written before pushing it towards Vegetius who quickly copied what was written.

Celer stood before the table and the centurion looked him up and down.

"Here to enlist, boy?" the centurion asked.

"Yes," replied Celer with a nod.

"Sir!" shouted the centurion, making both Celer and Vegetius jump. "You will address a superior officer as 'Sir' at all times, is that understood?"

"Yes, Sir," said Celer quickly, heart pounding in his chest.

"Very good," the officer said in a calm voice. "You learn quickly, lad, that's a good sign. Name?"

"Marcus Aelius Celer. Sir," he added quickly.

The centurion scratched the information on the tablet before him. "Age?"

"Sixteen, Sir."

The Centurion looked up from his tablet. "Little young to be joining the army, lad, aren't you?"

Celer stared straight ahead, not meeting the centurion's eye. "I turn seventeen in March, Sir."

The officer shrugged and wrote it down. "Profession?" he asked.

"I don't have one, Sir," Celer said nervously, but the officer seemed unconcerned with his answer.

"Father's profession?"

"He was a Senator of Rome," Celer answered stiffly.

The recruiting officer put his brass stylus down with a sigh and glared up at him. "The army is no place for fools or childish games, boy," he growled. Celer was about to reply to try to convince him of the truth when Vegetius leaned in and whispered in the officer's ear. The centurion eyed Celer suspiciously as he listened to the writer.

"And the General has approved that has he, Sir?" he asked Vegetius who nodded in response. Shrugging, he picked the stylus back up and wrote on his tablet. "First time for everything," he muttered under his breath.

"I take it you can read and write?"

"Yes, Sir."

"Languages?"

"Latin and Greek, Sir."

The centurion wrote it all down. Looking up, he beckoned with the stylus to Celer. "Step forward, lad."

Dutifully, Celer stepped forward and stood still as the centurion stood, picking up a measuring stick from where it leant against the campaign table. He planted the measuring stick next to Celer. "An inch off six feet," he said to Vegetius before pacing around Celer, prodding him in the shoulders, torso and buttocks with the end of the measuring stick. "On the skinny side but otherwise no obvious scars, injuries or deformities," he continued. "Teeth!" he said brusquely, coming to a halt in front of Celer.

Biting back his anger at being inspected like a horse for sale, Celer bared his teeth as the centurion inspected them, turning his head from side to side with a calloused hand.

"Where do you live?" asked the officer as he walked back to his chair.

"Here, at the palace, Sir," replied Celer.

"Of course you do," said the centurion with a glance at Vegetius.

"Very well, boy, you seem to be in good health and, since you seem to have come here voluntarily, I see no reason to refuse you as a recruit."

Celer felt a flush of elation at the centurion's words.

"Report to this location three days from today, at dawn. From here, you shall march to one of the army's training camps. If you complete your training, you shall be enrolled in one of his Imperial Excellency's legions, the finest fighting force in the known world. Standard pay is nine thousand sestertii'a year, paid in three instalments. Deductions will be made for food and clothing. Length of service is set at twenty years. If you understand and wish to proceed, make your mark here." He pushed the tablet across to Celer.

Celer wrote his name in the stiff wax and pushed the tablet back.

The centurion glanced down at the signature before pushing it over to Vegetius. "Welcome to the army. Next!"

Three days later Celer stood shivering in the cold morning drizzle alongside five hundred other recruits. The palace parade ground was a milling mass of men who stamped their feet against the wet; those that had cloaks hugged them tighter about themselves.

"Good morning, Gentlemen!"

The crowd immediately quietened at the booming parade-ground voice and Celer saw the swarthy centurion rise above the heads of the recruits as he mounted a podium before the palace walls.

"I am Senior Centurion Sirus. Third Cohort of the First Legion Italica." He looked about, eyeing the damp recruits who stared back with mixed expressions of fear or excitement upon their faces.

"This Cohort," Sirus went on, "is being raised as part of the army of His Excellency, Emperor Theodosius."

Celer's hands curled into fists by his sides.

"But, you are not soldiers yet," said Sirus with a smile. "Our training camp is located at the Legion's headquarters at Novae, on the Danube. Novae is two hundred and fifty miles from Constantinople and you are going to march there in less than two weeks. That is your first test."

Celer shuffled nervously alongside the rest of the recruits at the thought of marching such a long way. He steadied himself with the thought that it would not be as difficult as crossing the Apennines on foot.

"Quiet!" Roared Sirus, as a low murmur arose amongst the men gathered before him. They instantly fell silent.

"As I said, the march shall be your first test. Your first lesson begins now. You do not speak when on parade unless commanded to by a superior officer. When a superior addresses you, you will respond with 'Yes, Sir' or 'No, Sir', is that understood?"

Celer, along with half the recruits, responded with a half-hearted "Yes, Sir."

"Not fucking good enough, recruits!" screamed the centurion, making the front rows of the crowd jump back in surprise. "I asked you a question. Is that understood?"

"Yes, Sir!" the men shouted back at him.

"I've heard women cry louder, but it's a start," barked Sirus. "Your next lesson will be forming into ranks. When you name is called, step forward and stand in the position you are shown. Remember it. When the unit is called to ranks, that is the position you shall stand in."

As he spoke, optio's began forcing the front of the crowd back away from the podium. Once they had cleared a sizeable space, they began thrusting white pegs into the ground. When they were finished, Sirus beckoned to another centurion behind him. The officer stepped up beside the senior centurion and began to call off names from a list he carried.

Chaos soon ensued as men's' names were called and they had to force their way through the crush to get to the pegs. Once free of the crush, an optio would guide them into position on the correct peg.

"Marcus Aelius Celer," shouted the centurion. Suddenly feeling nervous, Celer began to force his way through the crush. Spotting him, the centurion pointed in his direction for the optios to help part the crowd, then moved onto the next name on his list.

"Make way, there, make way!" barked the optio impatiently, using a long wood staff to force the bodies to part quicker. Grabbing Celer, he pointed with his staff. "Head to Optio Longus at the front of the century."

Celer did as he was bid; as he moved to the front he saw that nearly all the pegs had a man stood on them. The century was ten pegs wide and eight deep. Optio Longus guided him to the last peg on the front rank, making minor adjustments until he was happy with Celer's position.

When the pegs behind Celer were filled, Centurion Sirus addressed them again.

"Gentlemen, you are now formed into the Third Cohort's First Century. It is an honour to serve in the First Century; see that you do it proud during your training. Fall in behind Optio Longus! Optio." He gave a nod to Longus who turned to face the recruits.

"Memorise your places, recruits. I don''t want to have to show you again." Longus wagged his staff menacingly before them. "When I give the order 'March!', you will follow me, right foot first. I will call the pace." He gave them a quick once over again to check their positions before turning on his heel to face the Senior Centurion on the podium. Longus threw a quick salute that Sirus returned and then called out "First Century, ready! March! One, two, one, two..." Trying to keep in time to the Optio's count, the recruits began to tramp their way out of the parade ground.

Longus lead them through the city streets and out of the gates, calling out the step all the way. He drew them up next to a mule train loaded with supplies; Celer guessed the mule train would follow them to the fortress. Off to his right, he could see the small chapel where they had buried Attianus. The memory of forcing his dead companion's mouth shut over the silver coin distracted him for a moment, so he didn't see Optio Longus stalk up in front of him.

"Eyes front, recruit!" Longus bellowed in his face, causing him to jump back in surprise.

"Did I give you permission to move?" The optio's staff flicked up and hovered in front of his face.

"No, Sir!" shouted Celer, stepping back into his position as his heart battered against his rib cage.

Longus stepped in close. "The army is no place for daydreamer's, boy!" he growled in Celer's ear as he rapped his staff against Celer's chest. "You keep your eyes ahead of you from now on, recruit, understood?"

"Yes, Sir," said Celer quickly, hoping that his body wasn't shaking as visibly as he thought it was.

Thankfully, Longus moved on to stalk through the ranks of the First Century as they waited for the other recruits to join them outside the city. Every so often, the optio would find a fault and would scream mercilessly at the unfortunate individual at full parade -ground volume.

Slowly, the Cohort took shape on the ground beyond the city.

Centurions and Optios eyed their new charges like hawks whilst the recruits tried to stand as still as possible so as to not attract any attention.

When all the centuries were assembled, Centurion Sirus, now astride a horse, led them onto the road and began leading them north.

For Celer, the days quickly blended into an aching routine.

They marched twenty miles the first day before making camp as the light faded.

They were permitted only quick rest stops and when they set about making camp they had to stand in the growing chill until the tent lines had been marked out.

Being placed at the front of the column of eight men made him a Decanus, a section leader, Longus informed him and the other men of the front rank of the First Century. As far as Celer could tell, the role came with no privileges and all the responsibilities of locating the section's tent each evening and making sure it was stowed properly in the morning before moving out.

Once the section leaders had found their tents in the mule train, the recruits could then erect their goatskin homes under the guidance of the optios. Each section then had to stand to attention whilst the tent was inspected for sturdiness by their centurion's before they were permitted to begin cooking the bland army rations they were given.

Adding to the hardships of the road, Celer struggled with being forced into such a close-knit group of men.

His life experiences up until that point had ill-prepared him for engaging with men of lower rank, he found. It was difficult to join in their conversations and he constantly felt awkward about how to act with them and quickly became envious of the ease with which they held themselves and quickly formed friendships.

In such close proximity, however, it was impossible to not pick up details about them all.

Sextus was the oldest at twenty-three. He, Magnus, Pulvillus and Cinna were all from Constantinople; a weaver's son, the youngest sons of city guardsmen and a mason's son respectively. Symmachus and Quintus were from the provinces of Cappadocia and Syria and had travelled to Constantinople to find work. Their failing to do so was mainly due to their non-Christian beliefs, Quintus stated one night, a comment that drew scowls from the four men from the capital who were devout Christians. Priscus, the final member of the section, was unusual in the cohort in that he, like Celer, hailed from the Western Empire.

Though they both hailed from different cities, the two felt a connection in being the only 'Westerners' in the century and Celer found it easier to talk to Priscus.

After almost a week of marching together he asked him what had brought him to Constantinople.

Celer was surprised to find Priscus's story was similar to his own.

He, too, had fled after Arbogast had seized power as his father had been one of the late Emperor Valentinian's freedmen. His father had led him from Mediolanum only for them to become separated outside the city. After days of searching, Priscus had found his father's body dumped in a ditch.

After that, a family connection on his mother's side had spirited him away to Athens but he had found his relatives unbearable and had made his way to Constantinople for work.

Priscus had not been long in the city when he heard the call for recruits and, lacking any other options, he found himself signing up.

Celer intended to speak little of his past at first, but his lack of simple practical skills, like how to cook, quickly became obvious. There was little privacy in a section and the others drew his past out of him over the course of the first few days and nights. At first, they didn't believe him. Celer thought it was likely they never would have had he not produced the wax tablet that Helva had given him back in Histonium. The tablet had reappeared on his bed the night before his departure from Constantinople with a simple note written into the tablets cover, "Lest you waver." None of his companions claimed knowledge of how it had come to be there and Celer presumed that it could only have been Stilicho.

His section-mates had various degrees of literacy but between them they managed to decipher the document; combined with Priscus's own tale and what they had heard of the events in the western half of the Empire, it convinced them of his claim.

The matter of his parentage and social rank became a source of awkwardness over the next few days as the others were unsure how to act around the son of a Senator. Cinna, who was a little less world-wise than the others, even tried to call him 'Sir' one morning as they stowed the tent away on their section's mule.

Celer was struggling with the straps that tied the tent securely to the mule's pack saddle.

"Please, don't ever call me that again," he said, finally succeeding in fastening the thick buckle. "My name is Celer, legionary recruit, the same as you. It doesn't matter who our fathers were now."

Cinna coloured with embarrassment but he never called Celer 'Sir' again and the other section members became more relaxed about him.

As the cohort of recruits marched further north, the weather deteriorated. Every morning, frost covered the tents and the men shivered in their civilian clothes. The officers, who wore padded jerkins as well as their long-sleeved military tunics under their armour, were better equipped to deal with the cold and took no mercy on any recruit that showed reluctance to crawl out from the relative warmth of the tents every morning.

Long marches and poor weather conditions took their toll on the men and by the end of the sixth day of the march the cohort was plagued by sickness. The recruits coughed painfully in the cold air with noses and eyes running and each man sweating profusely despite the cold.

The officers tried to contain it by taking sick men from their centuries and forming them into an ever-expanding group at the rear of the marching column, but after marching through rain and high winds for two days even the hardiest of the recruits was struck down.

Centurion Sirus begrudgingly called a halt outside the fortified town of Deultum which overlooked a narrow and marshy estuary that flowed into the Euxeinos Pontos. Any recruits too sick to march were taken to the infirmary at the town's barracks whilst the rest of the men were ordered to pitch their tents outside the city walls where they huddled over meagre fires. The town's garrison commander took pity on the recruits and drew them double rations from the town's stores.

The rain that had hounded them up the coast abated in the night so that when the centurions and optios kicked them from their tents they found the world bright and clear, the morning light reflecting off hundreds of pools. Feeling a little revived by the double rations, they broke camp and marched on, leaving any man too ill to march in Deultum to be shipped back to Constantinople.

As much as he still felt uncomfortable about them, Celer was glad that none of his section mates had fallen out of the march. Magnus had been the worst and had been barely able to stand as they pitched the tent outside the town the night before, yet the double rations at the evening and morning meal had worked wonders and he now marched along in the third rank of the century, pale and sweating but steady on his feet.

A light breeze carried the distant salt tang of the Euxeinos Pontos and Celer was delighted by being able to smell it. For two days he had been as miserable and cold as any day in the Apennine Mountains but now, with the weak rays of the autumnal sun on his neck and his sickness finally abating, he felt a sudden sense of freedom. The now familiar tramp of boots upon the road had become a comforting background noise as they marched through the countryside, heading ever north towards the frontier.

The rhythmic beat of their feet was interrupted around midday. At first, the front of the column was unaware of the approaching horsemen, but the officer at the rear of the column shouted a warning and Centurion Sirus turned in his saddle.

"Cohort! Halt!"

The column halted jerkily; the recruits were still getting used to obeying orders at a moment's notice. Optios instantly descended on the centuries, bawling at the recruits to dress their lines and the recruits hurried back into position in the churned mud that covered the road. Celer heard the horsemen draw nearer but Optio Longus was prowling nearby so he kept his eyes fixed firmly forward. Their identity was soon revealed. As the group of riders trotted down the side of the column, barely hushed whispers passed through the lines of men.

"It's the General!"

"Look, its Stilicho!"

"Quiet there. Silence in the ranks!" shouted Sirus as he turned his horse to meet the general. Stilicho was in full battle dress, silvered scale armour gleaming beneath a red cloak that matched the horsehair plume on his helmet.

"Centurion!" Stilicho called out cheerfully as Sirus and his hastily assembled officers saluted his approach. "I had hoped that we would catch up with you, though sooner than I expected?"

"The men, Sir. Many of them have fallen ill, Sir. The weather," the Senior Centurion explained hurriedly.

Stilicho was eyeing the pale faces of the men who continued to stare straight ahead; fear of their Optio's outweighed their curiosity to look at the General and his retinue.

"I did warn you, General," spoke a voice familiar to Celer. "Many of my sources have stated that men recruited from cities often lack the hardiness of men from more rural areas."

Stilicho sighed discreetly and turned towards the voice, ignoring the raised eyebrow of Centurion Sirus.

"I do remember you informing me of such things, Vegetius. Yet, as I explained to you then, the province of Thrace and the Danubian provinces have been a prime recruiting ground for many years. Our most recent conflicts have stripped much of the countryside of men suitable for service, hence our need to raise this cohort from the city or else risk aggravating the rural populace."

Vegetius's horse edged around Stilicho's and crept into Celer's peripheral vision.

"There appear to be fewer men than left Constantinople, Centurion?" asked the writer, eyeing the column, noting the uneven ranks of the centuries. Celer felt his gaze linger on him a moment but his friend said nothing and looked to Sirus.

"Yes, Sir, unfortunately some of the recruits were too sick to continue."

"You left them?" asked the writer, startled by the Centurion's apparent callousness.

"Those deemed too sick to continue were left at the garrison hospital at Deultum yesterday," explained Sirus patiently.

"How many?" asked Stilicho.

"Twelve, Sir. Cohort strength down to four hundred and sixty-eight" answered Sirus dutifully.

"Surely with such a shortage of men, would it not be prudent to slow the march to prevent losing more recruits before the Cohort even reaches Novae?" queried Vegetius.

Sirus shook his head. "No, Sir. These men will have to march harder than this, fully laden and possibly in worse conditions if they are to be an effective unit. I won't go easy on them now to have them fail in hostile territory. Wouldn't do them or the Empire any favours for that to happen."

"Well said, Centurion. I knew I picked you for a reason." Stilicho nodded approvingly.

Eyeing the sky, he said, "Still most of the day left; we shall see you and the Third Cohort at Novae, Centurion."

Sirus and the other officers snapped salutes and Optio Longus roared out from the front of the Cohort, "Cohort! Salute!"

Stilicho acknowledged the salute with a tip of the head before kicking his horse into a canter. His retinue, Vegetius, alongside a number of officers and a large squadron of heavily armoured clibanarii who were encased head to foot in armour and carrying long spears, followed.

Most of the men of the cohort steadily recovered from the sickness over the next week as they drew ever closer to Novae. They turned west, away from the coast, and headed cross-country as the weather grew steadily worse.

Exhaustion and the unfamiliar conditions caused more men to drop out of the marching column. These stragglers were chivvied along by the optios at the rear to struggle into the camp when night had fallen or else were loaded into the supply wagons that rumbled along with the mule train.

Thirteen days after they left Constantinople, the column sighted the fortress town. As they breasted a low ridge, the view opened out over a broad plain. Scattered farms dotted the landscape before them. Beyond that, smoke rose above the fortress walls and the town that surrounded it. The Danube lay like a black snake across the land, marking the end of Roman territory and the beginning of the barbarian lands of Dacia.

Stilicho and Vegetius, along with the garrison's commander, rode out to meet the column as it approached the city. Vegetius was shocked to see the state of the men. All had two weeks' growth of beard; they were dirty and ragged. Many had evidently worn out their boots as their feet were wrapped in strips torn from clothes or sacking.

Despite this, even his untrained eye could see that the men now marched in time better. When ordered to halt, they did so without falter and each man stood straight as a spear, eyes fixed firmly ahead until they were given the order to stand easy. The writer was pleased to see that Celer still stood at the front of the First Century. The boy was dishevelled and travel-stained, yet looked far better than when he had arrived at Helva's residence in Histonium barely two months before.

"Excellent progress, Centurion!" Stilicho called out to Sirus as they rode up to the column. "A day inside of two weeks."

"As promised, Sir," Sirus said proudly, snapping a quick salute.

"I trust the men's condition has improved since last we saw you?" asked the general.

"Sickness passed after a few days, Sir," replied Sirus. "Only eight more fell behind since we left Deultum."

Stilicho nodded approvingly and turned to the garrison commander at his side.

"What do you think of the Third Cohort, Prefect?"

"They did well to make the march in such conditions." The Prefect nodded towards the fields surrounding them. Snow had begun to fall almost a week before, mixed with icy rain storms, and the fields beyond the city were grey with slush and mud.

"I'm sure they'll make a fine body of troops."

Sirus dipped his head in acknowledgement of the praise.

"I agree, Prefect," said Stilicho. "Lead them on, Senior Centurion; get them out of the cold."

"Yes, Sir!" Sirus turned to Optio Longus who stood at the front of the Column and gave him a nod.

Turning about, Longus roared out the order, "Cohort, ready!

Advance!"

Stilicho, Vegetius and the Prefect stood their horses to one side of the road and watched as the recruits marched past. Vegetius raised his hand from the folds of his cloak to Celer as he marched past and Celer acknowledged with a tip of his head.

"Who was that?" asked Priscus, marching directly behind Celer.

"A friend," replied Celer loudly over the sound of their boots. "Flavius Vegetius; he was at Mediolanum when Eugenius took the purple. You might have heard of him?"

Priscus was quiet for a moment whilst he thought.

"Vegetius? There was a count of the third rank by that name, I think, a writer?"

Celer laughed. "Yes, that's Vegetius, no doubt about it."

"What's he doing here?" asked Priscus.

"He and the General know each other of old," Celer explained. "The General invited him to come with the army - something to do with training new recruits."

"He doesn't look like much of a soldier to me!" piped up Magnus from behind Priscus.

Celer shook his head. "He's not a soldier; I think the General had him going over old military manuals and accounts."

Magnus snorted derisively. "What use are books going to be in teaching us how to fight?"

Celer had wondered that himself. He shrugged as they neared the heavy oak gate of the fortress. "I don't know," he said honestly. "I guess we're about to find out."

The fortress was huge.

Celer later discovered it had been built in the days of the Emperor Vespasian who had deployed the First Legion to guard this section of the Danube. The fortress was now also home to Novae's civilian population. Gothic attacks had devastated the region and the fortress walls had been expanded. Much of the area that would have once housed the soldiers was now built over by simple brick dwellings and workshops. Celer struggled to keep his eyes forward as they marched through the streets, marvelling at his new home. Many of the workshops seemed to making glass and he caught sight of a craftsman manipulating a red blob of glass on a pole out of the corner of his eye.

The Third Cohort were shown to their barracks on the south side of the fortress, near the Legion's hospital and baths. The ground rose rapidly from the river to the north and the fort was terraced to accommodate the slope and, from their barracks, they could see over some of the buildings to the black snake of the Danube beyond. Novae's original layout had been for a garrison of nearly five thousand men but, even with the newly arrived cohort, the garrison now stood at little over a thousand. Now only the under-strength First Cohort and a unit of two hundred mounted archers were stationed at Novae. The Second Cohort, equally depleted of men, was deployed in a fort further to the east, defending an important crossing point of the river.

# XIII

Training began the day after their arrival. The recruits were taken by century to the fortress quartermaster, near the fortress headquarters. Their civilian clothing, dirty and torn from travel, was taken from them and the recruits shivered in the cold stone warehouse as the quartermaster's assistants handed out boots, thick long-sleeved tunics and woollen trousers.

For the first time in his life, Celer accepted the trousers readily. They felt awkward and scratchy against his legs but the warmth he felt was instantaneous and welcome in the frigid air.

Next, they were given military tunics and padded linen shirts, designed to lessen the force of any blow stopped by their armour, and the thick military belt that fastened round the waist and over one shoulder.

Lastly, each recruit was given a heavy, oiled cloak to protect them from the elements.

Thus attired, the recruits stood, expectantly looking at the quartermaster.

"Keep moving!" he shouted and pointed towards the door.

"What about our weapons?" a voice shouted from the back of the recruits.

"And our armour?" shouted another.

"Ha!" The quartermaster laughed and nudged one of his assistants who chuckled and shook his head.

"Weapon's are for soldiers, and you are not soldiers yet!"

Ignoring the indignant murmurs rising from the crowded recruits, he pointed again to the door.

"Move it along!"

Centurion Sirus was waiting for them outside.

"You may now be dressed like legionaries, but you still don't march like legionaries. No man shall even see a sword until he has mastered the use of his feet," the Senior Centurion told them.

He began drilling them daily in the different formations they would be required to perform in battle or upon a march. They learned to wheel and form battle lines by increasing the century's frontage. They learned to collapse the marching column into a hollow square or defensive circle the instructors called the orb.

For weeks, they marched back and forth across the parade ground, pounding fresh snowfall into brown sludge outside the fort until Sirus was happy they could perform the manoeuvres.

He and Vegetius watched as the recruits drilled in the swirling snow flurries. Despite coming from different worlds, the Senior Centurion and the writer had formed a creative partnership when it came to testing the recruits.

Confident in their marching, the instructors next issued the recruits with picks and shovels.

"The most deadly weapons of a legionary," Sirus called them.

Mornings were spent on the parade ground, honing manoeuvres, and after a brief stop at noon they were marched out into the frozen fields surrounding Novae.

They dug through drifts of snow and hacked into the frozen earth beneath to form ditches and earth ramparts for fortified camps. Each evening, the recruits marched back, cold and dirty, the fruits of their labours standing out in dark lines against the white backdrop. The soldiers of the Fist Cohort mocked them and dubbed them the 'Mud Warriors', for no frontier legionary in serving memory had been trained to dig ditches. Such a thing was no longer deemed necessary by the largely static troops of the frontier and the recruits grumbled that Vegetius and his history books were to blame as they nursed their sore and blistered hands.

As well as digging and marching, the would-be legionnaires were marched to the forests that bordered the farmland surrounding the fortress.

There they felled trees that fed the needs of the fortress and the town. Weeks of marches, digging, felling and carrying timber hardened the largely city-born recruits. Their hands grew calloused and their bodies hardened. Yet Vegetius was not finished with ideas. He had the instructors direct the men to dig trenches amongst the woods that they had yet to clear of felled trees. The resulting morass was a slippery nightmare of earth and timber barricades that separated the recruits from the road leading back to the fortress.

"Are you sure about this, Vegetius?" said Sirus, eyeing the tangle of tree trunks and ditches.

"Sallustius Crispus is quite clear on the importance of legionaries being able to move freely across broken ground, so that they might easily assault fortified positions," said Vegetius firmly. Seeing that the Centurion was still not convinced he added, "Sallustius insists that training such as this gave Pompey's soldiers victory over the forces of Sertorius."

Sirus grunted rather than alert Vegetius to his ignorance of battles fought so long ago, and gave the nod to Longus and the other instructors to begin.

The First and Second Centuries lined up facing the broken ground.

"Centuries will advance at my command!" shouted Longus, and the men eyed the muddy barricades nervously.

"At a run, Optio." Vegetius said quietly, so only the officers could hear. Longus looked to his superior but Sirus didn't move. With a shrug he turned back.

"Centuries will advance at double time!"

"Must be fucking joking," Priscus muttered behind Celer, and spat between his feet.

"Hear, hear," said the recruit to his left, as others grumbled their agreement.

"Centuries, Advance!" roared out Longus and the order was repeated by the other instructors along the line.

Celer set off at the steady run of the legion's double time but quickly found such a pace was impossible. Within seconds, the front rank encountered one of the ditches they had dug.

Celer, like the others, tried to leap across but his lack of a run-up meant he thumped into the opposite bank and began to slide into the swampy bottom. As he struggled to claw his way up the other side, Priscus, along with the others of the second rank, was forced to leap over by the ranks pushing on from behind. The ditch was soon a crawling mass of mud-streaked men, as they tried to haul themselves out of the way of the bodies that jumped in after them.

Sirus and the other officers watched aghast as the two centuries foundered so quickly at the first obstacle. The Centurion could well imagine any defender's glee at such a crush of men, jammed into such an enclosed space.

Celer finally scrambled free over the packed earth embankment on the far side of the ditch; he vaulted over a felled tree before him, but his hands were slick with mud and he crashed to the ground on the far side. Quickly, he got to his feet before the hobnailed boots of the men behind him came crashing down on his back.

By the time Celer and the rest of the two centuries reached the far side, the officers and Vegetius had walked around and were waiting for them. They stood in stony silence as the exhausted recruits reformed their ranks. All of them were caked in mud, many were bleeding from falls or jagged branches, and a few stood awkwardly on sprained ankles, eyes screwed in pain.

"Lead these men back to the barracks," Sirus said quietly. "And give the signal for the Third and Fourth Centuries to advance."

Longus nodded and raised an arm to the Centurion of the Third Century who was waiting with his men. As Longus lead the men off on the road to Novae, Celer heard the Centurion roar out the order for the next units to advance.

Celer's birthday came and went, lost in the exhaustive blur of their training. Celer didn't realise until a few days after it had passed. He was standing on the walls of Novae armed with a wooden cudgel, the only weapon the instructors would allow the recruits when they pulled sentry duty. It was a bitterly cold night and he had spent the day marching and cutting timber for firewood; his back ached but he found walking the walls helped to ease it. He stopped at a flickering brazier that offered a little heat in the frigid air on the north wall and looked out over the black expanse before him. His birthday made him think of his parents. With some shame, he realised he had not thought of them as much since he had come to Novae. His daily labours and the near constant presence of his section-mates offered plenty of distraction. Only rarely, now, did he dream of warriors silhouetted in the flames and of his mother's screams.

His mother would have made a fuss for his birthday, no doubt; she always had. He had come to be slightly embarrassed by it as he grew older, though now he would have traded anything for another day with her.

He closed his eyes, forcing his body to ignore the cold wind that bit at his exposed skin and tried to remember her face, happy and smiling as she would enter his room in Rome or one of their country villas. To his dismay, he couldn't. Every time he pictured her, no matter the setting, her face would always be frozen in terror, the way she had looked when Arbogast's men had raided their home.

He lashed out and struck the wall with his cudgel. Rage flashed through his chest, banishing the cold for a moment.

"Problem, Recruit?" came a voice from behind him.

Celer jumped and spun round, snapping to attention when he saw it was the watch officer for the evening.

"No, Sir."

The officer eyed him suspiciously for a moment, debating whether to give the lad a bollocking for daydreaming on watch. Another blast of wind swept along the wall and his thoughts instantly turned to the warm guardhouse and the dice game that was waiting for him.

"As you were, then," he snapped, waiting for the lad's salute before striding off towards the gate.

Celer gave a small sigh and hugged his cloak tight to him, moving off in the other direction. His watch wouldn't end for another few hours and his back still ached.

Throughout the winter, the recruits continued at their labours. Their formation drill continued to improve so much that even the most prolific teasers of the 'Mud Warriors' quietly acknowledged how impressed they were.

Sirus must have been impressed also, for he gave the order for the recruits to move onto weapon drill. Celer, along with the others, could not suppress his excitement when he first held the heavy wooden sword and the heavy shield made of woven withies.

They set up heavy posts along the edge of the parade ground like the ones Celer had watched the Scholae guardsmen training with at the palace barracks. They were bright in the winter sun, freshly cut, and the smell of sap was strong in the crisp air.

"Keep your shield up, Recruit!"

Longus stopped, facing Celer, who had stepped up to the post. The Optio aimed a swing at Celer's head with his staff that Celer only just managed to block with his heavy shield.

"Always up," said Longus, planting the butt of the staff between his feet. "You let it drop and your opponent will take your head off."

"Yes, Sir," Celer responded as he struggled with the dead weight of the shield, aiming another strike at the post before him.

Mornings were now occupied with sword drill, Centurion Sirus often shirking convention to lead the training himself. Absent his officer's cloak or helmet, he prowled the posts with his vine stick tucked beneath his arm. He showed them how to deliver a thrust so that their sword would be hidden behind their shield until the last moment and how to drive a punch with the heavy shield from the legs.

They trained until the posts and swords were splintered and cracked from the constant battering, then he began to square them off against one another. Remembering Nekar's advice, Celer payed close attention to Sirus's instruction and tried to emulate the speed and precision the Senior Centurion' showed when demonstrating an attack form to them.

Training at the post had lent strength to his arms but Celer quickly discovered there was more to fighting than brute strength. Whilst he was tall, he did not have the bulk of many the older recruits and so spent the first few bruising days being knocked to the ground, shield arm deadened from the battering of the heavy training swords.

Memories of his father being so easily beaten by Arbogast's soldiers made him force himself back to his feet each time. He studied Sirus and the other instructors religiously when they demonstrated technique. How to move, how to defend and attack. At night his dreams were dominated by their lessons; faceless attackers lunged and swung at him as he re-fought each match from the day's training, all to the symphony of wooden swords striking one another.

Soon he found himself progressing quicker than the others in his section. He discovered he could react and move faster than most of the recruits. Combined with his studious application of Sirus's teachings, he learned how to beat the bigger, stronger men of his century.

Sparring sessions quickly saw him land more blows than he received and he began to acquire a reputation amongst his century as a capable swordsman.

His newfound skills leant him a degree of confidence amongst his fellow recruits. They in turn became more open to the quiet, well-spoken Westerner. His section mates in particular became audibly proud of his prowess with a sword.

His skills were put to the test one morning thanks to the return of Stilicho. The General had spent only a few days at Novae before leaving on a tour of the frontier.

Having returned to Novae the night before, Stilicho walked out to the parade ground with Vegetius, his aides and a number of his heavy Clibanarii troopers to where Sirus was drilling the men. The General carried his crested helmet beneath his arm, his fair hair and beard matching the men about him as he joked and laughed. Clouds of steam rose above the group as they marched across the compacted ground. The recruits had just finished a session on the posts and the men were dripping with sweat despite the cold morning air as Sirus ordered them to pair off. Celer faced off against Symmachus; the Cappadocian was powerfully built, though shorter than Celer and he prepared himself for the heavy blows that Symmachus was becoming renowned for.

"Good morning, General." Sirus took his eyes away from the recruits at Stilicho's approach.

"Centurion." Stilicho dipped his head at Sirus's salute. "Vegetius tells me the men are progressing well."

"Very well, Sir."

"Perhaps we could see a demonstration, Centurion?"

"Yes, Sir." Sirus turned to the recruits "Cohort! Form Centuries!"

His cry was instantly echoed by the centurions of the other centuries as nearly five hundred men instantly ceased fighting and jogged into position.

Stilicho watched as Sirus put the cohort through the manoeuvres around the parade ground, the men completing each change with well-drilled precision.

"Very impressive, Senior Centurion," said Stilicho admiringly when the cohort halted before him.

"I trust they fight as well as they drill?"

"Equal to any unit in the Empire," Sirus replied without hesitation, bringing a smile to the general's face.

"Care to take a bet on that, Centurion?"

Now it was Sirus's face that flickered with a hint of a smile.

"I have a fine Falernian that I would be happy to wager Sir."

Stilicho shook his head. "As much as I would like to relieve you of such a wine, Centurion, usually I gamble for things of greater worth."

"Sir?" Sirus frowned, trying to think of what else he owned that was of greater worth than the hard to come by Falernian.

"Professional pride, Centurion," Stilicho explained. "I imagine it means more to you than a wine. I think the best way to test a man's convictions is to put what he favours most on the line."

Sirus nodded. "I stand by what I said, Sir."

"Excellent." Stilicho clapped his hands once. "Horatius!" One of his armoured guards stepped forward.

"Commander of my personal guard," he introduced Horatius to Sirus. Horatius stood beside Stilicho looking smugly at the ranks of recruits.

"My man against the best of your recruits," continued Stilicho.

"Yes, Sir," Sirus replied without hesitation. He turned to the waiting men. "Cohort! Form Square!"

When the men had formed the hollow defensive formation, Sirus had them about face so that every man faced into the centre. Sirus led the general and his party into the middle of the square and an optio handed Horatius a practice sword and training shield.

"Legionary recruit Celer! Step forward!" barked Sirus.

Celer pushed his way through the ranks to the hollow centre of the formation, heart pounding in his chest as he tried to keep his face clear of emotion. Hushed voices wished him luck as he pushed past the men.

Vegetius made a small noise in the back of his throat as if he started to say something but stopped himself as Celer walked across the open ground.

Stilicho kept his face expressionless as he watched the young man walk towards him.

The boy that had stood before him in the palace library three months before was quickly becoming a soldier. Relentless training had started to clad his thin frame in muscle so he appeared lean now, rather than skinny, and his sweat-streaked face was set with stone-hard determination.

"You're sure, Centurion?" asked the general.

"I am," said Sirus steadily.

Stilicho shrugged. "Very well, at your command, Centurion."

Sirus led Celer to the centre of the square.

"Remember," he said quietly to Celer as they walked, "he's a cavalryman so he'll swing rather than thrust and the weight of his armour will tire him quickly. Keep your shield up and do as I taught you."

"Yes, Sir," said Celer, taking a firm grip of his shield.

"You stand for me and the Cohort now," Sirus said, placing the padded leather sparring helmet on Celer's head. "Do not dishonour us."

Celer remembered the words his father had said to him the night before the attack and steadied himself.

"Yes, Sir."

They faced off a bare fifteen feet apart. Horatius had forgone his enamelled helmet, with its tall crest of ostrich feathers, in place of a leather training helm, but kept on the rest of his heavy armour. The clibanarius guardsman wore a long shirt of shining mail that split in two at his groin so that each leg was also wrapped in the iron links. A belt of vertical steel plates, gilded gold, covered his midriff and matching articulated plates covered his arms and legs, so that he appeared as a moving statue of silver and gold, a stark contrast to the dull wood of the practice sword and shield he held.

Celer felt nerves tighten his gut. The man opposite was the stuff of his nightmares; for months he had been hunted by warriors such as him. Horatius wore his hair short in the Roman style but it was blond all the same. Along with his blue eyes and towering stature, his appearance was shockingly similar to that of Eugenius's scholae guardsmen.

Celer raised his shield until he was looking over its rim, holding his sword horizontally at his hip so it was hidden from Horatius's view.

"Begin!" shouted Sirus.

Horatius smiled and began to circle Celer, his sword and shield held low at his side. Keeping his eyes on the guardsman, Celer slowly turned with him, shield up, feet spaced evenly and poised to anticipate his enemy's attack; Sirus's lessons rang in his ears.

Seeing no weakness in Celer's defence, Horatius shot a wink at his fellow guards standing by the general, then rushed forward to close the gap between them with a mighty shout and a sweeping blow of his sword.

Celer was ready for the rush; he countered by stepping into the cut. He caught the blow with his shield, grunting as the impact jolted down his arm, then his training took over and he delivered a quick thrust that almost connected before Horatius blocked it clumsily with his own shield.

Sirus had been right; Horatius was used to fighting from horseback and it showed. He advanced awkwardly, the weight of the steel and iron that covered his body slowing him, swinging powerful blows at Celer with his shield held low at his side. Wary of the German's strength, Celer used his speed to avoid the blows, deflecting any he couldn't with his shield. Jabbing with his own sword, he forced Horatius to jerk the heavy shield up to stop each attack.

Men of the cohort were calling out support for him but their cries slowly petered out as Horatius rained blow after blow at him, driving him across the makeshift arena.

It became clear to Celer that the fight had quickly gone beyond the realms of a training display. The failure of Horatius's initial onslaught in bringing a quick end to the fight, and the cheers that had echoed around the parade ground with every blow that Celer landed, rankled the guard's pride. He was a powerfully built man and he used that strength to deliver constant heavy blows upon Celer in an attempt to bludgeon him into submission.

Despite his footwork, the unwavering assault forced Celer to use his own shield to block many of the attacks until his arm went numb from the relentless battering.

Carefully sidestepping so that Horatius could not pin him against the ranks of men that formed the walls of the arena, he searched desperately for a way to retaliate.

His initial fear was gone, replaced by an icy calm he had not known he possessed. Watching each sword stroke and clumsy thrust like a hawk, he waited for a chance to strike back at the towering German.

Already sweating from the effort of swinging the heavy weight of the practice sword, Horatius grew madder as his blows achieved little more than glancing blows or slashing through thin air. His rage made him careless and each time Celer countered, he had to snatch his shield up to block the attack. Determined to knock his opponent off balance, he brought his sword down in an overhead swing, throwing all of his weight behind it.

Celer saw his opportunity and angled his shield so that the blow, which would have crushed his skull had it connected, glanced off to his left. Stepping in close to Horatius, he punched his sword forward as the guardsman's momentum carried him onto the point.

Caught off balance, Horatius somehow managed to haul his own shield up in front of the blunt sword tip in time. The jarring thrust hurt Celer's hand, but he felt a rush that the blow had nearly landed.

Celer gave him no time to recover as he followed with a series of cuts to the head that sent Horatius scuttling backwards across the square ducking behind his shield, as renewed cheers erupted all around them.

The guardsman was breathing hard from his attempts to batter Celer into submission, worn out from the unfamiliar weight of the training weapons. Furious, he slammed his own shield into Celer's and followed it with more blows and a few clumsy thrusts. Celer soaked it all up, not trying to contend with Horatius's strength. Weeks of training had put strength in his arm, helping him keep his shield steady before him. He feinted right then went left and Horatius chopped into the empty space where he had just been, leaving his right side exposed. Celer stabbed forward and Horatius could not jerk away in time; the rounded tip of the sword striking him hard in the stomach.

Layers of plate, mail and the padding beneath his armour meant that the thrust did no damage to Horatius, but it shook him none the less and Celer pressed his attack with a series of thrusts to his face and cuts to his torso, before slamming forward with his shield once more. Horatius caught the blow with his own shield and powered back. The man's strength was terrifying and quickly Celer had to scramble back as the clibanarii guardsman hammered at him once more.

"Cease!" roared Sirus above the noise of the men.

The voice of their commander silenced the men immediately and made Celer instantly step back. He stood, shield ready as Horatius looked as if he might continue.

"Impressive. Most impressive," said Stilicho, stepping forward.

Horatius reacted to the presence of his commander and stepped back, chest heaving.

Turning to Sirus, Stilicho said, "A remarkable effort, Senior Centurion; you seem to have formed an excellent unit of men in such a short space of time."

"Thank you, Sir."

"See the men to the quartermaster; they have proved themselves worthy of a soldier's attire."

"Yes, General."

Stilicho turned to Celer, who was wincing as the sensation returned to his battered shield arm.

"Well fought, young Celer. It seems Vegetius may have been right about you," the general said quietly.

Celer bowed his head at the General's praise. "Thank you, Sir."

"As you were, Senior Centurion," said Stilicho before turning and marching out of the hollow square, the recruits hastily parting to let him through. Horatius shot Celer a dirty look and spat on the ground between his feet before he followed the General. Vegetius's thin scholarly face broke into an uncharacteristically wide grin before he, too, followed the General back to the fortress.

"Get back to your section, Recruit," said Sirus gently to Celer.

"Yes, Sir." Celer hurried back to the front rank of his century, suddenly embarrassed by the grins and whispered congratulations from the men around him.

"What we saw here today, gentlemen, was a fine example of one-on-one combat," Sirus declared loudly, addressing the square around him. "However, in battle, you will not have the luxury of facing just one opponent. Nor will you likely have the opportunity to wait for him to tire before you make your move."

He turned in the square, eyeing the silent ranks. "Carpax," he pointed to one of the section leaders of the Second Century, "step forward."

Carpax dutifully trotted into the middle of the square until he faced Sirus. The Senior Centurion accepted a practice shield from Longus but refused the offered training sword, raising his vine stick instead.

"Defend yourself!" he suddenly shouted and lunged at Carpax. The recruits were all well-used to Sirus's style of instruction by now and Carpax had been ready. Each wild blow from the cane thumped harmlessly into his raised shield. Sirus, however, was unrelenting and he added blows from his own shield; the combination soon forced Carpax to shuffle back.

"There!" said Sirus, suddenly halting his attack and turning back to the recruits. "In battle," he continued, "you cannot step back, as you will expose your comrades on either side to the weapons of the enemy." He gestured to the imaginary men either side of Carpax.

"You must stand your ground; you must hold the line!" He turned to Carpax. "Attack me," he ordered. "Drive me back."

After a moment's hesitation, Carpax obliged. He stepped forward, hammering his shield into Sirus's, trying to drive the Centurion backwards. Sirus, however, dug his feet in and shunted back. They struggled for a moment before Carpax broke away. He attacked again, this time charging forward, hoping that speed would add power to his punch.

Again, Sirus dug in and absorbed the hit, his feet sliding only inches in the soft dirt. They strained against each other once more; this time Carpax tried to thrust over the Centurion's shield and find his head but Sirus ducked down and tucked into the curve of his shield. As Carpax's sword found nothing but air, the Centurion stabbed his vine cane below the recruit's shield. Carpax grunted in surprise as the cane raked across the back of his calves, then the grunt became a cry as Sirus heaved forward and tripped him with the cane. As Carpax sprawled in the mud, Sirus thrust his cane into the ground by his face.

"Remember," said Sirus, barely panting despite his exertions, "an attack to the legs can be just as lethal as one to the head."

He handed the shield back to Longus as Carpax shuffled ruefully back to his century.

"Form up!" shouted Sirus. "One section against another and, remember, hold the line!"

They trained without pausing until the sun began to dip and the training posts threw long shadows on the ground. Celer trudged wearily back along with the rest of the recruits, his arms leaden from the fight and bearing the weight of the training weapons all day. However, their exhaustion was momentarily forgotten as they stowed the wooden swords and training shields in the storage sheds attached to the quartermaster's building.

Sirus led them inside where the Quartermaster was waiting with his assistants.

Each recruit was issued an iron helmet, a heavy mail shirt, and leather guards for their forearms where the mail ended.

Priscus helped Celer into his mail shirt. The weight was extraordinary but he found that fastening his thick military belt helped spread the weight from his shoulders and made it more comfortable. He helped Priscus into his shirt then the two of them jammed the felt caps to be worn beneath the helmets on their heads and stood grinning at one another.

"You'll receive your weapons tomorrow morning, before the oath!" shouted the Quartermaster above the din, then the optios began herding the men outside and back to their barracks.

"The oath!" said Pulvillus excitedly, as they sat around their cooking fire that evening.

"Yes, we'll be proper soldiers then," said Sextus who was cheerfully polishing his new helmet, admiring how the flickering light from the fire reflected in its gleaming surface.

"Not just proper soldiers," Cinna said between mouthfuls, "the greatest soldiers in the whole Empire!"

They cheered at his words and Symmachus and Priscus raised their spoons to the ceiling as mock swords.

Celer chuckled quietly at their antics, still not comfortable enough to join in.

What would his father think, he thought to himself as he spooned more of the rough porridge they were eating into his mess tin. Would he approve of his only son swearing an oath to a Christian Emperor, to fight in his armies as a common soldier?

I do it for you, father, Celer thought as the others chattered about him. For you and mother, for Attianus and Varro and all the others.

He was broken from his thoughts by Cinna stealing Sextus's polished helmet. The older man tackled him to the ground and the two wrestled each other for possession as the others scrambled out of the way of their rolling bodies and called out encouragement to Sextus to teach the joker a lesson.

In the morning, Cinna sported a fresh black eye from the night's antics but it went unnoticed as he stood in his own gleaming armour. The recruits had spent all morning polishing and oiling their new equipment and stood proudly as they were handed their weapons for the first time.

Celer, like the others, held his sword reverently before him as he drew it from its sheath. After weeks of training with the weighted wooden swords, it felt as light as a feather; the grip seemed made for his hand as he held it before his face and watched the sunlight play upon the polished steel. They all admired their shields as much as their swords. They were made of birch boards and covered with painted blue leather, with a stripe of yellow running from the boss vertically down to the bottom rim of the shield. Above the boss, the Legion's insignia of a boar was painted.

The shields were taller and more oval than the crude willow shields that they had trained with. Celer found the slight curve of the shield offered comforting protection, whilst still allowing him to use his sword freely.

Once every man was armed, the cohort marched out onto the parade ground. The First Cohort and the unit of horse archers were drawn up, waiting for them to bear witness to the oath-taking. Celer could not help but notice that the frontier troops looked shabby in a motley array of armour and weapons compared to the men of the new cohort. Only the General's bodyguards outshone them, gleaming armour burnished to a silver sheen, with huge red horse-hair plumes and long red cloaks. Their horses were also armoured for the occasion, heads covered by three steel plates decorated with gold and silver, with protruding bronze eye-guards whilst their bodies were covered in iron scale trappers.

Stilicho stood flanked by his troopers, with the officers of all the units present ranked behind him.

The soldiers stood silently as Stilicho surveyed them with an approving eye.

He recited the military oath and the recruits repeated his words, each man's gaze locked firmly on the general. They swore obedience and loyalty to the Emperor Theodosius and his sons and to protect and defend the people of the Roman Empire. Because the East was officially a Christian Empire, the men swore their allegiance to the Christian God. Celer thought he was not alone in moving his lips soundlessly as others spoke about him, but none of the officers seemed to notice and Stilicho did not pause. Lastly, the men made their oaths to each other, never to abandon one another, never to flee in the face of an enemy.

As one, the men roared out "All this we swear!" to complete the oath. Swords were ripped from their sheaths and the glinting blades were thrust at the sky. The soldiers witnessing the ceremony were swept along in the moment and a forest of swords and bows were raised towards the heavens.

That night the newly sworn in legionaries were given leave to visit the town that lay outside Novae's walls. Word had also arrived from the capital that the Emperor had named his eight-year-old son Honorius as Emperor of the Western Empire. Many of the soldiers took this as further cause for celebration, with only a few more astute among them realising that this was a declaration of war against Eugenius's empire.

Vegetius argued against the leave but Sirus for once ignored the writer; this was one soldier's tradition not written in any history book, but one he would not refuse the men.

The various taverns and brothels often vied with one another for custom in Novae but that night there was no need for competition as the men of the Third Cohort flooded out from their barracks. The first instalment of their pay had been distributed after the oath ceremony and now men hurried to spend what little was left after the deductions the Legion's clerks had made.

Celer stuck close to his section-mates. On the training field he had established himself as a competent soldier and that gave him confidence. Out in the civilian world, he was out of his depth. Even the coin purse tied to his belt felt strange. Before he was forced to flee Rome, he had never had to pay for anything himself; such things were handled by his father's slaves. As they descended into the town, listening to the first roars of laughter echo about the tight streets, he felt painfully aware that this was a world he had never experienced before.

They muscled their way through a scrum of men to the counter of the nearest of the two taverns.

Sextus handed Celer a cup of sour wine, complaining loudly of the price. Celer just nodded along in agreement; the tavern owners were likely charging as much as they could get away with. There were almost a hundred men crammed into the cramped room with many more outside. The tavern's serving girls were working double time in an attempt to serve the mass of men forcing their way in. Even the tavern's whores had been enlisted to fetch drink out to the waiting legionaries, responding to the surge of custom before their other services were required.

It was hot in the tavern. Cinna and Priscus were pressed up tight to the counter and the others gratefully accepted the cups of wine they passed them, sending coin in the opposite direction. After a few cups the wine lost its sour taste. There was no room to lower their arms and the wine cups kept coming so, by the time Celer staggered outside to relieve himself, the world was reeling. He just managed to remember to unlace the still unfamiliar trousers before pissing against the side of the tavern.

As he fumbled the laces with wine-fuddled fingers, a body bumped into him, almost knocking him into the piss-soaked ground.

Celer flailed for a moment until he steadied himself and turned angrily but the drunk had already stumbled past into the dark alley between the tavern and the building beyond.

He forced his way back inside, pausing a moment to gawp at a tavern whore who was running her hands through the hair of a legionary from the First Century whilst his section-mates cheered and poured wine over her bared breasts.

He made it back to find Cinna, Symmachus and Quintus had disappeared. It was so loud that he had to shout in Magnus's ear to ask where they had gone. Magnus just shrugged and pushed another cup of wine into his hand, spilling some down his own front in the process.

Celer stumbled out of the tavern in the early hours of the morning. The night air was frigid but the wine in his stomach was making him feel hot and flushed. He took a deep breath of the cold air, smelling the homely aroma of wood smoke mixed with the sharp stench of vomit and urine and threw up in the street.

When he finally stopped retching, Celer wiped his mouth with a shaky hand and looked about him. The street was poorly lit by scattered torches and his eyes watered from vomiting but he could make out the slumped forms of men in doorways and in the back of a number of carts that sat at the entrance to alleyways.

He jerked around to see if any of the others had followed him out but he recognised none of the others staggering out of the doorway. His stomach heaved at the sudden movement and he threw up again, spattering the boots of the legionary retching next to him, but the man didn't notice.

A wave of tiredness washed over him, and it was only the icy blast that tore up the narrow street that stopped him from finding a doorway of his own. Torches flickered on the walls of the fortress looming over the town and he began to stumble towards the gate of the legionary's compound, trying not to think about what his boots slipped in on the road.

Few lights lit the approach to the main gate from the town but the moon was bright, bathing the simple stone houses in a silver glow. Shouting flared up behind him, swiftly followed by barking dogs, but the noise died out as he followed the curving street, grateful as the gate hove into sight.

Boots hammered at the street behind him and this time the sound grew louder. Celer staggered to one side as he tried to turn and see who was behind him and his drunkenness saved him. Horatius flew past him; his short-cropped hair appeared white in the moonlight and there was no mistaking him, even though he was absent his armour. The guard commander swivelled, staggered, then recovered his footing and came at Celer again. From the way he lurched towards him, Celer could tell he was drunk, too.

Sobering rapidly, Celer backed away, raising his hands as he went.

"Wa... wait! Stop!" he shouted. His voice sounded hoarse.

Surprisingly, Horatius did stop. Face screwed up with rage, he stared at Celer in a half crouch as he attempted to steady himself.

"You bastard!" he spat. "You stupid whoreson!"

"Horatius, whatever wrong I have done you," the words rushed from Celer's mouth as he struggled to speak coherently, "I did not mean it!"

"You, you!" Horatius raved and pointed an arm at him and Celer saw the blade of a dagger shine in the moonlight.

"You made a fool of me, in front of my men, in front of the General!"

Celer continued to back away, arms raised before him, the cold air and the imminent danger sobering him quickly.

"It was a training demonstration!" Celer protested. "I had no choi..."

"Cease your words!" Horatius screamed at him, strings of spittle running from his chin as he advanced with the knife held low.

"You made a mockery of me; no man does that and lives!"

Celer was ready for the lunge and threw himself to one side, sprawling hard on the paved street. The effects of the wine were rapidly wearing off as fear coursed through his body. He leapt up, nearly fell again, then took off in the direction of the tavern.

Horatius may have been drunk but he was also fast and strong and he pursued Celer doggedly.

Sober, Celer would have outstripped him easily, but his legs betrayed him barely a hundred feet from the tavern. His foot went out from under him, slipping on some ice hidden by the darkness, and he crashed to the ground. Unable to slow himself, Horatius careered into him and went down in a sprawl of limbs; the dagger clattered away into the darkness.

Celer kicked and writhed to escape the weight on top of him but Horatius recovered quickly and pulled him back. "Die, die, die!" roared the German who began shrieking something in his own tongue as he struck him over and over.

Out of the corner of his eye, Celer saw that the commotion had attracted several of the legionaries outside the tavern. Throwing his arms up, he tried to ride out the storm of blows as Horatius hammered at him with his fists. A scything blow slipped past his guard and the night erupted into a bright flash of white light. Then the darkness enveloped him totally and he felt no more.

# XIV

When Celer woke it was morning. Weak winter sunlight kissed his battered face and he could hear the now familiar sounds of the fortress, though they were strangely muted.

Groaning, he tried to raise his head. It felt heavy as lead and swam with dizziness. He retched and only just managed to turn his head so that he didn't choke on the hot vomit that filled his throat. He spat weakly and wiped his mouth with a bruised hand. His lips felt swollen beneath his shaky touch and the lightest contact made them sting.

One eye was sealed shut but the other opened enough for him to see that he was in the fortress hospital. All around him he could see the prostrate forms of men, the morning quiet punctuated by bouts of vomiting from the casualties of the Cohort's foray into town.

Feeling ashamed to find himself here amongst the other drunks, he allowed his head to sink back onto the cot. His whole body ached, worse than it had after any day of training. Closing his one good eye, he tried to remember what had happened. Fragmented memories flashed past his mind's eye. The crouched figure of Horatius silhouetted against the lights of the fortress. Running down the darkened streets, the low buildings of the town whipping past him, the cold night air on his skin. Being hurt, lying on the paved ground, gritty cobbles rough beneath his hands as he tried to rise. Then darkness, feeling blows thump into his body but not being able to see them coming, unable to strike back or protect himself.

He woke with a start. The sunlight no longer lay across his bed and several of the beds nearby were now empty. He felt clammy and cold. The rough blanket felt damp to the touch and he felt a mingling of horror and shame as he thought he had pissed himself. Furious, he forced himself into a sitting position, hands searching to discover the truth. To his immense relief he found no sign of such a shameful accident, though his tunic was wet through with sweat that stank of the tavern''s sour wine, making his tortured stomach want to retch once more.

Fighting to control his stomach, he quickly inspected himself. His arms and legs were cut and covered with bruises; looking beneath his sodden tunic he could see his torso, too, was a motley of purple and red bruising.

Carefully, Celer probed his head and face with his fingers, trying to ascertain the damage. His chin was almost too painful to touch but he still had all his teeth and, amazingly, none felt loose. His nose, too, was blessedly unbroken but the skin about his eyes was swollen and there was a thick bandage about his head.

He had just completed his inspection when he saw Vegetius striding down the aisle between the beds.

"My dear boy," the writer's face contorted at the site of the battered legionary, "you look dreadful!"

His old travel companion's evident concern felt so out of place amongst the brusque army setting that Celer could not help but snort with laughter at his words. Pain gripped his battered chest and his laughter dissolved into a wincing cough instead.

"Such kind words," he managed when the coughing stopped. "I feel dreadful."

Shuffling backwards, Celer propped himself against the wall and Vegetius settled onto the foot of the bed.

"I warned Centurion Sirus against allowing such foolishness; months of training designed to make soldiers worthy of the ancients, all undone by a night of wine and whores!" he remarked bitterly, gazing about the hospital. Many of the legionaries lay dead to the world on their beds; some were sitting up, wincing at various injuries or just at the churning sensations in their stomachs.

Looking back at his young friend, Vegetius eyed Celer's bandaged head. "The medicus tells me that your head was sliced open, most likely from a hobnail."

Gingerly, Celer felt the bandage on his head. "It was..."

"Horatius," Vegetius finished for him.

"What will happen to him?" asked Celer after a moment.

"He's to be flogged."

"Good," muttered Celer darkly, body aching as he shifted his position. "When?"

"In a few days, once the medicus has deemed him fit enough to receive the punishment." Seeing the question on Celer's lips, Vegetius explained. "It appears that the men who pulled him off you were members of your century, including a few of your section-mates. As soon as they saw what had happened, they took it upon themselves to enact some justice of their own before the provosts arrived."

Pride surged through Celer's veins and, for the first time since he had fled his family home, he felt a sense of belonging.

They sat in silence for a short while before Celer noticed that Vegetius was shifting uncomfortably at the foot of the bed, fidgeting with the hem of his tunic.

"What's wrong?" he asked.

The older man looked at him awkwardly for a moment. "It's not my place to say," Vegetius said, looking hastily away. "I am not your father."

His words made Celer sit up straighter. "You may not be my father, but you are my friend; say what you will."

Vegetius continued looking down the line of beds.

"You were fortunate last night," he said reproachfully.

Celer rubbed his bruised ribs and winced. "I do not feel fortunate." His voice strained a little as he shifted, trying to make himself more comfortable.

"You suffer the results of a single man's foolish pride," said Vegetius. Celer thought he heard a spark of anger as he spoke. "One drunken soldier managed to hospitalise you. God himself must only know what may have happened had your fellow soldiers not been present."

The writer turned to face him and Celer lowered his eyes rather than meet his gaze.

"I say you were fortunate," Vegetius continued, "for it could easily have been agents of Flavianus waiting for you on that dark street."

He laid a hand on Celer's leg. "You must be mindful of the dangers, even here. Do not forget the circumstances that forced you down this road."

"I will never forget!" said Celer vehemently, shame at the truth of his friend's words fuelling his anger.

Vegetius's face was instantly one of regret. "No, my dear boy," he

195

said sadly, shaking his head, "I don't believe you will. Forgive me my foolish words."

Now it was Celer's turn to shake his head. "There is nothing to forgive, my friend; you are right. It is I who is the fool. It shall not happen again, I swear it."

Vegetius gave him a small smile. "One day, there will be time for celebration, and you and I shall raise many a toast to all those we have lost along the way."

Returning the smile as best his damaged face would allow, Celer said, "I would like that, Vegetius; I pray that day comes soon."

"I shall add my own prayers. Between my God and yours we shall not have to wait long. Now I shall leave you to rest," he said, standing to leave. "Centurion Sirus has ordered training recommence at dawn tomorrow. He is adamant the Cohort will improve further before the spring campaigns begin."

"Spring campaigns?" Celer momentarily pushed all thoughts aside at the hint of news.

"But we don't march West until next spring!" he blurted out.

A wry smile crept across Vegetius's lips as he looked down at Celer. "And how does a legionary know when an Emperor plans to march his army against his enemies?"

Celer blushed, but thankfully the bruising on his face disguised it enough that Vegetius did not notice.

"Just rumours about the camp," he said airily, not wanting to lie to his friend, but also not wanting to betray the clerks and cooks who worked in the General's headquarters and often relayed titbits of information to the news-depraved soldiers.

Vegetius decided not to push for Celer's source; instead he smiled and tapped the side of his nose knowingly. "I fear it is not my place to tell you, dear boy. No doubt you will hear 'rumours' soon enough." He stood beside Celer and laid a hand on his shoulder for an instant. "Rest easy, my friend, and recover your strength."

As the writer turned to go, Celer snapped a mock salute, ignoring the ache that stabbed through his body. "Yes, Sir."

Vegetius smiled once more, then he strode off down the aisle, stepping neatly around a puddle of vomit that a bitter-looking orderly was mopping up.

They flogged Horatius a week later. Stilicho himself stood before the amassed troops of the fortress, his late guard commander lashed to a wagon in the centre of the parade ground. The General spoke briefly, his commanding voice unusually harsh; he harangued the soldiers about the severity of assaulting a fellow comrade, a man you were sworn to defend on the field of battle and declared that the punishment would also be severe.

Horatius slumped against the wheel throughout the speech and made no noise. Despite the hatred he felt for the man, Celer felt a small pang of pity for the swathe of bruises that covered the German's muscled torso. His own bruises had darkened in colour and the weight of his mail was almost unbearable at times and their pain soon quashed the pity he felt.

At the stroke of the first lash, Horatius came to life. His head whipped up as he bellowed in agony and Celer could see the bandage that covered most of his face. Whilst he had lain in his own hospital bed, an orderly had told Celer in hushed tones that Horatius's face had been so badly beaten by the men of the Third Cohort that he had lost the sight in one eye.

Celer had repeated the news once he re-joined his section. None of them showed any remorse for the injuries that would scar Horatius for life.

"Good riddance to the bastard," Magnus had spat that morning in their barrack block, carefully nursing swollen and bruised knuckles.

"I second that," Priscus had said. "That German pig-fucker would have happily kicked you to death. No doubt he'll piss off back to whatever wealthy family he comes from and live out his days in luxury amongst his own kind."

As the optio assigned to whip Horatius struck again, Celer thought that whilst the tall cavalryman might retire to some grand villa in the northern provinces, he would likely feel the sharp sting of shame of his punishment no matter what the luxuries.

Training had recommenced after only a day's respite from the Cohort's celebrations. Centurion Sirus drove them at a punishing pace and secretly Celer thought he might regret not following Vegetius's advice to omit that long held tradition of the legions.

Few men had been injured as badly as Celer during the night's frivolities, yet amongst those who had, three had broken limbs and one had died in a knife fight with an unknown assailant from a wound to the kidneys.

The men now trained in full armour at all times. Each man suddenly felt a raw recruit once again. Drills and exercises they thought mastered now pushed them to their limits as the heavy armour slowed them and their swords and shields encumbered them.

In addition to continued sword drill, the men were issued with the heavy darts that were weighted around their tips. They spent hours learning how much force was required to drop the heavy darts on the heads of their targets. Alongside this they were taught to fight with spears, javelins, slings and bows.

The legions also required that the men be able to manage a horse. Many of the freshly minted soldiers had gone their whole lives without sitting on a horse and the instructors had to begin with the basics. For Celer, the frustration he felt standing through the demonstrations was all worth it when he was finally allowed to mount up. The training was led by a decurion from the unit of mounted horse archers, a short, swarthy man hailing from the peoples beyond the frontier, with powerful shoulders from years of training with the recurve bows the unit used.

After putting the legionaries through their paces for a week on the parade ground outside Novae, he led them out into the countryside and put them through simple manoeuvres. Apart from being able to ride in a formation and follow commands, they were expected to know little else.

As they trotted back to the fortress that evening the decurion pulled in alongside Celer's section.

"You ride well, Roman," he said in the rough Latin that the soldiers had grown used to over the past week.

"If you were shorter, I would ask the name of your mother, for surely you could be one of mine!" he laughed and rode off to the head of the column.

Priscus was riding alongside Celer and burst out laughing at the look on his friend's face.

When at last the winter snows began to thaw, Sirus sprung his last test.

The Christians amongst the Cohort named it Hell; those who followed the old gods called it Hades or other names meaning much the same. They had revisited the series of ditches and felled trees they had constructed under Vegetius's supervision a few times over the months of training. The men came to fear and loathe such days. The ditches had filled with snow that barely thawed, creating a muddy morass that caked the men in a freezing layer of mud as they tried to haul themselves over the tangle of trunks and tree limbs. Once they were issued with their armour and weapons, their misery doubled. Not only did they have to struggle harder to make it to the other side, but they were denied sleep until the links of mail had been cleaned free of the cloying filth.

The long winter had finally passed and the first signs of spring were showing as they marched towards the site on the edge of the forest that the legion sourced its timber from. It had been dry all week and many of the men were praying to every god they knew for the broken ground to be dry. Celer shared their hopes but he knew that the ditches would be home to the last of the winter snows, long turned into icy slush; the trenches would be murder this fine spring morning.

"First Century! At the ready!" roared out Optio Longus, startling the crows form the nearby trees.

Celer tightened his grip on his shield and checked his sword's sheathe was firmly fastened. Like many of the legionaries, he had initially strapped on his sword on his left hip, the frontier garrison's no longer adhering to the old rules that only centurions could wear a sword in such a way. However, after a sixteen-mile training march, Celer had switched the sword to his right hip; the constant clunking of the pommel on the inside of his shield had almost driven him insane and he found he could still easily draw it from the right-hand side.

"First Century! Advance, at the double!" Longus bellowed and the order was repeated by the centurion of the Second Century. The front ranks rippled forward as the legionaries set off at a steady run. The first ditch came all too soon and Celer hurled himself forward. Even with the added weight of his armour and equipment, he sailed over to the other side, legs strengthened from the months of training, boots biting into the hard ground and churning through it as he powered up the embankment behind it. He was faced by a tangle of fallen trees. Keeping moving so as not to cause a bottleneck, he surged over and under the trunks, their bark long-stripped by the hands and boots of passing legionaries. Celer kept his shield held away from his body as he had been shown, angled forward so that it would block any missiles thrown at him.

Sirus and Vegetius watched from the far side. Vegetius saw Celer moving lithely through the maze of fallen trees, saw him leap into the air to clear a ditch then disappear once more behind a mound of brash and soil.

"They're good," commented the writer, looking down to jot something on a wax tablet he held.

Sirus grunted, watching the legionaries leap and duck around the obstacles. A shouted command, muffled by the trees and distance, indicated the next two centuries had been dispatched on the heels of the First and Second.

The front rank reappeared, Celer amongst them. Vegetius stopped writing on his tablet and the other accompanying officers halted their shushed conversations to watch the recruits face Sirus's final test.

The Third Cohort had constructed the ditches and felled the trees to create the obstacle course. Each time they had run it they had gained intimate knowledge of the muddy tangle. Which trunk to vault and which to duck under, what ditch could be crossed in a leap and which had to be slogged through.

They had become fast and efficient and secretly Sirus was proud of them as he watched them flow across ground that would have halted any hardened frontier unit in its tracks. But war was a fickle business, the veteran knew, and his men would have to be able to adapt if they were to survive and so he had created his final test.

An enormous ditch. More than twenty feet across and twice the height of a man, the vertical walls retained behind log piles that were slick with mud. It had taken a century of the First Cohort almost a week to construct and several of their officers now stood behind Sirus to see what the men of the Third would do in the face of their men's handiwork.

"What the fuck!" Celer panted, sliding to a halt.

Priscus almost crashed into him and spat his own curse as he saw why his friend had stopped so near the finish.

"Do not stop!" roared Sirus, so loudly he made Vegetius jump.

"Assault this position!" He turned to a section of dismounted horse archers he had requisitioned for this purpose. "Begin firing."

The horse archers nocked arrows to their powerful curved bows; the iron heads covered by heavy leather caps. Drawing the bowstrings back halfway to their cheeks, they loosed a volley at the growing number of men opposite them.

"Shields!" A voice cried out in the line and Celer quickly snatched his shield up in time to block the first volley.

"First Century will advance!" screamed Sirus again.

The men shuffled to the edge of the ditch, hesitant at the long drop below them.

"Fuck it," Celer muttered under his breath, then loudly, "On me, lads, on me!"

He dropped lightly off the edge, shield still raised against the steady volleys that clattered against the painted shields and smacked into the mud around him.

Priscus followed him without hesitation and the sight of Celer landing safely and wading his way across encouraged the other men to drop down.

Glutinous mud sucked at their boots but they managed to cross the ditch with their shields held above their heads as the archers alternated between those below and those arriving on the far bank.

"What now?" shouted Borus, the section leader who stood to Celer's left as the timber-clad wall loomed in front of them.

"The shields," said Celer, thinking quickly as an arrow thumped off his shield and clattered against the posts. "Make a ramp against the wall!"

The legionaries dressed their ranks instinctively. The section leaders braced the top edge of their shields against the wooden wall and overlapped the shields of the second rank so that the bottom edge rested on the shield boss of the man behind. This was repeated to the fourth rank where Cinna and the others crouched beneath their angled shields, bottom edges buried into the ditch base.

If Quintus or any of the other fifth rankers had any doubts about the flimsy ramp before them, they didn't stop to voice them. Struggling to hold their own shields above their heads, they scrambled up the ramp and climbed up the lip. Following their training, they quickly drew their swords and advanced upon the archers who continued to fire as they backed away from the mud-spattered legionaries.

Symmachus's sixth rank advanced to support their comrades and, under this protective screen, the rear two ranks turned and began hauling the ramp men up. Celer was last; groaning under the weight, he boosted Priscus up to the waiting arms of Pulvillus and Sextus. He threw his shield up, then held both hands up to grab Priscus who had shed his shield and sword and was being dangled by his belt over the edge.

Safely over the wall, the men drew their weapons and advanced to the battle line the Century was holding before Sirus and the officers.

Taking inspiration from the men of the First Century, the rest of the Cohort soon crossed the ditch until the whole unit was reformed in front of Sirus.

"Gentlemen," he addressed the legionaries, "well done. Training is now over, tomorrow we march from Novae to carry out missions along the frontier. It is important that the Legion secures the Empire's borders before we march West against the pretender Eugenius. Optio!"

"Sir," Longus snapped to attention.

"Lead the First Century back to the fortress."

"Yes, Sir! First Century, left face! Ready! March!"

Sirus turned to the gathered officers behind him. "To your centuries, Gentlemen."

They saluted and, one by one, the units marched away from the forest edge.

Vegetius remained alongside Sirus. The writer looked over the sea of ravaged earth, torn by hundreds of hobnailed boots.

"Well, Senior Centurion?"

Sirus was watching the column march away from them; he noted that, despite their tiredness, the men marched in perfect step.

"Send a dispatch to the General," he said to Vegetius. "Tell him that the Cohort is ready. We march at first light."

# XV

Two days after marching from Novae, the Cohort arrived at the fort of Sexaginta Prista. They were met on the road to the fort by a small detachment of the Second Cohort of the Legion led by Senior Centurion Proculus, who was the garrison commander.

After exchanging formal greetings, Centurion Sirus rode alongside Proculus as they headed for the fort. The escort from Second Cohort fell in behind the two officers and the Third marched behind them.

Celer inspected the backs of the men in front of him curiously. As with the legionaries of the First Cohort, the men of the Second had spent their entire army careers and, most likely, their lives on the frontier. They wore either mail or scale armour. Most had helmets like Celer but a few wore old pattern models with more protruding neck guards. They were all armed with long swords and heavy stabbing spears and a mixture of oval and round shields.

Longus and the centurions of the other centuries directed the Cohort to the construction of a fortified camp a short distance from the walls of the fort. The work progressed quickly in the soft ground and drew a crowd of onlookers from the small town that surrounded the fort.

The fort was small compared to Novae as it only housed the under-strength Second. Its squat towers overlooked the Danube and the large ferry barge that was the only means of crossing the river. On the far bank a timber tower stood stark and lonely, surrounded by scrub, but kept clear of trees by the Legion so as to see anyone approaching the river bank.

With the camp constructed and darkness rapidly approaching, the men were released from their duties for the night. The section's tent assembled, Celer walked to the edge of the camp that faced the river. Nodding a greeting to the men of the Second Century who were on sentry duty that night, he climbed the short earth rampart and looked north over the Danube.

Long shadows from the fort turned the river black as it flowed sluggishly past. Celer had thought the Tiber a big river but the here the far bank was almost half a mile away from him, the torches burning in the watch tower mere pinpricks in a vast dark landscape.

The sight of that dark emptiness made him shudder. For someone raised in the heart of the Empire, the land beyond the frontier was an alien world where civilisation ended and the rule of the barbarian began. Rugians, Alani, Huns, Goths and Vandals, all divided into countless tribes and small kingdoms. He had learned their names as a boy, wide-eyed as he listened to his tutors and read the histories of the enemies of Rome. Of the emperors and generals who had defeated them and those who had been defeated by them.

Celer returned to the lines and ate with his section-mates as usual. The mood, however, was different, tense; the men ate quietly and when the meal was done they crawled inside the tent without a word. Lying on his bed roll, Celer willed his body to sleep. Yet, despite the tiredness from marching for two days in full armour and carrying his weapons and gear, his mind would not quieten. Dark imaginings swirled in his mind. Warriors clad in furs and leather, armed with wicked blades, bursting from forests black as pitch to attack the small column of Romans.

He tried to suppress his fears and listened for the now comforting snores of his comrades about him to lull him to sleep. Only silence greeted his ears; his section mates lay quiet as the dead and the camp was ominously still. Little did he know that nearly all the men of the Cohort shared his worries. Few would sleep that night, and those that did would start awake often in a cold grip of dread.

Overcast skies come the morning did little to lift their spirits. The officers were summoned to a briefing in the fort as the men dismantled the tents and fortifications, once more drawing curious observers as the camp that had sprung from nothing the previous evening soon disappeared.

Sirus soon returned, the centurions and optios of the Cohort in tow as well as a half-century from the Second Cohort.

"Make ready," Celer called to Priscus and the others and they hurriedly packed the last of the tent away on their mule before fastening on their helmets and hefting their shields.

"Good to see the Second has our backs," Priscus muttered from behind him as the half-century marched down towards the ferry.

"They likely couldn't spare any more men," replied Celer, glancing up at the lonely sentries that patrolled the walls of the fort.

"Or they know what's waiting for us over there," said someone darkly from the ranks of the century.

Borus spat between his boots. "Makes no difference," he growled, "what's waiting for us or who's backing us up. We didn't go through all that training, hours of sword drill, to stand on the wall of some fort. We came here to fight and I don't plan on losing."

The legionaries stamped their feet and growled their assent at his words until Longus told them to shut up.

"Save your breath for marching." ordered the Optio.

He led them in column down to the river bank where ferrymen with skin tanned to leather by the sun waited to carry them beyond the Empire's border.

The watchtower loomed above them on the far bank. Its ground floor was built of stone, with the timber level above manned at all times by a section who watched the flat, treeless landscape that stretched half a mile beyond the Danube.

The watchmen followed the column's progress as they marched amongst the scrub and young saplings that resisted the Legion's efforts to tame the land, until they disappeared into woodland that marked the end of Rome's reach.

The Cohort marched in a guarded formation as soon as the watchtower disappeared from sight. The mule train was positioned between the first three centuries and the last; the half-century of the Second Cohort took the van. The mounted archers had remained at Novae so a section from the Second Cohort acted as forward scouts, their packs stowed on mules so they carried only their arms. Conscious of the need to season his troops quickly, Centurion Sirus began attaching a different section from his own Cohort each day to the scouts.

Ten days after crossing the Danube, Celer walked behind a wiry veteran named Iulianus, trying his best to step as quietly as the frontiersman.

"Is it true that a million souls live in Rome?" asked Iulianus, stepping lightly around a boulder, eyes constantly scanning their surroundings.

"Maybe once, or so my tutors taught me," Celer replied, keeping his voice low. They were far enough ahead of the column that the tramp of boots was little more than dull background noise and both legionaries strained their ears for any movement in the dense forest.

"Fewer live there now - perhaps half a million," continued Celer.

Iulianus, who had been born and raised in Novae, gave a derisive snort as if he didn't believe that so many people could exist in one place.

"I s'pose that you all lived in palaces and such?" the veteran asked mockingly.

Celer shook his head. "Only the Imperial Palace for the Emperor, should he visit. Many Senators and Equestrians live in grand houses but most of the people live in apartment blocks stacked on top of one another." He demonstrated with his hands when Iulianus looked at him questioningly, his shield and spear making his movements awkward.

"Apartments, eh?" The frontiersman repeated the unfamiliar word and tried to imagine buildings that sat atop one another.

"What are we looking for out here, anyway?" asked Celer, eager to change the topic before the older man could question him further about Rome, nervous that the questions would become more personal.

A pair of pigeons erupted from a nearby tree and both men instantly dropped into a crouch, their shields raised towards the noise and their spears levelled.

Confident after a few heartbeats that the bird's flight did not indicate nearby hostiles, Iulianus slowly straightened and continued on their line of march.

"There's always raiding bands in these areas, preparing to cross the Danube to plunder our fields and villages. Might be we find one of them," explained the veteran. "If not, then there's always settlers claiming land even though we pay their chiefs to keep them away. Normally we patrol and report any that grow too close to the frontier. The garrison at Novae usually sends the cavalry to chase them off. Now, though," he grinned and looked back at Celer, "we have our own little army. We're going to give the barbarians a good pasting."

"But why? Raiders, I understand, but what threat do settlers pose the frontier?"

"Because," explained the veteran patiently, "soon the frontier will be stripped of more troops to fight the Emperor's war in the West, when what it really needs, and has done for a long time, is more troops." He swept his spear in a wide arc before him. "There are tens of thousands of barbarians out here; all look to our fertile fields and the richness of our cities. If they knew how thinly stretched we are, they would be across the Danube before the last snow-melt and there would be no one to oppose them. So, to show them that the Empire is still strong, we do the unexpected; we raid with a larger force than many will have seen in a generation and remind them of why it pays to keep treaties with us."

"Surely there are other options," said Celer, uncomfortable at the thought of killing farmers.

Iulianus had sensed the tone of his voice and shot him a sideways glance. "Was your father a politician, boy? They usually spout that kind of shit. What other options do you see?"

Celer quickly turned to scan the trees so the veteran would not see the red flush of his face. Wishing he had never opened his mouth, Celer tried to think of a reply that his companion would not disregard immediately.

"What if we let them settle," he said carefully, "give them land on condition that they accept allied status and pay us tribute?"

"Let the tax men wear them down rather than us, eh? Not a bad idea lad, I'll give you that," said Iulianus, making Celer grin. "Won't work, though," he continued.

"Why not?" Asked Celer, quick to defend his idea.

Iulianus looked up at the sky through the still-bare branches of the trees then looked behind them to see if the column had halted for a midday break.

"One big flaw in your plan," he explained as Celer followed him back towards the column, "is that the people here don't want to be Roman. They were once, when this land was the province of Dacia, but they decided quick enough they would rather live like barbarians than civilised folk. And, like all barbarians, they hunger for land. We give them the land beyond the river and in a few years they"ll be crossing the Danube in their thousands."

They reported to Centurion Sirus and took the opportunity to down their weapons whilst they were safe inside the Cohort's picket lines. When Optio Longus bellowed out the order for the legionaries to make ready to march, Iulianus tapped Celer with the butt of his spear.

"Come on, lad, the woods won't watch themselves."

The column was following a narrow track through the forest that Iulianus claimed had once been a military road. Celer had said nothing at the time, not trusting the veteran's words.

Iulianus, like many of the army's veterans, enjoyed nothing more than winding up the new legionaries with false tales and information before roaring with laughter at how gullible new recruits were these days.

Yet Iulianus had seemed serious about the road, with none of the tell-tale laughter in his eyes that usually showed when he was trying to trick his young comrade. As they pushed off the track into the trees either side, Celer saw the faint remains of the drainage ditch running parallel to the track, now overgrown and silted up but an unmistakable mark of a Roman road.

The forest was young, Iulianus told him in hushed tones as they walked. A result of the buffer zone the Roman's paid the barbarians to keep free of people. The frontier had once been hundreds of miles to the north and the land had once been cleared and farmed. After the province had been abandoned under Emperor Aurelian to the Gepids, the farms had quickly been overrun by nature. Now only hunters, war bands or the occasional merchant convoy kept the old roads from becoming reclaimed by the wilderness.

Further north, the forest ended, the veteran said. People still farmed the plains between them and the Carpathian Mountains. Old Roman towns were now ruled by tribal chiefs.

That night, relived from his patrol duties for the day, Celer sat with the others around their section's small campfire. Centurion Sirus had halted the march earlier than usual when the scouts had reported a small clearing not far from the track.

Clearings like it cropped up throughout the forest, Iulianus had told Celer as they patrolled. Hunters created and maintained them as places that attracted game for the easy grazing and, in this case, access to the small stream that ran swift and clear through the heart of the glade.

The Cohort would not fit into the existing space so the men had set to work felling trees to create space for their camp and a killing ground beyond the rough palisade that they constructed from the felled timber, rather than hack through the tangle of roots to build the ditch and bank that normally encircled their marching camps.

Celer sat between Priscus and Quintus, hungrily watching Sextus tend the strips of venison cooking on a lattice work of green branches.

Celer had felled the young buck himself under the guidance of Iulianus. Unlike many of the men of the Third Cohort, Celer had hunted big game before. However, hunting boar on his father's country estate in the forested foothills above the northern shore of Lake Trasimene was a far cry from hunting with the Legions in foreign lands before the frontier. His father had taught him to hunt as the nobles hunt. On horseback, with a train of servants and beaters who would herd the boar down to where the hunters waited, slaves bearing spare spears should the first one miss. The estate manager, an experienced man, stood nearby with spear in hand should the boar prove to be too much for his noble masters. After the hunt, large sun shades would be erected and the choice cuts of meat would be prepared by his father's cooks as Cotta and his son lounged in chairs carried by slaves alongside their guests, sipping wine chilled in a nearby stream.

His hunt that late afternoon had been much different. As the Cohort set to, felling trees and drawing out the tent lines, Iulianus drew two bows and quivers from the mule train and led his young comrade back into the forest.

They did not have to go far. The noise in the clearing had deterred much of the game from drawing near, but sites with good grazing and fresh water were few amongst the trees and so the game lurked in the gathering gloom of the woods. Both legionaries still wore their mail armour and carried their swords but they had forgone their helmets and shields. Celer was focusing so hard on being as silent as Iulianus that he almost crashed into the back of the older man when he spotted the buck.

It was of a decent size. The last of its winter coat still clung on in tufts; patches of its russet red summer coat shone though where it had rubbed against trees and its new antlers were covered in velvet.

Iulianus had lowered himself to one knee. Raising his right hand slowly, he motioned for Celer to take the shot.

The deer was forty paces away and nibbling at the fresh young buds of a tree, hungry after winter's hardships. A breath of wind stirred the trees about them but Iulianus had chosen his approach well and they were downwind of the buck and he did not stir from his food.

Conscious that his shot would mean the difference between his century eating well that night or the men having to sup on their dwindling rations, Celer slowly stood. He was shielded from the deer by the broad trunk of a beech and he slowly inched round until he had a clear shot. Iulianus tapped his chest silently, indicating he should aim just above the shoulder to pierce its lungs.

Sirus had made sure they were all instructed in archery as part of their training and he had shot bows in the past as a boy, yet he had never had to rely on his own marksmanship in order to eat. Taking a deep breath to steady his nerves, he drew the string back to his ear. The buck still chewed at the branches. His shoulder tensed as he held the bowstring, sighting down the shaft.

"Breathe out. And let the arrow fly when your breath is gone," the squat instructor with narrow eyes from the eastern steppe beyond the Euxeinos Pontus had told them. "That is when you are most still, then your arrow will fly true."

Celer heeded his teacher's lesson. His let his breath out in a low sigh, felt his heart slow. The bucks head twitched up. He released the arrow with a dull thwack from the string. His shot struck true and, though the buck leapt forward, its legs gave before it could take another step and it crashed to the ground. Iulianus was by its side before its legs stopped kicking; he opened its throat with his dagger, whispering something in its ear as its blood rushed forth.

They buried the innards and carried the carcass back to the camp. Iulianus took a leg back to his section, leaving Celer to take the rest back to his century. Others had also been out hunting, returning with a brace of birds and an early wild piglet, but Celer's buck took pride of place. Centurion Sirus himself had come to sample it, refusing the choice cuts when Celer offered them, stating the spoils should always go to the victor who earned them.

"May the Lord forever smile upon you," said Cinna, a huge smile on his face as he eagerly accepted his share from Sextus.

The others were quick to agree with him.

"And may He bless us with a few more like this," said Sextus, laying more strips of meat onto the blackened framework. "The mules walk quicker each day; there can't be much food left."

"Iulianus believes Centurion Sirus is marching us towards new settlements," Celer said between bites of the delicious meat. "Says we'll likely take on supplies from the settlers."

"Why would they feed us if we mean to move them from their new home?" asked Magnus.

All the section raised their heads from the roasted meat.

"What?" Magnus looked around at them.

"I don't think the Centurion is going to give them much choice," said Sextus quietly.

Awkward silence descended upon them. Only the hiss of juices running off the meat into the fire could be heard.

"How long until we reach these settlements?" Priscus asked Celer quietly.

"Tomorrow, by Iulianus's reckoning, then two more days to the settlement where the chief resides."

Dawn broke slowly the next morning. The camp was wreathed in mist; ethereal trees loomed beyond the shivering sentries at the palisade. The legionaries broke their fast. Cooking fires were quickly rekindled from the embers of the previous night and soon added their smoke to the damp air.

Celer oversaw the section breaking down their tent, the routine now so flawless that the men did it without thought. All around them, the camp was stripped down with quick efficiency, left so that it would not offer any potential enemy an advantage against the Cohort.

When they first crossed the Danube, the forest had filled Celer with dread. In his imagination wild beasts prowled just beyond sight, waiting to strike down anyone who strayed too far from the column or camp and each clearing held an ambush of tribal warriors, eager to crush the Roman invaders.

Yet, as they marched on down the old Roman road, the rising sun slowly burning off the mist and bathing the trees in warm golden light, he found the forest held fewer terrors for him now.

His time scouting with Iulianus made him confident that no fur-clad warriors lurked in wait for them, and the only predator they had seen was a brief glimpse of a lynx as they stalked for deer. The cat had eyed them warily with amber eyes. Iulianus had slowly motioned them both to take a knee and the three hunters had stared at one another through the trees until the lynx turned abruptly and slunk away.

They found the first farms not long after leaving camp. Marching at the front of the Cohort, Celer saw the first of the scouts appear from amongst the trees and report to Sirus, who rode ahead of the legionaries with Centurion Decimus, the commander of the half-century of the Second Cohort.

Sirus did not seem worried by the scout's report and the column marched on. Signs of human habitation began to appear. Trees either side of the track had been felled and dragged along its stony surface and they soon came upon the first homestead.

The farmhouse was small and simply built. Its walls were made of undressed stone and rough-hewn timbers and its roof was dense thatch. The soft lowing of cows could be heard as the Column halted at the edge of the tree line. Here the forest had been heavily thinned to form small fields and Celer could see the distant shape of another farmhouse in the distance.

The scouts had already reached the building and they stood outside with the farmer and his two sons; one glowered at the legionaries, calloused fingers resting on the butt of a heavy axe.

Centurion Sirus spoke with Centurion Decimus briefly then turned his horse to his men.

"First Century, on me! Centurion Piso," he spoke to the leader of the second century of the Cohort.

"Sir."

"You have command of the Cohort, Centurion. See the men are stood down. Keep them out of sight and post a picket line."

Piso saluted and turned to the rest of the Cohort and began bawling out orders that were echoed by the other Centurions.

Optio Longus gave the order for the First Century to down packs and follow their Centurion with weapons only. Sirus rode ahead of them and the eighty men tramped towards the farmhouse. They marched straight through a patch of recently ploughed field but the sight of a fully armoured century marching towards him stilled any complaint the farmer may have raised.

Celer saw that Iulianus had pulled scout duty again; the wiry veteran was stood to one side of the farmer leaning on his spear. He straightened, as did the other veterans and the soldiers attached from the Third for that day, saluting Centurion Sirus as he approached.

"Century, halt!" Sirus barked before guiding his horse the last few paces towards the farmer.

Iulianus tipped a nod in Celer's direction, which he returned before the veteran's attention snapped back to the Centurion.

Celer had been taught the craft of diplomacy and negotiation from an early age as his class decreed. Yet here was a method of diplomacy he was sure his finely-spoken tutors never would have imagined happening.

Sirus walked his mare forward from his century until he towered above the farmer. He sat comfortably and looked past the farmer and his sons to where the legionaries stood, cloak splayed elegantly out behind him as if impervious to the chill morning air, looking more like a scion of a noble house than a lowly Imperial officer.

Sirus addressed Iulianus, the senior soldier amongst the scouts.

"Has our presence been questioned, Legionary?"

"No, Sir, they know why we're here," Iulianus replied, meeting Sirus's gaze.

"Do they have any Latin?"

Thinking the question addressed to him, the farmer replied in a broken accent, "Some Latin, Roman."

Iulianus ignored him and replied to his superior. "Some, Sir; barely enough to get by. Not much Greek, either."

Sirus continued to look past the farmer, whose face was growing red as the two Romans conversed in front of him. Celer recognised what the Senior Centurion was doing, the refusal to dismount, the casual air and dealing first with a common soldier were deliberate actions designed to establish a hierarchy to the negotiations. Sirus was the dominant figure, Iulianus and the other soldiers second and the farmer and his family firmly at the bottom.

"I don't suppose you know any of their barbarian language, legionary?"

Iulianus spat to one side. "Unfortunately I do, Sir."

"Excellent, you will translate my demands. This man and his family are in violation of a treaty between the people of Chieftain Theodoar and Theodosius, Emperor of the Romans. Under the terms of the treaty, habitation of this land is prohibited. By the rule of law, I have the right to confiscate all properties of those illegally occupying this land and demand that they leave immediately."

Iulianus hurriedly translated the Senior Centurion's words. The guttural Germanic tongue sounded harsh to Celer's ears.

The farmer listened angrily, glaring sullenly at Sirus. One of his sons spat as Iulianus spoke and shouted in words barely intelligible as Latin. "Roman law! Paah!" He undid his trousers and took a pace towards the mounted officer.

Sirus's horse took a step back as an arc of piss splashed about its hooves.

The centurion's gesture was minute but, in a heartbeat, one of the veteran soldiers had slammed the butt of his spear into the son's belly, dropping him, still urinating, to the ground. Swords and spears were levelled at the throats of the farmer and his other son who had raised his wood axe as his brother fell.

With razor-sharp steel hovering below his chin, the farmer shouted angrily at his son. The boy hesitated a moment, then one of the scouts rested the point of his sword at the base of his spine and the wood axe fell from his calloused hands.

Calmly, Sirus urged the horse forward a pace and continued speaking as if nothing had happened. "Emperor Theodosius is a merciful man. I have orders to resolve this matter with Chief Theodoar at his capital. Thanks to the Emperor, you have until I return in two days' time to leave this place. Should we find you here upon our return, you shall be removed by force."

Without waiting for a response from the farmer or his sons, Sirus turned his horse around. "Optio!"

Longus took a step forward. "Sir!"

"Have the men round up all livestock and foodstuffs; anything that cannot be carried away is to be destroyed."

"Yes, Sir. Sections one and two, see to the livestock. Sections three, four and five..."

Celer led his section past the glowering farmer who hauled his piss and dirt-stained son to his feet.

There were two cows behind the farmhouse, three pigs and a goat stood in a muddy pen beside them.

An ageing woman, skin turned a chestnut brown by the sun like the farmers, burst from the rear of the farmhouse when they began to urge the cattle out. Celer and Magnus met her with their shields and managed to force her back to the door as she pummelled the broad shields before her, screeching what Celer took to be curses in her own tongue.

Once the farmer's wife was barricaded inside, they turned to help the others with the livestock. Few of them, hailing largely from cities as they did, had ever handled large beasts other than horses. However, the cattle responded to the gentle prod of spear butts and ambled happily enough in the direction of the cohort, each guided by two legionaries.

The sows and goat were not so amiable. The men had to corral them in the corner of the pen and, even then, the goat nearly leapt the wooden fence in a bid for freedom. Priscus quickly hunted up some rope and they hog-tied all four.

As his animals were carried past him, the farmer began to spit angry words at the legionaries. Iulianus was still minding the men to make sure they did not try to intervene; the veteran clearly did not like whatever the farmer had said, for he struck him savagely in the face, knocking him to the ground.

By the time they left, the farm was a ruin. The legionaries had been ordered to burn the pens and small outbuildings and they had pulled thatch off the farmhouse to kindle their fires. The fields were transformed to muddy ruin. Little had managed to grow so early, so they piled the farmers tools and plough onto the flames. The woman's curses slowly turned to sobs as her home was pulled down around her and her bruised husband stood with his sons in silent fury as his livelihood burned about him. Several of the soldiers chatted happily as they went about their work but Celer found it hard to match their mood. For the first time, he questioned what he was doing here, out beyond the frontier, burning the homes of farmers so like those of the people who had helped him as he fled Rome.

He hardened himself to the woman's sobs. His tutors had taught him many times over the years the importance of Rome's treaties. He knew that vast swathes of the Empire had been won through such treaties, their peoples becoming Romanised and slowly incorporated into its structure. None of his tutors however had ever taught him this, the truth behind how such treaties were maintained. The cost people had to pay to ensure the safety of Roman lands.

They marched on, livestock now in tow alongside the mule train. They encountered many more small farms; some had clearly been established recently whilst others had been there a year or longer. Each time, Sirus led forth a different Century whilst Centurion Piso kept the rest of the Cohort out of sight. Each time, Iulianus translated the Senior Centurion's orders and each time they took all the food stores and cattle from the sullen farmers.

Only once was there blood-shed. One farm was home to a man and his wife and three daughters. The youngest was perhaps nine or ten but the oldest was a woman grown of about sixteen. When Sirus and the other officers had their backs turned, one of the legionaries grabbed the girl from behind, pulling her close to him. The girl cried out and struggled; her father heard the commotion and a thick-bladed hunting knife appeared in his hands as he threw himself at the legionary. Celer and his section heard the story later that night from one of the legionaries who had been there. Iulianus had turned, lighting fast, and thrown his own knife, near identical to the farmer's, burying the thick blade between the man's shoulder-blades.

The hysterical screams of the four women had been heard clearly in the small clearing where the cohort waited. Soldiers had jumped for their weapons as the farmer uttered his last gasping breaths, blood frothing on his lips.

Iulianus had yanked his blade form the farmer's back with disgust as Sirus turned on the legionary with terrible fury. The man had been stripped of his weapons and forced to march at the rear of the column with the promise of being whipped when the Cohort returned to Novae.

Just as dusk was settling in, they spied the distant sprawl of the Gepid's tribal capital, seat of Chieftain Theodoar. Many of the animals taken that day were slaughtered after the camp was erected. The rest were hobbled and left with the mules just beyond the camp's ditch with their own line of sentries.

Despite the sudden abundance of fresh food, the mood in the camp was tense. The day's deeds did not sit well with many alongside Celer and Sirus had ordered the watch doubled in case any tribesman chose to seek vengeance upon them.

Celer slept fitfully all night. In his dreams it was Decimus, the farmer who had taken he and Attianus in following the wolf attack in the Apennines, who stood before his farmhouse as ghostly legionaries led away his livestock and torched his buildings.

One faceless soldier grabbed Lucia, the girl whose stitches in Attianus's wounds had so impressed Timaeus; the girl's screams were so loud that Celer thought his head might burst. He saw Decimus turn, that stern face turning to fury, in his hand a long gleaming knife.

"No!" Celer cried out in the dream, charging forward to knock Decimus out the way, but it was too late. Cold steel burst from the farmer's chest and he crumbled into ash.

Furious, Celer turned to confront the thrower, expecting to see Iulianus. Yet it was not the wiry veteran but instead a nightmare in the scale armour of a scholae guardsmen. Suddenly afraid, Celer went for his sword but his arms were leaden and would not respond. Another armoured soldier appeared from the smoke of the burning farm and cruel laughter boomed out from the mail masks that hid their faces, filling the air as Lucia's screams turned to sobs.

The scholae advanced, bloodied swords in their armoured hands, and still Celer could not move.

Icy terror gripped him as the nightmarish pair raised their left hands and pulled the steel helms from their heads.

Flavianus the Elder stood before him, the same satisfied smile upon his face as when Varro and his family had been murdered. Beside him, eyes wide with a look that bordered on madness, was Horatius. The Prefect of Italy and the disgraced guardsmen raised their swords in unison, laughter growing all the louder, though their lips did not move.

Celer heard one more laboured sob from Lucia before the blades plunged down into his...

...chest. Celer sat bolt upright. It was black as pitch inside the tent and all around him his section-mates snored and mumbled in their sleep.

He put a clammy hand to his chest where the swords had pierced.

His skin was slick with sweat and growing cold quickly in the night air but there was no wound, only his heart pounding madly against his ribs.

His bedroll was soaked with sweat and he knew that sleep would not be easily forthcoming, so he grabbed his cloak from where it had been serving as a pillow and crawled forward, undoing the toggles that held the flaps of the tent shut.

The camp was as quiet as it ever got. Faint light in the east told him dawn was not far off so he knew he had slept most of the night.

Huddling into his cloak, he headed over to where a large pile of cut logs had been made after the camp had been built. He picked through the pile to find dryer wood to carry back. The others would welcome a fire already going when they were roused at dawn and he could save someone the long wait with the other sections as they queued for firewood.

The sentries acknowledged him with quiet greetings before turning back to the black landscape before them. Lonely lights could be seen to the north in the direction of the Gepid town and Celer imagined their own sentries eyeing the small pricks of light from the fires of the camp.

He busied himself in starting the fire, adding the new logs to still-hot embers from the night before. When the flames crackled into life, he sat back on a log serving as a camp stool and watched the sun rise above the palisade of the marching camp.

The sky turned through purple to pink, then a blood red as the sun breached the horizon. He added more wood to the fire and huddled in his cloak, the dream fresh and vivid in his mind's eye.

Ever a practical man, his father had never set much stock in dreams; it was to his mother he had always gone too as a child, frightened in the night.

Marcella would walk her son back to his room, telling him everything would be alright, that dreams came from the gods. If they were bad then they served as a warning and the bad things could be prevented and if the dream was good, she would look down on him with a loving smile and say, then it was simply something to look forward to.

Thinking of his mother filled him with anger and sadness all at once. She would have loved to see this sunrise, Celer thought; she would have appreciated the beauty of it in this land beyond the Empire.

"Up before the dawn, with a fire already built?" Priscus said quietly from behind him. "Surely I must have found the woman of my dreams."

Celer turned as his friend stretched and shivered in the cold morning air.

"I fear the only women you will ever find will be in your dreams," he replied mockingly.

Priscus adopted a grave face as he looked about the camp. "Fat chance of finding one here. Not a civilised woman, anyway."

"Perhaps this is the best place for you, then," said Celer as he filled their cooking pot with oats and water from a skin. "No civilised woman would have you."

Priscus trimmed the bark from a stick with his dagger and stirred their breakfast with it. "You know, I have often found educated men to be ruder than others."

"You are an educated man," Celer pointed out, to which Priscus flicked water at him from the pot in response.

Priscus did not ask why he had awoken so early. For a moment, Celer thought about telling his friend of the nightmare before swiftly dismissing the idea. Dreams were a subject for women and priests, not soldiers.

Between them, they soon had the section's morning meal ready as the others crawled from the tent as the horns announced the dawn call.

# XVI

After a hurried breakfast, Sirus led his century from the camp along with the half-century of veterans from the second cohort. Celer saw that Iulianus and the others did not carry their spears and shields, instead wearing only their swords, and each man carried a hunting bow and two quivers of arrows.

It was barely two miles to the Gepid town and the men carried only their weapons and the walled town soon loomed large in front of them.

They momentarily lost sight of the town in a low defile a mile from the main gate. Here, the fields were cross-cut with ditches that drained the fields into a small muddy river, spanned by a short wooden bridge.

Centurion Decimus barked orders and his half-century broke off from the marching column and Celer watched as the veterans quickly concealed themselves either side of the road.

A party of horsemen were waiting for them as they crested the brow of the last hill. Tall walls of finely dressed stone rose into the sky behind the Gepid lancers who sat still as statues in mail and tall iron helms, with horsehair plumes fluttering in the wind alongside snapping pennants on their long spears.

They were barely distinguishable from Roman cavalry, Celer thought as Sirus marched the century towards them. Up close, he could see the helmets were more conical than any Roman cavalry he had seen and, in place of the long sword all Romans carried, these men wore a variety of swords and long-handled axes; one of them even carried a brutal looking maul strapped to his saddle.

The captain of the lancers trotted out to meet Sirus with one of his men behind him. He bore no lance himself, but his armour and tack were richly decorated, Celer could just make of the figures of wolves and bears amongst strange geometric patterns and throughout it all were horses of gold and silver. His shield bore two black horses rearing at one another and when the wind snapped the pennant at the top of his companion's lance straight, Celer could see a black horse against the white fabric.

Sirus halted the century and rode forward, accompanied by the Cohort's standard bearer. The gilded eagle gleamed atop the staff in the morning sun.

The four men eyed each other in silence for a moment before Sirus spoke.

"Greetings, I am Senior Centurion Sirus of the Third Cohort, First Legion of the army of His Imperial Excellency, Theodosius Emperor of the Roman people. I am here to discuss..."

"I know why you are here, Roman," The Gepid captain replied in perfect Latin, spitting to the side of his horse at the last word. "Word of your advance from the frontier arrived ahead of you. I have been sent to escort you to my father."

"Your father is Chieftain Theodoar?"

"King Theodoar," corrected the captain forcefully, "is my father. I am Ardaric, Captain of the King's guards. Come!" He wheeled his horse about. "My father is waiting for you."

The century followed Ardaric and his lancers into the town. They were met at the gates by a challenge from the archers on the walls above. Ardaric shouted back in the harsh tongue Celer was beginning to recognise as Gothic and the gates swung open instantly. As they marched through, Celer could not help but notice the grim-eyed men atop the walls armed with bows and spears who stared down at them.

Borus, who led the section to his left, had noticed them as well and the two men shared an uneasy look as they followed Sirus down the paved street.

The town was tiny in the eyes of one who had grown up in Rome, yet the paved streets and stone buildings reminded him of his home city and gave a small sense of comfort. He even saw a much-eroded bust of Vesta on a street corner. The goddess had guarded Rome and her citizens for over a thousand years and Celer murmured a hurried prayer for her to protect them as they marched under her faded gaze, for he felt in need of divine protection as the marched past the hostile faces of the town's inhabitants. Their ancestors may have been called Roman once, but these people showed no kindness towards the soldiers of their former empire.

King Theodoar met them in the town forum, which, from the smell and the piles of dung, now evidently served as the town's livestock market.

The king was seated on the rostrum, the platform built from stone that the magistrate of the town would once have delivered public announcements from.

Ardaric dismounted and climbed the worn steps to stand beside his father.

Theodoar was an old man; white hair hung past his shoulders and a trimmed white beard covered a lined and weather-worn face. Yet he sat straight as his guardsmen's lances on his throne, clad in mail and leather armour more gorgeously decorated than his son's. A silver helmet with black horsetail plume rested on his lap beneath a gnarled hand.

Sirus dismounted and bowed stiffly towards the king.

"King Theodoar, I bring greetings from His Excellency, Emperor Theodosius of the Roman Empire."

Theodoar eyed the Centurion up and down.

"It is customary to kneel before a King," he said in lightly accented Latin. Sirus frowned but before he could reply the King continued. "Not that I expected a Roman to kneel; apart from your race's innate arrogance you have all seem to have an inherent dislike of kings."

"We have learnt from past experiences, your Highness," replied Sirus coolly.

"Ha!" Theodoar snorted. "To be ruled by an Emperor is much better than a King, I see. Perhaps I should change my title?"

Sirus ignored the jibe. "King Theodoar, I have travelled to your capital on the order of Emperor Theodosius to discuss matters regarding the treaty between the Empire and your Kingdom. Might we discuss these matters in private?" He looked about the forum where crowds of citizens watched silently.

The king shook his head slowly as the centurion spoke.

"We might have done so, Centurion, had you and your men marched here first rather than prowl the border lands like wolves, burning homes and murdering my people!"

There must have been people amongst the crowds with enough Latin to translate for, moments after the king delivered his tirade, the crowd erupted into angry shouts and Celer and the other legionaries had to force themselves not to flinch from the violence in their tones.

Sirus waited until the noise had receded before speaking in the same level tone as before.

"I acted in accordance with the law; those farms were in violation of a treaty that you signed and that you are paid handsomely to uphold. The man's death was regrettable, but he attacked one of my men, an act punishable by death. The legionary involved will be severely punished, you have my word."

King Theodoar's face grew red as Sirus spoke; powerful old hands gripped the arms of his throne.

"Your word!" he shouted. "I piss on your word, Roman. You say you acted under law; your law ends at the Danube. This is my land and they are my people and you have no right to act as such!"

"You are paid vast sums to keep your people away from the frontier zone," Sirus began again.

"It is no vast sum," growled the king in response. "What use is your Emperor's gold when the weather turns and there is not enough land to feed my people. Why should I deny them land their ancestors farmed, with plentiful timber and game? I think gold would flow aplenty should we have access to the great river and sea beyond."

The king's words raised cheers from the mob surrounding the legionaries.

Sirus waited once again until the noise has quietened enough for him to be heard.

"I have been ordered to remind you that trade stations have been established specifically for your merchants to use along the Danube."

"Stations where my people are only permitted under armed escort and are paid barely half of what their goods are worth whilst your Imperial brokers sell them on for double!" retorted the king.

"His Imperial Excellency understands your displeasure," said Sirus, raising his hands to calm the Gepid king. "The Emperor requires you to adhere to the current frontier but, in a gesture of good faith, he will build three more trade stations for your people to use and will increase his annual gift of silver to you by one third of its current amount."

Theodoar shook his head immediately. "These terms will not do," he said angrily, "not after the insults you have offered me by your actions. I demand the border lands be reduced by half in size so my people can farm and hunt in them and I want access to the river so we might establish a trade post of our own. Give me this, and the life of the man who killed my subject, and your Emperor and I shall remain allies."

Celer was suddenly fearful for Iulianus and was glad the veteran was safely outside the walls of the town.

Centurion Sirus shook his head. "I am afraid I cannot accept those terms. The legionary responsible for causing your subject's death is a Roman citizen and will be held responsible for his action under Roman military law. Furthermore, the Emperor will not permit the size of the frontier zone to change, nor will you be permitted to establish a base upon the Danube. I can offer you five new trade stations and an increase in the gift of silver by one half of its current amount, but no more."

Deathly silence met his words, though Celer thought he could hear the hushed whispers amongst the crowd as the centurion's words were translated.

"And if I were to refuse your Emperor's offer?" asked the king.

Sirus looked him dead in the eye, "Then, by the order of Emperor Theodosius, my men and I shall finish patrolling the frontier, removing any settlers that we find. Should we continue to discover new settlements then the Emperor shall consider it a termination of the treaty and a declaration of war."

An angry murmur swept the forum and Celer gripped the haft of his spear tightly, ready to turn to meet the crowd. Behind him he heard the shuffling of hobnailed boots as the rest of the century prepared themselves.

Instead, Theodoar laughed a great bellowing laugh that echoed around the forum and off the old Roman walls surrounding it.

"I think your Emperor cares for you not," he said, panting slightly when his laughter had subsided. "He must know I would not allow you to march across my lands, burning my farms, and do nothing."

"I cannot speak for the Emperor," said Sirus coldly, "but my men and I shall do as we are commanded."

Then he commands you to die," snarled the king, leaning forwards on his throne. "I have heard reports from each farmstead you have sacked; always just one unit of foot with a few held back in reserve. How many men do you have? Barely two hundred, I imagine. I have as many and more in my household guard alone." He indicated Ardaric and the other lancers who stood behind him. His son and the other guards chuckled at this and Celer saw their hands rested on the handles of swords and axes whilst others gripped spears tightly.

"Rumours had reached me of the dwindling strength of the great Empire, though I see your arrogance has not diminished."

With a grunt the king rose to his feet, gleaming silver helm clasped to his side.

"Should any of your men reach your precious frontier alive, tell your Emperor that I accept his treaty no longer; my people will take the land that belongs to them and the Danube with it!"

His people roared approval and the crowd about the century surged forward.

"Square!" bellowed Sirus above the din. "Form square!"

Training took over instinctively and the century quickly formed a compact hollow square. The front two ranks raised their shields and levelled their spears at the Gepids.

The broad shields and the razor-sharp spearheads halted the rush and the people spat and cursed the legionaries.

Theodoar strode down from the rostrum with Ardaric and the other lancers behind him.

The King raised his hand and Ardaric roared out something in his own tongue and the crowd receded at once.

"I will not have bloodshed in my streets," the King said as he approached Sirus. The Centurion stood rock solid as the aged ruler stopped before him. They eyed one another for a moment before the king smiled and nodded towards the main gate.

"Go, take my answer back to your Emperor." He stepped in close to the Roman officer, voice dropped so that only they could hear. "Pray that I never see you again."

They marched in the square formation, going a snail's pace through the streets to the gate. Sirus rode in the centre, eyes fixed ahead, ignoring the nocked arrows of the watchmen on the walls.

Once free of the town Sirus, quickly ordered them to form a column and head for the camp at the double pace. The sun had risen almost to its zenith in the sky and a cold wind blew across the fields from the north, but the men were soon sweating under their armour and the weight of their weapons.

They had just reached the foot of the hill where Ardaric and his lancers had met them an hour before when the air was rent by a ferocious roar from the Gepid settlement. Sirus urged his mount to the side of the road and turned in the saddle to look behind the small column. Several of the legionaries began to turn as well before Optio Longus's voice cracked like a whip.

"Eyes front!" he bellowed at them. "Come on; move yourselves, faster, faster!"

Fit as they were, the soldiers were panting by the time they crested the hill. Behind them, the air was filled with the thunder of hooves and cries of men and mounts.

Ahead of them, Celer could see Centurion Decimus standing alone on the short wooden bridge, sword in hand and urging them on with the other.

As the men reached the bridge, Sirus turned them about to face the enemy as their comrades streamed past. Sextus was forcing his way past Celer when the horsemen crested the brow of the hill.

First to appear were the fluttering pennants at the end of their long lances, then the horsehair plumes of the heavily armoured riders and the powerful mounts beneath them. Celer recognised the twin black horses on Ardaric's shield as the lancers lowered their gleaming points and thundered towards the century.

Centurion Sirus roared out the command to receive cavalry and the legionaries instinctively tightened their formation. The front rank narrowed until their shields overlapped and they thrust their spears over the rims towards the enemy. The second rank raised their shields to cover the front rank's heads and drew back their spears in an overhead grip.

"Hold, men!" Sirus roared from behind them. The discipline instilled in them over the winter months was such that even that simple command halted any who had begun to edge backwards.

Celer tightened his grip on his shield, heart thumping wildly in his chest from their forced dash over the hill. His mouth felt dry as parchment when he tried to swallow and he had a sudden, overwhelming urge to piss.

Fear gripped his bowels as the Gepid horsemen formed into a wedge without slowing their pace and hurtled down the slope towards them. The wild cries in their harsh tongue grew louder as they bore down on the First Century, confident in the imminent destruction of the small cluster of Romans.

Then the horses stumbled.

Or at least so it seemed to Celer.

One moment the road before him was a surging tide, the next it was awash with screaming horses and men. One of the riders in the point of the wedge was thrown forward as his horse fell beneath him. The man hit the ground hard, lance shattering beneath him. His senseless body smashed limply into the shields of the front rank, leaving a bloody smear on the road surface. The charge collapsed as chaos ensued. Riders continued to pour over the hill only to encounter the flailing limbs of the downed lancers and their horses and the milling ranks of those who reigned in behind them.

Then Sirus was screaming for the century to advance and Celer was swept forward as the legionaries screamed their battle cries and rushed the Gepids. Amongst the writhing bodies, Celer saw feathered arrow shafts. Out of the corner of his eye he saw one of the veterans of the Second Cohort rise from a ditch with an arrow nocked. The veteran drew and sighted quickly, then loosed his arrow into the broiling melee before dropping back out of sight.

Not all the lancers had been killed as the charge collapsed. A blood-stained rider staggered towards the legionaries with a sword in his left hand, right arm pinned to his side by a broken arrow. A spear thrust out from the advancing wall of shields and the rider went down, as did a screaming lancer whose shattered legs were bent at unnatural angles beneath him.

The legionaries kept a solid line as they charged into the horsemen. The lancers who had recovered or still remained ahorse threw themselves at the shield wall to no avail. The broad shields soaked up their blows as the razor-sharp spears flickered out at them like the tongues of a monstrous viper, boring into the press.

Celer's world shrank to a few feet before him and either side. His breathing sounded loud in his ears, amplified by the bowl of his shield and the small ear holes in his helmet. Peering over the rim of his shield, he pushed forward into the chaos. His arms seemed to have eyes of their own, shield rising to stop blows he never saw coming, spear darting forth into the scrum, blade dripping crimson as the century ploughed into the mounted men.

A rider charged him, a longsword flashing as it hacked at his head. Celer ducked, trusting the slash would be stopped by Priscus's raised shield behind him, thrusting his spear towards the Gepid's torso. The sword struck Priscus's shield boss with a loud clang that rang bright and clear for a moment in the tumult of the battle raging about them.

Celer's thrust took the lancer in the chest; the force of the rider's charge drove the point through the coat of overlapping iron disks he wore.

With a bloody hiss the rider dropped his sword and shield and tried to draw the spear from his side. His horse shied away from the advancing shields and the Gepid tipped from the saddle, ripping the spear from Celer's hand.

Shock at what he had just done almost froze him before his training kicked in.

Cursing, he quickly drew his sword and slashed at the legs of the next charging horse. The screaming animal tipped, reared, and fell backwards. Celer finished the trapped rider as another legionary silenced the horse.

The Roman advance slowed as a mound of bodies, man and horse alike, built up in front of them. Sirus and Longus urged them onward but the pause gave the Gepids a chance to reorganise.

Miraculously, Ardaric had survived the initial charge. His mount bled from cuts to its chest and a broken shaft sprouted from its haunch, but the prince remained unharmed. Rallying his horsemen, he led another charge as the Roman front line struggled to cross the corpses piled before them.

Once again, the world trembled to the thunder of hooves. Celer instinctively dropped to a crouch as he struggled to climb over a dead horse that lay atop its rider. A lance point hammered into his shield and scored over its angled surface. The force was enough to slam the shield back into his body, sending him sprawling backwards. Priscus and another second ranker were downed as he tumbled into their legs and only the barrier provided by the dead horse saved all three from being trampled.

The charge threw back the Roman line, for a moment.

Then, training honed over four centuries of near ceaseless conflict came to the fore and the First Century reformed its line as Longus and Sirus cursed and kicked the men back into a line. Those in the third and fourth ranks stepped over their stunned and dead comrades to meet the Gepid horsemen.

A deadly rain of arrows continued to pour into the flanks of the Gepid horse but several of the royal bodyguard carried bows as well as their long lances and several of the veterans of the Second Cohort tumbled back into the ditches, never to rise.

Struggling to his feet, Celer spat a glob of blood onto the rutted road. He hauled Priscus to his feet and retrieved his sword from where it had fallen. The century was still locked in deadly combat with Theodoar's royal guard and seemed to be holding their own for the moment. Dead from both sides lay strewn across the road and in the ditches either side. Blood was running down the channels and staining the waters a rusty red where they emptied into the small river.

Iulianus and the other veterans were falling back to the bridge, pursued by small groups of Gepids who jumped their horses across the ditches to try and run the legionaries down.

Armed only with swords and bows, the soldiers quickly fell back before the armoured riders.

The main Gepid body was slowly being forced back; the horsemen were ineffective in such a confined space where the broad shields and tight formation of the Romans could easily repel them.

The last of the veterans made it to the bridge but now the horsemen who had pursued them began massing into two large groups, poised to gain the road behind the First Century and attack the Romans in the rear.

Centurion Decimus saw the danger. He quickly organised his remaining men to fire their last arrows into the two groups of riders whilst one of the men sounded the recall on a trumpet.

Celer saw Sirus's crested helmet turn at the sharp blast and heard orders shouted. The sounds of fighting quickly died away as the century slowly disengaged, keeping their shields and weapons facing the Gepid cavalry.

Ardaric and his men let them go. Many of the horsemen were breathing heavily; they and their horses bled from dozens of wounds. Celer watched as one rider slipped from his horses back as the wounded animal tried to limp away from the legionaries.

Keeping a wary eye on the Romans, the rider held the horse's bridle and said something to it, rubbing its face affectionately with his bloody hand. His heavy axe flashed in the sunlight and the horse collapsed at his feet.

"Optio, form the men up for a fighting withdrawal," commanded Sirus, sounding as though they were back on the parade ground at Novae, though his arms and sword were drenched in gore and a blood dripped from the rim of his helmet.

"Sir!"

Optio Longus had not fared the fighting as well as his commanding officer. A red stain was already spreading through the hastily tied bandage on his sword arm and blood poured from his broken nose. The optio showed no hint of pain as he went about dressing the ranks, pushing and pulling the legionaries into their positions.

Celer shouldered his way through the century to his place in the front rank. The men stank of sweat and blood and more than once did he smell the sharp tang that told him a man had pissed himself.

Reformed, the century began to back away from the enemy. Hobnailed boots clattered against the worn planks of the bridge as they crossed the river whose waters now ran red with blood from the fighting.

It was slow going; the legionaries kept their shields facing the Gepids and Optio Longus had to keep dressing the lines as the terrain forced the century to bunch up.

Ardaric's men watched them go. The few with bows loosed some shafts after them but the broad shields rose and the arrows thudded home harmlessly.

They retraced their route from that morning. The road wound through the low hills, its sides formed by ditches or walls, and the fields either side were likewise crisscrossed, preventing the cavalry from encircling them.

The Gepids followed from a distance.

Twice more, Ardaric led charges against them and each time Centurion Sirus bellowed the order to receive cavalry and the withdraw would halt, spears would be passed to the fore, and the legionaries would brace their shields.

The Gepid horsemen had learned their lesson, however, and soon the royal guards became content to hound the Roman's' withdrawal, leading lightning-fast charges in to launch spears and arrows at the legionaries before turning and fleeing before the Romans could retaliate, knowing that soon the land would flatten and open up again.

Celer survived the charges. He had lost his own spear at the bridge so one had been passed forward to him. That spear shattered in the second attack Ardaric led, breaking off in the chest of a black stallion as its rider, growing overconfident, drove his lance into the compacted soldiers.

After that, there were no more spears, so he marched with his sword drawn. Around ten legionaries had fallen and many were wounded; the most severely wounded limped in the centre of the column or were carried by comrades less seriously hurt.

To bolster the ranks, Centurion Decimus had merged his veterans with the First Century; his men carried shields taken from the dead or those too wounded to carry them.

The cold wind from the morning died away as the men marched on into the afternoon. The spring sunshine was warm and the legionaries sweated under the weight of their armour.

Ardaric and his men walked their horses along well out of bowshot, so Celer took a hasty swig from his canteen; he was sorely tempted to drain the lot but the day was far from over and he did not know how long they must march so he stoppered the half-full canteen.

Worryingly, the land was beginning to flatten out. As new to warfare as he was, Celer had ridden horses for most of his life and knew that the more open ground favoured the cavalry over the Roman infantry. Worse, a steady trickle of horsemen had been arriving all afternoon. They were not as heavily armoured as the royal guard nor did they all bear the tall lances but nearly a hundred or so filled Ardaric's ranks, easily replacing the few he had lost.

With their numbers increased and the ground now turning in their favour, the Gepids grew bolder. They began spreading out until a long line faced the retreating Romans. Then the line split. Ardaric kept the majority of his lancers with him in the centre whilst the remainder broke into two flanking groups mixed in with the new arrivals.

Glancing over their shoulders, the Romans could see the outline of their camp on its low rise above the plain; small shapes that could only be sentries moved along its earth ramparts but no trumpets sounded to signal they had been seen.

Celer couldn't understand it. They must see them! How could they not? From the camp's ramparts the century would be clearly visible, sunlight reflecting off their helmets, stained even as they were with dirt and blood.

The Gepids would be even more visible. Several hundred men and horses moving like three angry swarms of bees about to converge on the small column.

The silence from the camp took its toll on the legionarie's' nerves. Men who had faced down cavalry charges began to lose their courage. They started to shuffle quicker, looking back over their shoulders at the safety of the camp more and more and the column become disjointed.

"Steady, men!" called out Centurion Sirus, with none of his usual bark and even Longus tried to steady them with calming words none of them would have dreamt to hear from his mouth.

The officers' words helped for a short while but then war-horns blared and a great cry went up from the Gepid horsemen as they surged forward.

"Century, halt!" cried Sirus.

"Form square and prepare to receive cavalry! Wounded to the centre!"

A few men were slow in taking their positions; one or two glanced up at the camp behind them as if thinking of making a run for it.

Optio Longus saw their looks. "You men are on a charge!" he screamed at them. "I'll have you digging latrines until your balls hang past your knees! Now get in formation!"

Wincing under the ferocity of the battered optio's glare, the shamed soldiers quickly hurried to their places.

Celer had thought the first attack by the bridge to be terrifying but this was something else.

Everywhere he looked there was a wall of charging horses, their riders blowing war-horns and bellowing in their strange tongue as they waved their weapons above their heads.

He pressed himself into the bowl of his battered shield, Priscus's held reassuringly above his head and held his sword ready to thrust.

The ground shook and the very air seemed to shiver to the pounding of hooves. Somewhere in the small square of Romans a legionary was uttering a relentless stream of the filthiest curses Celer had ever heard; others were hurriedly saying prayers in half a dozen tongues to half a dozen gods.

Celer thought he should pray himself, ask Mars to guide his sword and Jupiter to give him the courage to face death bravely with no fear. But all these thoughts were overwhelmed by bitter anger that he would not live to avenge his parents. That the men who had murdered them would live in power and luxury whilst he lay dead on a cracked and broken road in a land long abandoned by Rome.

Intent as they were on destroying the Romans, the Gepids recognised the dangers of charging the broad shields of the legionaries head on. On the first charge the three groups slashed past the compact square, arrows and thrown spears slammed into the shields and shrieks and cries of pain rang out as men were struck.

The Romans had too few spears and arrows to retaliate effectively so they all crouched behind their meagre protection and tried to weather the storm.

Many of the lancers rode right up to the small wall of shields, risking their mounts' legs to the protruding blades to drive their long lances into the static targets.

The power behind the thrusts knocked men off their feet.

Borus, who crouched at Celer's side, died as a lance point drove through the battered and hacked surface of his shield and pierced deeply through his mail into his guts.

The section leader's body was unceremoniously shoved out of the square and another legionary pushed forward to take his place.

When a second lancer charged along their face, Celer and the others hacked out with their swords and the Gepid's horse fell screaming. The lancer lay wounded a spear length away from the square but none dared leave the formation to finish him off.

In the end, his own countrymen ended his cries as riders continued to thunder past the square, regardless of their own injured they trampled.

Then, the storm passed.

Screams and groans of wounded men could be heard. The air stank of faeces and blood and the ground surrounding the square was black and churned; corpses lay strewn about it where riders had ridden within striking distance.

Celer peered out over the rim of his shield and saw the enemy reforming about two hundred paces away. They were quieter than before, he realised; so close to victory, they should have been cheering and eager.

Yet there was a haste in the way they turned their horses about and readied their weapons and then he heard the unmistakable noise of heavily armoured men running.

The rear side of the square were the first to start cheering.

"It's the Cohort!" one legionary cried.

"Gods above, we're saved!" another shouted.

Centurion Piso trotted at the head of the relief column as they hurried to the aid of the battered century. He and the other officers bellowed out orders as the other centuries formed up in front of the bloody square.

The Centurion of the Second Century hid his admiration behind a mask of stern professionalism as he broke off from the head of the column and approached the square, assailed by the cheers of the remnants of the First Century and Centurion Decimus's veterans.

Senior Centurion Sirus emerged from the bloody ranks of his men, sword and armour streaked in gore.

"You're a sight for sore eyes, Centurion," said Sirus, holding out his sword hand.

Piso clasped the offered forearm with no hesitation; no seasoned soldier was bothered by a bit of blood.

"Wouldn't miss it, Sir!" he said cheerfully, eyeing the massing horsemen beyond the fresh line of Romans.

"The plan seems to be working well, Sir?"

Sirus nodded. "They took the bait well enough; King Theodoar was furious, as predicted, though I did not anticipate them being able to muster so many horsemen so quickly."

"Matters not, Sir," said Piso confidently, "the men won't let you down."

"No, I think they will do quite well. Let's hope Prince Ardaric does not think the same; our orders were to destroy the core of Theodoar's forces and we will have no better opportunity than this."

Behind the Centurions, the survivors of the square continued to cheer and shout insults at the Gepid horsemen. The emotional relief of finding themselves still alive caused even the quietest of the men to lose all their normal restraint.

They had little time to enjoy their celebrations, however.

Eager to catch the Romans before they could fully form up, Ardaric led his cavalry in a massed charge. One again the Gepids split into three bodies, forcing the Cohort to form a hurried arc in front of the First Century.

The horsemen had used up their missiles on the square so they formed wedges and charged home with lances, swords and axes, screaming their battle cries in an attempt to shatter the Roman line.

Fearsome as the waves of horsemen were, the Romans' morale was buoyed by the survival of their First Century. Many also sought vengeance for their fallen comrades and they stood in a solid wall, weapons poised.

Spears flew as the Gepids thundered home. Their front rank rippled as horses and men were struck, then the wave broke against the shields of the cohort.

# XVII

It was late in the afternoon by the time the killing was done. Men stalked grim-faced through the battleground with bloodied swords, ending the cries of their enemies and calling out to the stretcher bearers where they found one of their own.

Celer limped amongst the piles of dead. He found a horse with a shattered foreleg and a spear buried in its back. The creature was kicking pitifully with its uninjured foreleg, eyes wide with pain and terror. He held its head and spoke soothingly as he raised the tip of his sword to the back of its skull and the eyes rolled towards him. Was it something else he saw in them, incomprehension perhaps? What had it done to deserve this fate?

He had no answers for it so he leant his weight into the blade and watched the life fade from its eyes.

A hushed groan made him straighten up from the horse. A Gepid horseman lay trapped beneath a dead horse, perhaps his own.

One side of his face was smeared with dirt and blood, the eye sealed shut, but the other stared at him.

Celer stood and turned towards him but the rider did not move apart from the ragged gasps that made his chest rise and fall rapidly. The man was lying on his right side so Celer placed his blade tip in his armpit where there was no armour, the point aimed at his heart. Still the Gepid did not move, nor did he make a sound; his one eye continued to stare.

Celer thought he saw the same look he had seen in the horse's eyes, fear, pain and questions. Why me? Why here? Why now? He doubted the man spoke Latin but he could see the questions all the same. He had read once that the eyes were gateways to a person's inner self and thoughts and all eyes spoke the same language; they could not lie.

He took a firm grip on the sword pommel but he could not find it in him to drive it home. Somehow, it was harder than the horse. In battle he had not had time to think when killing other men; it was either him or them. This was different though, somehow wrong.

Footsteps halted a short way from him and he looked up.

Iulianus stood leaning heavily on a bloodied spear. Through a blood-stained tear in his trousers Celer could see the white of a linen bandage.

"You'd be doing him a kindness, lad," he nodded to the motionless rider.

"Feels wrong," said Celer looking back down at the man. His voice sounded strained and cracked.

The veteran nodded and looked about the battle site. Already crows and ravens were hopping amongst the dead. Soon more birds would come and, at night, all manner of creatures would be feasting on the fallen.

"Nothing right about it, lad," he said gruffly before looking back to Celer. "Now don't make him suffer any longer and pray that if the time comes, someone will be willing to do you the same honour."

Celer listened to him walk away, one footstep heavier than the other.

His father has spoken often about honour but he doubted he had ever envisioned this. Nothing felt very honourable right now.

He took a deep breath and slid the blade into the rider's chest.

The horseman gasped then let out a rattling breath; his one eye remained fixed on Celer's. Before the eye glazed over, Celer thought he saw something that might have been thanks in the Gepid's stare.

It was nightfall by the time the dead were buried. Sirus sent men to bring the carts they had taken from the farmers down from the encampment on the hill. They transported the Roman wounded up to the camp before rumbling back down the hill to carry the dead to the burial site.

There were too few trees nearby to build pyres big enough for all the dead so they excavated two huge pits. The work was quickened by pressing the forty or so captives – men who had avoided wounds severe enough to earn them the merciful blades of the victors - into service.

The Gepid dead were stripped of anything of use and worth by the legionaries and thrown unceremoniously into one of the pits.

With their own dead the Romans took greater care. Any equipment was removed so that it could be reused again. Personal effects were taken from the bodies and entrusted to the Cohort's standard bearer who would guard them until the Cohort returned to Novae. There, the belongings would be distributed in accordance with any wills that the fallen may have made before the Cohort marched.

Carts were dispatched to the bridge on the way to the Gepid capital, escorted by two centuries should King Theodoar send out another force. They returned as the Romans began burying their dead whilst the captured Gepids shovelled soil over the bodies of their own comrades.

They bodies were laid out with the heads pointing west and the feet to the east, the army, after all, was a Christian institution now. Close friends whispered hurried prayers for anyone who held to other gods, performing the necessary rituals as best they could.

Sirus and the other officers turned a blind eye; any man who died for the Empire deserved to be buried with whatever rites he wanted, in their eyes.

The First Century had been placed on sentry duty whilst the other centuries dug the graves in shifts. Celer stood looking west, watching the sunset turn the sky red.

He was exhausted. Every part of him ached, worse than anything he had experienced before. His left leg was seizing up and he shifted a little to try and ease the tightness in his knee.

"Legionary Celer!"

He turned to see Optio Longus walking towards him, face bruised and swelling visibly now.

"Sir!" Celer saluted as best he could but it must have looked stiff because Longus waved his hand.

"At ease, legionary." He stepped towards him a pace. "It's time."

Celer nodded, grim faced. "Yes, Sir."

He followed the Optio towards the graves. The Gepid pit had been backfilled and tamped down. The prisoners were slumped in heaps, filthy and stripped of their armour and surrounded by cold-faced legionaries.

They walked past them all to the edge of the Roman burial pit where Celer's section waited.

Two bodies lay wrapped in cloaks at their feet. The others said nothing as Celer approached; there were no words for how they felt.

Quietly they arranged themselves around the body nearest to the grave, three either side. The shrouded body was shorter than the other, Quintus.

The stocky Syrian was lifted carefully onto their shoulders, aches temporarily ignored, and carried down the trampled ramp that lead into the grave. They placed him carefully down before walking back up for their next friend.

Cinna was bigger than Quintus, taller and with thicker arms and shoulders. His father had been a stonemason, Celer knew. Work had been hard to find, though, and stone masonry skills were appreciated in the army, Cinna had told them all.

Yet it would be another stonemason who would fashion the memorial they would erect back in Novae for them both, Celer thought sadly.

The six legionaries stood above the bodies, laid out side by side.

Pulvillus, Sextus, Priscus and Magnus said the Christian rites for Cinna. Then stood in respectful silence as Symmachus knelt beside Quintus and prayed in a language none of them had heard before.

When he had finished and risen, Celer knelt down and tucked a coin onto the fold of each cloak. As much as he respected their beliefs, he couldn't let his friends go without paying their fare to Charon.

The Roman grave took much longer to fill, though there were less of them to bury. The grave was backfilled by torchlight and Sirus led the eulogy for the fallen legionaries. Then the rest of the Cohort marched back to the fortified camp in a flickering sombre procession.

# XVIII

Morning came all too soon.

The Cohort rose to a grey drizzle that did little to lighten the men's spirits. Few had slept well during the night, each man tormented by his own thoughts and nightmares of the battle and the loss of close friends.

Throughout the night the cries and groans of wounded men could be heard throughout the camp.

The most severely wounded had been taken to a makeshift hospital in the centre of the camp, presided over by the Cohort surgeon and his assistants.

The walking wounded had been patched up by their section-mates or the surgeon and sent back to their tents. Celer could see them emerging from their tents to the morning summons, struggling with their armour or weapons, limbs or heads bandaged, wincing at every movement.

Celer felt their pain.

Overnight his left leg had swollen around the knee joint and his whole body was covered in bruises. Any skin that had not been protected by his armour was covered in nicks and cuts; the fresh scabs sent needles of pain into his flesh as they broke open with his movements.

His section mates were sullen and quiet. All of them were battered and bruised and Sextus had a bad gash along his jaw line that the surgeon had stitched the night before. Celer helped him remove the soiled bandaged, trying not to stare at the ragged wound that would no doubt heal into a vicious-looking scar and helped him to re-bandage it.

As they ate breakfast over a smoky fire, Celer could see the anguish in Symmachus's eyes. He knew that the Cappadocian had been particularly close to Quintus; the pair had often spent their evenings swapping stories of home and had taken comfort in both coming from the lands of the far Eastern Empire.

They were scraping their bowls clean when the call to arms sounded out across the camp, swiftly taken up by other sentries.

At once, the legionaries snatched up their weapons and jammed their helmets on their heads before moving to their assigned positions at the camp's ramparts.

King Theodoar rode at the head of a column of mixed foot and horse, maybe four hundred men, Celer thought as he took his position.

Sirus and the other officers were already on the rampart watching the King's advance. When the Gepids came within arrow range Sirus dismissed his officers to their stations, leaving him alone with Optio Longus and Centurion Decimus.

Theodoar raised his hand and his men halted. With arms spread wide to show he was not armed, the Gepid King rode forward, followed closely by a small group of followers bearing banners emblazoned with the twin horses.

"Optio." Sirus did not take his eyes off Theodoar, who had halted halfway between his force and the Cohort's camp.

"Sir?"

"Fetch the prisoner."

Longus saluted. "Right away, Sir."

Sirus looked out at the Gepids a moment more. Out of the corner of his eye, Celer thought he saw a faint smile play about his commander's lips.

"Legionary Celer!"

"Sir?" Celer turned to his superior and snapped to attention, ignoring his body's protest.

"Your section with me."

"Yes, Sir!"

The others responded without hesitation, wheeling as one and following their Centurion off the rampart and towards the camp entrance.

Centurion Decimus and a section of his veterans, Iulianus included, marched with them out to face Theodoar's party.

The King was angry, Celer saw. He shifted constantly in his saddle, hands clenching and unclenching as the Romans approached. His followers too were similarly agitated. They were all old men, with beards streaked with grey and gnarled hands gripping the tall lances from which the pennants fluttered. Most likely the fathers of the men they had fought yesterday, Celer thought.

Sirus was mounted and looked the king in the eye.

"King Theodoar, you grace us with your presence." He dipped his head in polite deference.

"Damn your pleasantries!" the King growled and spurred his horse forward.

At once, Celer and the other legionaries drew their swords. Sirus raised a calming hand before they moved forward and smiled at Theodoar, who sat barely an arm's length from him.

"Very well, your highness. What is it you want from us?"

"You know what it is I want, you thrice-cursed Roman. Where is my son's body and those of my men's son's?"

Sirus kept the smile fixed upon his face and slowly pointed a finger downhill towards the battlefield. The burial mounds could be seen clearly even through the drizzle.

"No doubt many of them lie at rest below."

Theodoar's hands were gripping his reigns so tight that his knuckles went white.

"Where does my son lie? Tell me and maybe I won't slaughter all of you."

Sirus shook his head. "There will be no slaughter, King Theodoar, especially not of my men. We shall leave here this very day and march back to our own lands so that I may report the success of our negotiations to my superiors."

"Success...?" Theodoar's face was twisted in rage and confusion.

"Yes, success. I shall report to my superiors how you agreed to obey the terms of our current treaty and that the current sum paid to you remains satisfactory for you to ensure your people adhere to it."

Theodoar exploded. "You will not leave here alive! Your men will be cut down and impaled on pikes; I will flay you and your officers alive in vengeance for my son!"

Sirus calmly wiped a globule of spittle from his horse's neck. "You are mistaken, King Theodoar. As I said, there will be no more slaughter, fortunately for you and your rabble of old men and green boys. You asked where your young men were and I told you that many of them lie in the graves down below us. However, I did not say that your son lay amongst them."

As he finished speaking, Centurion Decimus raised his right hand in signal and a gasp went through the Gepid party. The King's eyes were wide and Celer followed their gaze to where Optio Longus stood on the camp rampart with his sword tip at the throat of a bound prisoner.

With a start, Celer realised that the ragged Gepid was Ardaric, the King's son. He had not realised that the Prince had survived the battle, so grief-stricken had he been at the death of his friends.

Theodoar's mouth worked soundlessly, reigns dropping from limp fingers.

Sirus's face was cold and harsh.

"You spoke yesterday of rumours of the Empire's failing strength. Rumours have reached us also, of a certain Gepid King who dotes upon his last living son, a prince hailed by his people as their next great leader who will lead them to great victories. My superiors reasoned that such a prince would be a valuable hostage to ensure that the King and his people obey the treaty that they signed with the Emperor. Imagine their pleasure when I return with the Prince."

"I will kill you," croaked Theodoar.

"Only God himself may know the manner of my death but it will not be at your hand, not if you value your son's life."

"You would not dare!" raged the King. "My men would hunt you to the ends of the earth!"

"Only as far as the Danube," retorted Sirus. "No doubt the Emperor would be displeased were your son to die, yet, if I were a gambling man, I would back my men to reach the Empire undefeated. Your best men rode against us yesterday. It will be many years before more men of their calibre are of age and my men are more than capable of defeating the forces you have with you."

Theodoar shot a glance back at the men assemble behind him, as if noticing the grey beards and the smooth faces amongst them for the first time.

"Damn you," he snarled, turning back to the Centurion.

"You already did," replied Sirus.

The King's shoulders slumped and in an instant Celer thought he looked older.

"What will happen to my son?"

"He will be taken to Constantinople," said Sirus, his tone lighter now that Theodoar had accepted the situation.

"And the others?"

Sirus shrugged. "They will not be harmed."

Theodoar spat, "Very well, tell your Emperor the treaty still stands. The settlers will be gone by midsummer's eve."

Sirus inclined his head. "These terms are acceptable."

Theodoar took one last look at his son on the rampart then slowly turned his mount around and rode back towards his men. Several in his party gaped at him in surprise but their loyalty ran deep and none spoke. Instead they each shot the Romans furious looks before following their King.

Sirus gave the order to break camp as soon as he was back inside the ramparts. The men broke down the tents with quick efficiency then stood waiting as they watched the Gepid column disappear towards their capital.

Only when the enemy was several miles away did the Senior Centurion give the order for the defences to be torn down.

The prisoners were tied together with a series of nooses about their neck and were pressed into service backfilling the ditches with earth from the rampart.

When it was all done, the men picked up their equipment and formed a marching column.

Alongside the prisoners, the Cohort had captured a number of horses. Legionaries too injured to march were helped into the saddles whilst others were added to the mule train to carry soldier's provisions.

Men too wounded to even ride were loaded into the back of the wagons; each jolt at a rut in the track was followed by a chorus of groans and yelps.

Soon enough they re-entered the forest that marked the edge of the Gepid tribal lands. Wary of ambushes, Sirus had doubled the number of scouts and the column occasionally caught glimpses of the men moving through the woods either side of them.

Not content with just the scouts, Sirus had Ardaric separated from the other prisoners. The Gepid prince was assigned a personal guard drawn from the veterans of the Second Cohort; the legionaries surrounded him with drawn weapons whilst he marched at the head of the column with bound hands where any would be ambusher would see him.

For Celer and the other legionaries, the march back to the Danube was a hellish test of will and endurance.

The Cohort no longer needed to locate farmsteads so they took a more direct route back to the crossing. Even so, it took almost a week of long, tortuous hours of marching before they sighted the banks of the river frontier.

The wooden watch tower saw them emerge from the tree line and, moments later, they saw smoke rise from the signal fire. The sentries across the river in Sexaginta Prista responded moments later with two long trumpet blasts.

The men were stood down as they waited to be ferried back into Imperial lands.

Celer sank onto the grass with a sigh of relief. His bruises had darkened in colour and the marching had not helped his left leg. Each morning he awoke to find it inflamed and painful, forcing him to limp through the first few miles of the day before it loosened up.

Several times he had almost gone to the surgeon and asked to be put on a horse but each time he had stopped himself. There were others far more injured than he who needed those mounts and many more with injuries who marched alongside him with no complaint, only strained looks on their faces.

"I'd never have thought I would be so happy to see that miserable little fort again," said Priscus cheerfully, throwing himself down next to Celer.

"Agreed!" The fort was indeed a grim place, with crumbling old walls and a small town beside it inhabited by the people who scraped a living on the edge of the civilised world. Yet it represented safety and security they had only dreamt of beyond the frontier.

Priscus removed his helmet with a grateful sigh and stacked it atop his shield before falling onto his back with a thud.

"I can't wait to be clean again," he said, scratching at his head where the felt cap had matted his sweat-streaked hair. "Pretty sure my lice have lice."

Celer pulled off his own helmet and teased the knots from his scalp with his fingers.

"As soon as we get back to Novae, I'm going to the baths and I'm not coming out until I feel human again," he said with a sigh, leaning back against his shield.

The sun crept out from behind a cloud and for a short spell they were bathed in warm sunshine.

Drowsing with the sound of the river in their ears, they did not hear the arrival of the ferry, nor the approach of Optio Longus.

"On your feet, legionaries!"

Grumbling, the men of the First Century struggled to their feet and boarded the ferry. The boatmen eyed the young legionaries as they limped on, noticing the gouges on their shields and their travel-stained clothes. Their arms and armour, the ferrymen also noted, were pristine. The captain also noticed the extra room on the deck once they had finished boarding.

"Rough couple of weeks, eh, lads?" one of the young boatmen said jovially. He quailed under the deadpan stares of the soldiers and the captain cuffed him on the back of the head.

"Cast away!" the captain shouted and the crew hurried to pole the ferry out into the current.

The soldiers took a knee as the ferry rocked gently as it was poled across. Celer watched the trees grow more distant with a sense of relief and shame. He had marched beyond the frontier, fought and defeated the enemy and returned alive. Not all had, though, and he was all too aware of the space on the ferry deck, remembering clearly how cramped it had felt as they crossed the first time.

He heard a sniff to his side and saw a tear roll down Symmachus's face. Celer clapped his friend on the shoulder and together they watched the far bank grow smaller.

# XIX

"Cohort, attention!"

Over four hundred newly issued spear butts slammed into the hard-packed dirt of the parade ground.

General Stilicho surveyed the men before him. They stood like statues, polished armour and weapons gleaming even though the sky was dark and threatened rain.

Arrayed in their centuries it was immediately obvious the losses they had suffered beyond the Danube.

The butcher's bill had come back with forty-nine dead or wounded enough to require medical discharge. At first the loss of so many new recruits had angered him but after reading the Senior Centurion's report he was amazed that so many still stood.

The Third Cohort had returned to Novae two days before, arriving hours after the General himself had returned from another tour of the frontier fortresses.

Stilicho had received Sirus and his officers immediately, getting a verbal report from the tired and dirty officers before he dismissed them.

Ardaric's capture had been a huge bonus to the operation. When Stilicho had first outlined his plans with Sirus he had intended to merely inflict as much damage on the Gepid forces as possible, hoping a smaller force would entice them to be drawn into head-on conflict with the heavily armed men of the legion. The need to gain the newly-formed cohort some battlefield experience was another pressing concern and the General was pleased to see the men had performed to the standard his officers had promised.

His brief encounter with the Gepid prince had yielded little. Ardaric had been sullen and unresponsive to his questions and had made no move to ask about the welfare of his countrymen, from whom he had been separated.

Stilicho found his lack of interest for the men under his command unworthy of one blessed with a position of authority and had the prince and the other captives dispatched to Constantinople the next morning under heavy guard.

"Legionaries of the Third Cohort, of the First Legion Italica," Stilicho began, "you have acquitted yourselves admirably on your mission. You have the thanks of the Emperor and of myself. It shall be known that the Third Cohort upheld the reputation of the First Legion and, to acknowledge this, the Emperor has decreed that the Third Cohort be awarded with battle honours." He waited whilst one of his guardsmen marched out towards the cohort standard bearer and fixed the bronze disks onto the standard.

"Emperor Theodosius also commends the bravery of the men of the First Century for their role in the action fought against the Gepids. His Excellency has decreed that each man be awarded with a bronze phalerae as a reward."

A murmur went through the assembled legionaries as the General's guardsmen walked through the ranks of the First Century, pinning the bronze disks onto each legionary's harness.

Celer felt his chest swell with pride as the guardsman attached his and it took a huge effort not to look down at it but to keep staring straight ahead.

Each of the Cohort's officers was then brought forward and presented with a silver phalerae, whilst Sirus, as commander of the force, was presented with a golden torque by the General himself.

As the Senior Centurion bowed so that Stilicho could place the torque around his neck, Centurion Piso drew his sword and raised it above his head.

"For the Third!" he cried out.

A rippling forest of steel pointed towards the heavens as the legionaries roared back.

"For the Third! For the Third!"

After the ceremony the men were dismissed for the day.

Celer carefully stowed his polished armour and weapons and, wearing just his military tunic and boots, stepped out of the barrack block.

He strode down the main street of the fortress towards the

Headquarters, enjoying the spring sun on his bare legs, ignoring the bemused looks of the other soldiers who continued to wear their trousers despite the heat.

The duty guards searched him quickly before allowing him entry; even in the middle of a frontier fortress, theft was still rife and the security of the Cohort's standards and pay chests was a duty given only to the most trusted and experienced of soldiers.

Celer stood patiently through the search.

Confident he was unarmed apart from his dagger, and since he carried no bag, the guards admitted him into the massive stone building that dominated the centre of the fort.

Inside, the colonnaded atrium was cool and light, illuminated by the sun streaming through high windows filled with small panes of glass.

Much like every military building Celer had ever been in, the Headquarters was a seemingly chaotic hive of activity. Clerks and soldiers strode purposefully across the stone flagged floor, barely slowing as they dodged around one another in a silent dance that made Celer want to laugh at the absurdity of it.

Smiling to himself, he set off into the depths of the building, careful to avoid bumping into anyone.

He found Vegetius in a small office near to the treasury room.

His friend was seated behind a wooden desk that threatened to collapse under the weight of stacked tablets, scrolls and books heaped upon it.

In fact, so high were the piles that at first Celer almost walked on past the office door; at the last moment the writer straitened from whatever document he had been scrutinising and glanced at the doorway.

"Celer! Dear boy, what brings you to the madhouse?" he called out.

Carefully stepping over piles of tablets on the floor, Celer made his way into the office.

"I saw you at the ceremony," he explained as he cleared scrolls off a stool and took a seat opposite Vegetius. "I looked for you afterwards and one of the General's guards said I would find you in here."

With a sigh Vegetius looked down at his ink stained fingers.

"I'm afraid that the General is making full use of my previous experiences in administration and dealing with corrupt officials," he grumbled.

"Corrupt officials?" Celer asked, curious.

"Oh yes, frontier is full of them."

"Surely the Emperor doesn't know, he wouldn't allow it?"

Vegetius smiled at him.

"I am sure he is well aware, yet they are tolerated; such men often generate more revenue through taxes than those with a moral code, even if they are skimming off the top for themselves."

Celer looked about the piles in the office. "What is all this then?"

"Whilst in peacetime the Emperor and his governors may turn a blind eye to such things, in war they must be dealt with, lest they have damaging consequences for the campaign. General Stilicho has me going through mountains of documents relating to dealings by the frontier commanders, quartermasters and local civic administrators looking for anomalies so they can be brought to account before he leaves with the army. Speaking of armies," he gestured to a stack of tablets on his left with a sigh, "the General has also tasked me with dividing up the pool of new recruits to man the forts in the absence of the current garrisons, a matter usually undertaken by one with more of a military background than I, but then such men are in short supply and sorely needed elsewhere."

Celer smiled as he looked across the desk at Vegetius. It felt strange; he realised he had not smiled for some time.

"This life seems to suit you, my friend."

Vegetius made a fuss of the scrolls on his desk but Celer saw the look of pride upon his face.

"Yes," he nodded as he chased a quill across the wooden boards, "one of life's peculiarities; something I never thought I would do, in a place," he gestured about at the bare stone walls, "I never thought to find myself."

The writer looked solemn all of a sudden.

"And how do you find this life?" he asked Celer.

Celer dropped his eyes and studied his hands; they looked different to him, the hands of another man instead of the boy who had once lived in Rome. They looked bigger, thicker, covered with tough calluses. Hands that had found a talent in wielding a sword and shield, hands that had trembled as Gepid cavalry bore down upon him. Hands that had killed.

"I... I don't know," he answered truthfully at last.

"I read the report from Centurion Sirus. You lost many men beyond the frontier," Vegetius ventured gently.

Celer nodded. "I know why we were sent to Theodoar's kingdom, I understand the reasons, I understand the strategy behind it and what the Empire gains by it." He looked up and met Vegetius gaze, "But it still doesn't feel worth it. They were my friends." He almost said more but the words stuck in his throat.

Vegetius tactfully looked away as he steadied himself. The writer turned to rummage in a small wooden chest under the small window.

He reappeared with a small stoppered bottle of blown glass and two cups.

"Courtesy of our friend Helva in Constantinople," he explained as he poured.

He passed a glass to Celer and raised his own.

"To our fallen heroes."

Celer raised his own glass. "To friends no longer with us."

They drank and sat a moment in silence.

"How is Helva?" asked Celer, eager to change the conversation.

"He is well," said Vegetius cheerfully, "he wrote just last week. He, Timaeus and Nekar are staying with some friends of his in Constantinople. He complains of the noise and bustle of the capital and says he dreams of returning to the peace and quiet of his small seaside town."

Celer remembered the big house in Histonium fondly though he had only been there a short while.

"I can fully understand that desire," he said honestly.

Vegetius nodded wistfully. "I spent many a delightful week in the house of Helva. It seems another world from Constantinople or here." He eyed the walls and the constant stream of people beyond the open doorway.

"Yet!" he said, voice suddenly full of excitement, "the frontier is not without its charms, nor could it ever be said to be boring. In between my duties for the General and the planning that went into your training I have found the time to make some enquiries."

He stood quickly and began searching through stacks of scrolls on a shelf by the door. "Do you recall, that before we left Histonium in great haste, I was working on a treatise tasked with collating information regarding curing the ailments of animals?"

Celer opened his mouth to say that he vaguely recalled such a conversation but the writer had found his scroll and excitedly continued without waiting for his response.

"I found myself seated next to the commander of the cavalry detachment stationed here at Novae. Grim fellow, simply awful taste in wine as well, yet he proved to be a treasure trove of knowledge when it comes to keeping horses healthy..."

Celer rested an elbow on a tall stack of wax tablets and let Vegetius regale him with his discoveries, letting the stream of words flow over him as he nodded occasionally and asked a question whenever the writer paused for breath. The sunlight streaming through the high window was warm on his skin and for the time being he let his worries fall away.

# XX

Summer in the frontier arrived later in the year than Celer was used to. It was as if the seasons he had known in Rome did not obey the same laws on the Danube. The last traces of snow finally receded from the ditches and gullies, though the river remained ice-cold for a long time as if it was still fed by snow-melt from somewhere.

Wild flowers carpeted the borders of the fields that surrounded the fort and the stems of grain that would feed the soldiers steadily climbed towards the sun each day.

Beyond the Danube the zone kept free of trees was pushed back as the men of the Third Cohort added their muscle to the fort's manpower.

A riot of colour erupted from the freshly cleared ground as plants that had competed for patches of light amongst the trees were exposed to their new open world.

Yet the legionaries could only fell so many trees. Beyond their work sites the forest loomed, dark and cool.

Celer took every opportunity he could to develop the skills Iulianus had taught him, going hunting whenever volunteers were asked for.

Priscus and Sextus often accompanied him on his hunts. The three young soldiers became proficient stalkers and accurate bowmen; though Celer would never openly admit it, the others were the better shots.

Their other section-mates accompanied them whenever it was required or when they needed an escape from the fort and the monotonies of training and duties. All apart from Symmachus.

Since their return from the mission beyond the frontier the Cappadocian had become withdrawn and quiet, flatly refusing any invitation to go beyond the river. He had devoted himself to weapons training, sparring and practising with a dogged determination and ferocity that pleased their instructors but had the other legionaries grumbling over their bruises.

"He would have brained me had I not been wearing my helmet," complained Magnus to Celer, Sextus and Priscus the morning after a sparring session as they moved softly through the woods to one of their favourite stalking sites.

"That's why you wear the helmet," ribbed Celer, giving the bigger man a shove on the side of his head before neatly sidestepping the retaliating blow.

"The man fights like he's possessed," Magnus continued.

Celer couldn't disagree with that. It was a rare occurrence that one of his section mates or any other man in the Cohort managed to best him with a sword. Of late, though, Symmachus had become increasingly difficult to beat, a challenge that Celer had first welcomed, but he had begun to notice the madness in Symmachus's eyes whenever they fought that reminded him worryingly of Stilicho's ex-guardsman Horatius.

"He has not dealt with losing the others as well as us," said Sextus quietly. Though he was barely into his twenties he was still the oldest amongst them and the others often looked to him as the voice of reason and experience.

"Losing Quintus has hurt him deeply; they were closer, I think, than we imagined."

An awkward silence descended on them as they padded on through the trees. They all knew what went on sometimes in the late hours of the barracks but they rarely spoke of it. Mainly because, as long as it had no impact on how the legionaries fought together, it didn't matter, but also because it was difficult for young men to talk of things like love, especially in the brutal environment of the army.

"What do we do about him?" asked Priscus after a while.

When no one came forward with an answer Sextus shrugged and said simply, "Nothing different. He's still our friend, we watch his back." He glanced at Magnus and a small smile played about his lips. "And we keep our helmets on."

They soon arrived at a small brook that wound its way through the mossy tree stumps. Fanning out, they quickly discovered fresh scat telling them that deer were in the area.

Celer found signs of fresh grazing and they were soon trotting quietly in the direction the deer had gone. Each of them carried his sword and dagger alongside the bows they had drawn from the armoury for the hunt. Without their armour they could move swiftly and gracefully amongst the tangle of roots and leaves, barely making a sound; the swords were a nuisance but not one of them would step a foot on this side of the Danube without a weapon at their hip.

Priscus was the first to spot their prey. He slowed them all with a raised fist, then he slowly indicated the deer's location and silently knocked an arrow. He had lined up the shot when Sextus uttered a barely audible hiss that stopped him in his tracks.

In the dappled light of the forest floor the deer, three hinds with as many fawns, had raised their heads from the young sapling they had been grazing and were staring intently off into the trees.

Priscus grunted with the strain of holding the string to his cheek but Sextus shook his head and slowly pushed the point of Priscus's arrow towards the ground.

"What?" Priscus whispered angrily.

Sextus was about to answer when they heard a horse whinny nearby.

Instinct took over and all four legionaries dropped to the ground, all thoughts of hunting forgotten.

Their quarry stood still only a moment longer before bounding away into the undergrowth.

Celer pressed himself into the leaf litter that carpeted the ground and edged sideways until the large, moss covered roots of an oak shielded him from sight of the horsemen.

It was a raiding party, thirty something strong, riding in a column two-abreast along a faint game trail.

At first Celer thought they were Gepid warriors, but as they rode past he saw they were smaller in build than any Gepid warrior he had seen. Their ponies were smaller and shaggier as well than the mounts of Theodoar's people. Each rider carried a bow but otherwise they wore no distinguishable uniform. They wore leather and fur armour, though some rode just in light vests, displaying tanned arms that were thick with muscle, and they carried an assortment of lances, axes and swords alongside their curved bows.

"Who are they?" asked Celer in a whisper when the column had passed them by and faded amongst the trees.

"Huns?" Magnus ventured fearfully.

"Maybe," Sextus whispered as he carefully raised his head from the ground and looked about them. "Could be Sarmations or Alani?"

"Either way, we need to get back to the fort; the Commander needs to know there are raiders in the area," Priscus whispered as they rose to their feet.

In agreement, they headed back towards the ferry opposite the fort.

Haste made the distance pass quickly and they were soon at the tree line of the cleared zone. Half a mile away they could see the watchtower and, beyond it, the brown snake of the Danube.

Priscus stepped forward but Celer grabbed his sword belt and hauled him back to the tree they were stood next to.

"What now?" Priscus demanded.

"Over there." Celer pointed along the edge of the forest. The regrowth had been kept in check unevenly and a stand of young birch trees protruded like a peninsula into the cleared zone. In amongst the trees they saw sunlight glint off something metallic; moments later a shaggy pony appeared in a gap amongst the trees.

"They are too close to the river," murmured Sextus.

Celer nodded. The raiders were almost a third of the way closer to the ferry point behind the watch tower than they were, and they were mounted. Their horses looked smaller than the mounts the Roman and Gepid cavalry used but he doubted that they could outrun them either way.

"What do we do?" Magnus asked, turning to Celer.

"Why are you looking at me?" he asked, perplexed.

"You're section leader," Sextus pointed out.

"Highest ranker here, you give the orders," finished Priscus.

Celer looked for the glint in their eyes that they always got when they teased him but he couldn't see it. Each of them looked at him, serious and expectant.

Quickly looking back toward the hidden horsemen to buy himself time, he racked his brain; he could feel his friends' eyes on him and felt the pressure of the trust they put in him. Unexpectedly he found he liked the feeling, liked the fact that it was his decision to make.

"We wait," he decided at last. The others looked disappointed, so he explained.

"The alarm will be raised when we don't return at nightfall, maybe sooner; the others know how long it normally takes us. They won't risk a force in the forest in the dark but they will send men over to the watchtower to get their report and to strengthen the watch. Its standard procedure. Under cover of darkness, we make for the tower. Hopefully, the sight of the extra men there will keep the raiders away. We report in, be back in Novae by the third watch change."

"Good plan," decided Priscus, who stepped back deeper into the forest and settled down with his back to a trunk.

Celer looked to Magnus and Sextus but they both agreed it was a good plan so they all settled down to wait.

Rain started to fall in the late afternoon and none had bothered to bring cloaks. They built a crude hide with dead wood and covered it with leaf litter for them all to shelter under.

Once Celer thought he heard a horse approaching and they all leapt out into the rain with arrows knocked, succeeding in startling the wild pig that had been rooting amongst the base of the trees.

After the scare they built a second, smaller hide right in the tree line and kept a rotating watch on the stand of birch trees and the cleared zone.

When the sun had dipped so low it touched the horizon, they heard a trumpet blast from the fort that indicated to the tower that the ferry had been launched.

In the gathering darkness they saw small lights bobbing as the ferry made its way to the far bank.

"Any movement?" Celer asked Priscus who had been on watch.

"No, nothing. I kept catching glimpses of the horses, though, through that gap there, before the light faded." Priscus pointed with an arrow. "My guess is that there's a small clearing that they've corralled them in."

Celer stared at the birch stand for a long moment, trying to catch a glimpse of light that might indicate a torch or campfire, but he could see nothing. The darkness and rain made it impossible to see if any smoke rose above the trees and he knew the broken ground of the cleared zone would be inky black to any watchers amongst the birches.

"Grab your gear," he said quietly, "we're going."

He led his friends from the tree line. Even in the darkness they bent low as they moved, trying hard not to make any unnecessary noise, though he doubted anyone would hear them above the rain.

The heat of the day had long passed and all four of them were soon soaked and shivering as an icy wind blew in from the north.

Up ahead they could see the bright lights of the sentry's braziers in the tower and the smaller lights of the ferry as it neared the bank. They were halfway towards the tower when they heard the faint shouts as the ferry captain ordered his crew to make ready to dock.

Whether it was the darkness or fear of being caught so exposed, Celer did not know, but his senses seemed have heightened. He felt the raiders move before he saw or heard them.

The ground beneath his boots and the very air around seemed to shiver and it took him a moment to realise it was the beat of running horses.

"Down!" he hissed as loudly as he dared.

Something crashed through the low scrub a hundred paces to their left and he heard a muffled grunt in a foreign tongue.

The legionaries pressed themselves into the mud as the raiders hurtled past. Celer couldn't believe how fast they were pushing their horses in the dark and rain over such rough ground. The men, whoever they were, were clearly expert horsemen or completely lacking any sense of self preservation.

"What are they doing?" whispered Magnus, raising himself up to look after the raiders. "There's no way they could take the tower from horseback."

Realisation struck Celer like a hammer blow.

"It's not the tower!" he shouted, no longer caring about being heard. "They're going for the ferry!"

He leapt up and ran after the horsemen towards the ferry dock. Cursing, the others heaved themselves up and raced after him.

Lights flared up ahead of them and, with it, the sound of screaming men and horses and the clash of steel.

The soldiers in the watchtower were hurling burning faggots towards the dock; the oil-soaked bundles burned fiercely despite the rain and, in the flickering light, Celer could see the fierce battle on the waterfront.

Someone in the fort had dispatched two sections of legionaries to reinforce the watchtower beyond the river.

As the first men had been disembarking onto the wooden jetty, the raiders had hurtled out of the darkness, screaming war cries and loosing arrows towards them.

One section was made up of frontier veterans from the First Cohort. Surprised as they were, the legionaries reacted quickly and dropped behind their shields, forming a small shield-wall between their attackers and the unarmed boat crew.

The second section was made up of men from Celer's own Cohort. They were not as quick to act as their veteran counterparts but were mostly saved from the arrows by the shield-wall. One legionary toppled backwards into the Danube with a splash loud enough that Celer heard it two hundred paces away.

The two sections responded to the arrows with a volley of javelins, bringing down two horses, but unfortunately not their riders. They then lowered their spears and tried to back away onto the ferry.

With amazing gracefulness, the lead raiders slid from their mounts as they slewed past the jetty and hit the ground running. Tossing aside their bows, they hurled themselves at the legionaries, wielding their swords and axes, trying to smash through the shield-wall.

The sentries in the tower began firing at the horsemen with bows, unable to risk lowering the ladders they used to access the tower should the enemy be able to use them to take the tower.

Half of the raider group was still mounted and they wheeled away from the jetty and began circling the tower, loosing shafts at the sentries and forcing their heads back down behind the wooden parapet.

All this Celer took in as he ran towards the tower. He halted his small group just beyond the pool of light cast by the faggots.

Without pausing, he drew an arrow from his quiver, nocked, aimed and fired into the circling horsemen.

His arrow took a rider in the armpit and the man crashed to the ground. He fired a second arrow, this one joined by shots from his section-mates, and another rider slammed into the mud below the tower, thrown from his horse that screamed in pain as it writhed on the ground.

The dazed rider staggered upright, then went down straight away as

Priscus and Sextus found him with their second shots. Celer's third arrow missed his target but Magnus caught a raider in the hip and the man fell from his saddle, screaming until an arrow from the tower silenced him.

The remaining horsemen turned their mounts back towards the river. They knew that someone was on the ground but the light from the faggots had robbed them of their night vision and they were blind to what lay in the darkness.

Wary that the raiders might try and rush them, Celer cut right and circled the tower, whispering for the others to follow and be careful to stay beyond the reach of the light.

He could see the desperate struggle on the jetty was not going the Roman's' way. The raiders were lightly armoured compared to the legionaries, but they were formidable warriors and already several Romans lay on the rough wooden planks.

The horsemen had grouped near the river bank but they were vulnerable to the bows of the tower sentries and two more fell from the saddle as Celer's group moved round to flank them. As he had anticipated, the horsemen charged at where they had stood just moments before, desperate to locate whoever was shooting at them on the ground.

With the tower sentries growing bolder as more mounted men were hit, Celer turned his attention to the jetty.

Being directly in line with the jetty, no sentry had dared risk firing into the raiders as they risked a shot going too high and hitting one of their own men or one of the boat crew.

Standing on the bank of the Danube, Celer and his men had a side-on view of the vicious fight. He, Sextus and Magnus began to shoot into the rear of the raider group whilst Priscus kept a watch over the mounted men.

Lightly armoured and with few of them carrying shields, the raiders on the jetty were helpless before their bows.

Howling with rage, five warriors leapt from the jetty and charged towards them.

The three legionaries fired one last volley that brought down two raiders before hurriedly drawing their swords and shouting a warning to Priscus.

Combat training with the legion had focussed heavily on fighting with a shield and Celer felt horribly exposed without its weight.

Fortunately, the warrior that charged for him swung a scything blow with a curved sword that was easy to dodge. He responded with a back cut that sliced into the raider's side but did not bring him down.

They watched each other for a few seconds, waiting for an opening. The warrior leapt forward but Celer was ready, blocking an overhead cut, stepping past the warrior as he did so, then bringing his own sword down to bite deep into the man's hamstrings. He quickly dispatched him with a thrust then turned to help his friends.

Sextus was pressing his attack on another sword-armed raider and seemed to be getting the better of his opponent who was already bleeding from several wounds.

Magnus and Priscus, however, were fighting for their lives against a stocky bow-legged raider wielding a pair of war axes with terrifying speed.

Celer dashed forward but not before the raider disarmed Magnus with the blur of his axes.

Priscus bravely launched a desperate assault in an attempt to protect his friend but the warrior met each cut and thrust with comfortable ease.

The raider moved to the offensive, moving his axes with increasing speed and complexity, forcing Priscus to retreat.

The curved axe heads flashed in the wavering light, one high and one low. Priscus chose the high one, meeting it above his head with his sword just as the other bit deep into his thigh.

He fell howling back into the mud, tears of pain mingling with the rain as he clamped his hands onto the wound in his leg.

His attacker raised both axes for the killing blow, a wicked smile on his face, when Celer's sword punched through his chest.

Celer threw a quick glance in Sextus's direction in time to see him cut down the final raider, then he rushed to Priscus's side.

Magnus was already slicing strips from his own tunic with his dagger, hurriedly passing a wad to Celer who pressed them tightly against Priscus's wound.

He took small comfort to see that blood was oozing from the wound rather than spurting out, so he knew that no main arteries had been hit, but he could also see even in the near darkness that it was a deep cut.

Priscus's face was waxy pale in the weak light. He muttered a stream of feeble curses as Celer pressed the makeshift bandage into his wound, and shrieked when he tied it tightly with another strip that Magnus handed him before passing out.

The rain was pounding down about them, a blinding deluge that threatened to cut them off from the rest of the world.

Celer and Magnus hauled Priscus upright between them and began to slog their way through the downpour towards the jetty. After suffering heavy casualties, the surviving barbarians had broken off their battle for the ferry and had fled into the darkness.

Sextus led the way, calling out to the Romans on the jetty so that they wouldn't be mistaken for more raiders.

Suddenly, armour clad figures emerged before them and blood-stained hands helped them to bear Priscus's weight.

Hobnailed boots clattered along the boards of the jetty towards the barge. Wounded and dead legionaries had already been loaded onto the deck, which was awash with blood, rapidly being diluted in the rain.

As he lowered Priscus to the deck, Celer felt a strong hand on his shoulder and a familiar voice.

"You all right, lad?" asked Iulianus.

Celer felt anything but, yet the sight of the veteran's weathered face steadied him and he clasped the old legionary by the arm in welcome, noticing the blood and gore that caked his soaked sleeves.

"I'm fine," he shouted through the drumming downpour. "Priscus is hurt pretty badly, though!"

Iulianus knelt and quickly inspected the young legionary. He shouted to another veteran with the dark colouring of the eastern provinces who was crouched by a soldier with a vicious-looking facial wound.

Standing, Iulianus turned back to Celer.

"Ingenuus will take a look at him shortly, don't worry, he's in good hands."

"Thank you," said Celer gratefully. The others chorused their thanks which Iulianus waved away.

"What are you doing here?" asked Celer. The Second and Third Cohorts had parted ways on returning from the mission to Theodoar's kingdom and Celer had not thought to see Iulianus again.

"On detachment to Novae, General's orders. Arrived this morning.

When Centurion Decimus heard there were men missing beyond the frontier he volunteered our services."

"I'm glad he did," said Sextus honestly.

"What happened out there?" the veteran asked as the ferry captain roared out orders and the barge was pushed away from the bank.

Celer quickly recounted the day's events from the moment they saw the raiders in the forest up to Priscus being wounded.

"You did well," Iulianus said to them all when he was done.

"Not well enough," replied Sextus, gesturing to Priscus's prone form. Ingenuus was kneeling beside their friend, obstructing their view, but he seemed to be examining Priscus's leg wound.

"Your made it through with one seriously wounded and a few cuts and bruises," Iulianus said gruffly. "Not many can say they fought an Alani war band and came off so well."

"So they were Alani," Magnus mused aloud.

Iulianus nodded. "We think so. Hard to tell with the nomads, a lot of similarities between them, but the Alani are bad news; the General will have to be informed immediately."

As he spoke he looked at them all with new respect.

"I knew it had to be something bad. You lot aren't the usual idiots who get lost beyond the river; you proved that much, at least, with the Gepids."

Small lights from shuttered lanterns heralded the approach of the Roman bank.

"Go help get your friend ashore," Iulianus said to the young soldiers. "He has greater need of you than I do. Keep awake, though; Decimus and Sirus will have questions for you, no doubt."

# XXI

The hospital lay in the centre of Novae.

Originally built to cope with a far larger garrison, the old building had several sections that had long been abandoned.

They carried Priscus through into the same ward where Celer had recovered after being attacked by Horatius. It was warm compared to the freezing wet night and clean with the usual spartan furnishings that Celer had come to associate with military buildings.

He and the others were quickly ushered out of the ward to the open courtyard where they sheltered under one of the covered walkways as the medicus and his orderlies went to work on Priscus and the other wounded.

Rain rattled off the tiled roof and pooled on the worn flags of the courtyard as they waited. The night air was cold but an orderly took pity on them and brought them a worn blanket each and a cup of hot wine.

They had been there for over an hour when they heard approaching boot steps and they all leapt to their feet, ignoring the complaint of muscles fatigued from fighting and the cold.

Symmachus and Pulvillus came rushing through the main door that led out to the fortress.

"By the grace of the Lord," exclaimed Pulvillus when he caught sight of them, dark hair plastered to his skull by the rain. "You're all right! When we heard you'd all been brought to the hospital we thought..."

Symmachus said nothing; instead he marched right up to them and embraced each of them in a bear hug that threatened to break ribs.

"We're fine," gasped Sextus, clapping Symmachus on the back, "we're ok."

"Priscus?" asked Pulvillus, the worry apparent in his voice.

Magnus pointed towards the hospital ward. "In there, they won't let us in," he explained as Symmachus started towards the doorway.

"What happened to him, is he going to be ok?"

"The medicus never said anything to suggest he wouldn't pull through," Magnus said as calmly as he could, "but he took an axe to the thigh, lost a lot of blood before we could get back across the river."

Between the three of them they once again recounted the day's events.

When they spoke of seeing the mounted raiders in the forest, Symmachus broke his silence to ask if the warriors were Gepids.

Celer saw how he gripped the handle of his dagger tight enough to make his knuckles white and the vein that stood proud on his forehead.

"No," he answered, "Iulianus and the other veterans think they were an Alani war band."

This seemed to calm Symmachus somewhat, which did little to alleviate Celer's concern for his friend. Pulvillus cursed softly at the mention of the Alani but they remained quiet after that so that they could hear what happened after.

"We were lucky," said Magnus when they finished.

The others nodded but Symmachus shocked them all by sneering at him.

"If you were lucky, Priscus would be sat with us, not dying through there!" he shouted, pointing a quivering finger towards the ward.

Magnus was so surprised at the outburst that he said nothing so Sextus interjected.

"Priscus got hurt in battle, protecting his friend. That is a risk that all of us bear and don't you dare say that he is dying."

Symmachus pointed an accusing finger at Magnus. "He got hurt because Magnus left him to fight the enemy alone."

"I was disarmed!" retorted Magnus, angry now. "What would you have had me do, face his axes with my bare hands?"

"You should not have let yourself be robbed of your weapon in such a way," fumed Symmachus. "You should have fought harder!"

"Enough!" shouted Celer, pushing in between them. "Enough, Priscus is wounded in there and you two think it acceptable to squabble outside?"

Turning to Symmachus he spoke firmly. "You were not there, I was. They fought against a great warrior, highly skilled; he would have bested any of us. Even you," he added when Symmachus snorted derisively. "Now have some decency and remember where we are."

"Well said, Legionary Celer," said Senior Centurion Sirus from behind them.

Argument instantly forgotten, all five legionaries swivelled to face their commanding officer and slammed to attention.

Sirus was accompanied by Centurion Decimus from the Second Cohort detachment and by Prefect Cordus, the commander of the First Cohort based at Novae and the most senior officer in the Legion in the absence of a Tribune.

The officers had approached unheard due to the row and now eyed the young soldiers with steely glares.

Sirus paced forward until he stood before Symmachus. The Cappadocian trembled slightly before the Centurion but did not allow his gaze to drop

"I would watch that temper of yours, Legionary," warned Sirus softly.

"Yes, Sir!"

"Legionaries Symmachus and Pulvillus, you are dismissed. Return to barracks immediately."

Pulvillus and Symmachus saluted and marched away without question, though Celer saw their eyes flicker towards the hospital door as they marched past.

Once they were gone, Sirus turned back to Celer and the others.

Despite the late hour, Celer noticed that not one of the officers looked tired, nor did they look like they had just been roused from sleep. Instead, each man stood as if carved from marble, armour gleaming in the torchlight, not one buckle or strap out of place.

"Legionaries Celer, Magnus and Sextus, you will follow us," commanded Sirus.

Without waiting for a response, Prefect Cordus turned on his heal and marched from the Hospital.

Sirus and Decimus walked a respectful pace behind him, and Celer and his friends followed another pace behind them.

They marched through the rain and into the headquarters; the guards on the entrance slammed to attention as they passed.

Even late at night the Headquarters building was busy. Shadows danced on walls from small candles as scribes worked by the flickering light.

Cordus led the small procession to his office at the rear of the building next to the sacellum, which housed the standards of the Legion as well as the treasury for the garrison. Six battle-scarred veterans from the First Cohort, under the command of an optio, stood guard outside the barred door. Not one of them glanced at the party as it marched past them.

Prefect Cordus seated himself behind his solid oak desk and Centurions Sirus and Decimus positioned themselves either side of him.

Celer and his companions stood rigidly to attention before their superiors, each trying not to move as water ran off them and puddled on the stone floor.

The only other person present was a clerk seated at a small desk to Celer's right. Unlike the officers, the clerk looked as if he had been rudely awoken and seemed to be fighting back a yawn as he held his quill poised above the blank parchment before him.

"I have heard reports from the sentries in the tower and the men assigned to search for you," Cordus began, in a deep voice that suited his barrel-chested physique. "Now I would hear your version of tonight's events."

And so, for the third time in as many hours, Celer and the others recounted the day's events, beginning with the sighting of the horsemen in the forest and culminating as they boarded the ferry to return to Roman territory.

None of the officers interrupted as they spoke, instead appraising them with experienced eyes. The only other sound was the scratch of the clerk's quill as he furiously penned their report and the occasional echo of boots from the hallway.

When they were finished, they stood silently awaiting further orders, trying to ignore the ache in their bodies and the tiredness that pressed on their minds.

Prefect Cordus gave a curt nod. "It fits with the other reports."

Turning to the clerk he said, "Have all three reports copied in triplicate and have a compiled report sent to the General before first light."

The clerk saluted and left the room quickly. Celer felt a pang of sympathy for the man; there would be no chance of sleep tonight for him.

"I shall not mince my words," began the Prefect, "you have all performed remarkably well, upholding the honour and reputation of this Legion and for that, you have my thanks. By all accounts your discovery of the raiders and subsequent inability to return was a stroke of luck; the changing of the watch would not have been so heavily armed or prepared as the force sent to search for you and would have been overwhelmed with ease.

"With regard to your actions in the skirmish, your report matches that of the men in the tower and on the jetty. They all stated that without your intervention they would likely have lost control of the barge and placed the security of the crossing at risk."

He paused a moment to glance at Sirus, who continued to look unblinking at the young Legionaries.

"In light of this, and after discussion with your commander, I grant all three of you the position of immunes, making you exempt from all non-specialised duties."

Celer felt the others stiffen beside him but forced himself not to look or to allow any expression to show. Immune's privileges were much sought after amongst the men of the Legions, desired by all soldiers usually after they had pulled their first latrine duty.

"In addition," Cordus continued, looking at Celer directly. "I am promoting Legionary Celer to the rank of tesserarius. Senior Centurion Sirus informs me that this position has yet to be filled in the First Century of his cohort and your actions in tonight's skirmish and the mission to the Gepid Kingdom has convinced him of your suitability for the role."

The Prefect's tone hardened as he spoke. "Know that I am aware of whom and what you are, and I want it clear that I do not approve of men of your class serving with the Legions. However," his tone softened a little, "these are troubled times, and we have need of every man who has the ability to lead men and fight well. With that in mind, the promotion is well deserved, congratulations."

Celer struggled to keep his swirling emotions in check. "Thank you, Sir," he managed.

Cordus gave another of his curt nods and both Sirus and Decimus offered their congratulations, to which Celer was able to respond with more conviction.

"Now, the hour is late," the Prefect stated, matter of fact. "You are dismissed,; return to the barracks and await further orders."

"Yes, Sir!" all three chorused before turning on their heels smartly and filing from the room.

The torrential rain has lightened to a cold drizzle when they emerged from the Headquarter building.

Shivering in the cold night air and eager for dry clothes, they hurried towards their barrack block.

The urge to celebrate and congratulate each other on their improved status and promotion was dampened by the worry they all felt for their friend and by the weariness that weighed heavily upon each of them.

Quietly they entered the barracks, moving as softly as they could through the large communal cooking space, relishing the residual heat from the oven built into the walls that the other men of their century had cooked the evening bread in.

From the rooms they crept past came the sounds of sleeping men, snores and grunts and the occasional unintelligible mutter.

Faint light showed through the crack at the bottom of the door from the room their section shared.

Inside they found Symmachus and Pulvillus waiting up for them. Symmachus had been staring at the ceiling whilst Pulvillus was polishing his helmet with an oiled cloth. Both jumped to their feet as the three entered, unleashing a torrent of whispered questions.

"Patience a moment, brothers, let us get dry at least before you interrogate us," pleaded Sextus wearily.

Chastised for a moment, they stepped back to allow the others into the room.

As Magnus moved past him, Symmachus grabbed him by the arm.

"Forgive me for my words before," he said with what sounded like genuine regret. "I spoke harshly and out of turn; I have no doubt you fought bravely and better than I could have."

Magnus studied him for a moment, looking as if he might refuse Symmachus's apology. Pulvillus caught his eye over the Cappadocian's shoulder and gave him a small nod.

"We say things we do not mean when we are upset. I forgive you," he said graciously, in the end.

Once changed into their dry tunics and trousers, they sat on their bunks and recounted their report to the senior officers and their subsequent status changes.

"Immunes!" Pulvillus cried in mock outrage, loud enough for the others to shush him.

"No more latrine duty, no more ditch clearance or firewood collection! You always manage to land on your feet," he said accusingly to Sextus.

"Me?" whispered Sextus with a look of mock offence. "What about the century's new Tesserarius over here?" he pointed at Celer.

"Phah, a position well deserved," declared Pulvillus. "Celer has proved his worth before; the Cohort still love telling any who will listen how well he fought that pig's arse Horatius in front of the General."

Celer gripped the bedpost at the thought of the towering German. Yet another enemy who wanted him dead, he thought to himself, one who had come far closer than all the others.

They were interrupted by the sound of boot steps in the corridor.

Optio Longus emerged through the doorway, nose now forever distorted after the battle against the Gepids.

Hastily, the legionaries stood to attention before the officer.

"At ease," Longus ordered quietly, surprising the soldiers, who were used to his parade ground bellow.

"The Senior Centurion informed me of your new position," the optio said to Celer. "Report to me at first light to discuss your new duties."

"Yes, Sir."

Turning to the others, Longus continued, "I have also been informed of your new status as immunes, a status well-earned but not one to be abused. I expect great dedication to your other duties, is that understood?"

"Yes, Sir," they said in unison.

Longus nodded and turned to leave.

"As you were," he ordered, opening the door to their room.

"Sir?" Magnus took a half pace forward.

"Yes, Legionary?" Longus looked un-amused at being addressed out of turn.

"Is there any news on Legionary Priscus?" Magnus asked nervously.

The stern look on the optio's face faltered for a moment.

"The latest report from the Medicus stated that he seemed to be recovering, his wounds have been cleaned and bound. It is up to the Medicus to decide, of course, but I see no reason why you may not visit him tomorrow, off-duty, of course," he added.

Magnus's face split with a big grin which he quickly struggled to hide. "Yes, Sir. Of course, Sir."

"Good night, gentlemen. I expect to see you all on parade tomorrow. First light, Tesserarius." he said again to Celer, who nodded back.

"First light, Sir."

With that he was gone. They listened to his footsteps disappear down the stone corridor.

Sextus produced a wine skin and Pulvillus rooted around until each of them had a chipped pot cup before them on the rough-hewn tabletop.

"A quick celebration is in order, I think," said Sextus, raising his cup high. "To Priscus, may he have a speedy recovery."

"To the safe return of our friends," said Pulvillus, raising his cup.

"To our newest officer," said Symmachus with a small smile.

"And to never having to shovel shit again," finished Magnus happily.

"To never shovelling shit again," the others repeated with a laugh and drained their cups.

# XXII

The following weeks passed quickly for the men of the First Legion.

Worried by the boldness of the Alani raiders and fearful that they were the outriders of a much larger force, Stilicho ordered the Danube frontier be placed on high alert.

Detachments from all three cohorts were sent regularly across the river to hunt for signs of large forces moving towards Roman territory.

Stilicho also doubled the amount of river patrols and the legionaries spent the days cursing the summer sun as they rowed up and down the Danube, sweating from the heat and exertion with one eye always on the far bank. By evening they would swiftly turn to cursing the swarms of biting insects that clouded the river and its banks.

The heightened security meant that Celer had to learn his new responsibilities quickly.

As tesserarius, he ranked above his fellow legionaries but was still the most junior officer in the century after Sirus, Longus and the century's signifier.

In the unlikely event that all three men were killed or incapacitated, the command of the First Century would fall to him, a possibility that Sextus pointed out to him during one long day in a patrol boat and one that Celer fervently hoped never happened.

His main duty was command of the century's night watches. He would receive the watchwords for the night from Longus or occasionally Sirus and would then be left to deal with any incidents in the night hours.

Two weeks after the attack on the river barge, one of the sentries saw a dark shadow glide into the Roman bank of the Danube and figures illuminated in the silvery moonlight emerge.

Celer was forced to call out the entire garrison of Novae and then led a sortie from the fort whilst the two cohorts watched him from the walls.

Fortunately, it turned out to be two drunken locals from a village several miles upstream who had accidentally cast off and had been unable to land the boat until it crashed beneath the fort's walls.

Along with the fright of being dragged into Novae by a tense group of fully armed legionaries, the two men received a dressing down from Senior Centurion Sirus, so loud that it could apparently be heard in the village outside the fort.

As the watch commander on duty, the full weight of the First and Third Cohort's anger at being dragged from their beds in the middle of the night fell on Celer. Whilst the men gave him no end of grumbling abuse, he knew he had done the right thing and neither Sirus nor any of the other centurions chastised him for his actions.

Alongside their duties beyond the frontier, the Legion also had to maintain its presence within Roman lands.

As the son of a Senator of Rome, Celer had been schooled in the bureaucratic and political processes of the Empire since he could talk. Yet he had not fully appreciated the level of involvement the military had with local affairs within the provinces.

The Legion was required to police roads and villages to protect them from bandits, escort tax collectors to protect them from the villagers, maintain the main road-ways and deal with personal grievances amongst the populace that threatened to destabilise the peace.

There were state-run factories that produced weapons and clothing for the frontier and imperial forestry that supplied timber to the rest of the Empire that needed protection as well.

Emperor Theodosius's declaration of war against the Western Empire meant that resources became all the more valuable and all the more vulnerable to sabotage by enemy agents.

According to Iulianus, Theodosius's own agents and specialist military units would already be in enemy territory, disrupting supplies and the enemy's intelligence networks and targeting their infrastructure to make defence of the frontier as hard as possible.

Celer did not doubt the old soldier was right but he had little time to think on the war to come. The Legion had its work cut out defending its own frontier.

Boat patrols began coming into frequent contact with the enemy. Increasingly they found abandoned boats and rafts where small bands had crossed the river or came upon camps where barbarians were preparing to cross.

Here the legionaries would launch lightning raids from their own crafts, occasionally joining up with the mounted archers from Novae, launching two-pronged attacks on the raider camps.

Few of the raiders offered any real resistance; most laid down their arms at the sight of the heavily armed legionaries or in the face of the arrows of the Roman cavalry. The prisoners they took revealed that the raiders were not limited to Alani warriors. Most were Goths from various tribes beyond the frontier. At first many refused to talk, but hard words and harder blows from soldiers like Iulianus who could speak some of their tongue soon had them talking. The warriors had been called by their brothers across the great river, summoned to swell the ranks of the Goths who had revolted, once again, from Roman rule in the Thracian provinces.

Celer understood little of their barbarous tongue but he began to pick up a few words as the summer wore on and they captured more raiders. Time and time again he heard the same name from the tongues of the warriors, spat in the face of their Roman captors, the name of the man who had summoned them: Alaric.

In late summer, Celer and the men of two sections were placed under the command of Optio Longus and marched a day and a half south to the small city of Nicopolis ad Istrum.

They were being sent to relieve two sections from the First Cohort who had just completed their three-week posting to the small military compound just outside the city.

The word in Novae before they had left was that the situation elsewhere in Thrace was deteriorating fast as the Gothic revolt swelled. There were rumours that the Third would be marching soon to join the army that General Stilicho was forming to deal with the rebels and their chieftain Alaric.

The compound at Nicopolis acted as a reserve supply depot for Novae and the other frontier forts within a fifty-mile stretch of the river as well as housing a factory that produced armour for the frontier troops.

Their orders were to ensure the security of the compound. There had been rumours of hostile agents loyal to Arbogast that were believed to be in the area. Optio Longus had taken Celer aside before he led his men away from Novae.

"We watch our backs in Nicopolis," the optio warned him. "This isn't patrol duty like on the frontier. These agents will hide in plain sight, waiting for a moment of opportunity, then they will strike. Keep your eyes open and look after your men."

Longus's warning had set Celer's nerves on edge. Before the optio had taken him aside, he and the others had been praising their luck at landing the patrol duty.

They had just come off a three-week rotation on the patrol boats in baking heat; even the boat crews had stopped laughing and mocking the miserable soldiers sweating in their heavy armour as they pulled at the oars of the river boats.

They had come into contact with another raiding party but they were too far out in the river when they were spotted and the horsemen had melted back into the tree line.

Three weeks in an actual city, away from the demands of fortress life, had sounded like a blessing.

The other men had talked of little else than women and wine the entire march there, pausing only to grumble as to why they were carrying so much kit when they were heading away from the frontier zone.

Nicopolis ad Istrum was a small city, an old one by the look of the buildings and starting to show its age, Celer thought as they marched through its streets.

It had once been grand enough, by provincial standards, anyway.

As they marched through the forum, crowds parting before them with bored indifference, he saw a statue of the Emperor Trajan astride a horse and a vague memory from his history lessons reminded him that the Emperor had won several victories in the area before it was made into a Roman province.

After presenting themselves to the town magistrate, they made their way to the military compound which sat just outside the walls with its own timber palisade separating it from the other buildings that sprawled unrestrained beyond the city boundary.

Before they even reached the compound, they could hear the deafening ring of hammers and see the smoke climbing from the blacksmith's forges.

Inside the palisade they got their first look at their new temporary home.

The ground was hard-beaten earth, rutted by the heavy wagons that rolled in and out bearing either armour, timber or supplies.

A large stone granary ran down the middle of the compound, dividing it into two halves. Cats sunned themselves on the worn stonework and small black dogs dozed in shaded cages, waiting out the heat of the day before they were released to root out any vermin from beneath the granary. Before the granary entrance there was a large open area where goods were either loaded onto the carts and mule trains or unloaded and sent to their respective sides.

To the left of the granary were the stable blocks and beyond them the forges. Celer could see men stripped to the waist beneath scorched leather aprons with thick beards sweating in the glow of the hot coals, sparks flying to accompany the ring of their strikes.

To the right of the granary there was a wagon bay where unhitched vehicles stood awaiting repairs or use, and beyond them was the wood mill.

Now they were in the compound, Celer could hear the bite of axes and the tapping of chisels as raw trees were turned into beams and planks for construction.

The forges, like the granary, were largely made of stone, but the sheds for the wood mill were all made of timber.

Moving closer, Celer could see that much of the wood sheds were beautifully carved with figures of running animals, plants, trees, gods and a whole plethora of scenes.

No one paid any attention to the new arrivals, so whilst the others stood down and took in the scene before them, Celer accompanied the optio as he made his way to the small gatehouse to present his orders to the compound officer.

The officers ran the compound from a small room in the gatehouse that reminded Celer of the small clerk's' rooms in the military stations that they had rested in during the journey from Dyrrhachium to Constantinople.

It was small, sparsely furnished, but crammed with all manner of documents stored in every available space.

The compound officer was a civilian, a Greek, Celer thought by the look of him, and a grossly overweight one at that.

The soldiers snapped a quick salute, out of politeness rather than necessity, and Longus placed his orders on the officer's cluttered desk.

The Greek glanced at the tablet before looking up at them with small beady eyes.

"Gentlemen, I don't believe I've had the pleasure before?" he said in a high nasal tone.

"Optio Longus and Tesserarius Celer, Third Cohort, First Legion, reporting for duty," Longus replied. Strangely, the Greek suddenly looked up at Celer's name, studying him more intently; Celer even thought he saw a flash of recognition across the officer's sweaty face.

"Third Cohort? I don't remember there being a Third Cohort of the Legion," said the officer.

"We're newly raised," Longus explained.

"Not from around here, you're not; that's no Moesian accent." The Greek wagged a finger at him as he reached for the tablet of orders.

"The Cohort was raised in Constantinople," Longus explained calmly. Celer didn't think he'd heard the optio speak so calmly for so long without exploding at someone. He crushed a smile that threatened his lips at the thought and stared straight ahead at the plastered wall above the Greek officer's head.

"Where is Optio Antonius?"asked Longus.

"Ha!" the officer snorted, "no doubt preparing to brief you on the best wine sinks and flesh pots in the city, I wager, all you lot seem to do here, so much for guarding the compound."

Amazingly Longus ignored the jibe. "If you would direct us?" he said calmly, though Celer thought he heard a hint of steel creep into the optio's tone.

If the Greek heard it too, he made no sign. Seeming to lose interest in them, he waved absent-mindedly towards the door, their orders already lost amongst the mess of his desk.

"Go through the Tanner's Gate into the city, you'll find the street of whores not far from there; your Optio likes to frequent a place called the Golden Aphrodite as far as I know."

Longus did not thank the man and he did not salute again, but this seemed not to be noticed as the Greek reached for a papyrus scroll, so he turned heel instead and marched out of the office. Celer thought he heard the optio mutter something under his breath as they left but only caught the word "civilians". Longus said nothing to him, though, so Celer kept his mouth shut and followed his superior out of the compound.

As soon as he was gone, the officer looked up from his desk. His fat fingers moving nimbly, he grabbed a scrap of papyrus and a quill and hastily wrote a note.

He shouted loudly for his clerk, a wizened old Thracian with one milky white eye.

"Send this with the evening dispatches to Constantinople; see that the courier delivers it personally to the Egyptian. I believe I have found someone he's looking for."

Celer had been able to smell the city as they marched towards it. The stench of humanity combined with the reek of various industries had assailed his nostrils several miles away.

Walking through the Tanner's Gate, he was assailed by the smell as if it were a physical blow. After the cool, clean freshness of the frontier, the city was abhorrent and he wondered how anyone could stand to live here.

Briefly, he wondered if Rome would smell much like this were he ever to return. It saddened him to think that he might find the city of his birth intolerable and made him think that joining the Legion may have changed him more than he realised.

They found the Golden Aphrodite easily enough. Even during the hours of daylight, there was a steady stream of customers enjoying the establishment's wares.

Women in revealing dresses slashed almost to the hip eyed them as they approached; many were washing clothes and bedding in tubs along the side of the street whilst others nursed small infants as dirty children played around them.

A young woman with a pretty face smiled at him as he approached the doorway and pulled at her slit skirts to reveal the full length of her legs.

Celer felt his heart quicken a moment but the sight of the small child nestled in the crook of her arm, staring at him with wide blue eyes, left him feeling slightly disgusted and he quickly stepped through the threshold.

His eyes took a moment to adjust to the gloom. All around him were bodies sprawled on couches. Men, women, boys and girls. Some were busy with patrons whilst others reclined, patiently waiting for their next customer.

Celer spied the soldiers easily enough.

They had taken over the far corner of the room. Several of the men were playing dice with some of the whores on a table littered with wine cups whilst others were laid back on the couches.

Celer tried not to look too closely as they approached them, aiming instead for the dice-playing men.

At the sight of him and Longus, dressed in full armour and bearing weapons, the soldiers got to their feet. Some not too steadily.

The soldiers quickly noted Longus's long staff and saluted.

"Where is your officer?" the optio asked in his more familiar bark.

"Opito's in the nearest one. Wouldn't disturb him though, he don't like being interrupted," one of the legionaries responded drunkenly, pointing in the direction of some dark alcoves against the back wall, screened by stained red curtains.

"Why don't you sit and have a drink?" said another soldier from the table, slurring his words slightly.

One of the whores giggled and rose from the table. She ran her hands over Celer's armoured chest and took hold of his belt, starting to pull him towards the table.

"Legionary, you will stand at attention when you address a superior officer!" Longus roared in the drunken soldiers' faces.

The fact that Longus was not their commanding officer, nor even an officer of the First Cohort, mattered little. Even Celer slammed to attention at Longus's sudden outburst. The girl who had hold of his belt let go with a small cry of surprise and tumbled giggling back onto the couch.

Optio Antonius had heard Longus and chose that moment to emerge from his alcove.

Antonius was fastening his belt about his waist as he pushed though the red curtain. A young boy in his early teens and a girl about Celer's age followed him out nervously and headed hurriedly towards the couches by the entrance.

The optio was like many of the other veterans of the Legion Celer had met. A lifetime on the frontier exposed to the elements had given him a tanned and weathered face. Celer guessed he was in his late thirties or forties, but he had the wiry, powerful look of a much younger man.

Antonius gave Celer a cursory glance as he stepped past him. Celer noticed that, unlike his men, the optio did not appear to be suffering the effects of drink.

"What is the meaning of this?"

"I'm here to relive you," replied Longus, his voice iron as his eyes bored into the legionaries who swayed before him. The men were sobering fast under the optio's gaze, Celer thought, suddenly glad he was not on the receiving end.

"These men are under my command," Antonius said lazily.

"I was reminding your men of the proper way to address an officer," Longus responded coolly, turning to face Antonius. The Optio of the Third was bigger than Antonius and he looked down his bent and battered nose at him.

Antonius looked up at him and for a moment Celer wondered if the two officers would exchange blows. Then the moment passed and the optio of the First Cohort shrugged and reached past Longus for a jug of wine.

"Looks like the holiday is over, lads; pack up, we're moving out."

The drunken soldiers stumbled for the door, none of them raising their eyes to Longus as they passed him.

"Your handover report?" Longus asked as Antonius made for the exit.

The optio thought a moment, then smirked. "The booze is expensive but you won't find a cleaner woman anywhere else in Nicopolis." He laughed, raised his wine jug in mock salute, and left the building.

Longus shook his head in disgust. A girl swayed up to him drunkenly, but the optio turned his eyes to her and she quickly veered away.

"Food," he barked at a wizened serving man, "and clean cups." He sat himself on a wooden bench near the door where a breeze from outside helped combat the drunken fumes and perfumed oils of the brothel.

Celer followed him nervously, uncertain of whether to stay or go.

"Sit down, Celer," Longus said, gesturing to the bench across the table.

They sat in silence as the old man brought clean cups and a jug of wine with two plates of cured meats and bread with oil.

"Remember what you saw here today," Longus said as he poured wine into both their cups. "The frontier is a dangerous place but it can also make you soft. Soft officers like that", he waved a calloused hand to the door Antonius had left through, "make soft soldiers. And soft soldiers die quickly."

Celer didn't know what to say. No officer had ever spoken to him the way Longus was now. He drank some of his wine and started on his bread and meat.

The optio wasn't finished, however. "Men like that are the reason the First Cohort will stay in Novae, whilst the Third marches to fight with Stilicho against the Goths."

"So it's true, Sir," Celer asked quickly, eager for any news of the Cohort's plans, "we're marching to fight Alaric?"

"We can't head west with an enemy at our backs," the optio stated matter of factly. "We march at the end of the month."

"And after that we head west, Sir?"

Longus shrugged. "Can't see why they would wait much longer; the longer we wait the stronger the enemy grows."

"Good," Celer said, his hand curling into a fist on the tabletop at the thought.

Longus noticed and eyed the legionary as he drank from his cup.

"You have a lot of hate in you, boy," he remarked. "Don't let it rule you; your opponents can use it against you."

Celer looked up and met the optio's eye.

"Yes, Sir, I'll remember that."

"See that you do," Longus drained his cup and stood up. "Come, we have work to do."

As they headed out, Celer noticed the girl who had tried to pull him onto the couch. She caught him looking down at her and stretched, arching her back like a cat and winked up at him, patting the couch suggestively. Celer smiled back nervously and followed his optio out into the sunlight.

# XXIII

The small barracks block in the compound designated for the soldiers' use was badly dilapidated. Half of the building was roofless and the section with a roof had obviously been abandoned for a long time, the previous units stationed there having chosen to spend their nights in the city when they were not on duty.

Determined not to let his two sections slip into idleness, Optio Longus had the men rip the entire block down, something the legionaries stuck into with great relish.

They scavenged what they could from the remains to rebuild the walls, then, using wood from the compound, they raised a new roof for it. The new block was smaller than the original but more than adequate for the sixteen men.

With a new base in the compound the legionaries got to know their new home.

The wooden palisade only had a short walkway either side of the main gate. To patrol the entirety of the compound, the men had to walk around the exterior of the walls. During the day this was fine but was less popular at night when they had only a burning torch and the faint lights from the city walls to keep the inky blackness at bay. Though they had been soldiers for less than a year, their apprenticeship on the frontier had made them wary of moving unprotected in small numbers at night.

Once they had finished work on their barracks, Longus had them raise short sections of walkways around the interior of the compound; no longer would his men be risked in the shadows outside the palisade.

Despite the wariness of the legionaries, their time at Nicopolis passed without incident. The morning of the day their relief detail was due to arrive, Celer was sparring with Priscus outside the barrack block.

His friend had been returned to duty shortly before they departed for Nicopolis and the easy garrison duty had been a blessing for the injured legionary.

Celer had seen the huge knotted scar that roped its way across Priscus's thigh. Though it still caused him to limp a little, the medicus had deemed him fit enough to return to duty.

The pair of them were stripped to their tunics in the morning sun. Heavy training swords, made from wood purloined from the imperial timber stacks, clashed loudly even against the usual cacophony of the blacksmiths.

They fought without shields. After the desperate fight on the banks of the Danube, all the members of Celer's section had made the unspoken commitment to improve their swordsmanship so they wouldn't become reliant on the protection of a shield.

They had sparred every morning since arriving at the compound. Priscus was still weak from his wounds but had thrown himself into training with more devotion than ever before and his strength was slowly returning. The rest of their section trained around them, either sparring or practising with javelins and darts in the small range Longus had ordered built. The other section were on guard duty that morning and stood with their back to their comrades, looking out from the new platforms at the wagons that trundled in and out of the compound.

"Enough!"

Priscus stepped back, panting heavily, his left hand dropping to rub his thigh as he did after every training session. Celer did not ask him how it was. The hardness instilled in the legions had seemed harsh and even cruel when he first started training but was now becoming the norm for him, and Priscus would have waved aside his questions even if he had asked them.

"You're getting faster," said Celer truthfully. He was sweating in the morning heat and looked forward to dunking his head in a water butt they kept in the shade of the palisade for such a reason.

"I'd be faster still if my damn leg would stop seizing up," his friend grunted as he massaged the tissue around his leg. The scar was newly formed and vivid red.

"I know a medicus in Constantinople; I could write him and ask if he knows anything that would help?" Celer offered.

"I doubt my wages would cover the cost of your medicus," laughed Priscus.

The Cohort had received the second instalment of their pay before they left for Nicopolis and, after their deductions, there was little left, becoming a popular gripe amongst all the legionaries.

"He would not charge for advice," Celer assured him. "Besides, I do not want you hobbling around in a battle line; you'll slow us down more than usual," he teased.

Priscus swiped at him with the practice sword which Celer blocked easily, raising an eyebrow as if to prove his point.

Priscus swore. "very well. Write to your man. Can't be any worse than the sawbones back at Novae."

The rest of the day was spent preparing for their departure the following morning. Their relief party, another two sections from the First Cohort, arrived at midday and the compound suddenly seemed very cramped.

Celer's section pulled sentry duty for the afternoon. It was a pleasant day, with enough of a breeze to keep the worst of the heat at bay, and the legionaries enjoyed it as they scanned the activity beyond the compound.

They'd been at it for several hours when Symmachus gave a low whistle to attract Celer's attention and beckoned him over. Celer left Priscus overlooking the compound gate and trotted over to Symmachus's platform, halfway along the palisade on the wood mill side of the compound. The air was heavy with the scent of fresh green timber as Celer climbed the ladder to the newly constructed platform.

"What is it?" he asked.

"Probably nothing," said the Cappadocian, "but there are several men sneaking about amongst the houses down there. I catch them out of the corner of my eye darting between buildings every time I look over a different sector."

Celer scanned the ground beyond the compound. Like many Roman towns and cities, the limited space within the walls was reserved for those who could afford it. Nicopolis was no different. The poor erected their homes in an unplanned sprawl about the city. Many seemed to have decided that the legionary compound might act as extra security for them and the houses and workshops were built almost right up to the compound.

Longus had pointed out to them that in the event of an attack upon the compound or the city, any attacker would have adequate cover to approach the walls making the defenders' job all the harder.

"There!"

Symmachus shot a hand out, pointing with his spear to a narrow alley between two rickety-looking houses.

Celer thought he caught a glimpse of someone dart between the building, but he couldn't be sure if it was a man or a woman.

"I'll get the Optio; might as well play it by the book," said Celer. Protocol dictated that any suspicious activity was to be investigated.

Longus was in agreement when he reported to him. "You did the right thing coming to me. Get the rest of your section off the walls; we're going out there. I want the other sections on the platforms on full alert." He reached for his shield. "I'll meet you by the gate."

The section was formed up by their optio in moments; there was much last-minute tugging of buckles and straps before they moved out of the compound.

"Up front, Symmachus," Longus ordered. "Show us where you saw them."

"Sir." Symmachus trotted to the front of their small party and they set off at a trot, ignoring the strange look the civilians gave them as they jumped out of the way of the soldiers.

Symmachus slowed as they neared the alleyway. Celer looked up and saw the helmets of the other sections poking above the rampart; he could see some had armed themselves with bows and he was grateful of Longus's decision to build the extra platforms.

They had just started down the narrow alley when a shout from behind them turned their heads.

"Optio!" the shout came from one of the legionaries from the relief force. He was pointing to their left. "They're in the alley to your..." the rest of his warning was cut short as he dropped out of sight; they saw an object hurtle through the space where his head had been only an instant before. The men on the platform beside him had also ducked but now rose up with drawn bows and fired at something down at street level. Celer heard the dull thud of arrows striking home but heard no shouts or cries. In response, four blazing torches were thrown over the palisade wall, swiftly followed by four more.

"They're trying to set fire to the timber stacks! The whole compound could go up; quickly, with me!" shouted Longus, running around the corner of the building, Celer and the others hot on his heels.

Another salvo of burning torches arced over the palisade as they rounded the corner into another alley, wider than the last.

Four men stood in the alley, hooded despite the afternoon heat. A fire was burning merrily in what looked like a large copper pot behind them; next to it stood a wicker basket. Celer could see the wooden handles of the oil-soaked torches stacked within it.

He was surprised to see the men carried crude shields made of rough planks. Several arrows protruded from them, which accounted for the strikes Celer had heard.

The men fled at the sight of the legionaries, though one took a moment to kick the pot and the basket over as he passed. Burning logs spilled out on the muddy alley floor; the torches took almost instantly.

Longus led his men after the saboteurs, swerving round the blaze.

Though they were weighed down by their armour, shields and weapons, the legionaries were superbly fit and managed to keep sight of the men as they pounded through the rabbit-warren of tight streets.

Slowly, Longus began to fall back as his younger comrades gamely followed their quarry.

Suddenly, the men they chased split up; two veered left down a gap between two houses whilst the other two broke right, leaping over a series of low walls and disappearing through a large open door.

"Celer, Priscus and Magnus, follow them," Longus panted, pointing to the two who had gone right. "You three, with me. If you lose them, head back to the compound."

"Yes, Sir," said the three in unison before leaping over the first of the wall.

If the saboteurs had hoped it would slow them down, they were sorely mistaken. Low brick walls on dry flat ground were nothing compared to the nightmarish course the legionaries had trained on.

The building the two men had fled into was a tannery; the stench of ammonia from the vats was overwhelming and the three legionaries tried to breathe shallowly as they pushed on into the building.

It was hot inside. A long low brick building. Tanned hides were hung from the ceiling, obscuring their view more than a few yards in front of them.

"Something is wrong here," said Magnus warily. "Where are all the people?"

The building did seem to be deserted. Cautiously they moved forward, shields raised and spears held ready to thrust.

"There," said Celer, keeping his voice low, "up ahead."

Through a gap in the hanging hides he could see one of the men, leaning against a wooden post, panting heavily.

The three legionaries pushed through the screen of stinking leather and came into an open area; it was littered with foul-smelling barrows filled with grey congealing slime that Celer guessed from the stench was the hair and fats scraped from the hanging hides behind them.

The men they had been pursuing straightened at the sight of them. They had dropped their shields in the chase but now he could see long knives clenched in their fists.

They were not alone. Men began to appear from either side of the legionaries. They heard the hides behind them being batted aside and Magnus swivelled on the spot to guard their backs as more men appeared.

Up close, Celer could see the men they had chased were lean and hard with pockmarked faces filled with rotten teeth. The men surrounding them were similar in appearance; they all shared a half-starved look he had seen in beggars on the streets of Rome as a boy. They were all armed with knives or clubs. One or two wielded short hatchets but none were armoured. He counted quickly and came up with twelve. Not good odds, he thought; though he and his friends were better armed and well armoured, twelve men could easily overwhelm them with sheer force of numbers.

"Who are you?" demanded Magnus behind him angrily.

The men made no reply but formed a ring around the three legionaries.

Celer stepped further into the open space, feeling Priscus and Magnus move with him. He had seen that two of the large barrows had been abandoned close together; they would make an approach more difficult and would mean they had to defend themselves from one less direction.

A small side door opened and a man dressed in fine silk robes strode into the tannery. Celer was about to shout a warning to him when the men surrounding them gave way to allow the man into the ring they had formed.

He approached the soldiers, stopping two spear lengths from Priscus, and addressed them in Greek.

"Is Marcus Aelius Celer among you?"

The question took them all by surprise; Priscus unwittingly shot Celer a confused look.

The finely dressed man caught the look and clapped his hands.

"That was easy, wasn't it," he said cheerfully.

"Who are you?" Celer asked this time.

"I am known by many names. Most commonly I am simply referred to as the Egyptian."

"Why did you attack the compound? Who do you serve?" this was from Priscus, angry that he had betrayed his friend's identity so easily.

The Egyptian laughed lightly. "I care not for your quaint little fort; the theatrics were merely intended to draw you outside the palisade. You soldiers are so predictable."

"Eugenius sent you, didn't he," said Celer, realisation dawning on him.

"Your father's money was not wasted on your education, was it, clever boy," The Egyptian mocked. "Though not quite correct; one could only dream of such exalted patronage."

"Flavianus," spat Celer.

The Egyptian nodded. "The Prefect sends his regards. He was quite adamant that you should meet your end swiftly." His eyes narrowed and the light jovial tone disappeared. "Kill them," he ordered the ring of men.

Despair welled in Celer"s chest.

"I'm sorry," he started to say to the others.

"Save it for later," grunted Magnus, lunging forward to stab his spear into the chest of one of the men.

The men surged at them, knowing that the soldiers could only attack a few at once. Celer and Priscus threw their spears, preferring to fight with swords in such close confines. Priscus managed to wound a man with his throw but the attackers threw themselves aside and Celer's sailed through without touching anyone. The attack by the soldiers startled the men, more accustomed to fighting in the streets and alleyways with knives and clubs.

The legionaries fought with dogged determination, trusting in their armour and each other to ward off the blows of their attackers. They punched, hacked and stabbed at the press of men, desperately trying to stay on their feet. One of the men picked up Celer's spear and tried to stab them from a distance, but they had been trained to fight such a foe. As one unit they surged forward, punching with their shields and slashing with their long swords at any body-part exposed to them. When six men had fallen before them, the others began to back away, fearful of the blood-spattered legionaries. The soldiers were unrelenting in their ferocity; moving as a unit, they began singling out individuals, pinning them against the walls and barrows where one would kill the man whilst the others protected his back.

Celer was filled with a burning rage. Longus's words, said only weeks before, rang in his ears and he controlled the urge to lay about him like a mad man. Instead, he fought mechanically, using all his speed and sword skill.

Magnus killed the last man with a single thrust through the man's open mouth as he wept and begged for mercy. The legionaries, however, were beyond mercy, and Magnus did not hesitate in his thrust.

Celer cast about for a sign of the Egyptian but could not see him; the man must have fled as his men began to fall.

Exhausted, battered and bleeding from dozens of wounds, the legionaries stumbled out of the tannery, the stench of blood and opened bowels mingling with its already potent aroma, and gasped in the fresh air.

Magnus winced as the rush of battle faded and he began to feel his wounds.

"Someone really wants you dead, Celer. I think there's more to your past then you've let on."

"They were willing to attack an army compound just to get to you," added Priscus. "I know some of your past, more than the others, I think, but you owe us the truth."

Celer met his friend's eyes and nodded.

"You're right, I owe you the truth. I'm a danger to you all. I'm so sorry."

The pain was clear to see in his face and his section-mates clapped him on either shoulder with bloodied hands.

"You can tell us everything when we get back to the compound. That Egyptian might have more of his thugs with him," said Priscus gently.

They gathered their weapons and headed back towards the compound as quickly as they could manage.

Optio Longus debriefed them when they returned. He sat Celer's section down in the compound officer's office and sent the two sections from the First Cohort to the tannery to retrieve the bodies. His group had lost the men they were chasing not long after splitting from the other group and had been back in the compound for some time when the three legionaries returned.

After recounting what had happened, Celer told them why the men had been after them.

He told them the whole truth; his night escape from Rome, the message to Theodosius, his father's plan, the flight across Italy and northern Greece that had ended with Attianus's death in the imperial palace and the reasons for him joining the legion.

When he had finished, he sat silently, staring at the stone floor between his feet, unable to meet their eyes.

It was Longus who spoke first. The optio stood and walked over to the door. "I think I might trust you more than any man in the Cohort now, legionary."

"Sir?" Celer raised his head, puzzled.

"Now I know that when we face the armies of the western empire, you're the one man I can guarantee won't turn and run." With that he turned and left the guardhouse.

Celer turned to his friends. "I truly am sorry to have put you in danger."

"We lead such safe lives otherwise," said Sextus.

"I too know what it is to truly hate," said Symmachus quietly from where he sat on a stool. "I feel your pain, and," he said with a faint hint of a smile, "now I know why you fight so hard."

Priscus spoke next. "My father had no titles, nor the ears of emperor's and senators. But his death lies at the hands of Eugenius and Arbogast as much as your family's. I too would have my vengeance against them. You have nothing to apologize for in my eyes."

Celer looked at Magnus, still bloody, and Pulvillus who sat beside him.

"I think the would-be emperor and his puppeteer will think twice about having you killed after today. You have no need to apologise to me, Celer; I swore an oath to fight alongside you, after all, didn't I?" said Magnus and Pulvillus nodded his agreement.

"Come," said Sextus rising from his seat, "let's talk no more of plots and emperors. We'll get you fixed up; the optio will still want to leave at first light."

# XXIV

Blaring horns woke Celer and the rest of his section in the early hours. Stumbling and cursing in the half darkness, they quickly pulled on their armour and collected their weapons. All around them the encampment lurched to life as the field army roused itself for battle.

They had left Novae under the mid-summer sun and marched south-west until they reached the province of Dardania. The Gothic rebel army had been growing steadily whilst Stilicho had assembled his, and they terrorised the local town and cities into supplying them with food and money. Orders had quickly come down that units were to be deployed as garrisons to repel the Gothic raiding parties. The Third had been deployed to a city called Ulpiana to bolster its local garrison alongside a four-hundred-strong cavalry detachment.

The cavalry had provided scouts for the small Roman force and Celer could now see riders galloping to and from the command tent at the centre of the encampment.

The Third had been temporarily billeted in the middle of Ulpiana's amphitheatre whilst the cavalry had taken over the circus, as it already had adequate stabling for their mounts.

Now the legionaries hurried to their section markers in the assembly area that had been left open for them.

Celer quickly cast an eye over his section, as had become his habit, before heading off at a jog for the muster point.

"Looks like the bastards stole a march on us," commented Priscus as he jogged alongside.

"About time," said Pulvillus from behind them, "two weeks we've been waiting for them to show themselves."

"Hurry it up, lads!" Optio Longus shouted as they jogged up, pacing impatiently already even though they were the first section to arrive.

Out of the corner of his eye, Celer saw Centurion Sirus emerge from the command tent and salute to Prefect Verinianus, commander of the cavalry unit and the senior officer of the Roman force. Verinianus mounted and rode out of the amphitheatre and Sirus marched over to the assembling cohort.

The centurions left their optios to usher the stragglers into formations as they moved up to the front of the Cohort to receive the Senior Centurion's instructions.

When he was finished, the centurions trotted back to their centuries and Sirus mounted his horse that a slave had led out to him.

"Cohort, march!" Sirus bellowed out at full parade-ground volume.

As one the legionaries moved off, the noise of their boot steps muffled by the sandy floor of the theatre only to rise to a crescendo as they marched out onto the paved streets of Ulpiana. The morning rays had barely breached the horizon and the high city walls and tall buildings meant they marched through dimly lit streets towards the main gate. Their passage could not go unnoticed and Celer saw more than one nervous face peering from doorways and windows as they tramped past.

As they passed through the main gate, Celer could see the cavalry already waiting for them.

They marched forth from the city and followed the river north. Celer knew from patrol duty that there was a bridge about half a mile from the city that offered the only crossing place for many miles.

Sure enough, the bridge was soon sighted and the legionaries were deployed into battle lines on the south side. The cavalry unit, long lances gleaming in the morning sunlight, split themselves and took up station on either flank.

"Cohort! Ground shields!" bellowed Sirus, the ears of his mount flickering at the deafening shout. "Remove your helmets," the centurion ordered and the legionaries gratefully removed their iron helmets. Although the morning was cool and pleasant, the heat of the day grew quickly in high summer and the soldiers would soon be cooking in their heavy armour.

They had not been at the bridge long when they heard the tell-tale sound of a marching body of men. The legionaries stirred, some men jerking into alertness from where they had been half dozing, leaning on their spears.

Worried murmurs rippled through the men when they realised the noise was coming from behind them and several of them crammed their helmets back on their heads. At the front of the cohort Celer didn't bother to turn; tall as he was, it was difficult to see through the raised spears and helms of the men behind him. Instead, he looked to Centurion Sirus. His commander merely glanced back from where he sat on his horse in quiet discussion with Verinianus.

"Easy, lads!" called Optio Longus, other officers echoing his calls across the Roman force, "they're friendlies."

"You boys will never believe this," Sextus chuckled from the rear rank of the First Century. All around, Celer heard chuckles and laughter that turned into whoops and cheers as the mystery force came into full view of the legionaries. Two hundred men from Ulpiana's garrison marched up alongside the Cohort, awkwardly manoeuvring around the detachment of cavalry on their left flank

"Silence!" barked Sirus and the calls quickly stopped. Orosius, who had replaced Borus as section leader after he was killed beyond the Danube, stifled a second whistle.

"They don't look very happy, do they," he said with barely contained glee.

Celer couldn't argue that; the garrison troops looked nervously about them as they came to a ragged halt, lacking the precision and coordination of the Third Cohort's men.

Tensions had flared from the moment the Third had arrived at Ulpiana. The garrison troops were all local men. Many lived in their own homes rather in the dingy small barracks that the city grudgingly maintained for them and clearly thought themselves a cut above the legionaries from the barbarous frontier.

The legionaries in turn looked at the garrison troops as poor-quality troops who'd never done any hard fighting and were paid too much for what little duties they had.

Out in the field, the garrison men did look the poorer cousins of the frontier troops. Celer had gleaned from his short time in Ulpiana that the men of the garrison were expected to furnish their own armour from their wages, reducing the burden of the city, which was only expected to equip them with their weapons. As such, the men wore a mismatch of helmets, and varying forms of armour. Few wore complete panoplies of mail or scale with others wearing scraps of both backed onto leather vests. Some wore no armour that he could see bar their helmets.

"Commander," Celer heard Verinianus greet the leader of the garrison troops, a tall gaunt looking man who seemed to be struggling with the weight of his scale armour. "I was expecting you to have more men with you?"

"My apologies," the commander saluted awkwardly, "the City Prefect thought it best we not leave the city defenceless."

"Our purpose here is the defence of the city," said Sirus, stern and imposing as he looked down from his horse.

The commander was attempting to stammer a response when Verinianus waved a hand to silence him.

"Deploy your men to the rear of the Third Cohort; you shall act as a reserve force in the event that the enemy manages to force their way across."

The gaunt commander managed a shaky salute and bawled out orders to his men. More chuckles and hoots came from the ranks of the Third as the garrison force clumsily marched to their positions.

The morning heat was just beginning to make itself felt amongst the Romans when the enemy hove into view.

They appeared over the crest of a low hill, a quarter mile from the opposite bank to the Romans. Celer could see a mass of riders followed by a swarm of infantry marching in wide column. Behind them appeared a train of draught animals, ready to carry what supplies they could force the city into giving them.

At the sight of the Roman force, the Goths drew up in surprise. The two sides watched each other from afar for a short while and Celer could make out a cluster of riders form at the head of the war band.

Eventually, the Goths moved forward. The dry weather allowed the cavalry to push off the road and the Goths formed themselves into a formation mirroring the Romans as they neared the bridge.

Up close, the Goths made for an intimidating sight. They outnumbered the Romans; Celer thought they had almost twice as many infantry and as many horsemen, although they were not as well armed as the Cohort and Roman cavalry.

Four riders detached themselves from the Gothic force and rode out onto the bridge.

Verinianus and Sirus, accompanied by Ammianus, the standard bearer for the Third and the standard bearer of the cavalry, rode out to meet them.

The bridge was just wide enough for four men ahorse to sit aside one another, so the two parties faced off man to man.

Neither side greeted the other. Celer saw them silently staring at each other; neither side seemed willing to speak first.

Eventually one of the Goths grew impatient and uttered something in his own tongue, the strange words barely audible to the legionaries who waited, sweating in the sun.

Verinianus's standard bearer apparently spoke enough of whatever tribal dialect the Goths spoke, as he lent in his saddle to repeat what was said in his superior's ears.

Verinianus's reply was short but whatever he said riled up the Goths. The one who had spoken began gesturing towards the distant city walls, his voice louder and angrier than before. He stood in his stirrups to look over the Romans' heads at the waiting force of legionaries and cavalry and spat contemptuously over the side of the bridge.

Celer slid his helmet back onto his head and deftly tied the leather thongs beneath his chin. All around him he could hear his comrades doing the same. The legionaries could not hear or understand what was being said on the bridge, but some things translated better than words.

Verinianus's standard bearer said a final few words and then all eight men turned their horses and rode back to their waiting troops.

Sirus and Ammianus rode back to the Cohort, both dismounting before the men. Sirus allowed his horse to be led away by a slave and took his shield and a spear from another.

"The barbarians demand our silver and our supplies," cried Sirus. "We shall give them a taste of Roman steel! First Century, to the bridge, march!"

The legionaries marched up the edge of the bridge, their frontage easily spanning its width.

"Century, form shield wall!"

Celer raised his shield until he could barely see above its rim and levelled his spear forward. Feeling the rank of men to his left do the same, the sun was blotted out as Priscus and the other second rankers raised their shield to cover his head.

"Tighten it up, men, overlap shields!" called Sirus from his position in the middle of the front rank.

Celer edged sideways until the left rim of his shield overlapped Orosius's. The shields above their heads became a roof and he felt the heat of many bodies compacted together, heavy breathing reverberating in the bowls of the shields.

The Gothic infantry had started forward towards the bridge, urged on by their mounted leaders. At the site of the shield-wall waiting for them, many faltered, eyeing the wall of shields and protruding spear tips warily.

Angrily their commanders screamed at them from their horses. One even drew his sword and threatened the men at the rear, forcing them to move forward. Haltingly their column edged closer. Men bearing shields were shoved unceremoniously to the front and they formed their own shield-wall.

Celer had the benefit of being on the edge of the formation and he could see that a few Goths were armed with bows and were running to the edge of the riverbank. Before he could shout a warning, Optio Longus's voice roared out from behind him, "Century, form testudo!"

Celer pressed himself into his shield as he had been taught, feeling Priscus move closer behind him. They would be reliant on Magnus's shield to cover their exposed right side.

Fortunately, the officers of the cohort were prepared and, from behind him, Celer heard the Centurions commanding their men forward. The Third Century marched into position to Celer's right, their front two ranks raising their shields and covering him from enemy fire. Some legionaries had been armed with bows themselves and they began to shoot from the cover of the shield-walls.

The enemy infantry were advancing along the bridge. Arrows thudded into the mass; shrieks and cries let the Romans know that some were finding their mark whilst arrows thudded and skittered off their tightly locked shields.

The Goths faltered again, ten feet from the Roman shields. The narrow confines of the bridge meant that barely six men could stand together at the front and they were in no hurry to meet the Roman spears.

Through a crack between the shields, Celer could see the terror on their sun-darkened faces. A few souls, made braver by the distance between them and the legionaries, shouted battle cries and threw spears and axes at the shield-wall, but they clattered off the curved faces or bounced off to no effect.

More arrows from the legionaries peppered the Gothic column, which had too few shields to protect the mass of warriors, and Celer began to hear splashes as bodies either fell or were thrown over the stone parapets.

The Romans were not immune to fear, either. The stench within the closely packed formation was almost unbearable. Celer had never known that fear had its own smell before he joined the army, but he knew it well now. Every arrow or missile that hammered into the interlocked shields resulted in curses and sharp cries. Many of the men were muttering prayers in several languages; Symmachus's own voice could be heard almost hysterical three ranks behind him, chanting something in his native language.

Once again, as he had beyond the Danube, Sirus held them in place. The Centurion constantly issued words of encouragement, mixed with scorn and curses for their enemy. No legionary would dare break his position whilst the Centurion still stood. Many of them feared him more than any barbarian warrior, whilst others would not shame themselves in front of him.

One of the enemy commanders rode his horse into the mass of his warriors, trying to urge them on, whilst the others spurred their horses towards their own horsemen.

They passed out from Celer's narrow field of view and he barely heard shouted commands from his far right where half the Roman horse waited out of arrow-shot.

The two sides stared at each other for what seemed like hours as the missiles tore the air above them. Once or twice Celer heard the scream of a horse above the shouts of the infantry and he agonised over not being able to see what was going on elsewhere.

As his arms began to ache from holding his shield and spear at the ready for so long, the Gothic warriors charged.

A great chanting began to start from somewhere in the depths of the mass of enemy infantry that grew and grew until each chant was a blast of sound that assailed the Romans.

"Ready, men!" Sirus screamed above the noise. "We hold this line! They *do not* make it through!"

"For the Third!" someone bellowed from within the ranks.

"For the Third!" the legionaries roared back as the Goths surged like a tide and drove into the Roman line.

The impact was tremendous. The Romans were nearly driven off their feet as hundreds of men shunted towards them. Somehow the line held and then the killing began.

Celer slammed his spear into the mass of screaming men, each blow indistinguishable in the scrum; its blade ran red as it struck again and again.

Weapons hammered against his shield and he could hear the grunts and cries of men separated from him only by the thickness of their shields.

As soon as it had begun, the immense pressure eased and Celer's spear struck at thin air; the Romans drove forward and their front rank stumbled and collapsed over the piles of dead.

Celer scrambled to his feet, using his spear shaft as an aid. He shook as blood and gore mingled with his sweat as it trickled down the haft of his weapon. The clash had been as fierce as it was fast; maybe twenty Goths lay dead or dying along a clear line where the Roman infantry had held. Quickly glancing about, Celer could see no dead or injured men of the Cohort.

A great cheer went up as the Goths retreated. The soldiers armed with bows sent a few more volleys after them before Sirus commanded them to save their arrows.

Further along the river, Celer could see the Gothic horsemen had been probing the river for a place to cross. Even though the summer had been dry, the river was still wide and deep in places and the Roman cavalry copied their every move, waiting on the high ground for anyone foolish enough to attempt to cross.

Glancing at the sky, Celer was shocked to see that the sun had yet to reach its peak. It felt like they had been at the bridge the whole day.

"First Century, to the rear!" Sirus ordered. "Centurion Piso, your men have the bridge."

The second century, which had been massed behind the first, now moved into position at the front of the formation. The legionaries marched forward eagerly, their morale high at the sight of their uninjured comrades and enemy dead.

The Goths attacked only once more. The leaders of the war band managed to stir up their infantry's courage enough to get them onto the bridge and launch an attack against the Roman shield-wall. Once again, the heavily armoured legionaries mauled the Gothic column and the enemy's morale shattered; their men fled under a hail of arrows as the Romans cheered.

Verinianus led his cavalry across the bridge to harry the enemy retreat but the Gothic horsemen covered the retreat of their people until they reached the hills and eventually the Roman horse left them, returning to the bridge with unbloodied spears.

They stayed at the bridge the remainder of the day in case of an enemy feint, but the returning scouts told them that the Goths continued to retreat north empty-handed.

The Romans returned to Ulpiana victorious and rested for a week with no sign of further raiding parties. Legionaries gleaned news from the traders in the forum that other detachments in towns and cities across the province had also proved too much for the raiding war bands.

Eight days after the battle at the bridge, the orders arrived at Ulpiana and the legionaries took down their tents. Stilicho was massing his army to the north. Alaric's forces had been bottled up and the army was preparing to confront the rebels.

# XXV

High peaks surrounded the army camp, reaching upwards to an azure sky. When Celer had been on picket duty away from the camp he'd heard the cries of eagles as they soared on the wind and heard wolves howling through the night watches. It was a wild place; it was hard to believe that, were he to take a horse and ride due west, he would be on the shore of the Adriatic in a matter of days. From there only a short journey by ship would see him to Italy and the lands of his birth.

More than once he caught himself staring west, as if he could see through the mountains and forests, across the stretch of sea to Rome.

They had marched north and then west for ten days from Ulpiana. The cavalry detachment had gone on ahead leaving only a few men to act as scouts. Though they marched through Roman lands, Sirus seemed wary that there may be roaming bands of Goths still in the area.

They had reached the camp late in the day. The summer heat was still strong as darkness began to gather and all the legionaries were hot and tired. Their mouths and eyes gummed with dust and sweat. Even so, the sight of the army Stilicho had gathered made them forget their aches for a moment.

Thousands of campfires burned in neat rows, marking out a temporary camp that looked bigger than a city. Over ten thousand men had gathered in the valley floor, flanked by dark peaks.

The men all around him were murmuring with awe at the spectacle when Celer spotted something farther up the valley.

"Look!" He pointed with his spear point past the gathered host below them.

"What is it?" asked Priscus from behind him, straining to look past Celer without breaking formation.

"Another camp, to the north; you can see their fires."

The legionaries turned their gaze further north and looked at the distant glow. From such a distance it was impossible to make out individual fires and it was difficult to tell how big the camp was.

"Ours or theirs, do you think?" said Orosius next to Celer.

"Must be them. Remember what that trader said: Stilicho had Alaric like a rat in a barrel."

"It's a big barrel," the other section leader said dryly, eyeing the steep, dark slopes around them.

"Big rat," said Symmachus darkly from behind them.

The local trader had seen the Cohort marching past a small town that Celer had forgotten the name of as soon as they marched past its stone marker. Rushing after the soldiers with a laden cart, he had followed them until their midday break. Sirus had allowed the merchant to ply his wears, mostly fresh fruit which the legionaries eagerly bought as a respite from the stale marching rations they were used to. Even more eagerly they had questioned the merchant for news from the north, knowing his kind always had an ear to the ground. The merchant had answered their questions whilst continuing to sell his produce to them.

Alaric had moved his army north. As more and more war bands returned empty handed from the garrisoned towns, the Goths went searching for easier prey, knowing the Romans could not fortify every city in the empire. Stilicho had anticipated his move, however, and had blocked the passes in the mountains, funnelling Alaric deeper and deeper into the valleys whilst the mustering Roman army tailed them.

"You fine gentlemen will catch up with the rest in three days I would imagine," the trader had said happily from his empty cart as he turned the pair of asses hitched to his cart for home.

It had only taken them two days in the end, marching along hard paved roads that were strangely quiet. Few dared to travel when huge armies were on the move, Celer thought, feeling a pang of pity for the farmers who must live in the valley. He had instantly thought of Decimus and Lucia, which in turn made him think of Attianus and his parents. Time had not dampened the hate that flared in his chest and again his eyes turned west towards the sunset beyond the peaks.

Celer and the rest of the Third Cohort were relaxing in the shade of their tent awnings when war horns and trumpets blared out across the camp. The camp was instantly in chaos as men sprinted to their tents for their equipment and officers began bellowing for their men to form up.

"The Goths can't be attacking us?!" shouted Magnus over the noise as they scrambled into their armour.

It was well known in the camp that the Gothic forces numbered about eight thousand men, whilst the ever-growing Roman army numbered nearly twelve thousand and was still growing. With the numerical advantage and the enemy trapped with little supplies, Stilicho seemed happy enough to starve the Goths into submission.

"Maybe they're trying to break out?" replied Priscus as he jammed his helmet on his head and reached for his weapons. Celer had a vision of a column of Gothic horsemen smashing its way through the Roman camp before dismissing the idea.

"The camp's too fortified, they'd never break through," he said as they jogged towards the Cohort's assembly area.

The Third had been assigned a section of the valley to prepare for an enemy assault two days after arriving. The familiar tasks of digging ditches and felling trees and scrub for barricades was made harder by the oppressive heat and Celer found himself missing the freezing cold of a Danube winter. The combined efforts of many units had turned the ground north of the camp into a maze of ditches, earth ramparts and wooden barricades.

Once assembled, the Cohort marched through the camp on the wide roadway that had been left clear to allow such movement of large bodies of men quickly and formed up in their position on the right flank of the front battle line.

From their location atop an earth rampart, Celer could see the enemy army in the distance, spilling down from where they had encamped.

Despite the massive Roman force, the enemy army formed up and began to march towards them.

Units of archers ran through the gaps in the infantry lines and formed up on the faces of the ramparts, the height giving them a clear shot over the ditches and barricades before them.

"They must be mad," someone commented in the ranks behind Celer.

He agreed; their training had proved how difficult it was to assault a fortified position, let alone one with twelve thousand trained soldiers manning it. The Goths must be truly desperate, he thought.

It took a long time for the Gothic forces to reach the Roman position. They halted, far out of bow-shot, and stood there watching the Romans.

Celer heard a commotion amongst the Romans, far to his left. Craning his head, he saw that Stilicho had come to the ramparts a few hundred paces away from the Third Cohort. Celer looked to see if Vegetius was with him but the General had a mass of officers, aides and bodyguards surrounding him and he could not pick out his friend. Indeed, there seemed to be far more men attending the General than was normal with many of them in civilian clothing. Celer was wondering who they could be when there was movement amongst the enemy army.

A single horseman rode forth from the Gothic army. As soon as he was in range the Roman archers nocked their first arrows. In the still summer air, the noise was terrifyingly loud but, to his credit, the horseman rode on. He rode right up to the edge of the first ditch, well within bow-shot but too far for a javelin to reach.

The rider carried a long lance with a black horsetail hanging from it. He planted the lance firmly in the dry ground and cried out in perfect Latin.

"My Lord Alaric desires an audience with General Stilicho!"

Silence greeted him for a few moments before a Roman officer, resplendent in scale armour and with a red plumed helmet, stepped forward onto a rocky spur projecting out from the earth rampart.

"Rufinus, Praetorian Prefect of the East will speak with the voice of his Imperial Excellency Theodosius. What does the rebel Alaric hope to achieve by this audience?"

Rufinus! Celer remembered the name from the library at Constantinople. Stilicho had warned him that the Praetorian Prefect wished him dead as part of some plot or scheme. The general had spoken badly of Rufinus that day and Celer thought that only a command from Theodosius himself would have placed a civilian official in charge of the negotiations rather than the general.

"My Lord wishes peace between our people," the Gothic envoy replied. "He sees no reason for blood to be shed this day."

"Bloodshed can be avoided," shouted the red-plumed officer, "if your rebel army lays down its arms and surrenders!"

The Goth spread his arms. "Lord Alaric is willing to discuss terms, but only with the General."

"You will treat with the Prefect or not at all" shouted the officer.

"I was sent here to seek audience with General Stilicho," answered the horseman doggedly. "My Lord will discuss terms with the commander who has manoeuvred against him so well."

"We have a strong position here; we have more men and we have more supplies," the plumed officer responded cheerfully. "We can wait for your lord to change his mind. Or we need not parley at all and instead break you upon the field."

"All true," responded the Goth, "but if we are forced to fight, many will die, on both sides. My Lord believes such men could be useful in future conflicts."

"Celer," Pulvillus said in a stage whisper from four ranks behind him, "what's happening? Can't see a thing from back here."

"They're trying to make peace," said Celer over his shoulder.

"They can't," Symmachus began angrily.

"Quiet!" hissed Orosius

One of the civilians in the party behind the Roman officer stepped forward and spoke in his ear. The officer listened a moment then turned back towards the envoy. "The Prefect will receive your leader with General Stilicho in attendance," the Roman officer was shouting. "He is invited to the Prefect's tent where the matter can be discussed!"

"My Lord would see the meeting happen here," the Goth indicated the ground on which his horse stood, "between our armies, where all can see."

"You rebels are in no position to dictate terms." The officer raised an arm to the silently waiting legionaries at his back. "The meeting will take place in the Prefect's tent or not at all."

The Goth seemed to consider a moment before bowing his head. He ripped the lance from the ground and turned his horse to gallop back to the army.

Both armies stood and sweated in the sun as the Goth relayed his message to Alaric. The Gothic army began to move and many legionaries raised their shields in anticipation of an attack. As the Romans watched, the enemy army parted and a group of riders emerged from their midst.

Officers all along the ramparts called at their men to stand easy as the riders approached the defensive lines.

A young man rode at their head. It was hard to tell from a distance but Celer thought he must be no older than thirty and wondered if this could be Alaric?

The Goths tried to pick their way through the defences on horseback, but several of the horses shied at the steep-sided ditches and eventually the Goths were forced to dismount and continue on foot, much to the delight of the watching Roman army.

Stilicho and his retinue met them as they emerged from the last ditch and the large group made its way into the camp, leaving both armies to eye each other warily.

Hours passed and both sides stood down, legionaries and warriors alike trying to find some shade in the merciless heat, swatting at the flies that hovered in clouds above their heads.

Eventually trumpets blared behind them and the Romans were stood to once again. The Goths picked themselves off the ground at the sight of the Romans readying themselves.

Messengers galloped along the rear of the Roman lines, riding up to the commander of each unit.

"General's ordered the army to stand down, Senior Centurion," the young officer said to Sirus. "Your men are to return to their tent lines."

"And the enemy?" asked Sirus, looking out over the Goths.

"No longer our enemy; they've surrendered to the Prefect," replied the officer before riding off.

Sirus called his officers together and relayed the orders. If they were surprised, the centurions did not show it, instead turning back to their centuries bawling orders.

Within a short time the legionaries were stripping off their sweat-soaked kit back at the tents.

Only Symmachus remained fully armoured. The Cappadocian stood standing outside their tent looking north to where they could just see the Gothic forces returning to their camp.

"Stand any longer out there and you'll fry," Sextus said to him, taking a swig of warm water from a canteen and pulling a face at the taste before holding it out to Symmachus.

"How can we just let them go!" said the Cappadocian angrily, ignoring the offered canteen.

"We're not letting them go," said Priscus, eyeing how Symmachus's knuckles were white on the hilt of his sword. "They surrendered, we won."

"Won!" Symmachus's eyes blazed as he swung towards them. "We haven't won, not whilst those animals still live!" He was shouting now and soldiers from the surrounding tents were staring at him.

"You need to calm down," Sextus said calmly; he too had noticed his friend's hand on his sword.

"Don't tell me to be calm!" Symmachus roared, ripping his sword from its sheath.

As one the rest of the section rose behind Sextus. Celer, Magnus and Pulvillus snatched their shields from the ground.

In a rage, Symmachus swung his sword at Sextus who managed to leap away from the flashing blade.

Celer powered forward and caught the next blow on his shield. All around them the camp was erupting as the soldiers saw Symmachus go wild. He hacked madly at the shield before him as Celer doggedly blocked each blow. Magnus and Pulvillus rushed to his side and the three of them blocked Symmachus from the others.

"Grab your shields!" Celer shouted, "box him in!"

Doing as he said, the others grabbed their shields, they were joined by men from Orosius's section who were pitched next in the tent line.

Between them all, they hemmed Symmachus in, their broad shields blocking his wild slashes until they crushed in so tight that he could no longer swing his sword.

Someone wrestled the blade from his trapped hand then they all bore him to the ground. Symmachus screamed and sobbed hysterically as they took him down.

"What is the meaning of this!" roared Centurion Sirus.

Panting and shaking, the legionaries slammed to attention, leaving Symmachus curled in a ball on the floor. His body shook with heavy sobs and he clawed at the dust ground with one hand.

"I asked you a question, legionaries," said Sirus, his voice dangerously low.

Celer took a half step forward.

"We don't know, Sir, he just went mad."

"He attacked you?" Sirus glared at the legionaries, noting how many were just in their tunics and how none carried any weapons save a few with shields.

He looked down at the fully-armoured Symmachus at his feet.

"On your feet, legionary!"

Symmachus stayed where he was, shaking and crying.

Disgusted, Sirus turned to Longus at his shoulder.

"Optio, get this man out of my sight. Have him stripped of his armour and bind his hands so he can't harm anyone."

"Sir!" Longus saluted, grim faced. "You two," he pointed at two random legionaries from the crowd that had gathered behind them, "pick him up and follow me." The two legionaries hurried to comply. Roughly gripping Symmachus under each arm they hoisted him to his feet and half carried, half dragged him after the Optio.

"The rest of you, back to your tent's!" Sirus ordered, and the crowd dispersed until only Celer's section stood before him.

"You five, put down your shields and come with me."

He marched them through the Cohort's tent lines to his tent, slightly larger than their own. Inside, he sat behind a simple wooden desk whilst they stood to attention before him.

"Now, explain to me what happened," he ordered.

They quickly told him of what had happened, what Symmachus had said and how he had reacted.

Optio Longus came in as they were finishing and stood silently to one side.

"How long has he been acting in this way?" asked Sirus, his stern gaze sweeping over them.

"Ever since the mission across the Danube, Sir," replied Sextus, "when we lost Cinna and Quintus."

"The battle against Theodoar's men?"

They all nodded in response.

Sirus glanced at Longus.

"I have seen this happen before to men after a battle, after losing men, especially. It is a demon that seeps into a man's souls and eats away at him, day and night."

The section dared not look away from their officer, but Sirus could see the shared horror in their faces.

"Some men heal over time, others live with the demon, but a few men…" he paused, "a few men are destroyed by it."

"Sir?" Sextus took a half step forward. Sirus nodded his permission to speak.

"Is there anything we can do for him?"

Sirus sighed, "I am more adept at fighting men than demons of the soul. There are many priests who claim to have some success in dealing with such ailments, and many priests travel with the army. Optio Longus!"

"Sir," Longus stepped forward.

"You will ask after a priest to see the man here; perhaps they can do something before we march back to Novae."

"Yes, Sir," Longus left without a glance to the legionaries.

"We're going back to Novae, Sir?" Celer asked, wincing when he realised he had spoken out of turn.

Sirus gave him an admonishing look before answering. "Yes, legionary, our orders are to return to the frontier. There is still much preparation to be done before we can march west."

He stood to dismiss them, they all saluted as one before turning and marching neatly out of the tent.

"Poor Symmachus," Magnus was saying as they walked back. "I knew something was wrong with him, but a demon!"

"He should have said something," said Sextus angrily. "There was no need for it to go as far as it did."

They talked of demons and priests all the way back to the tent but Celer was only half listening. Long after they all went to sleep that night, he lay awake. Back to Novae! He wanted to scream at the thought. They could be in northern Italy within a month, he knew. Twelve thousand men, surely enough to take on what forces Arbogast and Eugenius could muster, he thought angrily.

After a while he calmed. The time could pass quickly. Now that Alaric was dealt with, the Eastern army would be free to prepare for war. So much had changed since he fled Rome little over a year ago. He could be patient for his vengeance. With that final thought, Celer drifted off to sleep. He dreamt of smoke and fire, of wolves in the shadows. Armoured men came for him through the smoke, rank upon rank, a whole legion of them. His mother's screams were loud in his ears and he heard his father shouting for him to run. He felt the familiar weight of his armour, and looking down he saw he held his sword. He looked up and the armoured ranks were closer. Wolves snarled on their shields and the smoke swirled about them. Celer raised his shield. Either side of him he felt other shields being raised; a whole army stood with him. In his sleep, Celer smiled. This time he would not run.

# XXVI

It took almost a month for the Cohort to march back to Novae. The mood amongst the marching column was light, the men in high spirits after their victories and the surrender of the Goths. Sirus and the other officers pushed the pace so that each night the legionaries fell into their tents exhausted from the day's march, eager to return to the frontier before the winter weather arrived.

When the snows did begin to fall, every man amongst the Cohort was glad of the long days marching. It was the coldest winter Celer had ever experienced. Even the colossal Danube froze over, the ice thick enough for a man to ride a horse on with no fear of falling through.

Sentries shivered on the fortress battlements, so thickly bundled that they could hardly move. Snow drifts built up high enough that it was possible to walk up to the parapets.

All thoughts of war and future campaigns were driven from everyone's minds by the biting cold, legionaries and townsfolk alike huddling close to their fires, only straying outside when necessary.

Aside from cold and snow, Celer's section were plagued with worry for Symmachus. Their friend had marched at the rear of the column all the way back to Novae, guarded by men drawn from the other centuries of the cohort. Sirus had not allowed anyone to see him until they had returned to the legionary fortress. Symmachus was kept in isolation at the hospital in a small cell with a tiny barred window, visited frequently by the priests of Novae's church.

What success the Christian priests were having with their prayers was hard to tell, Celer had thought to himself the last time he had visited. The medicus would only allow two visitors at a time, so he and Priscus had gone, wrapped in cloaks and thick scarves.

Their friend's cell was cold, warmed only by a small hearth that the orderlies fed meagrely. Symmachus shivered on his cot, wrapped in blankets and his cloak that Magnus had brought for him on a previous visit. He did not speak the entire time they were there, instead staring blankly at the far wall. His face was drawn, with hollow eyes. The medicus had told them that he ate very little, often refusing food at all. After a while, when none of their conversation had stirred a response, Priscus looked at him and nodded to the door. After unanswered farewells they banged on the door until an orderly let them out.

An icy wind was blowing over the northern wall as they left the hospital. Hurrying across freshly fallen snow that crunched beneath their boots, they headed back to the barracks.

"Would your medicus friend be able to help him?" Priscus shouted against the wind.

Guiltily, Celer remembered that he had meant to write to Timaeus about Priscus's injured leg before they left for Ulpiana. "I could try; nothing they are doing seems to be helping," he shouted back.

They changed direction and headed for the Principia. Passing the stable blocks, Celer could see the clouds of steam rising from the mounts of the horse archers.

The legion headquarters, like many of the military buildings in Novae, was a grand old structure from a time when the fortress housed an entire legion of five thousand men. It was still the most imposing structure in Novae, Celer thought as they passed through the brick archway and blessedly passed out of the wind.

They found a clerk and Celer requested writing materials. The clerk handed over birch shavings about the size of his hand and ink and a stylus.

Celer found an empty table in the corner and wrote out his letter. It felt strange to hold a stylus after all this time and his first few words were uncertain. He wrote the address that Vegetius had given him for Helva the last time they spoke. He gave the ink some time to dry before carefully sandwiching the two thin shavings together and tying them with some twine the clerk offered.

The clerk promised the letter would be sent south with the next courier as soon as the weather abated enough for them to travel.

Spring brought a response. Celer and the others were at formation drill on the parade ground beyond the fortress walls when they saw a small column advancing from the south.

"Supply column?" Celer said to Orosius.

The section leader shook his head. "More recruits. I heard from some lads in the First that they were sending more men to bolster the garrison when we're gone."

The Third cohort had lost almost a complete century's worth of men over the course of the year. Men had been lost in the skirmishes and battles they had fought, or to disease and injury that prevented them from fighting.

Young men from Novae, sons of the men of the First and Second Cohorts that had come of age, were enlisted into the ranks of the Third. The Prefect determined that the young men who had been raised on the frontier in the knowledge that they would one day serve as legionaries would be better replacements than conscripts and volunteers from the southern cities.

Celer and his section-mates were now veterans within their own cohort, though most, himself included, had yet to reach their twenties.

Three new boys had been attached to their section. Aurelius, Hadrianus and Severus were all sons of serving soldiers in the other Cohorts.

Magnus had quickly nicknamed them the 'Three Emperors' and the new arrivals had settled into the section well.

As to be expected from boys raised in a frontier fortress, they knew how to fight and march, needing only a few corrections from the officers. As the weather warmed and the last of the snows turned to slush in the ditches and in the shade of walls, the Third Cohort was put through its paces by Sirus and his centurions.

Long route marches put strength back in their legs and they sweated at the training posts and against one another to sharpen their reflexes and weapon skills. With the river thawing, the boat patrols had resumed and the centuries took their turns attached to the river fleet, patrolling amongst the slabs of ice that floated down from the mountains on the river swollen with snow-melt.

Little stirred in the lands beyond the frontier. The defeat of Alaric had stopped the arrival of war bands, flocking to his standards. Theodoar's son was still held in Constantinople and the Gepid king quietly brooded in his lands, unwilling to give the Romans cause to harm him.

The new column of recruits was small, maybe only a hundred men. They looked odd in their civilian garments, marching in a passable step. A few shot nervous glances at the legionaries tramping from one formation to the next like a giant beast that bristled with steel barbs and was armoured in heavy iron mail.

It was only as the formation formed into the defensive square that Celer got a good look at the column and noticed the riders at its head. Were it not for Nekar, Celer would never have recognised them. The giant Numidian would have stood out anywhere, especially this far north in the frontier. Celer saw Helva and Timaeus riding ahead of the bodyguard. All three were watching the legionaries but would not be able to see him, armoured as he was, just another soldier lost in the formation.

That evening, when the men were released by the centurions. Celer sought out his friends. The best lodgings, as might be expected in any town along the Danube, were situated close to the river front.

He found them in a large two storey inn, set far enough from the dock area that the smell of fish and tar was not overpowering. All three men were dining downstairs when he arrived. Nekar, ever watchful, noticed him as soon as he stepped through the door, leaning across the table to notify his master. Helva turned on his bench and rose beaming.

"Celer, so good to see you, my friend!"

Celer could not help but smile as the magistrate embraced him.

"And you, Helva," he said happily, returning the embrace.

He took Timaeus's offered hand and nodded his head to Nekar.

"It is good to see you, young Master," said the Numidian in his deep rumble.

"Please, join us." Helva gestured to the table. "More wine and food," he said to the serving girl who had come over.

Celer allowed Helva to usher him to a place beside him at the bench.

"It has been too long," exclaimed Helva, as Nekar poured Celer a cup of wine and passed it over. The cup looked tiny and as fragile as an eggshell in his massive hand.

"Indeed," agreed Timaeus. "It was fortunate that Nekar was on the lookout for you otherwise we might not have recognised you," said the medicus truthfully enough.

The slender young boy who had nearly fallen from his horse in exhaustion in Helva's courtyard was but a memory of the young man who sat before them. Celer had grown taller since they last saw him in Constantinople. Nearly two years of training had given strength to his frame and broadening shoulders filled his tunic below a face weathered by sun and wind that made him look older than his eighteen years.

Timaeus could not help but notice the small scars that covered his hands and forearms. His upper lip had a scar near the left corner from where it had been split by some blow and had long since healed.

"I had barely dared hope for a letter in response to mine, not for you to appear with the recruit column. What brings you to Novae?" asked Celer.

Helva grunted. "Life at court is not peaceful, especially when one has grown used to the pleasant quaintness of a small seaside town in Apulia. Besides, the good medicus here is quite bent of seeing this new patient of his."

Timaeus leant across to Celer. "His condition is still as you describe in your letter?"

"Worse," said Celer sadly. In truth, he had not visited Symmachus for over a week. His friend responded less and less to all visitors and had shunned most of his meals throughout the winter and spring. His now skeletal figure was hard to look upon and Celer and the rest of his section feared how long he had before the chief medicus at the hospital would medically discharge him and cast him out onto the streets.

Timaeus frowned. "I shall visit the hospital first thing tomorrow."

"Do you think you can help him?" asked Celer.

"I shall do what I can," promised the Greek, "although, ultimately, it may be in God"s hands."

"Meaning no offence, but I have little faith in your God," said Celer bitterly, thinking of the many visits of Novae"s priests that had yielded no results.

"Have faith in our medicus then, my friend," said Helva after an awkward pause. "I have never found fault in his skills."

"My apologies, Timaeus," said Celer. "I am grateful you have come. It has been," he struggled for a moment to try and find the word, "hard," he said lamely.

"You have chosen a hard path, young master," the medicus said gently. "No need for apologies."

The serving girl arrived with a plate of food for Celer and they ate in silence for a few moments.

"Let us talk of other things," suggested Helva. "How go preparations for the war against Eugenius?"

"Well enough," said Celer, grateful to not think of Symmachus for a while. "The cohort is ready to march, we're just waiting for our orders."

"They will come soon, no doubt," said Helva. "The whole capital is talking about it. Theodosius himself is readying forces to march out and join the rest of the army. Our friend Vegetius writes that Stilicho is to gather his forces to meet the emperor alongside the Gothic forces under Alaric."

Celer almost choked on his wine at that.

"Alaric is fighting alongside us?" he asked angrily.

Helva nodded. "As per terms of his treaty with Theodosius. I was there at court when it was ratified by the Emperor and the Eastern Senate. It seems Stilicho demanded that his men be answerable when the Emperor called them to war when he forced their surrender."

"I know about the surrender," said Celer darkly, "I was there." The others looked at him in surprise as he went on. "We fought the Goths before they could raid supplies from the towns and cities, forced them to retreat until we had them blockaded."

"A great victory over the rebels," said Helva, noting the distasteful look on Celer's face. "Many in the capital share your views on the Goths. Believing that Rome's enemies should be crushed, not allowed to lie in her lands and fight alongside them. Yet," he paused, "there are others who say the Empire is in dire need of fighting men. The wounds of Adrianople run deep and are yet to fully heal."

Celer had no answer to that. He knew of the great battle fought nearly two decades ago. Some veterans of the First Cohort had fought there as young men; they spoke little of the fighting but Celer knew from his tutors that the battle had been a heavy defeat for the Roman army at the cost of Emperor Valens's life and the lives of several thousand men.

Helva suddenly looked worried. "Perhaps I should not have

mentioned that; I would not want to cause a mutiny amongst your fellow soldiers." He hurriedly looked around to see who might have overheard them but the inn was largely deserted.

Celer could well imagine how the legionaries might react to the news. "Don't worry, I won't say a word," he promised.

A distant trumpet sounded the watch change. Celer rose from the bench. "Regretfully, I must beg my leave. I have sentry duty," he explained.

The others rose from their seats.

"Thank you, for the food," said Celer. "Truly, it has been good to see you all again. Will you stay long in Novae?"

Helva shrugged and glanced at Timaeus. "That depends on what the medicus makes of your friend."

"Thank you again," said Celer to the little Greek.

"I shall do what I can for your friend," said Timaeus, "you have my word."

"Enjoy sentry duty," said Helva with a smile. "I for one shall sleep all the better knowing you are out there."

As Helva predicted, their orders did come soon enough. Barely two weeks after Helva's small party had arrived with the new recruits, an imperial courier with an armed escort of two riders arrived at the fortress.

Word quickly spread and all off-duty legionaries soon gathered outside the Principia, eager for news.

Prefect Cordus eventually emerged with Sirus and the other centurions of the First and Third Cohorts. He stepped up onto a mounting block to better address the crowd.

"Men of the First Legion. His Excellency, Emperor Theodosius, has commanded that the Third Cohort of the First Legion Italica join his army at Salona. From there the army will retake the western provinces of the Empire from the Usurper Eugenius. Fight well and honour the First Legion."

Below him, Sirus drew his sword and raised it above his head. "For the First!"

"For the First!" the assembled men bellowed around him.

"This is it!" shouted Priscus over the din to Celer. "We're going home!"

# XXVII

Armies are slow lumbering beasts, Celer thought to himself as he spat the dust from his mouth once more. He could see nothing around him save the backs of the unit in front of him and the men of the Cohort to his left. The army Theodosius had assembled was vast, far outstripping the force that Stilicho had assembled to face Alaric.

As commanded, the Third Cohort had marched west and rendezvoused with the rest of Stilicho's forces at Salona where they had waited for the Emperor and the bulk of the army. Celer had said his goodbye's to Helva, Timaeus and Nekar at Novae the night before they marched. The little medicus had been spending long hours with Symmachus in his tiny cell and sounded tired but hopeful that the young legionary showed small signs of improvement. Helva had gripped his arm tightly as they said their farewells, promising to pray for Theodosius's victory and Celer's safe return.

The arrival of the Gothic forces under Alaric led to heightened tensions within the camp and only the threat of severe punishment from Stilicho prevented any bloodshed.

Salona was a huge port city, but it was unable to host so many troops, so the men had created a vast encampment to the north of the city. Mounted units scouted north towards territory controlled by Arbogast's forces but found no opposition. The summer heat and the cramped conditions of the camp only fuelled the sour mood of the legionaries. When the Emperor arrived, the camp was quickly broken and the whole army began a slow march north.

Unopposed, they pushed deeper into Dalmatia; the mass of men, horses and pack animals pounded along ancient roads. Huge dust clouds hung above the army from the moment it moved so that at the end of the day everyone was caked in a layer of dried sweat and dust.

They had entered the foothills of the Julian Alps three days ago. Climbing passes and descending through tight valleys, they drew ever closer to northern Italy itself.

"How many more days until we're through the mountains, do you think?" he asked Priscus, who marched behind him, almost shouting over the noise.

Priscus had come this way when he had fled from Mediolanum and seemed to have a vague idea of where they were in the mountains.

"Can't be more than a day. Hard to tell when you can't see anything!" his friend shouted back.

That night, Sirus walked amongst the tent lines of the First Century. The Senior Centurion spoke to each section as they ate their evening meals.

"Scouts are reporting that there is one more pass to cross tomorrow, then we descend into the lowlands. Arbogast's forces are nearby so you march in full battle gear tomorrow; leave your non essentials with the pack mule, understood?"

"Yes, Sir!" they chorused back, watching him move off to the next tent.

"Don't much fancy fighting in one of these valleys," mused Sextus, pointing with his spoon at the steep slopes surrounding the camp. "Not a lot of room to manoeuvre."

"Listen to the tactician over here," laughed Priscus.

"At least they won't be able to flank us," offered Aurelius, ever the boldest of the three newcomers.

"And we won't be able to flank them," said Sextus grimly.

Celer thought of the crushing tightness of the shield-wall, remembered the cries of dying men and stabbing blades of both sides; he shuddered.

"Cold?" offered Magnus, though the night was warm and still.

"A little," Celer lied. Looking around he saw they all knew it.

"We should get some sleep," said Pulvillus.

As they lay there, with the tent flaps open in the vain hope of a cooling breeze, Celer listened to the camp. Such a vast gathering of men and beast's was never truly quiet, but tonight the camp was eerily still. The officers had done their rounds and all the men knew that tomorrow they could face battle. Celer would have gambled what little money he had that every man was lying awake in their tent, wrestling with their fears the same as him. Just then, one of his section began to snore loudly. Stifling a laugh, Celer chastised himself. Fear of what may or may not happen would not help him and tiredness would more likely be the death of him. Calming his mind, he forced himself to sleep.

Dawn broke with a chill to the air that hinted at summer's near end. Celer was glad of his cloak as they quickly ate their morning meal and made their last checks of their armour and weapons. He checked the edges of his sword and spear as if they may have magically blunted since he put fresh edges on them the night before and found, unsurprisingly, that they were still sharp.

Together they dressed, helping each other with buckles and ties, making sure every piece was firmly strapped on. They hadn't been issued with throwing darts and carried only their shields, swords, and spears that were light enough to throw at close range or fight with in a melee.

Before they left, Sextus led them in a prayer, asking his god for his blessing and protection. As the only one left in the section who kept the old Roman gods, Celer bowed his head like the others and listened to the prayers. He had sacrificed a small portion of his ration the night before to Mars and Fortuna so he said nothing, waiting until they had finished.

It took an age for the army to form up into its marching column. Much to the disgruntlement of the Roman troops, the Gothic forces had been given the honour of the vanguard for the day and led the army up towards the pass.

The morning chill soon disappeared and soon enough the choking clouds of dust rose to obscure any view the legionaries might have had of where they were going. Celer kept his head bowed to protect his eyes as much as he could from the cloud, his armour and weapons feeling heavy as they climbed the steep slope. It was midday before the Third Cohort, positioned in the rear half of the marching column, breasted the summit of the pass. This high up a strong breeze was blowing and the visibility improved enough for the soldiers to see.

"Welcome to Italy," said Celer to the men around him, many of whom had never been this far west.

"So where's the welcome party?" said Orosius.

They marched two miles down a heavily forested slope before they saw the enemy.

To the west, an army was formed up at the exit of the pass, barring the way to a river that shimmered in the sunlight and the valley beyond. From what he could see, Celer thought that Arbogast's army must have numbered around fifty thousand men, an even match for the forces under Theodosius's command.

Ahead of them, trumpets and horns were blaring, the vanguard was already forming up. Shouts echoed up the column. Celer could see the men in the units ahead of them pointing up the slopes either side of them.

He swore under his breath when the trees cleared enough for him to see why. Arbogast had laid a trap for them. High on the slopes either side of the pass, the Frankish general had stationed small contingents of his forces. Individually, they were too small to harm the army but collectively they could pose a serious threat if they attacked alongside the bulk of the western army arrayed to the front of Theodosius's troops.

Riders thundered up and down the column with orders from the Emperor, somewhere near the head of his army.

The column halted as orders were issued. Eventually it was Stilicho himself who rode down the line to issue them.

"Senior Centurion." He reigned in alongside Sirus at the head of the cohort, his heavily armoured bodyguards in tow.

"Sir!" Sirus saluted.

"The Third Cohort is to move to position on the left flank alongside the Lanciarii and the Second Flavia's First Cohort." He pointed up at the western troops on the slope above. "You're to guard against any flanking manoeuvres by those troops."

"Yes, Sir." The general was already on the move as Sirus began bellowing orders. "Cohort, left face!"

They swung into position alongside the other two units from Stilicho's Thracian forces. Celer recognised the standard of the Lanciarii from the army in Dardania when they had faced Alaric, but the First Cohort from the Second Flavia were new to him.

Below them the Gothic vanguard, nearly twenty thousand strong, were forming up under their officers.

From his position at the front edge of the Cohort, Celer had a clear view down the slope towards Arbogast's army. The two forces were so large that they filled the valley floor. The Eastern cavalry and the Gothic horse sat uselessly, unable to manoeuvre to the flanks as the Gothic infantry began to advance towards the enemy lines.

"What are they doing!" exclaimed Priscus behind him, momentarily forgetting his animosity to the Gothic troops, "They'll be cut to pieces!"

"Quiet!" ordered Sirus. The Senior Centurion was stood a couple of paces in front of Celer, watching the formations below them. The Western troops above them were far enough away that he would have plenty of warning should they advance, so the officer largely ignored them.

Celer agreed with Priscus. From where he was stood it didn't look like Arbogast's men had prepared any fortifications beyond their camp. Even so, their infantry were formed into dense formations that, as he watched, formed a continuous shield-wall. The rattle of shields locking together was so loud that they could hear it almost half a mile away. Behind them were rank upon rank of archers. Already the gap between the Goths and the enemy shield-wall was dark with missiles; prone bodies were left behind the advancing warriors. The realisation of what Arbogast had done was beginning to dawn on Celer. He had allowed Theodosius to march unopposed through the mountains until he reached this valley. His army was drawn up in a strong position, giving Theodosius no room to manoeuvre his own forces. The soldiers on the high slopes meant that any retreat would be slowed, allowing his main force to catch the eastern army in the rear and inflict huge casualties, if not break them completely. The Eastern Emperor had been left with little choice, hence his command that the Gothic vanguard engage; Celer guessed that he meant to break through Arbogast's line with the fearsome warriors and move the fighting onto the more spacious plain beyond.

With a great roar the Goths hurtled across the last few yards and smashed into the Roman line. To the watchers higher up the pass it appeared as if a great wave broke along a rocky shoreline. Here and there the Western army was thrown back by the force of the charge, the line buckling whilst others held strong against the surge. Gothic ferocity, however, was not enough to break through the line and Arbogast's men held. Screams and cries rose from the valley, amplified by the tight slopes. All the while, arrows rose over the fighting men to pepper the waiting ranks behind. Celer knew the Goths were not as heavily armoured as the legionaries; the arrow storm would be inflicting huge casualties on the warriors.

Emperor Theodosius sat mounted on a grey stallion, surrounded by his Generals barely three hundred yards from where Celer was, positioned on a rocky knoll that gave a perfect viewpoint of the battle below. Celer saw riders powering their way up the slope towards the Emperor. He recognised Alaric's black horsetail standard streaming above them. The Gothic chieftain was shouting as he rode up, pointing with a lance down at the fighting below. Celer could not hear the response but watched as Alaric stared silently at the Emperor and his advisors before wrenching his mount around and leading his retinue back towards the fighting.

Hours passed as the fighting raged below. Wounded warriors stumbled back up the slope and a makeshift hospital emerged, surrounded by the legionaries who watched the troops who sat unmoving on the slopes above them.

Twice the Gothic horse led attempts to break the deadlock their countrymen were embroiled in. Twin charges were launched against the flanks of Arbogast's lines. The steep, wooded ground was unsuitable for mass cavalry charges and both times they were repulsed by the enemy infantry.

Eventually, failing light broke the two sides apart. Arbogast's line had held and the exhausted Gothic warriors were forced back up the slope. The supply train had arrived and tents were being erected halfway down from the summit of the pass. The Roman troops remained stationed around the camp until darkness had fallen and the enemy troops above them were hidden against the black slopes.

Picket lines were formed and the men stood down. The Third Cohort, along with the men of the Second Flavia's First Cohort were sent to the summit of the pass to guard the rear of the army.

The First Cohort were commanded by a Prefect named Cordulus. As the ranking officer, the Prefect decided that his men would have the first watch so Celer and the rest of the Third grabbed a few hours' sleep before being woken again at midnight.

There was no moon that night; the darkness was so complete that Celer could not see Magnus and Pulvillus in the next pair of their thin sentry line. He and Priscus were sitting amongst a pile of boulders forty yards from where the two Roman cohorts had made camp. Though the main camp was almost two miles away, he thought he could still hear the occasional scream of a wounded man being worked on by the army's team of medicus and their orderlies.

A strong breeze still blew and the night air was growing cold. Even the boulders they rested on had lost all the warmth of the sun and Celer felt his muscles begin to cramp. He was easing himself up to stretch when a fresh gust wafted the unmistakable smell of horses towards them. He dropped down instantly.

"Smell that?" he whispered.

"Yes," Priscus breathed.

They both strained their ears in the darkness but could hear nothing. Celer pressed his ear to the ground, trying a trick Iulianus had taught him back on the Danube. Sure enough he could feel rather than hear the tremors of a large group of men and horses moving somewhere close by.

"Get back and alert the Centurion," hissed Celer.

Priscus said nothing in reply. He slipped off into the darkness, quiet as a wraith.

Moments later, he reappeared.

"Report, legionary," whispered Sirus in the blackness.

"Sir, there's a body of men out there somewhere, with horses," said Celer.

He felt rather than saw Sirus drop to the ground and lie flat as Celer had done. The Centurion rose within seconds. "They're close," he breathed. "Gather the other pickets and form up on the right flank. Cordulus and his men are massing on the left; when he gives the order, we're going to ambush them."

"Yes, Sir," they both slipped into the darkness and quickly gathered the men as the Centurion had ordered.

As the enemy grew closer, so did their smell. Many were mounted, Celer thought, maybe all of them. He could barely hear their hoof beats and realised that they must have muffled the hooves of their mounts.

The men of the Third Cohort were massed amongst the boulders that Celer and Priscus had been watching from. From where he was crouched the sound of men breathing all about him was deafening and he hoped the enemy would not hear them.

At last he heard the scatter of small stones as the horses began to pass in front of his position. In the darkness he couldn't see a thing. He gripped the hilt of his sword, ready to rip it free of its sheath as soon as Cordulus gave the signal.

A horse whinnied barely twenty yards from where the legionaries were crouched, sounding abnormally loud in the darkness. The animal could smell the hiding legionaries, Celer knew. The Prefect would have to give the order soon if he was to catch them by surprise.

The enemy column halted. Celer could hear more horses snorting nervously as they caught the scent. He could hear riders shushing the animals quietly.

"Fellow Romans!" a voice called out, deafening to the legionaries who had been straining to hear the slightest noise. "We come in peace. We wish to surrender ourselves to the true Emperor, Theodosius."

Silence greeted him.

"My name is Gaius Marcellus, Commander of the Third Julian Legion. My men and I do not wish to fight you."

Celer heard the familiar noise of flint striking steel and light flared in the darkness, it's brightness so sudden that it was dazzling.

Prefect Cordulus rose from one knee, holding a burning torch before him. The Prefect stood alone in a pool of light, his men and the Third Cohort still hidden beyond the dancing shadows.

Commander Marcellus and his men squinted at the brightness; some raised their arms to shade their eyes and Celer could see that their weapons were sheathed, a mass of riders disappearing into shadow behind their commander.

"I will gladly accept your surrender," said Cordulus. "Dismount from your horses and lay down your arms."

"Might I know the name of the man I am surrendering to?" asked Marcellus.

"Prefect Cordulus, First Cohort, Second Flavia Legion." Cordulus inclined his head.

"Very well, Prefect." Marcellus signalled his men and dismounted, his men swiftly following suit.

The commander strode forward and stopped a spear's length from

Cordulus. The Prefect watched impassively, his right hand resting on the pommel of his sword as Marcellus slowly drew his own sword before reversing it and offering him the hilt.

Cordulus took the sword and reversed it, offering it back to Marcellus.

"My thanks, Prefect," said the commander as his men drew their own weapons and lay them at their feet.

"Torches!" Cordulus called out and flames blazed up as his men ignited torches where they had been hiding. Several horses tried to bolt at the sudden appearance of so many men, but their riders held them firmly.

Sirus led the Third Cohort forward, igniting their own torches until the darkness was forced back completely. Fully illuminated, Celer could see that the Third Julian Legion was a mixed force; nearly three hundred mounted men rode behind their commander whilst a column of legionaries, the rearmost ranks still hidden in the darkness, followed them.

Cordulus had detachments from his own forces move up and down the column, collecting weapons into piles from the surrendering soldiers. Celer tried not to stare too much at the men as he gathered their weapons. Their arms and armour were indistinguishable from that of any legionary in Theodosius's army. The men stood ramrod straight as the Eastern soldiers collected their weapons. Once disarmed, the captured legion was marched into the two cohorts' temporary camp. Their mounts were corralled on one side and them men were sat back to back on the other side.

"Senior Centurion," Cordulus called Sirus over to him when the prisoners were safely under guard. The Prefect stood with his officers and the captured Marcellus.

"Your men discovered the column; the honour of the capture should go to them. Gather an escort and take commander Marcellus here to headquarters."

Sirus saluted the senior officer. "You honour us, Sir."

He turned to his waiting men, "Optio, assemble two sections of the First Century to escort the Commander. Centurion Piso!"

Piso stepped forward. "Sir?"

"You have command of the Cohort until I return."

"Yes, Sir!"

Longus marched over to where the men of the First Century were back on picket duty.

"Celer, Orosius," Longus called out to them. The two legionaries came trotting out of the dark.

"Sir!" They saluted.

"Gather your sections; you'll be escorting the Centurion and the Commander to headquarters."

The men assembled quickly, eager to have such an honourable task. Sirus chose to march rather than ride the few miles to the main camp; the risk of a horse stumbling in the dark was high and Celer couldn't help but marvel that Marcellus and his men had been able to ride so silently up the pass without issue.

The Commander conversed happily with Sirus on the short march, seemingly unperturbed in his position as their prisoner.

They were stopped by the sentries several hundred yards from the camp; Sirus gave the password and the duty officer let them through.

The camp was lit by many fires and torches. Men were screaming in the makeshift hospital and Celer saw many legionaries and Gothic warriors sitting outside their tents, wrapped in cloaks and staring darkly into their fires rather than try and sleep. Morale was low amongst the men. Celer could feel the despair as if it were carried upon the breeze. Theodosius's men had suffered heavy casualties that day and Arbogast's army had shown no signs of wavering. As they marched down the wide road between the tent lines, Celer could hear the Christian priests leading large groups of soldiers in prayer, asking their god for victory.

The camp headquarters was huge, made of multiple large command tents joined together. Scores of elite scholae guarded the perimeter. Celer felt the old shiver of fear as the faceless guardsmen made them wait until an imperial official came to escort them through to the main tent.

They were instructed to wait in a courtyard formed by three tents. Light poured from open tent flaps and Celer could see clerks and soldiers moving in the lamplight.

It was Stilicho who came out to meet them in the end. Despite the late hour the General looked fresh and greeted Marcellus warmly, waving a hand as the Commander began to formally surrender once more.

"Enough, Marcellus. You have surrendered to my men already, have you not?"

"I have, General."

"Then there is no need for this. Keep your sword; you are most welcome."

"My gratitude, General Stilicho."

"I must admit, I am surprised to see you and your men were stopped at our rear. I take it Arbogast means to surround us here?" There was a probing tone to Stilicho's voice.

"Indeed, General. Many other units were dispatched to the smaller passes. My men and I, however, have no wish to fight for a man who favours barbarians over Romans."

Stilicho frowned. "Our reports say only Roman units were seen fighting in the battle line today."

Marcellus screwed up his mouth bitterly. "Arbogast has a core of men he trusts. Legionaries from the Gallic legions, but mainly Franks and Alamani from beyond the Rhine; he has been growing their forces these past years. He holds them in reserve, meaning to use them to crush you come the morning. It was Roman troops who held the line today against your foederati."

"Our losses were heavy today," said Stilicho sombrely. "We may have need of you and your men; our scouts reported a column arriving at Arbogast's encampment just before nightfall."

"That will be reinforcements arriving from Hispania. They arrived the same time as Consul Flavianus, the Prefect of Italy," said Marcellus.

Celer started, earning a withering glance from Sirus. He steadied himself, mind racing. Flavianus was here!

Stilicho had not noticed and was tapping the pommel of his sword thoughtfully.

"This is distressing news. I must inform the Emperor." He reached out and clapped Marcellus on the shoulder. "Your loyalty to the true Emperor shall not be forgotten. I will have your men escorted to the camp; they will bolster our forces for the fighting tomorrow."

Marcellus bowed his head. "As you wish, General."

Stilicho turned to Sirus. "Fine work once again, Centurion. I'm sending a cavalry detachment to relive your men. There will be hard work to do once day breaks so let them get some rest."

Sirus stood ramrod straight at the General's praise. "Yes, General."

"If you will excuse me, gentlemen, I must disturb the Emperor from his prayers." Stilicho turned and disappeared into the tent he had emerged from.

Marcellus was led away by an aide so the two sections from the Third Cohort marched back up the pass alone. The breeze that had been present all day was growing in strength and they had to bow their heads into the buffeting gusts as they neared the top of the pass.

They were overtaken by the cavalry detachment that Stilicho had sent on the way and, as they arrived at the small camp, the men of the Third Julian Legion were being escorted down the slope. Their weapons had been bundled together and lashed to the cavalry mounts as some troopers led them down the slope.

Sirus passed the General's orders to Cordulus and the infantry pickets were drawn back, the men falling gratefully into their tents to try and sleep a few hours before dawn.

Celer lay wrapped in his cloak as the wind made the goatskin walls of the tent billow above him.

"Flavianus is the man who killed your parents and your friends," said Sextus in the dark.

"He is."

"If we win tomorrow, what will you do?"

"I swore an oath," said Celer, "that I would do everything I could to avenge my family and all those who lie dead at the hands of Arbogast, Eugenius and Flavianus. If we win tomorrow, I will find the bastard and kill him."

"I pray for vengeance also," said Priscus in the dark. "My list shares names with yours; Flavianus will do for a start."

"Flavianus, then," said Sextus.

"Flavianus," the rest of the tent said in unison. If Theodosius's army survived the next day, the man's fate was sealed.

# XXVIII

Celer woke with a start. The tent above him shuddered violently; somewhere nearby a tent flap had broken loose and was slapping loudly against the leather walls as powerful gusts ripped through the camp.

Gingerly he undid one of the wooden toggles that held their flap shut and looked out. To the east a faint light was spreading over the jagged horizon of grey mountains. Dark clouds covered the sky, slowly turning pink and purple as the first rays of sun touched them. Dust and grit blasted his face as the wind stormed through the tent lines; he could see the horsemen that had relieved them on picket duty sheltering behind their mounts in their pairs. More dirt blasted his face and he quickly ducked back into the shelter of the tent, wiping it from his eyes. When he turned, he found seven pairs of eyes looking up at him from their bed rolls.

"A storm?" asked Magnus quietly.

"Could be," Celer nodded, wrapping his cloak more tightly around him, savouring it's warmth. "The wind is building from the north east."

"A storm is an ill omen," warned Sextus, falling back onto his roll, staring up at the walls that strained against their ropes.

Celer thought of Jupiter, lord of all, master of thunder and storms. The wind would be at their backs, after all. "I wouldn't be so sure," he said.

The others just looked at him, non-believing. To them, storms were sent as a punishment from their God, a means of cleansing the sinful.

Any thoughts of a fire were quashed by the wind, so they ate a simple meal of hard bread and dried figs to break their fast before dressing for battle. The weight of his armour, the smell of the oiled metal and leather was so familiar to Celer now that he often felt naked when he wasn't wearing it. The thick layers would be welcome to help ward of the blast of cold wind that ravaged the camp as they dressed.

By the time the sun was fully above the horizon the Third Cohort had broken down their camp and stood assembled in full battle gear. Fierce gusts buffeted them, so strong that the legionaries had to brace themselves so as not to be blown over. As soon as they were assembled, the order was given to march. Centurions resorted to hand signals rather than have their shouts snatched away by the wind.

Celer had hoped that descending to the main camp would take them out of the wind, but the pass only served to funnel it down the slope. Below them the whole army was assembling; legionaries battled to flatten their tents, whilst cavalrymen kept firm hold of their mounts which snorted and struggled against their halters, the storm making them skittish.

A subaltern from the Emperor's staff rode up to Sirus as the Cohort marched into camp. The young officer had to lean almost out of his saddle to give the Centurion his orders before guiding his mare over to the next unit.

Sirus led them through the camp on the main roadway; the hard, dusty ground had been battered and churned by thousands of boots and hooves, making a ragged dark scar that pointed straight at Arbogast's army.

Celer felt a sickening in his stomach as they marched down towards the battlefield. So many had fallen the previous day that the details sent to retrieve the bodies had barely made a scratch on the grisly piles. Here and there Celer thought he could hear faint moans and cries rising above the wind from men too wounded to move, fated to lie amongst the dead until someone found them or until their life ebbed away.

He found himself muttering a prayer to all the gods he knew that if he were to die today at least let it be a quick death.

All around them the army was forming up. The Third Cohort marched to the centre of the force that stretched from the northern slopes of the valley to the south. The First and Second centuries were ordered into the first battle line. The Third and Fourth centuries lined up directly behind them in the second line. A third line of reserve forces was positioned behind them all. To Celer's right a century of legionaries moved into position. They wore shirts of gleaming scale armour. Celer could see that the collars and cuffs had borders of bronze scales and their iron helmets were plated with bronze and silver. The soldier directly next to him had scenes etched into his silvered cheek guards; Celer could make out the image of a legionary standing over the body of a fallen enemy.

The legionary noticed him looking and turned. He was a powerfully built man, with a scarred, tanned face with a nose that had been broken in the past and set badly.

He grounded his spear and offered his right hand to Celer.

"Licinius."

Celer passed his own spear to his shield hand and shook Licinius's hand. "Celer."

"This your first fight, Celer?"

"No," Celer said. "Never in a battle this big, though," he admitted.

Licinius grinned, showing a gapped row of teeth. "Stick close to me. Keep it tight and you'll be fine. We're going to break that wall of theirs."

As he said it, the legionaries around him thumped their spears on the inside bowls of their shields twice.

Licinius laughed. "Didn't even flinch! You boys will do fine."

Archers began filtering through the gaps between the men. Dark-skinned men from Egypt and Syria, they looked cold, Celer thought, as they formed up in front of the infantry, their faces and necks wrapped in scarves beneath their conical helmets, shoulders hunched against the wind that had begun to pick up dust and grit in swirling clouds.

Priests appeared before the army. Many of the legionaries bowed their heads as they spoke their prayers, their voices taken by the wind that blew their words towards Arbogast's army.

The Western forces occupied the same ground as the day before. Their men seemed eager despite the blasts that blew great clouds of dust towards them. Celer could see them making crude gestures towards the eastern army, their morale high after their victory over the Gothic warriors.

When the sermons were delivered trumpets blared, their notes strangled and distorted.

"Spears to the rear!" Sirus bellowed, his voice a match for the storm. Celer and Priscus, along with all the other men in the first two ranks, passed their spears back to the men behind. They would launch the spears in volleys before the shield-walls clashed whilst the front ranks absorbed the enemy missiles.

Officers prowled in front of their men one last time before the trumpets sounded once more and the army of Theodosius lurched forward.

The archers ran ahead of the main force. As soon as they were within range, they began launching their shafts towards the enemy. Western archers moved forward to meet them. Celer watched as they nocked their arrows.

"Shields up!" came the order from Sirus and the other officers.

Celer raised his shield to just below his eyes, ready to snatch it higher when he saw the arrows begin to fall. He watched the air darken above the enemy lines as the swarm of missiles was released and covered his head. Nothing happened. The legions marched on across the valley floor. No arrows thudded into the shields or landed in the ground before them. Warily, Celer lowered his shield and looked across at Arbogast's lines. The enemy was in disarray. The archers bent their bows to release another volley. Taut bowstrings snapped as they were released and the second swarm rose only to be blown apart in the sky. Celer watched in disbelief as the missiles were scattered as if by an invisible hand; many slammed into the ground between the two forces but others fell amongst the archers who had launched them.

Theodosius's archers too had noticed the effect the wind was having on their volleys. They were shooting at a far flatter angle than Celer had ever seen them, sending volley after volley into their western counterparts. The enemy archer core was being ripped apart. Unable to retaliate, they retreated behind the shields of their infantry which quickly bristled with arrows.

The eastern army's front line had advanced through their own archers and was swiftly closing the gap. Shouted orders echoed down the line to form a shield-wall, barely audible over the howling gale that swept down behind them, driving them towards the enemy ranks.

Celer's stomach churned and icy fists gripped his chest as they neared the enemy, Orosius and Licinius either side of him. Someone in Licinius's century howled something and the legionaries banged the bowls of their shields in response. Another ten paces and they did it again, five paces and again; now the thunderous banging was continuous,

Celer found himself following suit, the men of the Third Cohort taking up the rhythm that swelled in volume until it almost drowned out the gale. Officers screamed to be heard above the noise as they closed to thirty yards of the enemy line. Celer could see the eyes of the men amongst the enemy shield-wall. The eastern legionaries launched their spears at a trot over the heads of their front ranks; the missiles slammed home into the enemy ranks, the heavy weapons able to punch through the shields of their foes and render them useless.

Celer saw arms drawn back as the enemy responded with their own volleys and raised his shield. Once again, the gale-force winds saved Theodosius's army from the worst of the volley; the rearmost ranks injured their own men as the wind robbed the force from their throws and brought them down on the undefended necks and backs of their comrades. The nearest ranks cleared their own lines but the buffeting wind blew many off course to thump harmlessly to the turf or struck with so little impact that many bounced off the curved shield faces.

Unhindered, Celer and the rest of the front rank smashed into the enemy. Taking a last glance over the lip of his shield, Celer aimed for the weak spot where two enemy shields met. Dropping his shoulder into the bowl of his shield, he drove forward with all his might. The collision was earth-shattering. The point he had struck gave a little before the ranks behind steadied it for a moment, then the force of the men behind him drove him onwards. He forgot all about trying to use his sword and focussed on staying upright and keeping his shield up. Stars flashed across his vision when his head slammed into his shield and he could taste blood in his mouth.

To fall was to die, Sirus had taught them. So he stumbled over the writhing bodies beneath his feet, fighting to maintain his balance. Blows hammered into his shield and something glanced off his helmet.

All around him men were screaming and shouting. Both lines had held. Licinius was to his right, roaring at the top of his lungs as he thrust his sword into the gap between their shields. A spear flashed past Celer's face and he heard a cry behind him but he could not look back. There was no place for compassion in a shield-wall; to stop for another was to weaken the line and doom them all. He thrust his own sword forward between the gaps in the shield wall, felt it bite and ripped it back. The front few inches were wet and red, he saw, before thrusting forward once more.

Time lost all meaning as they pushed on, a great beast with steel fangs that slowly gnawed its way into Arbogast's army. Celer punched and thrust his way into the mass of men. An enemy blade had raked his sword arm and his blood mingled with that of his enemies as the churned ground soaked it up eagerly.

Their momentum had slowed but they had broken the front ranks and the men they faced began to give way before them. Space appeared in front of him, filled with fleeing men whilst a few brave souls stood their ground only to be hacked to pieces by Theodosius's legionaries.

Dust swirled around them, hiding the rest of the battlefield. Celer was vaguely aware that arrows and javelins arced above his head, but his eyes were fixed firmly on what lay before him.

A fresh line of shields faced them, emblazoned with strange beasts and strange designs. Arbogast was committing his loyal core of Franks and Alamani. The men who had ransacked his home and killed his parents could have stood among them, Celer thought as he felt that old rage burn away his fear. Orosius was gone; another man he did not recognise stood to his left. Licinius was on his right still, battered face painted with blood. Red rivulets ran down his silvered helmet; the etchings ran red, bringing the scenes to life.

"Reform, First Century! Reform the line!" Sirus roared form somewhere to his left, and the advance paused as other officers checked the line.

Celer tore his eyes from the barbarian soldiers and looked behind him. Pulvillus stood behind him, panting and spattered with blood. He looked grimly back at Celer's questioning look. Priscus and Magnus must have fallen, either injured or dead, for Pulvillus to stand behind him.

"You fight well, boy," gasped Licinius, "ready to do it again?"

Celer spat blood from his mouth. "Are you, old man?"

Licinius grinned his broken smile. "We're going to break their wall!" he shouted.

The men either side of him beat the inside of their shields.

The Franks and Alamani shouted and spat, banging their own shields as the Romans resumed their rhythmic beat. The double thump reverberated off the battered shields as they began to edge forward.

Dust clouds blasted the front ranks of Arbogast's army. Scavenged javelins and the last few arrows were loosed, hammering the barbarians until the last possible moment.

"Century, form a boar's head!" Sirus shouted.

The legionaries responded on instinct, forming into a wedge pointed straight at the enemy line with Sirus at its head. All along the front line, other officers were forming their own. Troops from the rear rushed forward to fill any gaps.

With a roar, the blood-soaked legionaries surged forward. The wedges punctured the enemy line. Each man pressing his shield into the back of the one in front, their weight bore the point man through the enemy shields, ripping their formation apart or simply running straight over any man who could not keep his feet. More soldiers funnelled into the wedges, driving them deeper and wider, the men at the front almost running as they staggered over fallen bodies and tried to protect themselves as best they could.

Celer was swept along in the formation; he thrust and hacked at anything that moved before him, his shield a moving extension of his body that shuddered under countless blows.

The barbarians who fought for Arbogast were fearsome warriors; though their line had been broken, they counter-attacked. Small companies of warriors formed their own wedges, splintering the Eastern formations and isolating groups of legionaries that were surrounded and hacked to pieces. All along the valley floor, all semblance of order was lost and the fighting descended into a mass melee, both commanders desperately throwing in their reserves to turn the tide.

One minute Celer was hacking his way through broken files of men, the next he was back-to-back with another legionary, fending off multiple attackers that came at him with swords and axes. The fighting was desperate and his arms grew so tired that he could barely fend off blows. The ground was so torn and littered with bodies and equipment that he could not dodge their attacks. Only another armoured wedge smashing into the flank of his adversaries saved him from death.

There was no respite though. In front of him, Optio Longus appeared from the turmoil. The optio was screaming for men to form on him.

Rushing forward Celer positioned himself behind his optio at the point of a wedge. Longus glanced over his shoulder at him and nodded. When enough men were massed behind him, the optio led them forwards. They hurled themselves at a mass of warriors. The legionary beside Celer was killed by a massive battleaxe that split his helmet open as if it were eggshell. Another soldier instantly took up the dead man's place, and he and Celer pressed forward, carrying the dead legionary on their shields into the waiting swords.

Little by little the eastern army forced its way across the valley floor. Both sides sustained heavy casualties, but Theodosius's men had the momentum. Driven by the howling wind, they ground down the western army until it broke.

Amidst the mass of fighting men, Celer did not understand what was happening at first. Instead of a wall of men, he could see gaps between fighting warriors. The enemy seemed to sense that there were less and less men behind them. A few shot nervous glances over their shoulders and began to back away.

Slowly the two exhausted lines broke apart, Theodosius's men too spent to carry on. Celer felt the ground shift beneath his feet, and thought for a moment that he was going to collapse before he realised what it was. Battered officers and legionaries alike shouted warnings, barely heard above the roaring gale, and men threw themselves out the way as the eastern cavalry thundered across the field. For nearly two days they had stood uselessly as the infantry slogged it out, but now the lines had been broken and the horsemen were let loose. Heavy cataphract cavalry thundered through the hastily made gaps, falling like wolves upon the shattered western infantry. Clibanarii, man and mount armoured in iron, rumbled across the torn valley floor in wedge formations. They made straight for Arbogast's cavalry reserves that were valiantly trying to cover the retreat of their infantry. Fresh screams of men and horses added to the din as Arbogast's horsemen broke under the charge. A seemingly endless tide of lighter horsemen and mounted archers surged down the valley, hounding the last remnants of Arbogast's formations.

With a ragged cheer the tired infantry followed the cavalry towards the enemy camp.

"Celer!" He turned at the sound of Sextus's shout.

His friend was stumbling towards him, tripping on the piles of dead and wounded men. Celer went to him and the two stopped feet from one another, panting. Sextus was so covering in blood and gore that Celer could not tell if he was wounded or not.

"Where are the others?" asked Sextus, leaning for a moment on his shield.

"I don't know. I lost Pulvillus when we broke the second line," croaked Celer. His throat was dry and his voice was breaking.

"I was with Aurelius and Hadrianus when Aurelius took a sword through the shoulder," said Sextus, wiping blood from his face with a shaking hand. "Hadrianus took him to the rear."

"Priscus and Severus?" asked Celer, but Sextus just shook his head wearily.

"I don't know what happened to them. Priscus went down when we broke the first line. Severus was still fighting the last time I saw him, but we got separated."

Celer cursed aloud. Part of him wanted nothing more than to return to the camp to see if his friends were alive but he could see men fighting on the edge of the camp ahead of them.

"If Flavianus is in that camp, I must find him."

Sextus looked at the camp and nodded, picking up his shield. "I'm coming with you."

Together they picked their way across the corpse-strewn field. The camp was massive, larger than Theodosius's camp. Celer made for the centre, trusting that Arbogast would follow the same layout that all Roman armies did. The senior commanders would have their tents immediately surrounding the main headquarters tent at the centre of the camp. If Flavianus was still here that was where they would find him.

Soldiers from both sides ran through the lanes between the tents. Vicious fights erupted everywhere as small, determined bodies of Arbogast's troops tried to hold back the eastern troops. Lancers thundered between tents and more than once they had to dodge out of the way or be ridden down.

They found the centre of the camp quickly; resistance here was stronger. Elite troops had rallied to their commanders and were fighting doggedly on the main approaches.

"Through here!" Celer led Sextus into an abandoned tent and slashed a way through the far side. They did this several more times until they were past the fighting.

A soldier was fleeing through the gaps between tents, his shield and weapons abandoned. Celer jumped out and slammed his shield forward. The blow flattened the soldier, who lay groaning on the beaten ground.

They levelled their swords to his throat.

"Where is the tent of the Prefect Flavianus!" shouted Celer.

"What? I don't know!" protested the soldier, trying to press his head further back into the ground away from the blood-encrusted blades.

"Try again," growled Sextus, applying more weight to his blade.

"Err... Prefect Flavianus..." the soldier's hands fluttered nervously at his sides, "west side of the command tent."

"If you're lying," Celer threatened pressing harder.

"No, I swear that's his tent," gasped the soldier.

They lifted their blades from him.

"Go," said Sextus.

The soldier needed no further urging; he scrambled away from them and disappeared around a corner.

They hurried to where he had said Flavianus's tent was. The few remaining soldiers of Arbogast's forces were being forced back and they had to be careful to avoid the groups of men who rushed towards the fighting.

"This is it," pointed Sextus, his sword blade focused on the open flap of a large, luxurious looking tent, bowed and straining against its ropes as the gale buffeted its canvas walls.

Celer checked to see if they were any guards posted but saw no one.

"Let's go."

Walking quickly, they crossed the wide thoroughfare and took up position either side of the open tent flap. Despite the wind and noise of battle, Celer heard something move within the tent.

He nodded to Sextus and mouthed, counting down from three. On one they both stepped through the open flap, shields raised and blades held low.

The tent was vast. The area they had entered was dominated by a large wooden table at the far end with comfy looking couches before it and expensive rugs covering the floor. To their left, thrown-back partition drapes showed a sleeping area with a bed and an empty stand that may have been for hanging a suit of armour on.

On their right their view was hidden by more linen drapes. Two armoured scholae guardsmen stood before them with drawn swords.

The drapes were thrown open and Flavianus emerged, dressed in an ornate cuirass. He was carrying a small chest and stopped dead at the sight of the two legionaries.

"Kill them," he ordered in a flat voice, eyeing them with distaste, "and be quick about it."

The two guardsmen advanced, their faces hidden behind silvered masks with only eye slits for them to see through. Scale armour covered them from neck to mid-thigh and they wore articulated steel armour on their arms whilst their shins were wrapped in enamelled greaves.

Celer and Sextus met them in the centre of the tent. The guardsmen were fearsome warriors, but they carried no shields and Sextus and Celer had faced worse that day.

Celer's man thrust at him with lightning speed. Celer blocked the cut with his shield. The guardsman followed with a backhand cut that he ducked, then caught the follow-up slash on his shield. As the blow landed Celer dropped one knee and stabbed his blade between the guardsman's legs. Powering up, he slammed his shield into the faceless man whilst drawing his blade across the unprotected back of the man's right knee. With an agonised cry the guardsman fell back. Trying to rise on his uninjured leg, he thrust at Celer again, but the young legionary easily parried the blade with his own. Knocking it aside, he stepped in close and hacked his sword into the guardsman's neck. A mail coif stopped the cut from severing the man's head from his shoulders, but the force knocked him sideways, where he lay gasping for breath through his broken throat. Celer quickly placed the tip of his blade in the guardsman's armpit, unprotected by the iron scales, and thrust the blade into his chest.

Turning he saw that Sextus had also brought his opponent to the ground. His friend contemptuously kicked the guardsman's sword away and brought the rim of his shield down on the masked face. The thin metal gave way at the first blow but Sextus made sure and brought his shield down once more as the scholae's body jerked on the expensive rugs that covered the floor.

Flavianus took a step back as the two legionaries straightened before him.

"If it is valuables you want, that can be arranged," he said in a calm voice, "I would be worth a small fortune in ransom. It would pay for you to let me live."

"You are worth far more to me dead," said Celer, his voice shaking with emotion.

Flavianus frowned. "I assure you that is not so. I could make you both wealthy beyond your wildest dreams."

Celer laughed bitterly. "You do not recognise me, Flavianus, but I remember your face very well."

"Who are you?" asked the prefect, startled at the mention of his name.

Celer leant his shield against one of the couches and stabbed his sword through the rug so that it stood quivering before him. Slowly, he undid the chinstrap and eased his helmet of his head, then he pulled off the felt cap and let them both fall at his feet.

"Recognise me now, Prefect?" he spat.

Flavianus stared unknowingly for a moment before his gaze turned into one of fear. He shrank back another step, the chest he held falling from his fingers.

"You," he whispered.

Celer smiled, a ghastly vision, his face painted with the blood of others as he pulled his sword from the ground.

"I have waited a long time for this, Flavianus. I have remembered the faces of those that you took from me; I swore to avenge their deaths." He took a step forward.

"Your family were traitors," snarled Flavianus. He unsheathed his sword and held it before him.

"My family were not traitors!" roared Celer. He lashed out blindingly fast and the Prefect's sword was knocked from his hands. "My mother, Varro, his sister; tell me, Flavianus, how were they traitors?"

"Guilty by association," spat the Prefect. "Your father knew what he risked with his plots."

"My father wanted nothing more than to free Rome from a barbarian warlord who favoured his own people over those of the Empire."

"Don't be so naïve, boy," said Flavianus. "Yes, Arbogast let Franks settle in Gaul and rule themselves. But their men fight for Rome and protect our borders from other, more hostile peoples, no different to how Theodosius treats with the Goths. Eugenius would have been a good Emperor."

"A puppet," retorted Celer.

"And what will Honorius be?" asked Flavianus mockingly. "A boy of ten knows how to rule, does he? Theodosius will leave him with a guardian. No doubt one of his trusted generals, like Stilicho."

"Stilicho is a good man," answered Celer, his words sounding childish in his own ears.

Flavianus laughed. "Know him well, do you? The man's father was a Vandal nobleman. What makes you think he would be any different to Arbogast? The truth is, boy, Rome has few true sons left; men like you and I are a dying breed."

"I am nothing like you," Celer said coldly.

"Clearly," Flavianus sneered, then lunged for his sword.

Celer let him reach the blade. The Prefect jumped back, the sword raised before him.

"So what now?" asked Flavianus. "You and companion here cut me down? Trust a son of Cotta to have no honour."

Celer ignored the barb. He turned his head to Sextus, who had watched the whole exchange.

"I'll guard the door," said Sextus, turning and walking away.

"That was foolish, boy," snarled Flavianus, drawing a dagger from his belt.

"I swore an oath to kill you," said Celer. "I intend to keep it."

The Prefect of Italy was nearly sixty years old, but he possessed a bullish strength that he tried to use to batter through Celer's guard. Each swing of his sword would have severed a limb or disembowelled him, but Celer saw each attack coming. He remembered Optio Longus's advice and fought with cold, mechanical efficiency, suppressing his emotions as he turned each sword stroke and watched the dagger held in the Prefect's left hand.

When Celer parried an overhead cut, the Prefect saw his opportunity, launching himself forward to plunge the dagger into Celer's throat.

Ready for the attack, Celer stepped deftly to his left. He lashed out with his free hand and struck Flavianus hard in the face, staggering him. As the Prefect lurched back towards him, swinging wildly, Celer drove his sword point hard into the man's guts, putting all his weight behind the hardened tip and punching it through the muscled cuirass.

Flavianus collapsed, almost pulling the sword from Celer's grip. With a savage pull, the blade came free, releasing with it a powerful odour as Flavianus's bowels emptied.

Panting and gasping, the Prefect hauled himself up until he was propped against a couch. Groaning with pain, he tried to press his hands to his wound, but the cuirass blocked him. Sweat broke out on his brow as he raised his dagger with shaking hands and cut the straps holding the armour to him, tossing it to one side. The dagger fell from his grip and he pressed his fingers to the growing red stain on his tunic.

"My son will avenge me," he gasped, eyes wide with pain as he glared up at Celer.

Celer crouched before him, careful to knock the dagger out of Flavianus's reach.

"Your son shall know the pain that I have felt every day since you took my parents from me." Forcefully, he reached out and grabbed Flavianus's hand, ignoring the Prefect's cry of pain. Brushing away Flavianus's feeble attempts to stop him, he pulled the Prefect's family ring from his finger. His own father had owned such a ring, solid gold, in the family's possession for centuries, passed from father to son. Celer would never hold his father's ring again, and now neither would Flavianus's son.

Celer stood, tucking the ring into a pouch on his belt. Stepping out into the main area of the tent, he knelt and pulled on his felt cap and helmet and grabbed his shield from where he had left it.

He paused at the tent flap and looked over at the dying prefect. Flavianus watched him through slitted eyes, his face distorted with pain and hatred. Dark red blood oozed through his fingers from his stomach wound and pink bubbles frothed at the corners of his mouth. Celer took it all in, watching every grimace and hearing every hiss of pain. His oath

343

was fulfilled; the man responsible for his parent's deaths lay dying before him but he felt no elation. Rage still burned deep within him, a burning, swirling anger at what he had lost. Flavianus's death barely dampened the flames. He hoped that the spirits of his mother and father would find some solace now that their deaths were avenged. Flavianus began coughing violently. Blood and spittle hung in long tendrils from his lips, shuddering with every movement. With one last wheezing breath he lurched to one side and slumped limply against the couch. Already, the expensive rugs were greedily drinking in the blood that seeped from the prefect, their colours slowly turning red as the life flowed out of him. Hefting his weapons, Celer pushed his way out of the tent and into the wind.

Sextus turned as he stepped outside, blade raised.

"It's done then?" his friend asked, lowering his sword.

"It's done," Celer confirmed

"What now?" asked Sextus, looking at the chaos that raged about them. Eastern soldiers were pouring through the camp now; the final resistance had been crushed and all about them Arbogast's men were surrendering or dying.

Celer was about to answer when a voice hailed them.

"Sextus, Celer, over here!" They both turned to see Pulvillus beckoning them from a cluster of legionaries. They trotted over, bowing their heads into the gale.

"Where have you two been?" demanded Sirus. The Centurion was caked in dried blood and was leaning heavily on a legionary.

"Apologies, Centurion," Celer said as the two snapped a salute to their officer. "We got separated in the battle."

Sirus never got a chance to respond. A party of men appeared from the main command tent. Sirus saw that Stilicho was at their head and quickly called the group of legionaries to attention.

"At ease, legionaries," said the general. "Centurion, you are injured." He pointed at Sirus's leg.

"Just a scratch, Sir," said Sirus, wincing.

"I need as many of your men as are still fit to march. Do you have someone who can lead them?"

"Yes, Sir; Optio Longus will fill in for me"

Longus stepped forward and saluted the General. Stilicho nodded. "Very good. Optio, assemble your men on the west side of the camp immediately; gather what supplies you can. Arbogast has escaped. Reports have him leaving the camp heading west with a body of mixed foot and horse. I don't mean for him to get away."

"Yes, General, right away," said Longus. "Right, lads, form up; let's get to the muster point."

Not daring to complain in front of the General, the exhausted legionaries formed into a column three wide behind the optio.

"Who do I report to, Sir?" asked Longus.

"I will be leading the force myself," said Stilicho. "I will meet you shortly." He climbed into the saddle. "Make haste, gentlemen; the battle is not yet done."

# Epilogue

Soft rain pattered off the browning leaves, the only sound that could be heard in the damp wooded defile.

Stilicho and his men had pursed Arbogast and his followers for a day and a night. The remnants of the Western army had fled west, then north, deep into the mountains. Arbogast's men were a mixed force of scholae guardsmen and barbarian allies.

Stilicho had more horsemen in his small force; they kept Arbogast and his mounted arm from fleeing but were unable to break his small infantry force. They played a cat and mouse game through twisting valleys and over steep passes.

Celer and the other legionaries struggled along behind the horsemen, pushing their tired and battered bodies to their limit to keep their quarry in sight.

The driving wind had intensified following the battle, until it was all they could do to stay upright and fight to place one foot in front of the other. Mercifully it began to ease as darkness fell, bringing with it the soft late summer rain that quickly soaked the miserable men as they huddled beneath their shields through the dark hours.

Come the dawn, they had set off after Arbogast once again, tracking the Frankish General to a dead-end valley, heavily forested on all sides with broadleaf woodland.

They found the abandoned mounts of his men at the foot of a small stream that spilled down the hillside. Stilicho ordered his cavalry to dismount and left a small party of five men to watch the horses. Unclasping his sodden cloak from his shoulders, the General set off up the hill.

The defile was halfway up the valley side. A depression in the hillside, carved out by the small stream that ran through the middle. Arbogast's men rained what missiles they could down on the climbing eastern soldiers; javelins, axes and even rocks thudded into their raised shields.

The fight was bloody and swift. Stilicho had brought more men and he sent parties to either side of the defile to flank the western troops. The small stream ran red as the rain washed the blood from the corpses.

"Where is Arbogast?" asked Stilicho wearily, leaning on his shield. "Find me his body," he ordered.

The men fanned out, turning over bodies of slain men. Swords rose and fell when they found a soldier not yet dead, and the strangled cries were the only interruption to the relentless drumming on the canopy above them.

"General!" A group of legionaries were standing by the trunk of a large fallen ash tree; everyone turned and saw a body slumped up against the pale trunk.

Stilicho straightened and began moving towards them. He walked past Celer without a glance, his eyes firmly fixed on the body of his old comrade.

A movement off to the left caught Celer's eye. A body rose up from amongst the dead, leaf litter falling from its frame, an axe held high in one hand.

"General!" Celer shouted, throwing himself forward as the soldier launched the axe at Stilicho's back.

The general began to turn at Celer's warning; his eyes widened as the axe hurtled towards his chest. Celer ploughed into Stilicho at full tilt. The breath was knocked from both of them as the axe-head hammered into Celer's battered shield. The young legionary landed on top of the general and pinned him down as the other legionaries swarmed the western soldier. Within seconds the man lay dead amongst the leaves.

Celer rolled off the general and climbed to his feet, leaving the ruined shield where it had fallen. Stilicho's personal guard were quick to his side and helped the general to his feet, uneasily aware that they had failed in their duty. Stilicho waved them off with a glare and the guards sheepishly retreated, busying themselves making sure no further corpses would rise up.

"My gratitude to you, Celer. I see fate guided my decision the day I permitted you to join this army."

Celer was too exhausted to think of a response; he stood there dumbly before the general as Stilicho appraised him.

"Come," Stilicho beckoned towards Arbogast, "you have proven more adept than my guards. Let us see the face of our enemy."

Arbogast was propped against the trunk of the ash tree. No dead soldiers lay nearby and his sword lay in its sheath at his side. He had removed his red crested helmet and had placed it neatly by his sword. Mouse-brown hair, streaked with grey like a badger's back, clung to his temples. Celer noted the faint shadow of stubble covering the General's pale cheeks and the pale blue eyes that stared emptily up at the green canopy above them. Stepping closer, Celer saw the Frankish General had unbuckled his belt and lifted his mail shirt; the hilt of a knife protruded from the white of his belly. His trousers and lacquered thigh guards were dyed red with blood that had ceased to run from the wound.

"He took his own life," said Celer, feeling cheated that the Frank had chosen his own death.

"He was ever a proud man," said Stilicho, with what Celer thought was a hint of sadness. "I could not imagine he would submit to capture."

Stilicho turned to the watching men. "Wrap his body and prepare it to be carried back to the camp; the Emperor will wish to see it. Bury the others."

As the soldiers wrapped Arbogast in a cloak and began clearing a space for a mass grave, Stilicho turned to Celer.

"I told you in the palace library that I had no need for soft, privileged boys, only soldiers. You have proven yourself in that regard to be a man of ability. Rome has a need for men of ability. Hard times are ahead, Celer. The Empire balances upon a knife's edge; all those wise enough can see it." He looked Celer in the eye. "You have avenged your family and your friends, now I would offer you a chance to fight for something more. Serve under me and help me defend the Empire itself."

Celer was taken aback by the offer. A position on a General's staff was a position of high honour that few achieved. His father's words echoed in his mind.

"A man's duty is to his family and to Rome," he said. "I would be honoured to serve under you, General."

Stilicho nodded as Arbogast's wrapped body was carried past them.

"Come then," said the general, "the Emperor will be waiting."

Together, they followed the body down the mountain side.

# Historical note

It is easy to fall into the trap of thinking that the Roman Empire remained largely the same throughout its long existence. In truth, much had changed in the four centuries since the establishment of the imperial period under Augustus.

The Roman Senate, once the driving force behind Rome's aggressive expansion, was no longer actively involved in the military due to laws passed by Emperor Diocletian. Presumably, these laws were intended to limit the contact these wealthy and influential men could have with the armed forces, the aim being to limit the number of civil wars that plagued the empire. This, combined with the increasing need for a more 'professional' officer class, led to the rise of the equestrian class as the dominant military class of the late empire. They also fulfilled many of the civilian roles needed for the vast administrative needs of the empire.

The Empire itself was now divided into two halves. Though this was done for logistical and defensive reasons, as it was far easier for the two emperors to face threats on multiple fronts. The division was therefore not a result of a fracturing of political identities within the empire. The citizens contemporary with Celer would have regarded the two Empires as two sides of the same coin, with apparent freedom of movement between the two.

The faith of Christianity had been growing steadily since the reign of Constantine in the early fourth century and by the end of the century it had become increasingly powerful, prompting conflict between Christians and worshippers of the old Roman pantheon. The battle of the Frigidus has been seen by many as the deciding factor in which religion would emerge as dominant, although at the time this is likely not to have been much of a consideration and Christians and pagans would have fought on both sides. Eugenius himself is believed to have been a Christian, and his support of pagan beliefs was more a way of buying political favour with the largely traditional Italian aristocracy than a sign of a pagan restoration.

The army of the late empire had also changed from its earlier incarnation. The new military model was based around static frontier troops called limitanei and mobile field armies called comitatenses evidence suggests that these troops were formed into units much smaller than their predecessors with some legions perhaps numbering only a thousand as opposed to the nearly five thousand strong legions of the early empire. These forces were still highly trained and equipped professional soldiers and they continued to defend the Empire throughout the fourth century, despite often being outnumbered by their enemies.

Printed in Great Britain
by Amazon

79890557R00201